The
Body
in the
Dales

OTHER TITLES BY J. R. ELLIS

The Quartet Murders

The
Body
in the
Dales

A YORKSHIRE MURDER MYSTERY

J.R. ELLIS

THOMAS & MERCER

Text copyright © 2017, 2018 by J. R. Ellis
All rights reserved.

Previously self-published as *The Body in Jingling Pot* in Great Britain in 2017. This edition contains editorial revisions.

Published by Thomas & Mercer, Seattle

www.apub.com

Amazon, the Amazon logo, and Thomas & Mercer are trademarks of Amazon.com, Inc., or its affiliates.

ISBN-13: 9781503903111
ISBN-10: 1503903117

Cover design by Ghost Design

Printed in the United States of America

To Jackie

Prologue

Unless tha's careful on thi ways,
Providence Pot will end thi days.

Deep under the Yorkshire Dales, cavers were scrambling along dark passageways. Apart from the eerie echoing of their voices, the only sounds came from water dripping on to their heads and gurgling down the shallow streams. There was the distant roar of an underground river. The dancing lights from their helmets illuminated the rocky walls and cast huge shadows into the heights above them.

They were walking through a strange underground world of rock, mud and slime where the temperature remained at the same chilly level throughout the year and intricate systems of interconnecting tunnels plunged hundreds of feet below the surface. The slow action of water dissolving limestone over thousands of years had sculpted shapes like the cave art of a strange subterranean civilisation: long fingers of stalactites hung from the cavern roofs and stalagmites thrust in opposition from the floor.

The cavers were still only halfway through the system. They were entering a long and fairly straight passage with a shallow stream in the bottom, about twenty feet high with rocky, uneven walls.

The leader called back, 'Easy bit here. We'll stop for a rest soon.'

Echoing replies reached him in his forward position. As he splashed down the tunnel, he calculated the time and distance. Two and a half hours to get here, stop for food, another two and a half hours to get through to the end. It was a big responsibility, leading an inexperienced party like this. So many things could go wrong. People fell and broke limbs and it was hours before Cave Rescue could reach them. Reckless amateurs got lost in the labyrinth of passages and sometimes died of exhaustion and hypothermia.

Suddenly his foot struck something and he tripped forward. His first thought was how stupid he'd been to allow himself to get distracted. *He'd* be the one who broke his ankle, and then they'd all be in serious difficulties. Whatever he'd stumbled against had moved and seemed soft. He looked down to illuminate the object and staggered back in shock. His lamp was shining on to a human head. The body of a man lay across the floor of the passage. Congealed blood covered the matted hair and the skull was smashed at the back. Two facts immediately struck the caver.

First: the dead man was not wearing any caving gear.

Second: he knew who it was.

One

Watch out when striding over th'ill,
Especially near to Gaping Ghyll.

Detective Sergeant Andrew Carter would never forget his first day with the Harrogate Division of West Riding Police. It was a sunny day after heavy rains and he arrived early, smartly dressed in an Italian designer suit and his favourite Armani shoes. He was tall with a handsome face and a dazzling smile. He had short blond hair and was powerfully built, with a slight tendency to be overweight.

Carter hesitated outside for a while, fiddling with his tie before finally going through the door. Inside, everything seemed quiet compared to the bustle of the Met. There was a reception desk with a middle-aged female officer, who smiled at him in welcome.

He was filling in a form for his security pass when he heard a voice call out in a strident northern tone.

'Ah, the lad from the Great Smoke!'

Carter turned to see a figure walking purposefully towards him down the corridor. It was a man wearing what looked to Carter like a battered old anorak and heavy boots. He stopped and looked the new boy up and down with grey eyes that were both warm and penetrating.

'Come on, then, no time to lose, do your form-filling later. And we're going over rough ground; I'm afraid that smart suit could get crumpled.' With that, he walked off towards the door, calling back, 'As for those shoes!' He laughed as he disappeared out of the building.

Carter gave the receptionist a bemused look. She laughed too.

'You'd better follow him; that's Chief Inspector Oldroyd. Here, take this.' She handed him a temporary pass. 'Just fill in your name.'

Carter's eyes widened. Detective Chief Inspector Oldroyd was his new boss. Hastily he put the pen down, apologised, stuffed the temporary pass in his pocket and rushed out of the door.

Oldroyd was already starting the engine of a shabby old Saab saloon. Carter got in and they drove off through the gated entrance.

'DCI Oldroyd, lad; pleased to meet you. We'll shake hands later. It's Andrew Carter, isn't it? Do you go by Andy?'

'Yes, sir.'

'Good. Well, Andy, this is going to be a very interesting first case for you. I've just had a call from Inspector Craven from the Skipton station; a body has been found down Jingling Pot.'

'In a pot, sir?'

'A pot *'ole.*'

Carter looked bemused. Oldroyd shook his head.

'Come on, lad, frame thisen.'

'I beg your pardon, sir?'

'Tha's come to t'county o' t'broad acres, so don tha thinking cap and get thisen ackled.'

Carter had a strange feeling of dislocation: was his hearing scrambled or was his new boss a lunatic? He opened his mouth to reply when Oldroyd burst out laughing.

'Sorry, it's my little joke, just a bit of Yorkshire dialect. They call me "Yorkshire" Oldroyd round here but don't worry, people don't speak like that much any more. More's the pity.'

Carter was still confused. 'Right, sir, but, er, what were you saying?'

'Just teasing. The important thing is that the body was discovered in a pothole; that's an underground cave system. That's not a very common occurrence, even round here where there're hundreds of caves. I've got a feeling we might have something unusual on our hands.'

Carter hadn't thought of Yorkshire as a place full of caves. He looked out of the window on to the landscape. After a while, the picturesque countryside around Harrogate, which reminded him of some parts of Surrey or Kent, started to change into something much more unusual. The hedgerows were replaced by rough stone walls that criss-crossed intensely green fields full of cows and sheep. Dotted in the fields were squat rectangular stone buildings. Oldroyd slowed as the road narrowed between walls at either side. Carter saw a sign with the words 'Yorkshire Dales National Park' and a sheep's head.

'This is Wharfedale, Andy, and we're now in the Dales National Park – oops, better slow down.'

A flock of sheep filled the road ahead. A farmer sauntered along behind them and two black-and-white sheepdogs darted backwards and forwards on either side of the flock. Carter thought of Streatham High Road, clogged with traffic throughout the day.

'They can be a nuisance if you're in a hurry but we all love them, really. They keep the landscape looking the way it is.'

The sheep started to disappear through a gate. Oldroyd waved to the farmer as the car sped on past one of the collie dogs, crouched in the road blocking the path of any sheep considering escape.

The road undulated up the fellside and then down.

'I'll slow down here so you can see the view.'

A spectacular landscape spread out before Carter's gaze. Grey stone cottages clustered around a village green. There was an old church by a bridge. In the distance, the landscape looked even wilder. The river was still very swollen after the recent rains and some of the low-lying fields were flooded.

'That's Burnthwaite and Upper Wharfedale in the distance.'

'Not bad that, sir.'

Oldroyd laughed.

'You'd better watch it, lad, or you'll fall in love with it. Alf Wight was hooked the first day he saw this landscape.'

'Alf Wight, sir?'

'James Herriot to you. He lived way over those fells in the town of Thirsk.'

'He wrote those vet books, didn't he?'

'That's right.'

Carter had never spent much time in the countryside and he had a clichéd view of it: just a lot of fields stinking of cow muck and 'local yokels' grunting 'oo-aa' as they downed their cider. But there was something about this that was different, something grand and sweeping in the landscape.

The car went through the village and past two police cars, the first sign that something was happening. After about a mile up a steep road, Carter could see more police cars squashed by the wall, and a van that had 'Wharfedale Cave Rescue' on the side. He noted that the police cars here were Range Rovers, a model more suited to rough terrain than fast pursuits through the city. As they stopped, a police officer came over.

'This is the local inspector, Bob Craven. We pull his leg about this area being called the Craven District.' He opened the window and mimicked an upper-class English accent. 'Ah, Lord Craven of Craven. I hear nasty things are happening in your patch today?'

Craven grinned. He had a large red face and looked like a weather-beaten farmer.

'Hello, Jim, good to see you. You're right there and I'll tell you something, I'll bet even you've never seen one like this; it's a real puzzler.'

'We'd better get out and have a look at it then.'

He introduced Carter and the three men climbed over a stile and walked along a path across the field, Craven looking rather quizzically at Carter's expensive suit and shoes.

'So fill me in then, Bob.'

Craven consulted his notes.

'The victim was male, late thirties; found by the leader of a party of potholers, a Geoffrey Whitaker.'

'A party of what?' asked Carter.

'Potholers are cavers. This lad's from the south, Bob; don't assume anything. Carry on.'

'The body was lying across the passage with the water flowing around it.'

'Couldn't it have been an accident? A fall?'

'Very unlikely, Jim. The deceased wasn't wearing any caving gear and he'd no equipment. The wounds suggest he was hit on the back of the head with something fairly small and sharp, like a hammer. Not the kind of wound you get from a fall.'

'So someone murdered him and dumped the body in the pothole?'

'So it seems, but the point is, the cavers found the body when they were about halfway through. It takes over two hours from either end of the system to reach that point. Why would anybody take a body down so far and then just leave it where the next time anybody passes through they're going to walk straight into it? It doesn't make sense.'

Oldroyd frowned; it was an unlikely scenario.

'But that's not all, Jim. Listen to this. Two of the blokes who went down to help to retrieve the body swear they went through the same place only three days ago and saw nothing.'

'So?'

'But when you see the body I think you'll agree that it's been in the cave much longer than that.'

'I see what you mean. Well,' he rubbed his hands together, 'this sounds like the kind of case I like: plenty to think about. What do you say, Andy?'

Carter had been looking around at the grassy fells rising up; he felt the breeze on his face and saw the white clouds moving across the blue sky. The earth was so firm; it was difficult to believe that beneath their feet was a dark underworld. Now he was thinking fast, eager to make a good impression on his first day.

'I know this sounds obvious, sir, but couldn't he have been murdered down there? Why are we assuming he was killed elsewhere and the body taken down the pot?'

'Pothole,' corrected Oldroyd.

'That's extremely unlikely,' said Craven, consulting his notes again. 'The victim's already been identified as David Atkins of Burnthwaite, apparently a very experienced caver, so the chances of him going so far down a cave system without any equipment are nil, I would say.'

'So that rules out him being murdered on a descent with someone else?'

'I'd say so, yes.'

'But he could have been forced down the cave by somebody at knife point or something and then killed,' continued Carter, 'and he could have had all his gear removed after he was murdered.'

'That's not impossible,' conceded Oldroyd, 'but it's very unlikely. You'd be struggling for a long time, forcing somebody along narrow passages. Then you kill them, then you remove all their climbing gear and carry it all out again. Why bother?'

The path entered a steep and gloomy valley. Carter shook his head. 'No,' he concluded. 'I agree; it doesn't make sense.'

They turned a sharp corner and suddenly Carter could see their destination. About halfway up the fellside was the dark opening of a cave.

'That cave is the entrance to the Jingling Pot system,' said Oldroyd, 'and I see the body. Come on.'

In front of the cave was a collection of boulders of various sizes and piles of scree tumbling down to a stream in the valley bottom. Carter imagined this was normally a lonely place but today a large group of people had gathered at the mouth of the cave, some wearing helmets and waterproof clothing. Attention seemed to be focussed on a stretcher laid on the ground covered with a plastic sheet.

The narrow path drifted up the fellside and Oldroyd walked at a surprising pace, obviously eager to see the evidence for himself. Carter began to see why Oldroyd was wearing his boots. The path was wet and muddy. His shoes were already caked with mud and he kept skidding off the path.

At the mouth of the cave, a group of men dressed in caving gear were sitting on the grass or the rocks looking exhausted. Some had removed their helmets and one was drinking hot tea from a thermos flask.

'I could do with something a bit stronger after that,' he remarked to the others.

'Aye,' a few mumbled in reply. Their faces were filthy with mud, their gear wet and grimy. They looked dazed.

Two police constables were standing by the stretcher and Craven went over to them.

'OK, you've met Chief Inspector Oldroyd before and this is Detective Sergeant Carter.'

The constables nodded and acknowledged Oldroyd with a brief 'Sir'.

'Let's have a look then,' said Oldroyd. He put on plastic gloves and gave a pair to Carter, then pulled back the sheet covering the stretcher.

The body of a medium-sized but powerfully built man with dark hair and beard was revealed. He was dressed only in a blood-splattered T-shirt, jeans and trainers. His skull had been crushed at the back and his hair was clotted with a blackened mass of blood. The wetness was the most striking thing about the body. Everything, from the head to

9

the clothes, was damp and when Oldroyd touched the skin it had an unusual texture. It was not icy but clammy. In many ways it was like bodies dragged out of lakes and yet not quite. It had not been cleaned by submersion in water, but was as grimy and muddy as the Cave Rescue men who'd brought it out. Oldroyd covered it up again and frowned.

'Found two hours into a cave system in jeans and T-shirt and he's been down there a while if I'm not mistaken. Any more ideas, Andy?'

Carter was perplexed. Just my luck, he thought, to come up against a case like this on my first day. The whole thing was bizarre. He decided rightly that there was no point trying to pretend to the chief inspector.

'I don't know, sir; it's right outside my experience. We don't have caves and potholes in London.'

'Come on then, you'll have to use your imagination. Anyway, don't bodies occasionally turn up in the sewer systems down there?'

'I'm sure they do, sir, but I haven't seen one.'

'No.' Oldroyd's brief and distracted reply seemed more to himself. He looked down at the stretcher again and shook his head. There was a pause as all three men went quiet, reflecting on the puzzle.

Craven went over to the rescuers; Oldroyd and Carter followed.

'Thanks for your help. We couldn't have done this so quickly without you. A bit of a nasty job though. Who's been leading?'

'That's me. Williams, Alan Williams,' one of the group replied, wiping drops of tea from his grimy beard, 'and you're right; we're used to bringing people out on stretchers and sometimes they're dead, but not murdered. But it's only to be expected, Inspector; these caves are always likely to spring a nasty surprise on you.'

He turned to look at the black mouth of the entrance and his face took on an expression of reverence. 'They've been feared for centuries, well before they were explored. People thought there were creatures from hell down there; if you went too far in you'd be caught in their lair and never get out again.' He looked down at the body. 'If you don't show respect, well . . .'

It all sounded a bit fanciful to Carter and he dived in rather recklessly.

'What do you mean exactly? He was killed by the cave itself? By a goblin or something? What're you talking about?'

Williams shot Carter a hostile look, taking in his accent and dress.

'No, I mean that, where these caves are concerned, death is never far away if you're not careful. What's happened here is weird, but weird things happen down there.'

Carter still had no idea what the man was talking about but decided not to pursue it.

'I don't know how those two found it all.' Williams gestured to two of the group who looked more exhausted than the others. One was carrying a case that looked as if it contained photographic equipment. 'They're used to bodies but not the caves.'

'Those are the crime scene officers who went down with the cavers,' Craven informed Oldroyd. 'As you can imagine, it's a highly unusual crime scene.'

'Even so, it's a pity we couldn't see the body where it was found,' said Oldroyd, 'though I appreciate the difficulties.'

'Impossible to seal off the scene, Jim; you couldn't be sure that there aren't any other cavers around who could interfere with things. We couldn't leave any officers down there; they'd get exposure if they stayed too long.'

'I understand. I assume you got plenty of pictures?' He addressed this to the CSI with the camera.

'Yes, sir. Good job I had a powerful flash. It's pitch black down there. There was really nothing except a dark muddy passage with a stream passing through.'

'Did you search around thoroughly?'

'Yes, sir,' replied the other officer. 'There was just mud and stones. The only thing we found was this.'

He produced a plastic bag containing a small hooked piece of metal, rusty and ancient-looking.

'Good man,' said Oldroyd, examining the find. Carter looked on curiously.

'What do you think it is, sir?'

Oldroyd twisted and turned the object around.

'I don't know; maybe we'd better ask these gentlemen.'

Oldroyd walked back over to the cavers, now in conversation with each other.

'Sorry to interrupt. I'm Detective Chief Inspector Oldroyd and I'm in charge of the investigation. Any of you know what this might be? It was found at the crime scene.'

Williams took the bag and they all examined it closely. They shook their heads and he handed it back.

'It looks like a hook or something.'

'Is it anything you would use?'

'No. All of our stuff is made of steel or alloy. This looks like a piece of old iron, a bit primitive.'

Carter looked very sceptically at the bit of metal.

'I can't see how this is relevant, sir.'

'Bits of metal don't generally find their way deep into cave systems without a reason. This isn't just a piece of litter.' Oldroyd continued to look at it closely.

'Inspector?'

Oldroyd and Carter turned to see that the Cave Rescue team were on their feet.

'Is it all right if we go now?' asked Williams.

'Have a word with Inspector Craven; he's organised the recovery and he'll be taking statements.'

'We all knew him, you know.' Williams pointed to the stretcher.

'Yes, I understand he's a local man; must be a shock to you all. Did he have any enemies?'

Williams grunted and frowned. 'His death's a shock but no great surprise. Dave Atkins wasn't exactly popular.'

The two detectives were instantly on the alert.

'Why was that?' asked Carter.

'He was what my dad would have called a dead wrong 'un. Always up to something dodgy to make money and messin' about with other people's wives and girlfriends,' said another of the rescue team.

'I see.'

'I don't think you'd have to look far to find people who had a motive for doing him in.'

'Was it you then?' Oldroyd was suddenly direct and serious. The caver looked taken aback, until Oldroyd smiled.

'Don't worry, I've no evidence against you – yet,' he added with another smile. 'It sounds like we might have ourselves a lot of suspects.'

Another of the team called out, 'He was an absolute bastard.'

'I get the message,' said Oldroyd, 'but wasn't he one of you lot? I mean, a caver?'

'Yes, he was in the Wharfedale Club but he wasn't in the rescue team. He wouldn't put himself out for anybody else even if they were trapped down a system,' replied Williams.

'Not everyone who's in the club is also in the rescue team then?'

'No, but most are. We think it right that we should use our skill and knowledge to save other people's lives, even if they are a bunch of idiots who go down without the proper equipment and get lost. Like I said, people who don't show respect to these ancient caves.'

'Very noble.'

'Atkins just laughed at the idea, of course; thought we were the idiots. He would have just left them to die.'

'Ironic that he ended up dead down there himself then.'

Williams shook his head. 'Did I hear you say he's been down there a while?'

'Well, I'm not sure, we'll have to wait for forensics, but from my experience I would say he must have been down there for several days at least.'

'You see, Chief Inspector, that doesn't make sense.'

'Why?'

Williams glanced at his companion.

'Today is Monday. We went through this system following the same route on Friday, wasn't it?' The other caver nodded.

'So I understand from Inspector Craven. And you didn't see anything?'

'No, there was no body in Sump Passage at that point, I can assure you.'

'Are you absolutely certain about that?' Carter was fed up with all this 'mystery of the caves' stuff. 'I understand there are lots of holes and passages down there, so how can you be sure that you were in the same one?'

It was immediately obvious that Carter had said the wrong thing again. For the second time Williams's bearded face looked with contempt at the young detective.

'Look . . . officer, we know these systems better than anyone else. Jingling Pot is a pretty straightforward one. We know where we were – Sump Passage – and I'm telling you, there was no body.' He stabbed his finger at Carter to emphasise the point.

'Why is it called Sump Passage?'

'You've never been down a cave system, have you?'

'No,' admitted Carter.

'The sump is the name for the deepest part of the system where water collects. Am I right?' Oldroyd joined the conversation.

'Yes,' replied the caver. 'Sump Passage is right at the bottom of the Jingling Pot system, one of the reasons why the stream in the passage constantly flows strongly. At the end of the passage, the stream goes off down a fairly narrow hole into an underground lake and there's no way through.'

'How do you know?'

'It's been explored with diving equipment.'

'Diving?' said Carter. 'You mean people go underwater down there?'

'Yes.'

'That must be very dangerous.'

'Yes, underwater and completely dark. We've lost a lot of cavers in the flooded systems.'

Carter was struggling to make sense of this and he wasn't sure how relevant it was, but Oldroyd was listening intently.

'So no passages have been found out of the lake?' he asked.

'Only small ones, not large enough for anyone to get through. That lake has been well explored and it's a dead end.'

'What about the route through the system?'

'After Sump Passage it starts to go up again; fairly easy route until you come out at Mossy Bottom Cave.'

'So you're absolutely sure you were in that, er, Sump Passage three days ago and there was no body?' Carter still sounded sceptical.

'Yes.'

Oldroyd was looking thoughtful.

'Are there any other ways to get into that system?' he asked.

'Only one. There's a branch on the Wether Ridge Hole system that comes into Jingling Pot before Sump Passage, but that won't help you. It takes just as long to get to Sump Passage if you go that way.'

'And no other routes?'

'No. Jingling Pot's a well-known system and it's been thoroughly explored in the last fifty years. We would know if there were any other ways to get down there.'

'Was there anything different about Sump Passage today from when you went through on Friday – apart from the body, of course?'

'Nothing apart from a bit of a rock fall, but they're happening all the time.'

'So there were some rocks and stones in the passage today which you didn't see on Friday?'

'Yes, but nothing major.'

Oldroyd drifted off into a reverie for a few moments, then he turned to Williams again.

'Is there anyone around here who you'd say was an expert in the history of caving? You know, someone who might know just a bit more about the systems and how they've been explored over the years?'

Williams bridled a little at the implication.

'You could try Simon Hardiman up at the hall. He's quite well up on things like that, but I'm telling you, Chief Inspector, there are no other ways into that system and Simon won't be able to tell you about any.'

'I'm sure you're right, but we have to explore all the possibilities, of course. When you say "hall" do you mean Garthwaite Hall?'

'That's right, him and his wife run an outdoor-pursuits centre there.'

'I know it, and I know someone else who may be able to help too.' He turned to Carter. 'Come on, we can't do any more here now. We'll have to wait for the forensics report to confirm what I think. Let's go back to Burnthwaite and I'll buy you a spot of lunch at the Red Horse.'

The short steep drive back down to Burnthwaite passed in near silence. Carter wasn't sure that conversation would be welcome; the senior detective had lost his lively manner and had become distracted.

Back in the village, Oldroyd parked alongside a smooth village green surrounded by old limestone cottages. Carter looked up at the fells rising steeply behind the village but Oldroyd, who had come to life again, hurried him on.

'Come on, let's have a quick look at the river.'

He led the way along a narrow footpath by the road on to an ancient stone packhorse bridge. Triangular refuges jutted out from either side of the bridge, used originally by pedestrians to allow the laden animals to pass and now providing a convenient vantage point for the two detectives.

'The River Wharfe,' said Oldroyd in a reverential tone.

Carter looked over to see the water tinged with brown. It gurgled and lapped against the pillar of the bridge, sticks and branches bobbing on the surface and speeding along on the fast current.

'The water's very high at the moment after all the rain. It's a pity really; when it's low you can watch trout swimming slowly upstream under the bridge, though it's not easy to pick them out against the stones on the river bed.'

'The water doesn't look very pure.'

'That's peat brought down from the moors after the rain. Normally the water's crystal clear and fresh.'

Carter looked at Oldroyd. 'You're very fond of this place, aren't you, sir?'

'I should say so,' he replied. 'I used to come to this very spot as a child with my family for picnics. My sister and I used to catch bull heads and crayfish and play skim stones across the river.'

'What's a bull head, sir?'

Oldroyd was back to his teasing. He looked at Carter with his head on one side.

'What a deprived childhood the poor lad had! I suppose your experience of rivers is confined to the mucky old Thames?'

'The Thames is pretty nice up at Oxford. My dad took us out on a punt there once.'

'That would more likely have been on the Cherwell.'

'Do you know Oxford, then?'

'I was at university there, but that's a long time ago. A bull head, Carter, is a small, fat, lazy fish that you can catch with your hands if you're quick enough. And come on, I'll show you how we used to skim.'

Oldroyd went back across the bridge and down to the water's edge.

'There are hardly any stones here today. Normally there's a kind of pebble beach here. You find a flat pebble. Let's have a look.' He picked away at the few pebbles still above the water level.

'This will do. Let's see if I can still do it.' He held the stone between finger and thumb and threw it horizontally. The stone hit the water on its flat surface, bounced off, hit the water and bounced again. Altogether, the stone bounced five times before it hit the other bank, where it narrowly missed a duck. The bird quacked and flapped away.

'Fantastic. I haven't lost my touch,' Oldroyd announced with a flourish. 'That's pretty good for these conditions. You have a go.'

With some reluctance, Carter selected what he thought was a good stone, braced his strong shoulders and strode quickly to the water's edge. He threw the stone hard but it splashed into the water and disappeared immediately beneath the surface.

'Sorry.'

'Wrong trajectory, lad, you have to have your arm down and throw horizontally like this.'

He threw another stone with the same result.

'Try again.'

Carter made another selection and followed Oldroyd's advice. This time, the stone completed an honourable three bounces on the water before sinking.

'Very good!' cried Oldroyd. He turned from the river. 'Come on into the pub. I'm driving, so I'll buy you a drink. You want to try some northern beer.'

Carter shook his head in disbelief as he walked behind Oldroyd towards the pub. The last thing he'd expected to find himself doing with his new boss on his first day was throwing stones into a river like a couple of kids.

Soon they were sitting in the stone-flagged bar of the Red Horse. Carter had a pint of bitter in front of him. It had a creamy head and the taste was rich and strong.

'Sup up, Andy, as we say round here. We don't normally drink like this when we're on duty, but it's a special day, your first in the team. So cheers.' Oldroyd's knowing expression seemed to indicate that in fact drinking like this was not at all unusual.

He held up his glass of orange juice and soda water and Carter brought up his pint.

'Cheers. Anyway, as we had to leave the station so abruptly I've had no chance to ask you to tell me a bit more about yourself.'

'What kind of things, sir?'

'Your past, your family, where you were brought up, things like that. I like to know people's life story; it tells you a lot about them.'

Carter began an autobiographical outline, which he'd intended to keep brief. But he was prompted by frequent questions from Oldroyd, who seemed to want to know everything. He spoke about his boyhood in Croydon and how his father had died when he was only ten.

'He was a policeman too, sir. He was shot in Soho by a drug dealer.'

'Was he in the drugs squad?'

'No, he was on patrol and he approached this bloke in a car that was illegally parked. He just got out, shot Dad and ran off.' Carter paused and looked down before continuing. 'It turned out the car was stuffed with heroin, but they never caught the gunman; disappeared without trace.'

'Probably out of the country within hours. He's unlikely to come back, either.'

'No.'

'Were you close?'

'Yeah, he used to take me to matches at Upton Park – West Ham, you know. He was brought up in the East End, a real cockney. Do you follow football, sir?'

'A bit, just on television now and again. I don't go to matches any more. I used to watch the great Leeds side in the 1970s – you know, Billy Bremner, Johnny Giles, Jack Charlton. But about your father; was that why you wanted to go into the police force?'

'It was always my ambition. I'm sure a lot of people thought it was just a dream, a way of connecting with my dad again, or that I thought I could catch his murderer, you know, that kind of kids' stuff. I never wavered, although I wanted to be a detective, not in the uniform branch like him.'

'Why was that?'

'Because his murderer was never found. My mother's never got over it. It made me realise how important it is that crimes are solved and people brought to justice, even if we can't lessen the pain of the crime.'

Oldroyd clapped. 'Very good!' he cried, then saw Carter's rather crestfallen expression.

'Sorry, lad, I meant it,' he laughed. 'I wasn't making fun of you. People say I'm difficult to deal with at first until they get to know me: blunt speaking, unpredictable, things like that. But you'll see for yourself no doubt.'

A waitress brought two large steak sandwiches and a huge bowl of chips.

'Well, what a first day!' continued Oldroyd, changing the subject back to work. 'Any further thoughts on the case?'

Carter took a bite of his sandwich and another big pull on his beer while he struggled to marshal his thoughts.

'Well, sir – this is very good by the way, thanks.'

'You're welcome; local beer, brewed in Keighley.' He stroked his own glass of orange juice and looked longingly at Carter's beer.

Carter began again. 'There're a lot of things we don't know yet and there are a number of possibilities. As I don't believe in magic, there's obviously some practical explanation as to how the body got down there.'

'Have you now ruled out the possibility that he was murdered down there?'

'Not entirely, but I accept that it's very unlikely.'

'Cautious and sensible,' said Oldroyd with a smile.

'We know that he was a caver himself, so he's not going to go any-where near a pothole without equipment. We know he was unpopular, which is going to give us plenty of suspects. It strikes me as almost impossible that anyone who didn't know anything about caves would hump a body down there, so it's reasonable to assume he was bashed on the head by one of his fellow cavers. What I don't understand is how or why they took the body so far down the cave system and plonked it where it was obviously going to be found. And this other thing about these cavers going through and not finding a body. That's very suspicious.'

'Suspicious?'

'Are they saying that to try to confuse us? They could be involved in it. You said the body had been underground for several days.'

'I could be wrong. We'll have to wait for forensics.'

'But if you're right, what they said is impossible.'

'It seems like it, but if they were involved in the murder why spin us such a clumsy story? And they all backed each other up, which means that all four of them would be involved.'

'But if this bloke had lots of enemies, that's possible.'

'True.' Oldroyd did not sound convinced. 'I think it's likely we are dealing with more than one person, but four is a bit excessive.'

'Four people could have got the body down there. Maybe they did it in a kind of relay.'

'Yes, it would have been easier, but you're still left with your other question: why?'

'Obviously whoever did it wanted to conceal the body, but they seem to have gone about it in the daftest way I've ever come across.'

'I agree, and it suggests to me something went wrong with the plan.'

'How do you mean, sir?'

'I don't think we were meant to discover the body at all, and certainly not in the way we did.'

'You mean somebody went down and moved it? That sounds even weirder to me.'

'Well, we really are speculating now, but it's possible, maybe to incriminate the killer.'

'But if you knew somebody had committed a murder why not just report them? And nothing about the body tells us who did it.'

'That's true, but there's one thing you've forgotten.'

Oldroyd produced the bag containing the strange hook.

'I don't know what to make of that, sir,' admitted Carter.

Oldroyd looked again at the rusty piece of metal. 'What was it used for and why was it down there? I think this little object holds some of the keys to this mystery.'

They'd finished their sandwiches.

'Drink up, Andy. I'm leaving you here in Burnthwaite. I'll pick you up later on. Find out about Atkins and the people who knew him. Find out when he was last seen. You also need to interview the man who found the body; Geoff Whitaker, I think Craven said his name was. Craven will help you.'

'What about you, sir?'

'I'm going to study speleology.'

'Caves.'

'Indeed. We need to find out a lot more about these cave systems. I'm going to start with a visit to this Simon Hardiman at Garthwaite Hall.'

'Where's that?'

'A little way up the dale from here; it's a nineteenth-century hall and it's now an outdoor-pursuit centre. You know, the kind of place where parties of schoolkids go to stay and they take them out walking and caving.'

'I went with the school once to Wales. It rained all the time we were there. I just remember coming back soaked every day after trudging over muddy paths. We had a good time in the dorm though, drinking cans of lager that we smuggled in.'

'You sound like a bit of a tearaway.'

Carter laughed. 'Not really, sir. Just one of the lads, you know.' He didn't dare tell Oldroyd yet how badly he'd gone off the rails for a while after his father died. Some people had laughed when he had decided to join the police force and he'd had to endure plenty of comments of the 'takes one to know one' and 'poacher turned gamekeeper' type.

'Let's get on then.' Oldroyd got to his feet. 'And don't be too laddish when Steph gets back.'

'Who, sir?'

'Stephanie Johnson, Detective Sergeant Stephanie Johnson to be precise. Your colleague, and the other sergeant normally in my team. She's been away on leave but she's back tomorrow. Quite a character, so be careful what you say, but I think you'll get on well. You'll have to spend more time getting to know people back at HQ if you get much chance while we're on this case. It'll be a nice job for you tomorrow to brief Steph on what we know so far.' Oldroyd's eyes glinted mischievously for a moment.

They began to walk down a narrow passageway to the outer door.

'And don't forget to check the statements from those cavers who claim to have gone through the system and not seen a body. Craven's team will have got to work on it. Find out who they all are and see if their statements are consistent. If we're not happy we'll have to interview them all separately and—'

He broke off suddenly as the door opened in front of them and they were confronted by a burly figure.

'Nah then, are you t'police? I 'ear Atkins 'as been done in. They said you'd come in 'ere.'

'And who are you?'

Oldroyd stood firm, not giving way to the hostile presence and looking the man in the eyes. Those eyes were narrowed and his teeth were bared almost like a dog snarling. His face was dirty and his big rough hands were black with what looked like oil or grease. He wore ragged jeans and a jumper riddled with holes.

'That bugger owed me money, a lot o' money, and if you lot were doing yer job right you'd be getting it back for me.'

His arm rose and he began to punch his index finger at Oldroyd as he moved closer to him. Carter sprung instantly into action. This was his territory; he had encountered hundreds of thugs in his time in the Met. He moved between Oldroyd and the newcomer.

'Calm down now, sir, and watch it; we're police officers.'

'What? Yer young bugger. It's Atkins yer should have arrested years ago, not me!'

'Right.' Carter was going for his handcuffs and was ready to struggle with the man.

'All right, Carter, go steady.' To Carter's surprise, Oldroyd put a hand on the shoulder of each of them. He faced the man again.

'Look, I know you're angry, but don't do anything silly. Calm down and come into the bar with us now. Tell us all about it and I'll buy you a pint.'

The effect was immediate. The man backed down and the snarl left his face, although he continued to glare at Carter.

'Reet then, I'll have a pint o' bitter.'

They walked back into the bar, Carter bringing up the rear, still with a hand on the cuffs in his pocket.

They sat in the corner of the bar and Oldroyd ordered a pint. The landlord had clearly heard the scuffle in the passage and glanced over.

'No trouble, I hope?' he asked.

'Don't worry, we'll handle him.'

Oldroyd walked over and placed the beer in front of the man, who remained in a grim silence.

'Ta,' was all he said. Then he picked up the glass and downed half of the contents in one gulp.

'Now,' said Oldroyd. 'I asked you your name.'

'Cartwright, Sam Cartwright.' He wiped foam from his mouth with the dirty sleeve of his jumper. 'I've a garage just outside t'village.'

'And how do you know Dave Atkins?'

'He had an old Morris Countryman and I did it up for 'im.'

'You mean the model with a wooden frame at the back?'

'Aye, that's it. I had to replace all t'rotten wood and I overhauled th'engine an' everything; put a new drive shaft in.'

'And he didn't pay?'

Cartwright's hand formed a fist.

'No, the bugger didn't. It took weeks to do t'job and I had to send off for some new parts. I wasn't overcharging 'im but he argued about it, said I'd taken too long, the bastard.'

Cartwright banged his fist down on the table.

'Steady on,' said Oldroyd. 'You said earlier you knew he'd been done in. How did you know it was murder?'

'I've been talking to Alan Williams. He was one of them that brought t'body up this morning.'

'Did you do him in?'

Oldroyd asked the blunt question again. Cartwright was as unabashed as if Oldroyd had asked him if he wanted another pint.

'No, but I'll tell you this. You'll have a bloody job on trying to find out who killed that bugger. I wouldn't be surprised if there weren't celebrations in t'village tonight.'

'He was that unpopular, was he?'

'He was, and I can see I'm not going to get me brass. That's what you should be doing. It's no good bothering about him: he's dead now. You want to bother with them that's living.'

'We can't do anything about that. You'll have to go to a solicitor.'

'Huh,' Cartwright scoffed contemptuously. 'And if I go to one of them money-grabbing buggers I'll be worse off at th'end than when I started.'

'It's the only thing you can do. I'm afraid our job is to catch who killed the victim.' Oldroyd was firm but friendly. He seemed to have tamed the beast.

The beast grunted, drained the rest of its beer and fondled the glass in a self-conscious way as if hoping Oldroyd might buy it another. The latter, however, was intent on winding up this conversation.

'I'm sorry about what happened to you,' he said, 'but I'm afraid we must be getting off. As you knew Mr Atkins, someone will be coming round to give you a formal interview. And please take my advice: don't get nasty with policemen. We're only doing our job.'

Cartwright grunted again and got heavily to his feet.

'Thanks for t'beer. I can't say I wish you luck in finding out who did it. They did a bloody good job, getting rid of that sod.'

With that, he walked straight down the passageway and out of the pub.

Carter shook his head.

'I thought we were going to have real trouble there.'

'You can do a lot with a man round here if you offer him a drink. It's better to avoid conflict if you can; keep them on your side. You never know when they could be useful. I bet we'll find he's never far from this pub. I've seen that garage of his: full of battered old classic cars, forecourt blackened with oil and grease. It's not on the tourist circuit, but he'll know plenty about the locals.'

'I couldn't tell what he was saying half the time.'

Oldroyd laughed. 'I'm not surprised. We might have to send an interpreter round with you if you interview some of these broad Yorkshire types. It's not as difficult for people like you as it used to be. I doubt if you'd have understood a word my grandfather said; I had to struggle sometimes. Anyway, it's time we were off.'

The two detectives were about to leave when they were stopped again, this time by the landlord, a florid-faced man with a large paunch, who looked rather concerned.

'Can I have a quick word?' he said.

'Sure,' said Oldroyd, and they followed him into a tiny snug, which at that moment was empty.

'I'm Trevor Booth, the landlord. I think we've met before, Chief Inspector.'

'Yes, I've been in most pubs round here. Most publicans know me.'

Despite Oldroyd's affability, the man still seemed uncomfortable.

'Well, we've all heard about what's happened. Dave Atkins was found in Jingling Pot, wasn't he?'

'That's right. I assume you knew him. Did you have any connection with him?'

'Oh no, except that he was a regular in here; not a well-liked individual though. But I really wanted to ask about Geoff.'

'Who?'

'Geoff Whitaker. I understand he found the body?'

'He did.'

'He works for me here in the kitchen; he's a chef.'

'I see; well, I don't think he'll be in to work today after the shock he's had.'

'No. He's not due in until tonight, but I'm not expecting him now. It's just that . . .' He paused. 'I hate saying this, but something's been wrong with Geoff recently and I think it had something to do with Atkins.'

'Would you like to explain?'

'Well, for the last few weeks, Geoff has seemed to be always short of money, which is unusual for him. I mean, I've never known him to have money worries before. He and his wife seem to manage all right, you know.'

'OK. So when did things change?'

'As I say, two or three weeks ago, he started to come in looking worried and asking me if there was any overtime available. Then one night I overheard him having a row with someone out at the back. I looked through a window in the bar and it was Atkins. After a bit, Atkins stormed off and Geoff came back in, red faced and looking furious. I don't think it meant anything, really. I mean, I'm sure Geoff wouldn't have done anything. Anyway, he found the body, didn't he? Which probably means—'

Oldroyd interrupted him. 'Thank you, Mr Booth; you leave us to find out what happened and who was responsible. You've done the right thing in telling us.'

The landlord looked relieved.

'Oh, right, well, that's it then.' He made to return into the main bar.

'Just before you go, Mr Booth.'

'Yes?'

'I realise from what everyone is telling me that Mr Atkins was not popular. As the landlord here in the village, you probably have a better view than anyone of who gets on with who. Who would you say were the people who disliked him the most? Or, to put it bluntly, had a reason to kill him?'

Booth now looked very uncomfortable.

'Well . . . I . . . well, Inspector, I don't really like to say. I might be incriminating people.'

He looked pleadingly at Oldroyd, but found no relief in the implacable look on the detective's face.

'Well, there's obviously Sam Cartwright, as you already know. Other than that, I suppose it would be those whose wives he had affairs with. There were lots of those, I think, but the one that was fairly well known recently was Anne Watson, Bill Watson's wife. They run the Wharfedale Gift Shop.'

Carter noted the details.

'There were also rumours that he was involved with some dodgy dealings with money, but I don't know anything about it; it's probably all gossip.'

'Well, thank you, Mr Booth,' said Oldroyd. 'Can I ask you when you last saw David Atkins alive?'

Booth thought for a moment.

'I haven't seen him for about a week. He was in here with a few of his mates, loud-mouthed and bragging as usual. It beats me what women see in men like that – such a bloody big-head.' He smiled wryly. 'I always thought women were supposed to be more discerning.'

Oldroyd looked at Carter.

'What do you think about that then, Andy?' he said, looking at his new detective. 'Give us the benefit of your experience. I'll bet it's not inconsiderable.'

'Sir, you're making me blush. Well, I think some women, you know, they like men who make them laugh, give them a good time, know what I mean? They don't want boring, steady blokes; they want a bit of excitement.'

'I see.' Oldroyd reflected. 'Well, Atkins must have had something going for him, but it could have been his downfall in the end.' He turned to the landlord again. 'That night was close to when we think he died. It could have been the last time he was seen in public. Do you remember when he left, and if he left alone?'

'Actually I do. He'd been talking about having a new woman. And he made a big thing about leaving by himself as if he was going to meet her. All his mates were calling out to him as he left. They got a bit crude, you know: "Give her one from me", and all that stuff.'

'Can you remember what time that was?'

'It was fairly late I think, nearly eleven o'clock.'

'Who else was in here that night?'

'Lots of people, Inspector. It was busy, holiday season you know, plenty of tourists in the village, but I remember Sam was in, and Alan Williams – the man in charge of Cave Rescue.'

'Yes, we met him earlier today. Was Geoff Whitaker working in the kitchen all evening?'

'To be honest, I can't remember for sure, but I think he probably was because it was a Monday, so he would have been doing the evening shift. He's usually here until about midnight. I don't think he left early, but, as I said, I'm sure Geoff had nothing to do with it.'

Oldroyd ignored the last comment.

'Anyway, thanks again, and if you remember anything else significant, let us know.'

Oldroyd and Carter finally made their delayed exit from the pub.

'Well, that was all very interesting,' remarked Oldroyd as they walked out past the parked cars. 'The landlord of the local pub can always be relied upon for useful information.'

'Yes, sir, but it all seems to make it more complicated. The number of people with a motive seems to grow all the time.'

'At least we have some leads. I would say that night in the pub here was probably his last alive. That meeting with a woman was his last with the fair sex. We have to find out who she was. I wonder if he told anybody?'

'Probably not; she might have sworn him to secrecy to keep it from her husband, if she had one. What did you think of the landlord, sir? Why do you think he was so keen to deny that this Geoff Whitaker had anything to do with it? Do you think he's protecting him?'

'Could be, but I suspect it's nothing more mundane than he's worried he'll lose his chef if the man gets into any trouble. A good chef is hard to replace. The whole reputation of your pub these days can depend on the quality of the food. I'll be interested to know what you make of him in your interview.'

They had reached the car parked by the village green. Inspector Craven was waiting with some of his officers, so Oldroyd briefed them on what had happened in the Red Horse before driving off in the direction of Garthwaite Hall.

Back in the Red Horse, Trevor Booth was polishing glasses and thinking about the impact this was going to have on the village. The barmaid who worked in the adjacent bar appeared in the connecting archway.

'Was that the police, Trevor?'

'Yes.'

'What did they want?'

'Haven't you heard? It's Dave Atkins. He's dead; they found his body in Jingling Pot.'

'What? Down the pothole?'

'Yes. Are you OK?'

She looked alarmed and her face had turned pale.

'Fine; it's just . . . a shock, isn't it?' And she went back into the other bar before he could reply.

Two

If tha wants to keep all thi bones 'ole,
Don't go fallin' into Boggart's 'Ole.

Oldroyd got out of the car and looked at the impressive house and grounds of Garthwaite Hall, which had been built in the early nineteenth century by the Ingleby family, who had owned it for generations until they declined into the minor aristocracy and could no longer afford to maintain it. The house wasn't that big but had been skilfully designed to produce that sense of artistry and grandeur the upper classes considered so important in those times. There were, however, distinct signs of neglect. Paint was peeling from the woodwork and, although the framework of what must have once been extensive gardens was still there, everything was overgrown, with only the roughly cut lawn showing any signs of attention.

His knock was answered by an athletically built woman in a white shirt and blue tracksuit bottoms, her blonde hair tied back in a ponytail.

'Can I help you?' She didn't sound very enthusiastic or welcoming, thought Oldroyd, and she seemed very tired for someone so obviously strong and fit. He produced his ID.

'Detective Chief Inspector Oldroyd, West Riding Police. I'm afraid I'm investigating a murder and I'd like to come in and ask a few questions. I presume you are Caroline Hardiman? Is your husband at home?'

Not surprisingly, the woman looked startled. 'A murder? But who?'

'A Mr David Atkins.'

'Dave Atkins from Burnthwaite?'

'Yes.'

'Oh, but that's terrible!'

She looked genuinely shocked.

'Did you know him?' asked Oldroyd.

'Well, yes, he used to work for us. You'd better come in, sorry.'

She led the way into a large room which had somewhat faded-looking sofas and chairs around the walls and a very outdated television set in the corner. It was obviously some kind of lounge for the use of the guests.

'Please, sit down. Can I get you a drink?'

'No, thank you, I've just come from the Red Horse at Burnthwaite.'

Oldroyd settled into a dusty armchair. He studied her for a moment and then asked, 'You said he used to work for you. I take it he hasn't recently?'

'No.'

'Why is that?'

She shuffled uncomfortably in the chair before answering.

'He and my husband didn't really get on.'

'Why was that? Was his work unsatisfactory?'

'No. Dave was an experienced caver and fully qualified. The groups he took out enjoyed themselves.' She seemed unhappy at the line of questioning. 'Let's say some other issues cropped up and Simon was not happy. Dave was only given temporary contracts for the work he did and Simon stopped employing him.'

'What issues were those?' Oldroyd was insistent.

'I'd rather not say.' She was calm and assertive, but Oldroyd was having none of it.

'Mrs Hardiman, this is a murder enquiry. I must ask you to answer my questions fully and honestly.'

Caroline folded her arms and frowned.

Oldroyd continued, 'I am aware that Mr Atkins was something of a womaniser. Did you have an affair with him?' Oldroyd was in his inter-rogative mode. His keen eyes had become even more penetrating, his voice commanding and his posture alert. It all generated a force that few interviewees could withstand. Caroline Hardiman was no exception.

'No, I didn't, but he did make sort of . . . advances, and Simon didn't like it.'

'Is your husband a violent man, Mrs Hardiman?'

'No! Look, Inspector, this is all a bit too much. You've only just told me that Dave is dead; nothing happened between us.'

'But your husband didn't like his attentions?'

'No.'

Oldroyd was satisfied with her answer and softened. He sat back in the chair for a moment and looked around.

'I suppose it's very hard work, running this place. You look tired.'

Caroline relaxed and crossed her legs.

'It is – harder than we thought. We took a risk coming here; we were teachers in Leeds, but we'd always fancied running one of these centres and this place seemed ideal. We managed to get the money together somehow to buy the hall, but there's always so much to do and so much that needs to be spent. You know: leaking roofs, big utility bills, all that stuff. And then there's all the Health and Safety paperwork. It's a struggle.' She looked around the room at the faded wallpaper, which was starting to peel off in places.

'Look at this place. It's not exactly a five-star hotel, is it? When we show people around, I can see that many of them are not impressed.'

'It seems quiet. Do you have any parties in at the moment?'

'Only one small group of five come up from Cambridge to do some potholing. We've got bookings for the bank holiday weekend next week but it's the school holidays and our main clients are the schools. We're cheap and cheerful and can accommodate large parties in basic dormitories. The teachers like it because we take responsibility for all the activities and they just look after the kids in the evenings.'

'They don't like it when things go wrong, do they?'

'No, they don't.' A haunted look passed across her face.

Oldroyd's eyes flickered imperceptibly. 'Anyway,' he continued, 'when did you last see Dave Atkins?'

'I can't remember. I must have seen him around the village or in the Red Horse but Simon and I don't, didn't, have any contact with him any more; he wasn't a pleasant man.'

'So everyone keeps telling me,' replied Oldroyd. 'I think the whole village must have conspired to kill him.'

Caroline gave him a wan smile.

'Well, thank you for answering my questions. Actually, I really came to talk to your husband, if he's available. I wanted to ask him about the caves around here.'

'The caves?'

'Yes, not that I want to go caving myself, but you see David Atkins's body was found in Jingling Pot.'

'Jingling Pot? I didn't realise, but that's the last place I'd have expected. Are you sure it wasn't an accident? Those systems are very dangerous. Even those of us who go down regularly know that it's always risky in the dark with rock falls, water rising and things like that.'

'We're pretty sure it wasn't. You see, when he was found, he was not wearing any headgear or carrying any equipment.'

35

'That's impossible. He was a very experienced caver. He would never have gone down like that.'

'The murderer, or more likely murderers, obviously took the body there.'

'But why would they take a body down into a cave system?' She shuddered. 'That's awful.'

'It's certainly a mystery, but don't worry, we'll solve it. Now, your husband.'

Caroline looked hesitant.

'Look, Inspector, after what happened, Simon doesn't like talking about Dave Atkins. It's a sore point, male pride and all that. He gets angry if you mention it, so . . .'

'Don't worry, I don't need to go into any of the details of how Atkins behaved here.'

She looked relieved. 'Good. I'll take you across. He's sorting some of the equipment. We store it in what used to be the stables.'

They left the room and Caroline led the way out of a side door and across a stone courtyard to a rectangular building. She opened a door and they entered a long, narrow room. On both walls Oldroyd could see clothing and equipment hanging on pegs and stacked in rows on shelves: helmets, anoraks, boots and waterproof leggings. He could imagine groups of excited schoolchildren laughing and giggling as they donned these unusual outfits and made ready to step into a frightening but thrilling world of darkness.

A tall, powerful man with short blond hair was hanging newly washed waterproofs and anoraks on pegs.

'Simon,' Caroline called to him as the man looked up, 'this is Detective Chief Inspector Oldroyd. Something terrible has happened. Dave Atkins has been murdered. His body was found in Jingling Pot.'

Simon Hardiman dropped the anorak he was holding and looked from his wife to Oldroyd. He seemed speechless for a moment.

'Good God!' he finally said. 'But that's incredible. How? How do you know he was murdered? Couldn't it have been an accident?'

He sat down on a bench as if the shock had taken all his energy.

'I've just been explaining to your wife, Mr Hardiman. He was found in ordinary clothes deep in the system with a nasty knock on the back of the head; blunt instrument, as we say.'

'Bloody hell, Dave Atkins.' He shook his head as if he couldn't take it in. 'But what about a rock fall?'

'I don't think so, and anyway he wouldn't have gone down there dressed like that without any equipment, would he?'

'No, you're right, he certainly wouldn't.' His puzzled expression showed that he found the facts of the case as baffling as everybody else did.

'That's absolutely incredible,' he repeated. 'I suppose people have been telling you that he wasn't popular round here.'

'Yes. Your wife has also explained that he wasn't really welcome here any more although he used to work for you.'

'It's all right, Simon, I told the Inspector about Dave's behaviour,' Caroline intervened.

'Well, you know everything then. You can't go on employing a man who is trying to seduce your wife.'

'Very difficult,' agreed Oldroyd.

'Not that there was anything wrong with his work, you understand, and I got on quite well with him; very experienced caver and good with the kids, although he did flirt with one or two of the teenage girls. He was like that; couldn't keep his eyes or his hands off any female he fancied.'

'Did he ever do anything unprofessional with the girls?'

'No, he wasn't a paedophile or anything like that. He was checked out like everyone is. He just liked showing off; thought every woman fancied him.'

Oldroyd noticed a brief blaze of anger – or was it hatred? – in Hardiman's eyes.

'I don't need to ask you any more about Atkins at the moment,' Oldroyd went on, 'your wife has given me the details, although you will also be required to make a statement about your relationship with him and what happened while he worked here.'

'I suppose as the jealous husband I must be a suspect.' Hardiman did not sound particularly worried at the prospect.

'It's far too early yet for us to have any idea who the chief suspects are. We have a lot of people to interview and we've hardly started.'

'I see.'

'The reason I'm here is to ask you for help.'

'Oh? With what?'

'I need to find out more about Jingling Pot and the other cave systems around it. I was told by one of the Cave Rescue team who helped us recover the body that you were one of the experts.'

'Well, it's very nice of him to say that. I don't claim to be any more knowledgeable than many others.'

'But you have spent a lot of time exploring these systems.'

'Yes, it's been a hobby of mine for many years and now it's my job.'

'I'm also told that you know quite a bit about the history of caving.'

'A bit, yes.'

'In that case, have you got any idea what this is?'

Oldroyd produced the plastic bag containing the rusty iron hook and gave it to Hardiman, who furrowed his brow and shook his head as he turned the object over in his hands just as Oldroyd had done outside Jingling Pot.

'I've no idea. Why do you ask?'

'It was discovered in Jingling Pot, Sump Passage to be exact, which was where Atkins's body was found.'

Hardiman shrugged. 'It's just a piece of metal.'

'Could it be a piece of equipment used in caving? I don't mean nowadays but in the past.'

Hardiman looked intently at the object again.

'Possibly, but I've really no idea, Inspector. I'm sorry. Why do you think it's anything to do with caving, anyway? It could be something that was just dropped by someone going through the passage.'

'Just a hunch, that's all.' Oldroyd took the hook and placed it back in the plastic bag.

'Thanks for your help, anyway. Now, do you have any detailed caving maps of the area?'

'Yes, of course. Let's go back into the office.'

The three retraced the route back into the house. Oldroyd noticed that the Hardimans held hands. They were obviously a very close couple and their relationship seemed to have survived anything that had happened with Atkins.

In the office, Simon went to the bookshelf and selected a volume. He flicked through it and handed it to Oldroyd open at a certain page.

'Here you go.'

The book was entitled *Caves of Upper Wharfedale* and the page showed a plan of Jingling Pot and the adjacent caves.

'Very good.' Oldroyd examined the map intently. 'So is this the most complete map of these systems that exists?'

'Absolutely, that's the most recent, based on the 2004 surveys.'

Oldroyd looked carefully at the page.

'So I can see from this, correct me if I'm wrong, that none of the other cave systems have any connection with Jingling Pot other than Wether Ridge Hole.'

'Correct.'

Oldroyd traced the Wether Ridge system and saw that what Alan Williams had told him was true; it was just as far to Sump Passage if you went through the Wether Ridge system as if you approached through Jingling Pot. He frowned.

'This confirms what I was told. There is no quick way of getting to Sump Passage, is there?'

'Who told you?'

'Alan Williams. You'll know him. Short and stocky, black hair and beard.'

'Of course, a very committed caver and a stalwart of the Cave Rescue team. By the way, Chief Inspector, if the Cave Rescue were involved, why wasn't I called out?'

'That was organised by Inspector Craven of the Skipton station. I suspect he used the first few people he could contact.'

'I see. Caroline and I were out in Skipton on a shopping trip this morning and I forgot my phone. Buying in provisions, you know.'

'Quite a big job, I should think, when you've got a lot of people staying.'

'Yes, and by the way, Alan was absolutely right. There is no other way of getting to Sump Passage.'

Oldroyd looked at the map again.

'What about this system here?' He pointed to a small network of caves adjacent to the Jingling Pot system. Hardiman looked.

'Winter's Gill Hole? No, Chief Inspector. There's no link into Jingling Pot from there. It's all been well explored, although no one goes down there much any more.'

'Why's that?'

'Too dangerous; it's one of the systems that's very wet and the rocks are loose. There've been accidents in there and, quite frankly, it's boring: nothing to see; no spectacular caverns or lakes; just a wet, low, dripping passage which comes to a fairly standard cavern and then a dead end. There's no through route.'

'And you might come to a dead end too?' observed Oldroyd sardonically.

'Yes, if you're not careful, and why risk it down there where there's nothing of interest anyway? Also,' he paused, 'you might think this odd, but what also puts people off is that there's a long tradition that Winter's Gill Hole is haunted.'

'Is there indeed? I didn't think cavers were the type to believe in ghosts.'

'I don't think they do as such, but they do believe in bad luck – I think that's the case with all dangerous activities. Cavers tend to be a bit of a superstitious bunch of people; you know, "This is my lucky helmet" and stuff like that. It's a way humans have of trying to control what we really can't control, isn't it?'

'True.' Oldroyd still seemed absorbed in the map until, as was his habit, he suddenly sprang out of his reverie.

'Well, thank you both very much. You've been extremely helpful. One of my detectives may call round to interview you again. I must be getting off now. There's just one thing. Can you do me a photocopy of this page?'

'Borrow the book if you need it for your investigation.'

'That's very useful. Thank you. It will be returned to you in due course. There's just one thing I need to ask. Can you tell me where you both were last Monday? That was the night Atkins disappeared.'

The Hardimans exchanged glances.

'Here, Chief Inspector. We don't get out much. I can't remember the last time we've managed to have a night out together.'

The interview over, they both showed him out, and as he drove away, Oldroyd's last view of them was in his rear-view mirror as they stood together by the big door and watched him disappear down the drive.

Back in Burnthwaite, news was spreading about the grisly find in Jingling Pot. The villagers were used to pothole rescues and the occasional accidental death. Murder was a different matter, especially of a man known as the local rogue. This was no outsider's crime where the body had been brought in and dumped. This, in all likelihood, had been committed by one of them. Whispered conversations were taking place in shops and on street corners as speculation mounted as to who the perpetrator might be. A farmer driving his tractor along the main street acknowledged a friend standing on the pavement with a frown and a shake of his head. He didn't stop and no words were spoken.

Carter's first task in the village was to interview Geoff Whitaker. He walked through the village on the narrow pavement admiring the old grey stone buildings. He passed some gift boutiques and a shop selling walking gear and outdoor clothing. The Wharfedale Café was reasonably full and people easily identifiable as walkers, wearing boots, carrying rucksacks and looking at maps, were strolling up and down. For a Monday it was pretty busy and Carter concluded rightly that Burnthwaite was what the tourist authorities called a 'honey pot' and that on bank holidays it would be unpleasantly crowded. 'Busy', though, was relative. It was nothing like the constant bustle of London and he was still adjusting to the quiet everywhere. He'd worried that he might find it boring, but so far quite the contrary. He felt as relaxed as if he was on holiday in the countryside and didn't feel he was missing London at all.

He passed an ancient church and a small sixteenth-century gram- mar school complete with mullioned windows. Late brooding swallows swooped up to nests under the eaves to feed their young but other- wise there was a school holiday silence about the place. The sign read 'Burnthwaite Primary School'. A little further on, a cobbled street called Dawson Row went off at a right angle. There was a row of low cottages on one side and a wall on the other. Out of the sun, there was a sudden unexpectedly chilly draught and Carter pressed on quickly, looking for No. 12, which turned out to be right at the end.

The cottages opened straight on to the street and many had pots and containers with shade-tolerant flowers and ferns that could flour- ish in the somewhat gloomy aspect. No. 12 was enhanced with a vari- ety of small azaleas, hostas and unusual ferns. Someone was keen on gardening, thought Carter. There were also a couple of children's bikes leaning against the wall.

The door was opened by a dark-haired woman in her late thirties, casually but tastefully dressed.

'Yes?' she enquired in a rather hesitant manner.

Carter produced his identification.

'Detective Sergeant Carter, madam, investigating the murder of David Atkins. I understand Mr Geoffrey Whitaker lives here?'

She took in a deep breath and seemed to be steeling herself. Clearly, she'd been expecting this.

'Yes. I'm his wife, Helen Whitaker. Please come in.' There was relief in her voice as if she'd been expecting an ordeal and was now glad to be getting it over with.

Carter stepped into a narrow hallway with steps leading steeply up to the next floor. Helen Whitaker led him into a small but stylish sitting room with a polished wooden floor and modern furnishings. A boy who looked about ten was playing on a games console and various electronic noises were issuing from the television.

'Take that upstairs, Mark.'

The boy groaned. 'Do I have to?'

'Yes.'

Reluctantly, he pulled out all the wires and left the room clutching the console and the box without even looking at Carter.

'I'm sorry about that. I'll be glad when they get back to school; it won't be long now, thank goodness.'

'Don't worry, I was like that myself, but it wasn't so sophisticated in my day. I just had a little Nintendo Game Boy but I sent my mother mad, playing on it all the time.'

She smiled and seemed to relax.

'Please have a seat, Sergeant. Geoff is upstairs lying down. It was very upsetting for him to find the body, especially in those circumstances.'

'Yes, I can imagine. It won't take long, just a few routine questions at this stage. I can come back again if necessary.'

She went upstairs. Carter watched her go. She was rather thin and plain and not an obvious target for Atkins's womanising, but it was only a small village so the chances were still high. Maybe Whitaker was one of the jealous husbands and had not only discovered the body but had also placed it there. Carter frowned: that seemed implausible somehow. Why go to all the trouble to hide the body down there and then find it yourself? Nevertheless, this case was proving to be so bizarre that almost anything seemed possible.

His ruminations were interrupted by the entrance of Geoff Whitaker, who turned out to be another chunkily built and bearded individual, this time wearing glasses. Was a beard part of the uniform of a caver? Maybe it kept them warm down in those subterranean depths.

Geoff Whitaker looked at Carter with a dazed and sleepy expression as the detective got up to greet him, then he sat down and began an account of how he'd found the body. His manner was a little shaky and uncertain and he avoided eye contact with the detective.

'It was bad enough finding a body there, totally unexpected, but when I saw who it was and realised I knew him, that was even more of a shock. To see him there, dead, wearing ordinary clothing and no gear, it was so sort of weird and horrific. I could hardly believe it was true. It seemed unreal.' He paused and looked around as if checking his feelings and sensations. 'It still does.'

'So the body was laid across the floor of this passage.'

'Sump Passage, yes. There was quite a heavy flow of water and it was pooling against the body.'

'Did you see anything else unusual?'

Whitaker thought for a moment.

'Not really. I mean, I knew he'd been murdered and it was no accident.'

Carter looked up. 'Why?'

'Because it was impossible for a man like Atkins to go down there without equipment. Believe me, all of us who are experienced know that a caver would never do that.'

'Was there any other reason why you think he was murdered?'

Whitaker looked uneasy. His hand was repetitively stroking the velvety fabric of the sofa arm.

'What do you mean?'

'Well, he wasn't exactly popular round here, was he? I understand he was one for the women and also a bit of a wide boy, unreliable with money, things like that.'

Whitaker glanced at his wife, who was sitting in silence opposite him in an armchair. The glance was so fleeting that only a detective as sharp as Carter would have noticed it or realised its possible significance.

'Well, there was that side to him.'

'Did you have much to do with him yourself?' Carter continued to probe. Again, there was a slight hesitation and Whitaker looked down.

'Only through the Caving Club. I got on reasonably well with him but he wasn't someone who I'd have wanted to strike up a friendship with. In fact, I don't think he had any real close friends, at least not in the village, only his drinking cronies in the Red Horse.'

'You didn't have any reason to really dislike him then?'

'It sounds as if you're searching for a motive for Geoff to have been the murderer, Sergeant,' Helen Whitaker intervened. Carter wondered if she was trying to help her husband, having sensed he was struggling.

'Everyone who had a grudge against Atkins is a suspect at this moment, Mrs Whitaker, and you're right, I'm trying to discover whether your husband had a motive. That's my job.'

His tone was friendly but firm.

Helen Whitaker persisted. 'How could Geoff be both the murderer and the person who found the body down there? That's ridiculous.'

Carter looked out of the window. From where he was sitting he had a good view of the surrounding fells, some of which were purple with heather. The changing pattern of light caused by the scudding clouds produced a scene of calm beauty quite at odds with the tension in the room.

'I'm not making any accusations, Mrs Whitaker. It's still very early in the investigation. We're still finding out all about the victim and the people who knew him.' He turned to Whitaker again and looked at his notebook.

'Mr Trevor Booth, the landlord at the Red Horse, reports that he saw you having an argument with David Atkins at the back of the pub. Is that true, sir?'

Whitaker didn't reply; his hand stopped stroking the sofa arm.

His wife intervened again.

'Why did he say that? Is he trying to implicate Geoff in this?'

Carter ignored her and waited for Whitaker's reply.

'Yes, it's true,' he finally confessed, but didn't say more.

'When was that, sir?'

'About two weeks ago.'

'And what were you arguing about?'

Whitaker sighed.

'It was money, Sergeant. I lent Atkins some money and he hadn't repaid me. I confronted him that night because I was fed up of waiting for him to pay me back.'

'I see,' said Carter. 'Did you often lend him money?'

'No, that's the only time.'

'You see, Mr Booth also said he thought that, recently, you were a bit short of cash, offering to do overtime and things like that.'

'That bloke wants to mind his own business,' Helen interjected before Whitaker continued.

'We've been a bit short, partly because I lent Atkins that money, partly because we've spent a bit on the house; probably a bit more than we could afford.'

'Why were you down in those caves, Mr Whitaker?'

'I was leading a group of people. I often earn a bit of extra money that way, and it's coming in handy at the moment. The club's regularly contacted by groups who want to do some proper potholing and realise that they need someone with qualifications and experience to lead them through.'

'Were the rest of the party all behind you?'

'Yes, but obviously we don't lead a party like that alone. There was also a bloke from the club who was at the rear, but I was the leader, and I found the body.'

'Do you know that cave system well?'

'Yes, we all do; everyone in the club knows Jingling Pot. It's a classic one for taking inexperienced groups down: challenging, plenty to see, but not really dangerous as long as you're sensible.'

'You mean not taking any risks?'

'Yes.'

'Did you see anything else unusual?'

Whitaker considered this question as a shaft of sunlight lit up the room.

'Not really.'

'It's just that Alan Williams of the Cave Rescue team who went down to get the body out says there had been a recent rock fall.'

Whitaker considered. He actually seemed more relaxed now they were back on the discovery of the body.

'Can't say I noticed anything, but something like that wouldn't be unusual; rocks are moving all the time down there, that's one of the main dangers.'

'Mr Williams also says that he and some other cavers went through a few days before and saw no body, nothing unusual. What do you think of that?'

'What about it?'

'But it looks like the body had been down there a while.'

Whitaker shrugged.

'I can't see why Alan should make that up. I don't know.'

His voice tailed off. Carter realised he could not pursue that point any more and anyway he knew virtually nothing about caving. The only pot he had any knowledge of was the kind you smoked. That was another part of his past that he tried to keep secret now that he was in the police.

'OK, Mr Whitaker, I realise you've had a pretty heavy time, so that's all for the moment. We will require you to make a full statement and I'll send a detective constable round for that. Just one last question. Mr Booth says you were working in the kitchens at the Red Horse last Monday night. Can you confirm that?'

'Yes, I work evenings on Mondays. I remember catching a glimpse of Atkins in the bar when I walked through for something. I didn't know it was going to be his last time in there.'

'Neither did he.' Carter got up and smiled. 'I hope you're soon fully recovered; you're obviously a valued employee at the Red Horse.'

'Huh!' Helen Whitaker was contemptuous. 'If that's true, Trevor Booth could start paying Geoff a bit more. He's a stingy so and so.'

Carter laughed.

'Well, I won't report that back to him.'

Carter looked intently at Whitaker, who had slumped further into the sofa. Was his tiredness just because of the shock of discovering the body?

Helen Whitaker showed Carter to the door and gave him a rather curt goodbye.

Helen Whitaker watched as Carter walked back towards the main street, then closed the door and returned to the living room. The changing sky had darkened again and the room was gloomy. She stood in the doorway and stared at her husband, who returned her gaze in silence.

'I still can't believe you got involved with that man after what happened,' she said. 'Anyway, it's all over and done with now.'

'It's not. You know there's someone else involved.'

'Well, you'd better get them sorted out.'

From the Whitakers, Carter reported back to Inspector Craven and then went to search Dave Atkins's house. He'd lived in a small cottage in a row similar to the Whitakers'. Looking at the outside, Carter could see signs of neglect and a general air of shabbiness. Grass was growing between the old cobblestones. Right down at the bottom of the lane was the old Morris Minor Countryman Sam Cartwright had repaired, partially covered with tarpaulin. Craven had lent him two DCs and one of them unlocked the door using a key found on Atkins's body.

In the small hallway was a motorbike, which they could just squeeze past, and a pile of mail, which they picked up. They smelled the mustiness of the uninhabited house. The kitchen was old and scruffy but reasonably clean and tidy. The same was true of the other downstairs room, which showed clear signs of a bachelor existence and a rough-and-ready attitude to cleanliness and order.

While he went upstairs, Carter sent the DCs to examine the kitchen and waste bin: often the best guide to someone's last movements. One bedroom was empty except for a single bed and a cheap bedside cabinet with a lamp. The other bedroom was obviously Atkins's and here Carter found what he was looking for. The dead man had clearly used this room as a kind of office as well as a bedroom. There was a computer and some shelves containing files. Why did he have all this in his bedroom when there was ample room downstairs? Did he feel safer in the night sleeping near to whatever the hard drive and box files contained? He looked back at the door and saw that there was a lock on it, unlike the other bedroom. Clearly, the contents of this room were important to him. But the door had not been locked, suggesting that he'd expected to return in reasonable time after he'd left home. Had anything happened to change his mind? And who had changed it for him? They still had very little information about the victim's final movements after he left the Red Horse.

Carter looked at the row of box files and randomly selected one. It seemed to contain mostly technical information on land acquisition and property developments. There were some glossy brochures promising big returns on investments. Clearly, Atkins was a speculator; this must have been how he made his money as no one had mentioned any kind of regular job or career. All this stuff would have to go back to HQ.

Carter was beginning to form a picture of the man. Sharp with money but not to be trusted; a bit of a loner in life but also a woman-iser. Not a man to make any commitments. He preferred illicit liaisons with women committed to other relationships. He didn't want to take them from their husbands; that was the last thing on his mind. A self-centred, charming, rather unpleasant individual. He was just the kind of person to make lots of enemies, but it probably wouldn't concern him in the slightest.

Carter went downstairs and instructed the DCs to pack up the files and computer in the bedroom, then went outside. Another important source of information in these circumstances was the neighbours.

He knocked on the door of the cottage next to Atkins's. It was opened by a surly-looking man in his late thirties. He had a fat belly, tattooed arms and a pierced nose.

'Yeah?'

'DS Carter, West Riding Police. Unfortunately, I have to tell you that your neighbour has been found murdered.'

'What? Bloody hell!' Despite these expletives, the man did not seem very surprised or shocked. Everyone in this village seemed almost to have expected Atkins to be murdered. Did they all have a hand in it? Was it a gruesome group pagan affair like that film *The Wicker Man*?

Maybe they all went down that pothole thing and performed some ritual in the darkness before committing the poor bloke's body to the subterranean gods.

'When did you last see Mr Atkins?'

'He hasn't been around for a few days.' He thought for a moment. 'Today's Monday. I'd say I last saw him a week ago, maybe. Just a minute.' He turned and shouted into the house. 'Oi, Carol, come here, will you? There's a copper here wants to know when we last saw Dave.'

Carter heard a muffled 'Just a minute'; a toilet flushed and then a woman appeared. She was clearly even more enthusiastic about piercing than her partner. Her ears were double pierced. Her eyebrows and nose contained huge rings and when she spoke, a tongue stud was clearly in evidence. She also sported tattoos on her upper arms. Carter was unable to prevent himself speculating about their sexual liaisons. How could you do anything with all that metal in the way? The risk of injury must be quite considerable.

'What's happened?' she said.

'Dave's been done in.'

'What?'

'Done in, murdered.'

'Bloody hell!' she said, repeating her partner's response.

'Yes, his body was found down a pothole. We're trying to establish his last movements. When did you last see him?' asked Carter.

'It was last Monday, wasn't it?' The man turned to his partner.

She thought for a moment.

'Yeah, Monday afternoon he was playing about with his bike in the yard. He was always doing that and the bloody oil went all over the place.'

'Yeah, that's right.'

'But hold on. I think I heard him leave later on. I heard the door bang. He was probably off to the Red Horse. He went down there quite a lot.'

'What time would that be then?'

'Mmm, about eight, I think. It was starting to get dark, anyway.'

'He hasn't been back since then?'

'No.'

'Did you think that was strange?'

'No, he was always going off for days on end on that bike of his. He used to visit his children over Burnley way. He was divorced.'

'That's useful, thank you. Did you get on OK, I mean as neighbours?'

There was a pause.

'He wasn't bad, I suppose,' replied the woman. 'Not much trouble really. We didn't have much to do with him; although you used to get a few noises coming through the wall now and again.'

'What kind of noises?'

'You know, people . . .'

'She means when he was shagging women.' The man laughed and his partner giggled.

'Shut up, Gary!'

'I see. Did he do a lot of that then?'

'Quite a lot, yes, and sometimes women from the village.'

'Did you see any of these women going in and out?'

'No, but we heard him going in and out.' The fat bloke burst into raucous laughter again.

'Seriously, Mr . . . ?'

'Shaw, Gary Shaw.'

'I'm Carol.'

'Did either of you see them?'

'Well, if we did that would be telling. It's none of our business. We don't go telling business round the village like some busybodies do.'

Carter toughened his stance and his language turned formal.

'Mr Shaw, Mrs Shaw. This is a murder enquiry. I have reason to believe that you possess important information in relation to this investigation and I must ask you not to withhold it; if you do, you may be committing an offence.'

This made an impact.

'You'd better come inside a minute,' said Carol, 'and by the way I'm not Mrs Shaw, Carol Anderson's the name. I wouldn't get married to that fat git.' At this, the pair of them burst out into laughter yet again.

'Inside' proved to be quite an experience. The living-room walls were painted a darkish shade of purple and the pictures hung up were a vivid combination of sci-fi horror and pornography. Faded African throws covered a dusty sofa and the worn carpet looked as if it hadn't been vacuumed for weeks. The air was heavy with the scent of joss sticks and other unmistakable odours, which meant that Carter didn't need to ask what this pair grew in their garden. However, in the circumstances he decided to overlook it. He sat on a chair while the couple sank into the sofa.

'What can you tell me?'

'I haven't seen anybody and I don't spread rumours.' Gary Shaw was still insistent. He turned to Carol. 'But you said you once saw somebody you recognised.'

Carol leaned forward and whispered as if they could be overheard through the walls.

'I saw a woman leaving the house. I went downstairs for a glass of water; I heard a noise outside and had a peep through the window. She and Dave were kissing, then he went back inside and she left. It must have been about two in the morning.'

'You definitely recognised her?'

'Yes. I was quite close to them but there was no light on in the room so they never thought there was anybody there looking.'

'She likes watching other people at it.'

'Shut up!' bawled Carol and they both roared with laughter again.

'And who was this woman?'

Gary answered.

'Anne Watson. Her and her husband Bill run the gift shop just down the road. It's called the Wharfedale Gift Shop.'

'Thank you.' Carter took down the information in his notebook. That was confirmation of what Trevor Booth of the Red Horse had said.

'Did Mr Watson know about the affair?'

'We never said anything,' said Gary defensively.

'No, sir, I wasn't implying that you did.'

'I think he did get to know,' said Carol. 'There was a bit of trouble, you know, but they're still together.'

'Was there anyone else you recognised who made night-time visits?'

'No, but there were definitely other women. You could hear voices, but they always got into the house without being seen.'

Despite your best efforts, thought Carter.

'Did he have any other regular visitors?'

'He didn't seem to have many friends. I think he did a lot of shady stuff with money. One or two of those caving people dropped in now and again.'

'Yeah, those hairy blokes who do it underground with a helmet on.' Gary exploded with laughter at his own joke. This time his partner ignored him.

'What made you think that Atkins was involved with anything illegal to do with money?'

Carol Anderson pulled back.

'I don't know for certain, but it seemed funny to me that Dave seemed to live quite well but he never had a regular job. Where did he get his money from?'

'I see. Who in particular did you suspect might be involved?'

'That Geoff Whitaker used to call round quite a lot at one time. He's a chef at the Red Horse.'

'Yes, we've interviewed him. He found the body.'

'What?'

'Yes, so any reason you know of as to why he came to the house regularly?'

'No, but it was probably dodgy deals of some kind and I'll bet something went wrong. Remember that time we heard them arguing, Gary?'

Gary was still reluctant to give any information but muttered a grudging 'Yeah.'

'When was that?' asked Carter.

'It was a few months ago now. Whitaker had been in the house a while, then we heard raised voices. Suddenly the door slammed; I ran to the window and saw him striding off down the lane.'

Again, confirmation of what Trevor Booth had said. Some things were firming up a little. Carter decided he'd got enough information for the moment and was glad to make his escape.

'Well, thank you for your help. If you think of anything else that might be relevant let us know.' He handed over his card.

'I'll show you out,' said Carol and they left Gary slumped in the sofa. Carter heard the television being switched on.

Carter was about to walk through the door when he found Carol blocking his way.

'Nice of you to call round, Sergeant, I hope we'll see you again sometime.' She leered over Carter in an unmistakable manner. Close up, the blue of her tattoos was somehow revolting and her perfume was suffocating.

'Yes, well, thank you again,' was all he could think of in reply. A terrible image of tangling with all that metal had appeared in his mind and he left the house as swiftly as he could.

In the late afternoon Oldroyd picked Carter up for the journey back to Harrogate.

'Any luck?' asked Oldroyd.

Carter held up his well-used notebook. 'Yes, lots of useful stuff, sir.'

'OK, jump in. Give me a brief account now and save the detail until we have a case meeting tomorrow. There's something I want to show you.'

As they drove out of Burnthwaite, Carter looked again with renewed interest at the green landscape with the fields and barns.

'Why are there so many caves round here then, sir?'

Oldroyd replied eagerly.

'Because of the rocks beneath us. It's limestone; carboniferous limestone, to be exact. It's a pervious rock – water passes through and dissolves it. Over thousands of years the water has carved out the caves.'

Carter remembered all this vaguely from his geography lessons. The problem was that the teacher had sat him next to one of the prettiest girls in the class and he'd spent most of his time trying to chat her up. He strained to remember what he'd learned.

'Is that where you have those things that hang down? Stalactites or something?'

'Well done. Stalactites hang from the roof of the cave and stalagmites grow from the floor. They're both made up of calcite deposits left by dripping water.'

'That's it, sir, we used to remember that by thinking "tites" come down, you know, like a girl's—'

'I think I've got the idea, Andy. You sound like you were a bit laddish in your schooldays.'

'Oh, I was, sir, a right little sparky character till my dad died. That changed me.'

'No wonder,' said Oldroyd. 'Anyway, we'll just stop here.'

Due to the conversation, Carter hadn't noticed that Oldroyd had taken a different route back. The roadside walls had gone. They were driving on a lonely road across a bare landscape, flattish on either side with low hills rising in the near distance.

Oldroyd drove off the road and stopped on the sheep-cropped grass.

'Out you get; we're going for a little walk. This is real limestone country.'

The two men followed a path and Carter noticed that a stream came under the road and continued across the field. The path took them by the stream across smooth green turf cropped close by the sheep that were randomly scattered around.

'Limestone landscape,' continued Oldroyd, 'is both beautiful and strange.'

He said nothing else for a while as they walked towards what appeared to be a narrow gap between the hills.

Carter was aware of the atmosphere changing. He looked up: there were white lines high above but no aircraft noise. The sun was getting low in the sky. The black shape of some kind of bird of prey circled slowly over the hills. They approached the gap.

'Stop,' said Oldroyd quietly. 'Listen. What can you hear?'

Carter listened but could hear nothing except the slight hissing of the wind.

'Nothing, sir.'

'Exactly. Wonderful, isn't it? It's strange because we're not used to it. I think it's something to do with these hills cutting out the noise. You're in a kind of amphitheatre.'

Carter was used to an environment of constant noise. Silence in London was virtually unobtainable. Even if you went out into the countryside of Kent or Sussex, you were never far from a trunk road or motorway and planes were passing overhead.

'You also get this kind of effect.' Oldroyd stopped and turned to the hills.

'Hello!' he shouted towards the distant craggy limestone cliff. A second later the clearest echo Carter had ever heard returned eerily over the fields.

'That's incredible, sir.'

'Try it.'

Carter shouted his name, which duly returned to him teasingly, like a child who repeats everything you say.

'I've never heard one like that before.'

Oldroyd smiled archly. 'By the way,' he said, 'what's happened to the stream?'

Carter had been gazing at the hills and the sky and had forgotten the stream they were following. He looked down only to see that the rocky bed was dry. The water was gone; a substantial stream had completely disappeared!

'What the . . . ?'

Oldroyd laughed. 'It's another limestone trick. It's disappeared bit by bit down holes into the underground cave system.'

'This place could give you the creeps,' said Carter, who was nevertheless absorbing the strange compelling beauty.

'Just a bit further,' said Oldroyd.

They entered a dry valley which grew narrower until they were walking down a waterless stream bed that twisted and turned. Carter could imagine the torrent of water that must have once flowed through to create the gorge they were in. Suddenly it opened out and they stepped on to yet another weird landscape. The greyish white limestone was completely exposed and deep fissures had been weathered into it so that it resembled a giant fossilised human brain. This expanse of rock was bare of surface vegetation except for a solitary wind-blown tree growing in the middle of a stone plateau.

'This is a limestone pavement,' announced Oldroyd with pride and enthusiasm. 'Let's have a quick walk on to it. There are some beautiful ferns growing in these grykes – those are the spaces and . . .'

He stopped abruptly as a sound broke the silence. To their left, a little way up the hillside, was an old drystone wall with a small scree slope below. A stone had fallen off the top of the wall and was rattling down across the rocks below. As Oldroyd glanced up sharply, he caught a brief glimpse of a figure crouching behind the wall.

'Hold on, Andy,' Oldroyd said quietly. 'I think we're being watched.'

'Out here, sir?'

'They could have followed us.'

Carter thought of frantic chases through the crowded streets of the capital and looked around at the empty landscape.

'How, sir? There's nowhere to hide.'

'The walls; there were walls all across those fields parallel to the path. They could have hidden behind them and tracked us. There's someone over there behind that wall. I saw him duck down quickly when that stone clattered down. Let's walk over slowly in that direction while we're talking.'

The detectives walked across the edge of the limestone pavement with assumed nonchalance, but halfway towards the wall Carter stopped.

'You were right, sir; look, he's making a run for it.'

A head appeared occasionally above the top of the wall as the figure stooped and ran along the other side.

'I'll get after him, sir.' Carter prepared to run.

'Don't bother, Andy, he's already too far off to catch.'

Carter relaxed again. 'It could've just been someone messing around.'

'Possibly, but it's a bit suspicious in the circumstances. A bit of a coincidence: the day we find a body, someone seems to be watching us. Anyway, it's probably to our advantage for him to think we didn't see him. We'll ask Craven to get his people out here and do a search; see if they come up with anything.'

Carter looked across the corrugated plateau of the limestone pavement as the silence re-established itself. The sun had now sunk below the hills and the temperature had dropped. Everything was coloured in austere grey and pallid greens. The smoothness of the fields was broken only by the walls, randomly scattered boulders and the craggy cliffs of exposed limestone on steeper hillsides in the distance. Even Oldroyd seemed to be feeling the strange loneliness as he shuddered slightly and fastened his jacket.

'Let's get back,' he said.

Later that evening, Carter was trying to sort out his new flat although he was feeling tired after his long day. He had brought back a pizza as he had no food in and no time in the day to go to the supermarket.

He was very pleased with his new home. He had a good-sized kitchen, spacious living room and two bedrooms for a rent that was laughably low compared with London, where he'd paid more for a cramped two-roomed flat in Croydon. The flat was just out of the centre of the town and he could walk across the Stray, a wide expanse of green, every morning to West Riding Police HQ. No queues or long journeys on the Underground. Life should be much less stressful in some ways at least, although he was still not sure yet how he would adjust to the small-town atmosphere of Harrogate.

He kicked his shoes off and smiled as he saw that they were still mud stained from the walk across the fellside. He stretched himself out on the sofa and thought again about his new boss. He had taken to Oldroyd straight away. He felt comfortable with his unpredictable, teasing style, which he imagined could disconcert others. He had just begun to eat the pizza out of the box when his mobile phone rang.

'Hey, how's it going?' The voice was familiar: Jason Harris, one of his oldest friends. They'd been at school together in Croydon and had played in the same school football teams. Jason was an archetypal lad-dish extrovert, exuberant and hedonistic. They'd had many memorable nights out together, and those were only the ones he could remember.

When Carter joined the police force, Jason went to the LSE to do a degree in Economics. He was bright but totally idle and enjoyed his time 'getting pissed for three years with state funding', as he summed up his time as an undergraduate. His mediocre degree didn't prevent him from securing a job in a City firm of bank analysts and making rapid progress to a position in which he made substantial amounts of money. He promptly blew it all on cars, drink and women in no particular order.

The fast lifestyle showed no sign of abating as the years went by and he had survived the recent crash in the financial world apparently unscathed. 'It only got the idiots who didn't know what they were doing,' he would say. Carter lived in fear of being on duty one night and having to arrest Jason after he'd been involved in some drunken fracas. He had slowly reduced the amount of time he spent with his riotous friend, whose activities were so potentially at odds with his role as a police officer. In recent times, after his promotions, he'd chosen the nights out even more judiciously and always departed before the excesses of the early hours.

Jason didn't seem at all offended by Carter's more sober behaviour. He understood the reasons, but seemed to pity rather than resent Carter's changed attitude. He was constantly ringing him to say what an amazing time he'd missed, what a boring life it must be as a copper, etc. When Carter had announced that he was moving to Harrogate, Jason was astonished. His ignorance about anywhere outside London was as complete as his lack of interest. The north of England may as well have been Outer Mongolia.

'Can you understand what they're saying?'

Carter laughed.

'Where do you think I am, you daft sod? It's only two hundred miles away. People don't have two heads up here.' He started to tell Jason about the Jingling Pot case, but he soon realised that his friend wasn't really interested.

'You missed a great party on Saturday mate: Tony Hammond's birthday. You know Tony, bit of a lightweight, gets wasted on one JD and Coke. God, was he pissed! We ended up at this house off Mitcham Road. He took all his clothes off and ran out of the door. He'd have been off down the street starkers if we hadn't stopped him. We hauled him back and threw him in this pond they had in the front garden. That sobered him up a bit. Then he ran round the garden with his dick all covered with waterweed. You should've seen it, mate. I haven't laughed so much in years.'

Carter smiled at this account of a typical piece of Jason high jinks, but it seemed rather a long way from him now, and not only geographically. A part of him was beginning to feel that blokes like him and Jason, pushing thirty, ought not to be behaving as if they were still nineteen or twenty. Perhaps there was something in this notion of maturity. He didn't say as much to Jason, as the latter would have scoffed at the idea, but he felt a certain distance growing between them.

'Anyway, can't talk to you all night, I'm off out. There's a new bar opened on North End; meeting Gary and Simon there. What you up to, then? Cosy night in? Mug of cocoa? Do they have any proper bars up there or is it all real ale and packets of pork scratchings?'

'I've seen some places worth exploring when I get the time.' It was difficult to explain to Jason, who seemed to be able to go out every night of the week and go to work the next day, that his commitments precluded midweek carousing unless he was off duty. Also, he'd lied; seeking out bars in Harrogate had not been uppermost in his mind during his brief time in the town.

Jason rang off and left for his night out with his customary cheeriness, but Carter did not feel envious. He was content to be where he was.

At the same time, Oldroyd was sitting in Café Nico near the bus station reading the *Guardian* and drinking coffee. He was waiting rather nervously for his wife to arrive. When they separated they'd agreed to meet occasionally to discuss things. What things, exactly, they had left open but they usually talked about the children, what was happening at work and then some family memory. She'd been away over the summer so he hadn't seen her now for quite a while. The children were no real problem any more, apart from money. Robert was at Birmingham University studying Engineering and Louise was doing A levels and had recently started to discover the night life in Leeds.

Julia had moved out of Harrogate and now lived in a terraced house in Chapel Allerton, which was much nearer to her job as a History lecturer in a sixth-form college in Leeds. Louise had agreed to move from her Harrogate school sixth form to the same college as long as her mother didn't teach her for anything. Louise shared her mother's flair for History and her parents were both hoping that she would follow in their footsteps to Oxford.

Oldroyd sat and thought about the past. He'd met Julia at Oxford at a disco dance. They'd married soon after graduating and moved back to the north, where Oldroyd began his career in the police force. It seemed strange to many people that someone so individualistic, so witty and sharp, should want to join a somewhat regimented organisation, but Oldroyd was fascinated by the challenge of solving puzzles, not simply intellectual puzzles but puzzles concerning people and their motives, and he believed that a strong but humane police force was necessary in a civilised society to uphold the rule of law.

But it was this same love of police work that had caused problems in their relationship. As he progressed through the ranks, he spent more and more time on investigations. He'd been selfish. Julia had her own demanding job, but he'd tended to leave most of the domestic work and childcare to her. Their relationship had slowly deteriorated until the break had come three years before. He didn't think there was anyone else involved; she'd just tired of coming second all the time to his work. The separation had taught him that he did value his family more than anything but the realisation had come too late. He glanced up from the newspaper. He could see down the street from where he was sitting but there was no sign of her yet. He felt a tingle of excitement, waiting for her arrival.

'Hello, Jim.'

The sound of her voice was unexpected but pleasant. She'd entered by a different door. His initial elation was succeeded by disappointment. There was a distance and formality in the way she spoke. The intimacy that had once existed between them was gone.

'Hi . . . I . . .' It was rare to see Oldroyd at a loss for words.

'I'm sorry I'm late, I've just been doing a bit of shopping. It's so relaxing to come here after the crowds of Leeds.'

'Cappuccino?'

'That would be nice, thanks.'

Oldroyd had a good look at her as he got up to fetch the coffee. She was over fifty now, very slim and attractive and sporting a suntan after her summer holiday. She settled herself in an armchair opposite his, pulling her green cashmere cardigan around herself.

Oldroyd returned with the coffee. This was always a difficult moment.

'How are things?'

She sighed before replying. 'Oh, not bad. I can't say I'm looking forward to going back to college next term.'

'Why's that?'

'It's not the students. I still enjoy the teaching. It's all the bureau-cracy and paperwork.'

'I know, it's the same in the police now and everybody I speak to says the same about their job. It's all targets, performance criteria, the business culture and managerialism. I think all senior managers from all the professions have been taken away to some government indoctrination centre and had a chip inserted so they stay on message about targets, performance management and all the rest of the bloody nonsense.'

She laughed. He'd always been able to make her laugh and he loved her smile. There was a pause as she sipped her coffee. Oldroyd felt uncomfortable; there was still a rapport between them, but also a barrier.

'We'll probably get an OFSTED inspection this year; that's another thing to look forward to. Anyway, not to worry; we had a great time in Cephalonia.'

'Oh yes, you went with Janet, didn't you?'

'Yes. It was great fun. We stayed in this little hotel on a cliff top overlooking the sea; spectacular views. We really went because it's the setting for *Captain Corelli's Mandolin*. It reminded me of Crete. Do you remember we went that last summer before Robert was born?'

'Of course.'

'Have you been away at all?'

'No, not this summer. I might try to go somewhere in the autumn, but . . . I don't know where yet.' He had been going to say that he had no one to go with, but that sounded too self-pitying.

'Work still comes first then?'

'I didn't say that.'

'No, but what does it say, Jim, if you can't ever get away for a holiday?'

They'd strayed on to the taboo subject.

Julia finished her coffee and put the cup down on to the table.

'Anyway,' she said with a smile that brightened the atmosphere again, 'let's go across the Stray, shall we? It's a nice evening.'

They left the café and walked a short way through the pleasant streets to the Stray. This was their usual route whenever the weather was decent, especially in summer. They always ended up sitting on a particular bench talking about the children and what they were doing, although Oldroyd, who kept in regular contact with his son and daughter, knew most of it anyway.

They walked across the green sward, which at this moment reminded Oldroyd of the University Parks in Oxford. It had been one of their favourite places to go walking in their student days.

'Has Robert told you about his latest girlfriend?'

'Yes, he's mentioned her; says he might bring her up when he next pays us a visit.'

Robert shared a house with friends in Birmingham and tended to stay there over holiday periods. He didn't come home much any more. Oldroyd felt sad and somehow responsible for this, feeling that his son was escaping his unhappy family.

'I've been getting the attic room ready for them.'

Oldroyd thought how the world was different now, remembering the times he had crept across the landing at night to Julia's room when they were staying with her parents before they were married. Who would really want to go back to the falsity and hypocrisy of those times?

'How's Louise? I spoke to her the other day; she didn't sound tremendously enthusiastic about the new term.'

'No, but she's got to get down to it.' Louise had got top marks in all her subjects at AS, without working very hard. Her parents were still convinced that she was going to be 'found out' at some point.

'Has she done any reading over the summer?'

'Not much, I don't think. She's been working at that café nearly every day and blowing the money at night in the clubs.'

Oldroyd sighed. He wasn't so much worried about his daughter drinking under age, although that could cause him embarrassment if she ever got into some kind of scrape and the press got hold of it. It was more that he didn't want her to waste her potential. He took consolation in the knowledge that this was a perennial concern of middle-class parents.

'She's got that History aptitude test for Oxford in November, hasn't she?'

'Yes, but it's up to her, Jim. If she's serious about it she'll do the work. Anyway, it's nice to hear that you're so concerned about her progress after all those years when I had to go to their parents' evenings and sports events by myself because you were always too busy.'

'I know; you don't have to remind me.'

They arrived at their bench and sat in silence looking across the Stray towards the distant road and hearing a faint hum of traffic. As dusk settled, coloured lights twinkled in the trees that lined the road.

When she'd finally gone, Oldroyd was left wondering in a puzzled and wistful way what the real meaning of these meetings was. He enjoyed them. Did she? Did she just want to keep him involved with the family or was she assessing him to see if he had changed? Or sending a message that somehow he wasn't receiving? Did she still care for him? He enjoyed his professional tussling with problems but found these deeply personal questions very painful to contemplate. He walked slowly back again over the grass in darkness to his flat which overlooked the Stray. Standing at his sitting-room window and feeling lonely again, he could just make out the dark shape of the wooden bench where they'd sat.

Three

If on th'edge tha tries to sit,
Tha'll be dahn Hunt Pot, that evil slit.

It was early in the morning of the day after the discovery of the body. The village of Burnthwaite was still in shock. In the quiet streets, people with sombre expressions were conducting whispered conversations. The normal air of rural tranquillity had been replaced by shock and fear.

However, not everyone was concerned by recent events. At Fell Farm, just outside Burnthwaite, Fred Clark, utterly indifferent to the discovery of Atkins's body, had been up and working since 5 a.m. and was now waiting for his cowman, Stuart Tinsley, to arrive for work. The cows were still in the sheds, but should have been out in the fields by now.

Clark ran a mixed-stock farm, the biggest in the area. It had been in his family for generations, but he'd built it into a very successful enterprise through a combination of traditional farming knowledge and shrewd business sense. He had cows down in the rich pastures of the dale bottom and sheep on the high and rougher fell slopes. He looked after the sheep himself in addition to the other work of organising the farm; those hardy animals roamed happily over the hillsides in all weathers. The cows were more complicated, with milking regimes and additional health issues. He needed some specialist help with that.

Tinsley had always been a good, reliable worker. He was well qualified and knowledgeable, lived locally and knew the area. That was until the last few days, during which his behaviour had become odd. He was morose and uncommunicative, and he'd started to arrive late; a cardinal sin in Fred Clark's book.

A farm was a business, which was what a lot of townies didn't realise when they walked over the fields in spring looking at the cows and sheep and the wild flowers and thinking how pretty it all was. To him those animals represented income and the grass was a raw material used in the production process. In a business everyone had to pull their weight; no one could be carried.

It was time to have a word with Tinsley, he thought, as the cowman came into view cycling furiously up the farm track. Tinsley jumped off the bike and leaned it against the wall of the farmhouse. Then he saw Fred Clark watching him. Clark was six feet two and built like one of the bulls in his fields. He was not noted among his employees for his humour. He paid well and was fair, but was not the kind of man to joke with. It was all a serious business to him.

It was impossible for Tinsley to avoid saying something. So he spoke while walking purposefully towards the cowshed.

'Morning, Mr Clark; sorry I'm late.'

'You'd better come over here. I want a word wi' thi.'

Clark's gravelly voice was flat and menacing, one that brooked no argument. He looked at Tinsley with his craggy, expressionless face.

'This is t'second time tha's been late this week, and tha were off yesterday morning bringing that body up.'

Tinsley was a member of the Cave Rescue and had been involved in the operation of the previous day.

'Yeah, I'm sorry. I've been having a few problems.'

Clark frowned. He noticed Tinsley was walking with a bit of a limp. 'What's wrong wi' thi leg?'

'I twisted my ankle yesterday.'

This did not produce a favourable response. It was a general agreement among employers in the dale that members of the Cave Rescue, like lifeboat men, could take time off work if they were called out. Clark, of course, didn't think much of the arrangement. Scrooge-like, he begrudged anything that took up time for which he was paying, and part of his functional view of the countryside was a disdain bordering on contempt for activities like potholing. To Clark and farmers like him, those 'bloody 'oles in t'ground' were a nuisance mainly because an occasional hapless sheep was apt to stray too near the edge and plummet to its death, which was money lost. Idiots who climbed down to where it was dangerous, mostly a load of townies again, deserved all they got. He didn't even bother to ask Tinsley about how he had found the experience of bringing the body of a local murder victim to the surface.

'Tha should have more bloody sense. Anyway, tha'd better get on with thi work. Don't be late again. Those beasts need looking after. I've got my eye on those milk yields and if they go down I'll be on to thi.'

After delivering this laconic warning, he turned away and strode back into the farmhouse.

Stuart Tinsley hurried miserably on to the cows. Getting on the wrong side of his employer didn't help. His life had been messy enough in recent times, but in the last two days it had become infinitely worse.

He quickly opened the gate to each stall and cajoled the cows out of the shed. A house martin flew with terrific speed past his head and arced up to its neat little mud nest stuck to the wall. Normally he enjoyed the sight of such things but today he was too preoccupied and distressed.

As he followed the lumbering animals along the track, splodgy with cow muck, down to the field, he thought again about the previous day and the trauma of bringing Atkins's body to the surface. He'd never expected that. He felt a spasm of anger and he kicked the metal gate as he closed it behind the last of the cows to enter the field. It was really all that bastard's fault anyway. He wished he'd never heard of the man. Tinsley was yet another person in Burnthwaite whose life had been affected by the activities of David Atkins; another person who was not sorry to see him dead, however disturbing the retrieval of the body had been.

When Carter arrived for his second morning at West Riding Police HQ in Harrogate he was much less nervous than on the previous day and took more notice of his surroundings. It was a beautiful and unusual building for a police station. Constructed of brick in a curiously formal Queen Anne style, it was low-lying with two symmetrical wings at each end built at right angles to the main building. It looked more like a minor stately home than a police station and totally unlike the modern high rise, functional workplaces Carter was used to. The effect was completed by a set of ornamental gates, which opened up on to a small car park.

Inside, security was very relaxed compared with the Met. He said hello again to the woman officer at reception and this time was able to complete his forms for an identity card. On his way to the CID section, he passed a group of uniformed officers starting their shift and filing in a relaxed manner into a room to receive their briefing.

The day began with another meeting in Oldroyd's office. As he entered, he saw that there was a young, smartly dressed woman who gave him what might be called a half smile. Oldroyd waved him over.

'Ah, Andy, this is Detective Sergeant Stephanie Johnson. Stephanie is the third part of our team. I'm sure you'll find her an excellent colleague. Stephanie, Detective Sergeant Andrew Carter.'

They shook hands and exchanged greetings.

'Call me Andy,' said Carter.

'And I'm Steph. Welcome to Harrogate. You're not from around here, are you?' she asked in pleasant northern tones. She was dressed in linen trousers and had curly dark blonde hair.

'No, London. I was in the Met.'

'Ooo, the Met. That's where they think all the real police work gets done, don't they, sir?'

'Now Steph, have you ever heard me say anything like that?' Oldroyd teased. 'Anyway, I'm going to leave you two together for a while as I've just been summoned to see the super. Fill her in on the Jingling Pot business, Andy, and we'll meet up again at eleven.'

He promptly left the room and there was a short, awkward silence. Carter felt as if he had been put well and truly on the spot. They sat down on the easy chairs and Carter shuffled his notes. He felt a little intimidated as she was obviously more experienced than him as a detective sergeant and was used to working with Oldroyd.

'Er, I hear you've been on holiday?'

She gave him another half smile. 'Yes, we went to the south of France, to a water-sports centre.'

'Great, did you have a good time?'

'Yeah, we've been before. It's always fantastic fun.' Carter wanted to ask who 'we' were but thought that was too personal at this stage. He wasn't sure what to say next.

'So,' Steph broke the silence. 'You'd better bring me up to speed with the investigation.'

Carter began a rather halting account of the previous day's events. There was something about the situation that disrupted his normal fluency. He felt a certain uneasiness beneath the surface, as if she was trying too hard to be pleasant.

Steph listened intently and made her own notes. When he had completed his account, she put down her notebook and shook her head.

'What a first day you had! I'll bet you've never worked on a case like this before.'

'Too right; I didn't even know what a pothole was until yesterday.'

'Don't worry, you'll soon pick it all up, especially after your training at the Met.'

Carter wasn't sure whether she was being sarcastic or encouraging so he didn't reply.

'Anyway, I think the boss has taken to you, so you'll be fine.'

Carter was surprised.

'What makes you think that? I've only been here for one day.'

'Well, I've known him for quite a few years now and I can tell straight away when he likes people. He's not the sort of person to get on the wrong side of. Not that he's nasty, vindictive or anything. He just doesn't like people who he doesn't think are genuine or committed, you know. He wants people around him he can rely on, who share the same passion for the job.'

'Well, I'm glad if he thinks that of me already.'

'I'm sure he does. You notice he said *our* team? He's already regarding you as part of things. I think you're in.'

Steph's analysis gave Carter a warm feeling.

'Thanks,' he said and gave his new colleague a smile.

Detective Chief Superintendent Tom Walker was not the easiest person to get along with. He was a portly, moustachioed man in his early sixties who had risen through the ranks. A long career in detective work in the tougher parts of industrial Yorkshire had made him as hard as nails beneath a rather bluff exterior. He was usually very suspicious of what he called 'college boys': men (being of the old school, he didn't really think of women as detectives), who came into the force after university. However, he and Oldroyd shared the same background and love of

Yorkshire and they enjoyed throwing bits of dialect into their conversation. He still liked to tease Oldroyd about his Oxford education, and if he wanted action rather than analysis from him he would exhort him to 'get thi cap and gown off and get summat done'.

In private, they were on first-name terms and Oldroyd had a lot of respect for Walker, who'd proved himself in a demanding profession without the benefit of Oldroyd's education. Nor did he consider the super's mind inferior to his own. It might be less sophisticated in some ways, but no less sharp. Tom Walker was also a man of legendary experience who had worked on some of Yorkshire's most notorious cases during his years with West Riding Police in the Leeds and Bradford Division, including that of Peter Sutcliffe, the Yorkshire Ripper. He sometimes referred to his coming to Harrogate Division as 'semi-retirement' in comparison, although he'd begun his career there.

Oldroyd tapped on the door and immediately heard, 'Come in, Jim.'

Oldroyd entered to see Walker seated at his big desk wearing reading glasses and dressed in the same worn and shabby suit and tie that he seemed to have been wearing all the time Oldroyd had known him.

'Sit down, Jim,' he said, but went on reading what looked like some kind of report. Oldroyd glanced around the office: a forlorn and rather empty affair. There was one small and slightly sad picture of York Minster on the dull walls, dwarfed by the vast areas of magnolia. There was a hook behind the door, on which Walker's coat hung, and two battered old filing cabinets. His large desk was almost completely empty. There was a rough pen-and-pencil holder, which had been made at school by one of his children thirty years before, and a paperweight with a small model of Blackpool Tower imprisoned in the glass: clearly a present from the famous Lancashire resort, that probably predated even the pen-and-pencil holder. His computer didn't appear to be switched on. Altogether, it was the workspace of a man who didn't like offices or administration, and this described Walker exactly.

His climb to the top had not been very happy. It had seemed to happen almost in spite of himself; he'd been the most experienced person available when jobs came up and had been persuaded to apply for them. Oldroyd suspected that he secretly yearned for the days when he was on the ground as a working detective back in the city.

There were advantages in all this for Oldroyd. Walker was a man who had absolute contempt for modern management jargon and practices. He looked after his detectives and annoyed his superiors by ignoring them as much as possible.

As Oldroyd watched him reading, Walker's brow became more and more furrowed. Suddenly he let out a huge grunt of contempt. He almost seemed to have forgotten that Oldroyd was there.

'Huh! Sorry, Jim, I was just finishing this . . . this unbelievable thing here. What an absolute pile of bloody claptrap! This idiot here says that we need more of a business culture in the police. What the hell does he mean? Can you imagine it? The criminal as customer? Maybe they'll be able to choose which force to be arrested by. "Sorry, but I prefer to be arrested by Toy Town police as their conviction rates are lower than yours." And do you know what? Surprise surprise, he's never been in the police force! He's probably some kind of business guru like that bloke I told you about at that wretched conference. Wasted a whole afternoon flouncing around on the platform with a microphone like a bloody failed comedian prattling on about "How to be a Leader". And he charged three grand for the privilege. Just like the chief to shell out money for something like that.'

The chief in question was the chief constable of West Riding Police, Matthew Watkins, a forty-something whiz-kid: ambitious, political and full of what Walker graphically called 'management bullshit'. Walker held him in such deep contempt that the mere mention of Watkins's name could render his face red and make the veins in his forehead stand out.

Walker shook his head, threw the report down and changed the subject.

'Anyway, I wanted you to tell me about this Jingling Pot business. Sounds an odd affair to me, bloke found down a pothole. Why would anyone take a body down there? I take it he was bumped off somewhere else?'

'You're right, Tom, we've discounted murder in the cave. He was an experienced potholer, but wasn't wearing any equipment.'

'So I understand. Bloody funny business, isn't it? Have you got any leads?'

'Nothing firm yet, but I've got a few ideas I'm working on.' With some detectives, Walker would have come down hard on that as vague and evasive, but he knew the quality of Oldroyd's mind. Oldroyd's ideas usually led somewhere.

'Who've you got working on it? That new lad from London started yesterday, didn't he? Any good? Came with good reports, I believe.'

'It's a bit early, but give t'lad a chance and he'll be reight.'

Walker smiled. Oldroyd knew that a bit of dialect always defused the tension with the super.

'He's on the case with Steph,' continued Oldroyd.

'Well, she's a good lass, so you should be fine. The thing is, the chief always gets edgy when a case starts to get a lot of publicity, and this one already has; even got into one of the nationals this morning. The press love it: a mystery the police can't solve; they'll be on it for a while. If the TV want to do an interview, you'd better do one. It'll all die down if nothing happens; they'll lose interest like they always do.' Walker's face contorted into a snarl. His contempt for the chief was exceeded only by his contempt for the press. He looked at Oldroyd.

'What do you think happened? What's your instinct?'

Oldroyd frowned and shrugged.

'I must admit it's a puzzler, Tom. I've never met one quite like it before. There's plenty of suspects and motives, but quite how and why it was done like this is still not clear to me.'

Walker grunted again. 'Hm, well, you'd better get on with it then. Tell me if you think you need more help.'

Oldroyd got up to leave.

'By the way, on Sunday we're having a round over at Moortown in Leeds; do you fancy coming? Oh, I keep forgetting, you're not a golfer, are you?'

'No, Tom, it's not for me but I'm on for a drink out at the Black Cat sometime.'

'Oh, right. Well, how about Friday week?'

'That works for me; I'll see you then.'

Oldroyd had the occasional social meeting with the super, which he thought judicious, but he didn't want to see him too often, especially not with his whisky-drinking golf cronies. These evening drink sessions were not unpleasant as he knew the superintendent, liked him, and they usually had a good evening in some nice rural pub if Oldroyd could keep Walker off Watkins, the press and any of his other pet hates. With this, he departed to continue his quest to solve the mystery and to keep the press at bay.

'So let's review what we know.'

Oldroyd, Carter and Steph were gathered in Oldroyd's office for a briefing session. Jackets were off and Oldroyd was ensconced in his favourite chair. There was a large cafetière of coffee on the table and a plate of chocolate biscuits. The latter were being consumed mainly by Carter, who gradually munched his way through the plateful as the meeting progressed.

'Andy, go over what you think we've established.'

Another gently enforced but quite rigorous test, thought Carter.

'OK, sir. Well, we know who the victim is and that he was killed by a blow to the back of the head, probably a hammer but we're still waiting for forensic reports on that.'

'Correct,' muttered Oldroyd, who had put his head back on his hands and closed his eyes. His legs were supported on a chair.

'Due to the lack of equipment and what the victim was wearing, we're pretty sure that he was murdered elsewhere and taken down into the cave, but we're no further forward in understanding why or how he was taken so far in. According to that Williams bloke, of course, the cave or some monster in it could have just swallowed him up.'

'Yes, a man with an over-fanciful imagination, but very knowledgeable; we might need him again before we've finished. Anyway, I've got one or two ideas about how the body ended up there, but I'm not sharing them yet until I've got more information. They may just be blind alleys which will confuse the investigation.'

'Was there any important forensic evidence from where the body was found?' asked Steph.

'Very little,' replied Oldroyd. 'Just a lot of rocks and water around the body, except for this.' Oldroyd went over to his desk and again produced the plastic bag with the rusty piece of iron.

'You really think that's important, don't you, sir?' Carter still sounded unconvinced.

'Yes, I do, and I'm going to send it to forensics. As far as the evidence from the crime scene goes, it will be very interesting to get the report, but also the photographs the CSIs took. They should have uploaded them on to the system by now. We'll have a look in a minute, but carry on with your summary. What about the suspects?'

'We know that Atkins was a very unpopular man and we may find more people who had a grudge against him as we go on. Although there are a number of suspects, the one thing we have in our favour is that at least one person, and presumably more than one, must have had knowledge of the caves and the physical strength to move the body all that distance. I can't believe that one person could have done it, so I think we're looking for at least two people, and at least one must be a caver.'

'Good logic. What do you think, Steph?'

'I agree, sir, but it doesn't solve the problem of why. Why take the body so far? It's hard enough getting through those caves without carrying or dragging a body.'

There was a brief silence as everyone again contemplated the central puzzle of the crime.

'Go on, Andy – suspects?'

'There's Sam Cartwright the mechanic. Atkins owed him money and he's volatile enough to commit a violent crime. He's not a caver as far as we know. We've got lists of all the members of the Wharfedale Club and the Cave Rescue and his name doesn't appear.'

'Well done.'

'But that proves nothing. He could be in another club somewhere and I suppose he's the kind of local bloke who's lived there all his life and would know something about the caves anyway. But we're still back to the problem of why.'

Oldroyd pursued the point. 'Also, those passages are narrow in places and I'm not sure that Cartwright might not be too wide to get through some of them. I'm expecting a report from Craven, who's been speaking to Alan Williams. When we get that we'll have a better idea of what would have been involved in getting a body down there to that point. More coffee, anyone?'

Oldroyd replenished his own cup and Carter's. Steph drank from a glass of water.

'Carry on, Andy.'

Carter consulted his notebook once more.

'Then there's the man who found the body: Geoffrey Whitaker. I interviewed him and his wife and they were clearly concealing something. He was working in the pub that night and he could have followed Atkins out later and killed him. He made a big thing over being upset by finding the body but he admitted that he had had an argument at the pub with Atkins, said that Atkins owed him money and hadn't paid it back. His wife didn't seem to know anything about it, but I'm not sure. I don't know whether she had anything going with Atkins, but I learned from Atkins's neighbours that they had seen Whitaker visiting the house a number of times, and the last time there was a row.'

'Did they know what about?'

'No, but my guess is that it was either about Helen Whitaker or the money. It was obvious from all the stuff in Atkins's bedroom that he was involved in some kind of shady financial stuff in property or shares or something. We removed all his files and his computer and I'm having them all analysed.'

'Good.'

'It could be that Whitaker had been cheated or let down by Atkins and maybe lost a lot of money.'

'And you say he was the one who found the body?' asked Steph.

'Yes.'

'That's a bit strange then, isn't it? Surely he would be the last person to want to discover the body if he was the murderer?'

'That's exactly what his wife said, and I suppose it's true, but she sounded very defensive about it somehow.'

'Lots of people who discover bodies turn out to be the murderers. There may be a reason why he wanted it to be discovered there.'

Oldroyd paused for a thoughtful moment after this observation and drank some coffee.

'Did the neighbours have any more useful information?'

'They did; they obviously enjoyed having their ears to the wall when Atkins was entertaining women. They gave me a graphic account but I'll spare you the details.'

'Well, well, a couple of voyeurs in Burnthwaite,' said Steph archly. 'Isn't it amazing what goes on in these little Dales villages?'

'I'm sure,' continued Carter, 'but the main thing is that they recognised one of these women as,' he consulted his notebook again, 'Anne Watson; she and her husband own a gift shop in the village. Apparently there was some trouble about it.'

'Good; that confirms what the landlord was telling us at the Red Horse. Anything else?'

'Not at the moment, but we've got more people to interview.'

'Right. There's also the question of who Atkins was going to meet on what I think was his last night alive. We've nothing on that yet. Of course, if any of his former lady friends knew about that it could have provided a motive. OK. Good.' He turned to report his own investigations.

'Well, I visited Garthwaite Hall and spoke to the Hardimans and found out more than I expected. They employed Atkins on a casual basis in their outdoor-pursuit business but got rid of him when he started making advances to the wife, Caroline. So we can add them, or at least the husband, to the list. Their alibi is weak too; they claim to have been together at the hall on the night Atkins disappeared.'

'Did the wife have an affair with Atkins?'

'Not according to them, but there could have been more to it than they will admit to. What I really went to Garthwaite Hall for was to find out more about the caves. Simon Hardiman confirmed that there are no quicker ways into the Jingling Pot system. He lent me some books for further research.'

'What do you think you might find, sir?' asked Steph. 'If Jingling Pot is a well-known and well-explored system, any other linking passages would have been discovered by now, wouldn't they?'

'Yes.' Oldroyd narrowed his eyes a little. 'But you see, if someone did discover a linking passage like that it would create a bit of a stir, wouldn't it?'

'I suppose so.'

'That's what caving's all about to the real fanatics,' continued Oldroyd. 'It's exploration, pushing the frontiers forward and trying to find new caves. The biggest challenge of all is to link systems together. I remember 1983, when they finally made the underwater connection between Gaping Ghyll and Ingleborough Cave. It made the national news.'

Carter was not quite sure what Oldroyd was driving at but at that moment there was a knock on the door and a DC entered.

'The forensic report, sir, on the murder victim found in Jingling Pot, and also a report from Inspector Craven.'

'Excellent, Stevens, thank you.' Oldroyd read the forensic report quickly and pushed it over to Carter. He took a deep breath.

'Well, it confirms what I thought. The body had been down there for several days at least, so we have the added problem of explaining how those potholers could have got through the system on Friday and not seen it.'

'I'm not sure I believe them, sir, it's just not possible.'

'Any ideas, Steph?'

Steph shook her head. She had been quiet and thoughtful for much of the time, trying to take in the events of the previous day.

'No, sir. The whole business of the body being down there baffles me too. But all this talk of caves, and then when you mentioned the news, it's stirred some memory in me, although I can't remember exactly what.'

Things went quiet. Carter looked at the forensic report while Oldroyd was skimming through what Craven had to say. Oldroyd laughed.

'Well, it looks like we've got even more problems.'

'Why's that, sir?' asked Steph.

'According to Alan Williams, the Jingling Pot system would be virtually impassable if you were trying to drag a body along with you. Apparently, some of the passages are only just wide enough to crawl through. There are also one or two ducks. It took a team of six of them and four CSIs to get the body up to the surface. Dead bodies are difficult to move, as I'm sure you're aware.'

'What are ducks, sir?' asked Carter.

'Passages partly filled with water where you have to duck down into it and maybe turn your head to breathe. The idea of dragging a body through all that is, well, unbelievable, unless he was also murdered by a team of ten, which is also just about unbelievable. It was bad enough when we thought the four from the Cave Rescue could be in a conspiracy, but ten? And even if there were ten of them, why do it anyway?' He frowned with frustration and then looked defiant.

'Well, someone got the bloody thing down there and they had a reason for doing it. It's our job to find out how. I enjoy watching illusions performed but I don't believe in magic. There's an explanation and we're going to find it. Now let's have a look at those photographs.'

Oldroyd went to his desk and logged on to the computer, and all three of them gathered around the monitor. He clicked on the file and the photographs followed in a slideshow sequence.

The periphery of each shot was a sinister black and the subject was illuminated by the powerful flash of the CSI's cameras. There was a series of gruesome images of the body in close-up sprawled across the passage, neck bent at an unnatural angle. The casual dress of the corpse struck an incongruous note in that subterranean landscape.

'He doesn't look too happy down there, does he? And he looks completely out of place,' Oldroyd observed sardonically. In the next shots, the camera zoomed out and the body could be seen at the end of a straight passage. Water was flowing and the flash reflected brightly on the ripples. Finally, the camera panned around the passage and then up to the roof. The walls and roof were very uneven, casting numerous overlapping shadows. The roof seemed as much as twenty feet above the floor of the passage in places. Oldroyd used his mouse to click through each photograph again. He pointed to one that showed a number of smallish rocks lying on the floor of the passage.

'That's that rock fall Alan Williams told us about. That was the only thing he said was different from when they went through on the previous Friday, apart from the body.'

'Whitaker mentioned that as well, sir,' said Carter, 'but do you think it's significant? Rock falls are common in those caves aren't they?'

'True, that's also what Williams said,' replied Oldroyd, still examining the picture, 'but we've so little to go on that everything has to be considered.' He clicked on through the photographs. 'I've also read the CSI's report and that piece of metal I'm fond of was found near those rocks too. You can see it there in that photograph.'

Carter and Johnson looked on, rather bemused and unsure about what was going through Oldroyd's mind. There was a knowing smile on Oldroyd's face and Carter noticed that Steph was smiling too.

'Are we playing games again, sir?' she said.

Oldroyd raised an eyebrow, rolled his head from side to side but said nothing.

Carter was puzzled and not sure how to react.

They continued going through the photographs, but none showed anything strikingly different: dark passage, water, rocks, body. There was something chillingly stark about it all, so different from the standard scene-of-crime shot showing a body on a living-room floor or sprawled on the ground by a car down a back street. The scene was bare, dark and alien.

'Right,' announced Oldroyd after a while. 'We're not going to get any further looking at these. Let's get back to work in the field. This afternoon I want you both back in Burnthwaite. Steph, you go to the gift shop and interview the Watsons, and Andy, take DC Robinson and start following up Cartwright. We've got Bob Craven following up the caving fraternity and the rescue team that brought up the body. By the way, do you still suspect them of being the murderers?'

'Not really, sir,' replied Carter. 'I still think the murder could have been some kind of conspiracy, but it's odd they claim not to have seen a body only two days before it was found. I can't think why they would tell us that if they were the murderers. There's also the problem of motive – surely not all of the Cave Rescue team could want Atkins dead?'

'Well, at least one of them seemed to have a pretty strong dislike. He shouted out something nasty about Atkins, didn't he?'

'That's a fairly general feeling though, sir, but I think I agree with you that murder by a conspiracy of ten people is very unlikely.'

'But not impossible, remember *Murder on the Orient Express*? Anyway, you've a lot to follow up. I'm staying here to think.'

'To what, sir?'

'Think, Carter. Use the "little grey cells", as Agatha Christie's Poirot says in the stories. All the great detectives spent time reflecting on the case. Remember Sherlock Holmes playing his violin far into the night.'

'And injecting himself with cocaine?' interjected Steph. 'You won't be doing that, will you, sir?' she asked cheekily.

'No,' replied Oldroyd. 'The similarities between myself and Conan Doyle's creation are few, apart from our brilliantly perceptive minds.'

'And exceptional modesty,' laughed Steph.

Oldroyd laughed too, then slapped his legs decisively and got up.

'Right, off you go. We need to get on with this; the super's been asking me how it's all going, worried about the media coverage as usual. There'll be people ringing in from Wharfedale complaining about the slow progress.'

'Slow progress, sir? This is only day two.'

'I know, but they think it's bad for the tourist trade to have a murder in the area; not good for the image of the place.'

'Right.'

'Not that I think it makes a damned bit of difference. In fact, if you ask me I'd say it increases the number of visitors. There's nothing the ghoulish public like more than gawping at the scene of a murder. No doubt some enterprising caver could make quite a bit of money by organising trips to where the body was found.'

Carter and Johnson left the chief inspector in his office and their last image was of him seated at the computer again concentrating hard on the macabre pictures of the body in Jingling Pot.

'Do you fancy a bit of lunch in the canteen?' Carter asked as they made their way down the corridor.

'No thanks,' Steph replied and Carter felt a little pang of rejection which was thankfully brief.

'But they do nice sandwiches at the Royal Oak. I can't stand the canteen, it reminds me too much of school dinners.'

Carter's mood immediately rose again.

They left the building and walked the short distance into the town centre.

'You seem to be very well in with Oldroyd,' Carter began.

'How do you mean?'

'Well, you know, what you can say to him and get away with.'

'I suppose so. He's got a good sense of humour and he doesn't mind being teased.'

'Do you like working for him?'

'Yeah. He's great. He can be demanding and he doesn't always tell you what he knows, but he's a genius when it comes to solving crimes.'

'Is that what you meant when you said he was playing games?'

'Yes. He won't share his theories with you until he's sure. He expects you to work it out too, so it's like a little game you play with him.'

'That's not working by the rules, is it? Aren't we all supposed to share information?'

'He doesn't always work by the rules, but he gets results. And it makes you think. I like it; he treats you as an equal. You're not just there to do all the routine interviews and stuff like that. He expects you to have an angle on the case.'

'Good, I'm up for that; had enough of boring drudgery. There must be a downside to working with him.' Carter immediately regretted saying this as it could be construed as inviting her to be disloyal.

'Not really. He can get quite depressed. I think that's because he's separated from his wife.'

'OK. Not surprising then.'

'No. He's talked to me about it a bit. He's always very frank and open about personal things and he helped me a lot when I . . .'

Steph didn't continue and they walked on in silence. Carter felt that something was wrong. Her mood suddenly seemed very subdued. He wondered what she had been about to say but didn't want to probe any further. She seemed preoccupied.

They came to an old, low building with a narrow pavement outside.

'Here we are,' said Steph.

They walked down a few old steps and into a little bar. It was rather gloomy owing to the stone-framed windows but when Carter's eyes adjusted he sensed a cosy local-pub atmosphere. There was a pleasant hum of conversation and laughter.

They managed to find a small unoccupied table in the corner. Carter got the drinks: orange juice for him as the driver that afternoon. When he returned to the table he felt a sense of pride that he was here with this attractive woman and he couldn't stop himself from gazing at her.

'Stop looking at my tits and sit down.' Her tone was mocking but not hostile. The directness gave him a jolt, but he remembered that Oldroyd had warned him that she was a woman who wouldn't accept any nonsense.

'Sorry.'

Steph sipped her half-pint of Stella and looked away from him towards the bar. Carter took the menu and scanned it.

'What do you fancy then?' he asked.

'I usually have the light tuna mayo sandwich with salad.'

She still seemed distracted, looking at her glass, not really connecting with him.

'OK, I'll go with that but I'll have mine with chips. I'll order then.'

There was no reply.

The bar was very busy and it took a long time for Carter to return to the table. They sat for a while in silence. Steph's face looked downcast and she seemed depressed. Suddenly she sighed.

'I'm sorry.'

'For what?'

'For being poor company, not very welcoming when you're so new. It's just that things this morning have reminded me of some issues I have and it's upset me a bit, that's all.'

'That's OK. I didn't realise.' Carter was reassuring, but although he was curious, he felt it would be wrong to push for more information.

'How are you finding things in Harrogate, anyway?'

Carter sensed she was making a big effort to keep the conversation going, even though she was not in the mood.

'Fine. I've got a little place near that big field thing – what's it called?'

'The Stray.' She laughed but it sounded strained. They sat quietly for a while and then Carter saw that tears were welling in her eyes.

'Are you OK to work this afternoon?'

She dabbed her eyes with a tissue.

'Sure, I'm fine. I soon get over these little episodes.'

'If you like, we could do some interviews together.'

'No, honestly; we wouldn't be able to interview enough people and the boss wouldn't be pleased.'

The sandwiches arrived and her mood improved. She began to ask him about himself and where he came from and then she told him a bit about herself. She was a local girl, brought up in Starbeck.

'I was always very sporty at school and very responsible and confident; not particularly academic but good enough. I didn't really want to go to university and I hadn't thought about the police until a careers officer suggested it.'

'My dad was in the police, that's why I wanted to join. What did your father do?'

'He was a salesman, cars.'

Something barely perceptible in the tone told Carter that he had hit a raw nerve.

'But he's not around any more.'

'I see.'

'So what do you make of "oop north" then? Did you expect to find us all wearing flat caps and headscarves?'

She obviously liked to tease. Maybe she had learned this from her boss.

'So far I like it. It's very different from London and a nice change. I think Wharfedale is, well, cool.' He couldn't think of a better word.

She laughed. 'The Dales, "cool"! Well, I've never heard them called that, but you're right, they are.'

'Burnthwaite's a pretty village. Oldroyd took me into a pub, the Red something?'

'Red Horse.'

'Yeah, that's it. That's where we met that mad mechanic. I thought he was going to start messing with me.'

'I'm sure you would have coped, with your experience and a big bloke like you. You must have tackled some hard cases at the Met.'

Was there a hint of a compliment there, thought Carter.

'Aren't you going to miss the big city?' she went on. 'Harrogate must seem like a very small town.'

'We'll see. It's certainly different, but I think I can live without the club scene, and to be honest I'm getting a bit old for that now. They say Leeds has a good nightlife anyway, and that's not far from here, is it?'

'Forty minutes by car and there's also trains and buses.'

'There you are then, cool.'

'Too old? You don't look it.'

'Thanks, but I'm going to be twenty-eight next month. I was starting to feel out of place with all those eighteen-year-olds.'

'I'm sure a lot of them liked you.'

'Well, thanks, maybe.' Carter wasn't sure how to respond to this. He glanced at his watch.

'Better be getting back, pick up the DCs and get over to Burnthwaite. You'll have to direct me; I can't remember the way.'

'No worries. I know my way around here. We used to go up the Dales a lot when we were kids. Burnthwaite is one of my favourite spots.'

'It's one of Oldroyd's too. He had me skimming stones there.'

Steph laughed.

'Anyway, I couldn't do it, but he got one right across to the other bank.'

'I remember when I was little, Mum said I took my first steps on that village green by the river.'

She sounded a little nostalgic, so maybe her early childhood had been happy. Something must have happened since, but what?

He was still wondering as he paid the bill and they left the pub.

Throughout the afternoon Oldroyd sat in front of the computer looking hard at the digital photographs and thinking. He clicked the mouse and went backwards and forwards through the series, glancing intermittently at the small rusty piece of metal. After a while he went out for a walk through the Valley Gardens to clear his mind. This was one of his favourite strolls and he liked to think of himself as following in the footsteps of Sir Edward Elgar who had also frequented the Valley Gardens on his visits to Harrogate.

He passed between the formal flower beds and the Arcadian wildness of the stream running through the gardens, deep in thought. Going off into distracted ruminations had been a characteristic of Oldroyd since childhood. It was a valuable tool in solving crimes, but it could also lead him into a gloomy state of mind if he strayed on to his current loneliness or on to some of the perennial existential problems his mind tended to gnaw at rather obsessively.

He reached the decorative little pavilion café, where he was a regular customer, and ordered a cup of tea. The café was full of young parents with their small children, and through a window he could see the model boating pool behind the café. This brought a wave of nostalgia and sadness as he remembered bringing his son and daughter when they were little to float their boats in the pond. Once, his son had stepped into the water in his eagerness and Oldroyd had had to wring out his socks. He frowned. Those happy days were gone for ever, and what did he have to look forward to now? At times like this he felt bleak about the future and the brevity of life. A line from Edward Thomas would come to haunt him: 'How dreary-swift with naught to travel to is time?' He shook his head, dismissed the thoughts and the self-pity and brought his mind back to the case.

He was trying to solve the puzzle of how the body had got down there. Why was it not there just days before it was discovered when all the evidence confirmed that it had been down in that damp cold world for some time? He didn't believe the other potholers were lying, but that seemed to leave the impossible scenario of a body appearing from nowhere.

He drank his tea slowly, then left the happy young families and went back to the station. In the late afternoon, feeling frustrated, he phoned forensics and spoke to Tim Groves, a tall bespectacled pathologist whom he had known a long time. They had great respect for one another.

'No, Jim, I'm afraid there's no possibility that the body had been down there for only a day or so.'

'How can you be so sure?'

'The discoloured and saturated state of the clothing; we actually found traces of the early stages of fungal growth on the material. The condition of the body indicated that the victim had been dead for about ten days, but only the first stages of decomposition had occurred. That was obviously due to the unusual conditions down there. The temperature is low so it acts like partial refrigeration and the number of bacteria is much lower than at the surface. I doubt if a body would ever properly decompose down there. It would probably just eventually dry out and sort of mummify.'

'Right, so it must have been there a while?'

'Yes.' Tim Groves was insistent, but as if he sensed Oldroyd's frustration and wished to help, he added, 'I don't normally make suggestions like this, Jim, but don't we have to assume the body had been moved to the passage where it was found from somewhere else in the caves?'

'We've already thought of that, but why? You make the effort to get it down there in the first place, goodness knows why, you presumably conceal it, then you go back later and dump it smack in the middle of the passage where the next person passing through the system is going to walk straight into it.'

'It doesn't seem likely, but it got there somehow. It's almost as if someone wanted it to be discovered. Anyway, I'll leave you to it. Bye.'

Oldroyd remained silent.

'Jim? Are you there?'

Oldroyd's eyes were narrowed thoughtfully.

'Yes, Tim, sorry. I was just thinking.'

Groves smiled; he was used to Oldroyd's sense of drama and enigma.

'OK. I'll leave you to it then. Bye again.'

'Bye.' Oldroyd pressed the button on the phone to end the call.

Something Tim had said had made him think; odd how sometimes the most ordinary comment could suddenly give you a new perspective. Feeling a little more encouraged, he decided to go to his favourite Italian restaurant near the theatre to see if a plate of ravioli and a glass of wine would help.

After their lunch at the Royal Oak, Steph and Andy drove back to Burnthwaite together with DC Peter Robinson and DC Julie Lloyd. During the journey Steph was distracted again, but this time it was nothing to do with any personal issues. She was puzzling about what it was on the edge of her memory that concerned the case. It continued, however, to elude her and she had to abandon the effort as they arrived in Burnthwaite.

With DC Lloyd she made her way up the short main street away from the Red Horse. It was a warm afternoon and there were a number of people sauntering up and down eating ice creams or gazing at the neat, attractive cottages and gardens. Many of them were making for the Wharfedale Gift Shop. A barn at right angles to the road had been converted into a shop and art gallery. Stone steps led up to the first floor, which housed paintings by local artists in an airy room in which the wooden rafters had been exposed. The ground floor was packed with the usual variety of local craft wares, everything from cards, pottery and clothing to walking sticks and sweets. Outside was a small plant-sales area specialising in herbs.

Steph glanced at a few items of jewellery and a woollen jumper. It was good quality but very pricey. This place must be a goldmine in summer, but winter might be different, especially in bad weather. Steph's practical mind was analysing these issues as she approached the counter. She showed her ID to the young assistant, whose eyes widened with fear.

'Detective Sergeant Stephanie Johnson, West Riding Police. Can I speak to Mrs Anne Watson, please?'

The girl didn't say a word in reply, simply bolted through a door behind her. In a moment a dark-haired woman in her late thirties dressed in expensive-looking jeans and a strappy top appeared.

'Yes, how can I help?' She met Steph's gaze with composure.

'Are you Mrs Anne Watson?'

'Yes.'

'Detective Sergeant Stephanie Johnson. I'm investigating the murder of David Atkins.'

The woman's gaze dropped and she sighed.

'You'd better come through here.'

The two detectives followed her into a rather cramped office and then through another door which led into the living room of the adjoining house. Here large white leather sofas stood on a wooden floor and there were imaginatively designed metal lamps and abstract paintings on the walls.

Anne sprawled over one of the sofas and pointed to another.

'Take a seat. This is called living near your work. It certainly cuts down on the costs of commuting.' She laughed cynically. 'But it's too damn near for me. Like everything else in this bloody village, it's all on top of you and you can't breathe.'

'Is Mr Watson at home?'

'No, he's out, as usual, probably visiting some urban escapee artist who has a studio in a freezing old barn somewhere, though why anyone would want to escape to this place is beyond me. My husband does all the purchasing of that stuff out there and I run the shop.'

'I take it you're not happy here.'

Anne lit a cigarette and offered one to the two officers without acceptance. She inhaled deeply and blew out the smoke. DC Lloyd, whom Steph knew had a particular aversion to cigarette smoke, grimaced but remained silent.

'Well, Sergeant, I can't congratulate you on great powers of deduction. Yes, you're right, it's not my idea of heaven. I trained as an interior designer and didn't think I'd end up selling postcards, fudge and soft-toy sheep.'

'Is that why you had an affair with Dave Atkins?'

For the first time Anne Watson was thrown off balance, but she had a strong pull on her cigarette and soon recovered herself. Steph, having Oldroyd as her boss, knew something of the power of direct speaking.

Anne replied, 'I could ask you how you knew about that but I can guess. You've been talking to those weirdos next door to Dave.'

'If you mean Gary Shaw and Carol Anderson, that's correct. They both reported to my colleague that they had seen you late at night coming out of Mr Atkins's house.'

Anne sniffed contemptuously.

'I'll bet they did. Just a couple of dirty-minded junkies, those two. Anyway, it's no use denying it. They weren't the only people who either knew or guessed what was happening.'

'How long did the affair last?'

'Is this really necessary?'

'I'm afraid it is. We have to establish the facts. This is a murder enquiry.'

'Yes, I'm sure you do.'

She gave Steph a searching stare and Steph knew what the woman was thinking: what's a pretty girl like you doing in a job like this? Curiously, she had this response more often from women than from men, especially the ones who considered themselves arty or alternative. They thought everything to do with the police was demeaning to women who had to conform to a man's world of regimentation. They didn't seem to appreciate, as Steph did, that women were needed in the police force for many reasons, not least of which was the importance of countering the male tendency to macho behaviour.

Anne gave a weary sigh.

'OK, if you want the gruesome details. Maybe I should get it published in the *Wharfedale Gazette* or some other pathetic little local rag. It will give all the farmers' wives and the boring retired couples something to gossip about.'

Steph did not reply but waited professionally and impassively for the information. Anne saw that she would not be diverted from her purpose.

'I met Dave about three years ago when we took on this place but we were only lovers for about a year until . . .' She stopped and seemed to be genuinely affected by a moment of sorrow. Steph's eyes narrowed slightly. It was difficult to tell just how genuine it was.

'A lot of people will tell you he was a rogue, up to all kinds of shady business with money but I didn't care about that. I liked his humour and his cynicism. He felt the same way about the people in these villages as I do and he could be so funny when he was imitating them and sending them up.'

'Did he have any particular enemies that you were aware of?'

'He had plenty, to be honest. He was too wild a character for a place like this. I bet you've already got lots of suspects.'

'What about your husband?'

Again, the question stopped Anne in her tracks and she hesitated. Steph pursued her advantage.

'I presume he knew about your affair?'

Anne stubbed out her cigarette and immediately lit another. She was very anxious but still retained control. Did she suspect that her husband had done it?

'He did,' she said quietly.

'And how did he react?'

The strain finally cracked her composure.

'How do you expect?' she said angrily. 'He was fucking furious, obviously.'

'Angry enough to commit murder?'

'I didn't say that. You realise he was one of the team that brought Dave's body to the surface yesterday.'

Steph remembered Oldroyd's words earlier that day to the effect that many discoverers of bodies turn out to be murderers. 'Yes.'

'Well, why would anyone volunteer to remove the body of someone they'd murdered?'

'You'd be surprised, Mrs Watson. It would draw attention away from them for one thing, wouldn't it, as you're suggesting?' Anne didn't reply. 'Also, since your husband was a member of the Cave Rescue team, he would have to respond to a call-out. It would have looked strange if he hadn't, wouldn't it?'

Anne looked again at Steph, who was tight-lipped and grim.

'I simply can't believe that Bill would do anything like that. He's just too placid. We've had our disagreements, obviously, but he's not a murderer.'

Steph was not impressed by this either. How often did the calm and quiet man prove to be the cold-hearted killer, the one who could plan a deadly revenge? She thought of the mild-mannered Dr Crippen, who murdered his wife and tried to escape with his lover disguised as a boy. Where passion and jealousy were involved, who knew what the most unassuming person was capable of? She decided it was time to soft pedal slightly.

'I appreciate that this is painful for you, Mrs Watson, but I'm sure you're aware that it is our job to follow up every lead we have.'

'Oh, I know that.' Her tone was now rather bitter.

'Have you noticed any change in your husband's behaviour recently?'

'No.'

'We believe that the body had been in the cave system for over a week.'

Anne Watson raised her eyebrows.

'Does that surprise you?'

'Well, yes. Bill said that some of the cavers had been through the system only three days before and found nothing.'

'We can't explain that yet, but we're working on it. Were there any particular days just over a week ago when he was out of the shop or away from home for a long time? Did he behave strangely?'

Anne was silent and seemed to be thinking.

'No,' she finally replied.

Steph glanced sharply at her face and was not sure that she was telling the truth.

'And finally, I need to ask you where you and your husband were on the night of Monday the seventeenth of August. We believe that was the last time Mr Atkins was seen alive.'

Anne shrugged.

'I think I was here as usual. If it was Monday, Bill was out. He likes to go to different pubs round here, but I don't know which one he went to.'

'Thank you, Mrs Watson, you've been very cooperative. We'll need to speak to your husband when he returns. When are you expecting him?'

'I'm afraid I'm not sure.'

'OK, we'll be in touch.'

The detectives were about to get up to leave when Anne Watson suddenly said, 'You'll probably be wasting your time.'

'Why?'

'Sergeant, I wasn't telling the truth earlier. I haven't seen Bill since yesterday morning when the body was recovered. He came straight back here, told me about it and then went out again. He seemed very upset, which is not surprising as he'd just helped to bring Dave's body to the surface, but he didn't return last night.'

'I thought you said his behaviour has been normal.'

'It is; he's gone off before when we've had rows. He usually goes to his sister's in Ripon. I thought it had brought all the business of the affair back to him and he was angry about it again. It's just that . . .'

She looked directly at Steph and now there was definitely fear in her expression.

'I've rung his sister and he's not there. I don't know where he's gone.'

Carter and DC Robinson found Burnthwaite Motors quite easily. In a tidy village with neat cottages and gardens, the place stuck out as dirty, old-fashioned and definitely not trying to attract any tourists. In the blackened forecourt stood an ancient petrol pump advertising Esso, and a tin sign for Castrol was fixed to a wall. The whole building, which was not much more than a glorified shed, was squeezed between houses and set back a little from the road. Down either side of the building were crammed ancient cars; Carter spotted two Morris Minors and a Ford Anglia. Others were beyond recognition. Some had been there so long that grass was growing through the rusted bodywork and their empty headlight sockets made them look like human skulls. The doors to the workshop were propped wide open with a brick on either side. Music was blaring from a radio, which, combined with the sound of a hammer banging hard on metal, made conversation impossible.

Carter peered into the gloomy interior, lit by two bare bulbs. Rickety shelves lined the grimy walls, full of grease guns, oil cans, socket sets and dirty boxes. Over everything there was a film of dirt and grease, ancient and ingrained. The rusty, oily smell was overpowering.

Carter ventured in, trying to keep his smart suit and shoes away from the oily filth.

'Mr Cartwright!' he shouted.

There was no reply. DC Robinson came up behind him, shaking his head and smiling.

'Mr Cartwright!' Carter bellowed at the top of his voice.

As their eyes adjusted to the relative darkness, the two police officers could see a van stationed over an inspection pit. Suddenly the banging stopped, sparks flew up from beneath the vehicle and a bright purple light lit up the pit. They could see the large outline of Cartwright holding a welding torch.

'He's doing a spot of welding on the chassis, Sarge,' said DC Robinson.

'I can see that,' replied Carter grumpily, trying to dodge sparks as they flew towards him.

The sizzling of the welding torch seemed almost as loud as the hammering.

'What are we going to do?'

'Leave it to me, sir,' replied Robinson. The DC picked up a probably rarely used broom and, crouching down, tapped Cartwright gently on the shoulder with the end of the handle. The light went out abruptly.

'Who the hell's that?' boomed a voice.

'Police, Mr Cartwright.' Carter still had to raise his voice above the blare of the radio.

'What?'

A huge head with a grimy face and hair appeared between the wheels of the van. It was wearing goggles that had been pushed up on to the forehead. Sam Cartwright looked up at Carter and his brow furrowed.

'Oh, it's you again. What the 'ell do you want? Haven't you caught who did it yet?'

'We want to ask you a few questions, Mr Cartwright. Can you . . . ?' Carter gestured towards the radio.

'No, I bloody can't. I haven't got the time to be talking to the likes o' thee, I've got work to do. I've got to get this chassis fixed before five o'clock.'

With that, he disappeared under the van again. Carter looked at Robinson and shook his head.

'Just go over and switch it off.'

Robinson walked around to the workbench on which the paint-stained radio was perched and switched it off. Luckily, there were no banging or sizzling noises from beneath the vehicle.

Carter crouched down so that his head was almost level with Cartwright's. He tried to speak assertively but calmly.

'Sir, I am asking you to cooperate. This is a murder investigation.'

Cartwright's eyes glared through the goggles and for a moment Carter thought he was going to turn the welding torch on him. However, he suddenly tore the goggles off angrily and hauled his great frame out of the pit. He threw the welding torch on to the floor.

'I've told you already, I don't know owt abaht it. The only thing I know is that I'll never get me brass now.'

This bloke's definitely got a temper, thought Carter. He could imagine Cartwright being capable of smashing Atkins on the back of the head. But could he plan a murder? Had it been a spur-of-the-moment thing and then, when he'd realised Atkins was dead, he'd taken him down the pothole? He would still have been cursing the body for not paying him what he was owed as he'd dragged it to its final resting place. If Atkins had been killed in anger, then Cartwright must be one of the chief suspects.

'I understand that, sir. Now, you told us that Atkins owed you money?'

Cartwright was about to launch into this subject again but Carter continued.

'But we want to ask you some more questions. Are you a member of the caving club?'

'Not round here, no.'

'You mean you're not in the Wharfedale Club.'

'No.'

'Why's that?'

'I fell out with that clever sod at Garthwaite Hall.'

'Simon Hardiman?'

'Aye, thinks he knows it all, that bugger, because he's got a certificate in everything. Some of us were going down them caves when we were nobbut nippers.'

'He means when they were just kids, Sarge,' interposed Robinson, who was aware his superior needed a translation from time to time.

'So you were a member for a time?'

'Yes.'

'And so was Atkins, wasn't he? Did you fall out with him there as well?'

'No. I'd no argument with him except he didn't pay his bloody bills.'

'So, where are you a member then?'

'Over at t'Ribble Club.'

'So I assume you know this Jumbling Pot?'

'Jingling Pot,' said Cartwright with contempt.

'Yes.' Carter looked slightly embarrassed; blast all those cave systems and their peculiar names.

'Of course I do, I've been through there many a time. It's not difficult.'

'Have you been through there recently?'

'No, not for a few years.'

'And are you a member of the Cave Rescue team?'

'Not now.'

'Why's that? An experienced bloke like you?'

'How many bloody questions are you going to ask? What's all this to do with Atkins getting bumped off?'

Carter stayed firm.

'Just give me an answer, sir, please.'

Cartwright looked a little sheepish. After a pause he said, 'I used to be a member but they said I was getting too . . . big and I wasn't fit enough. Bloody cheeky buggers! Anyway, I told them to stuff it.'

I'll bet you used stronger language than that, thought Carter. He looked again at Cartwright's large bulk. Was he too big to get through the narrow passages? If so, maybe he had a thinner accomplice. How could you ever know unless you measured the man and then measured every narrow passage in the system? Carter frowned. He could foresee Oldroyd giving him a rather cold, wet and difficult task to oversee.

'So altogether, then, you don't have much to do with the caving people round here?'

'No, I don't.'

'But you know your way around the systems.'

'As well as anyone, I suppose.'

Carter moved in for the kill.

'Well enough to carry a body down there and dump it?'

Cartwright snorted with derision.

'So you think it was me?'

'I didn't say that, sir.'

'Why would I do him in, anyway? That would only make sure that I didn't get me money back.'

'You've got a bit of a temper though, haven't you, sir?'

'What do yer mean?' growled Cartwright, ironically confirming Carter's accusation. DC Robinson moved closer.

'I mean, sir, did you have an argument with Mr Atkins which got out of control and ended with you hitting him on the head with a hammer? I see you've got plenty of them.' Carter turned to the battered workbench on which lay a number of weighty ball-pein hammers with oily and blackened handles.

'I see. You think I bashed him over th'ead. Well, I'd a good mind to, but I didn't. I want anybody who owes me any brass to stay around and bloody well pay me.'

'So you don't deny that you had considered being violent towards him?'

'Of course, I wanted to tear t'bugger limb from limb, but I didn't.'

'When did you last see Mr Atkins?'

Cartwright sat on the bonnet of the van and considered.

'He was in t'Red Horse one night about a week since wi' some of his mates, loud-mouthed as ever.'

That was consistent with what Trevor Booth, the landlord of the Red Horse, had said.

'What was he bragging about?'

Cartwright grunted contemptuously.

'Money. He wor always going on abaht how much brass he 'ad, though 'ow he made it wor a mystery, and he didn't pay what he owed folk.' He glared at Carter as he emphasised the point for the umpteenth time. 'He wor going on abaht women too, saying he'd got a new one.'

'And that got on people's nerves?'

'It bloody did, 'cos most of his brass he owed to other folk and the women he had were other blokes' wives.'

'Who else was in the pub that night?'

'Plenty folk; it wor jam-packed as usual.'

'Any of Mr Atkins's particular enemies?'

Cartwright scowled.

'Besides me, yer mean? Aye, lots of 'em, probably everybody in t'bloody place apart from one or two of his drinking mates.'

'Did you see him leave?'

'No, I don't remember that. I think he was still in t'pub when I left.'

'Did you see anything else unusual that night?'

'Such as what?'

'Anything.'

Cartwright shook his head. 'No, but . . .'

'What?'

'The only thing I remember was when I left, I saw a woman standing in t'lane at t'side o' t'pub.'

'Could you see who it was?'

'No, she wor too much in t'dark, but I thought it were a bit funny, the way she wor just standing there. I've thought since that it might've been Atkins's new woman waiting for him; maybe she bumped him off.' Cartwright laughed heartily at this; he seemed to find the idea hilarious.

'Anyway,' he said when his laughter had subsided. 'Have you finished all these bloody questions? I've got work to do. And when are you going to do summat about me money?'

Carter smiled and decided it was time to bring the interview to an end before the conversation went down that road yet again.

'Thank you, Mr Cartwright, you've been very helpful. We won't keep you from your work for a moment longer.'

The big man grunted and pulled down his goggles. Then he grabbed the welding torch and disappeared back beneath the van without a word. Almost immediately, the hammering began again.

DC Robinson smiled at Carter, who shook his head. They had almost got out of the ramshackle place when a voice bellowed: 'Well, put t'radio back on!'

As Carter was dealing with Cartwright for the second time, Inspector Craven was in Ingleton. He didn't normally like working with CID people, especially if they came from one of the large cities like Leeds or Sheffield. He found their attitudes patronising. He felt they regarded him and his colleagues as country bumpkins policing tranquil places where nothing much of a criminal nature happened except tractors breaking the speed limit and visitors dropping litter.

The exception was DCI Oldroyd, who had a deep love for the Dales. Beneath the mild exterior he knew Oldroyd was a serious and tenacious character, but he liked his sense of humour and knew that, like him, he was Yorkshire through and through and very attached to the landscape.

So Craven didn't mind when Detective Sergeant Carter, the new member of Oldroyd's team, rang to ask for help in finding out more about the caving community. While his team took statements from all the members of the Cave Rescue team who had brought up the body, he made a visit to one of his favourite haunts: Johnny's Café in Ingleton, run by no less than Alan Williams, head of the Wharfedale Cave Rescue.

Craven was a child of the Dales. He'd been brought up in Grassington and his father and several generations before him had been farm workers. His earliest memories were of watching his father doing the milking and of climbing up into the lofts of the lathe barns where the hay was stored for the winter. He also remembered the village bobby (the community constable in today's jargon), a man they all feared and admired in about equal measure. He gave them Extra-Strong Mints, which made their eyes water, from a bag in his pocket, but woe betide them if he caught them doing something they shouldn't, like climbing on to the roof of a garage and firing stones at people from their catapults. Innocent days, thought Craven as he walked through Ingleton. That village policeman had undoubtedly inspired him to enter the police himself, but goodness knows what he would have made of the modern, bureaucratic and computerised force.

Craven walked under the impressive railway viaduct in the centre of the small town and thought of the first Dales tourists in Victorian times. Many were genteel visitors from the industrial towns and cities who must, especially the women, have discovered that they were inappropriately dressed even for the comparatively light demands of Ingleton's famous waterfall walk. But there were others, pioneering individuals who carried on the explorations begun by local people into the mysterious caves and potholes in the area and who went down with candles and ropes into the black, uncharted depths. Men like the Frenchman Edouard-Alfred Martel, who made the first successful descent of the 340-foot main shaft of Gaping Ghyll in 1895, using wood and rope ladders. He stayed in the huge main chamber – which must have been a terrifying spectacle to see for the first time, illuminated only by candlelight – for two hours and produced a sketch map.

Martel's modern successors gathered in places like Johnny's, a well-known climbers' and potholers' café. Tables were set out in front of a huge menu board that listed enormous breakfasts and fry-ups together with tea by the half-pint or pint.

Both sides of the room were festooned with climbing and potholing gear, cagoules, guidebooks, walking books, tents and Trangia stoves, ropes, karabiners and maillons. There was a counter for service if you wanted to buy any of these items and a hatch for ordering food. At the back was a corridor through to the toilets and to a shower, provided so that people returning from deep underground could clean off the mud and grime.

Johnny's was never empty. At any time through the day you could be guaranteed to find a group of men, and sometimes women too, sitting with mugs of tea and enjoying the craic. Craven was hoping to talk to some of the caving fraternity who might be able to shed some light on the mysterious crime, which he knew would have been deeply shocking to them. Death was, unfortunately, not rare in this dangerous pursuit, but murder: that was another matter. A caver found murdered in a cave meant that the murderer was almost certainly one of their number. This made the crime not only terrible in itself, but also a blow against the camaraderie of men and women who often trusted each other with their lives.

As Craven entered the café, he was relieved to see a group of men he vaguely knew, sitting around a table with the usual pots of tea. He went over to the hatch and ordered tea and a bacon sandwich before walking over to join them. Alan Williams was behind the shop counter and nodded a greeting to Craven. This would need careful handling. Cavers didn't always like to be interrupted, especially if they were doing some serious planning or comparing notes.

'Mind if I join you?'

Things immediately went quiet but the faces that turned to him were not unfriendly. Craven was respected; he had liaised many times with the fell rescue organisations in the area when there was a serious emergency. He was always careful to let the rescuers handle things their way and not to be the interfering policeman. After all, they were the experts.

'Inspector Craven.'

'Aye we know who you are.'

'And I think you probably know why I want to talk to you.'

'Aye.' A number of the men shook their heads glumly.

'We were just talking about it. It's a bloody awful business; bloke murdered in a cave.'

'We don't think he was actually murdered in the cave; his body was dumped down there after he was killed.'

'Whatever,' muttered a solidly built individual with a shaved head as he grasped his pint pot of tea and swigged from it.

'Dumped halfway through Jingling Pot?' broke in a wiry but strong-looking individual whom Craven could imagine crawling powerfully along through the narrowest of tunnels. 'That's bloody daft, isn't it?'

'I agree with you, but that's where he was found.'

'And who the hell do you think did it?'

Craven sat down at the end of his table as his tea arrived.

'That's where I thought some of you lads might be able to give me a hand,' he said, and immediately regretted the way he'd phrased it.

'What the 'ell do you mean by that?' A burly man with shaggy black hair turned a mean-looking face on Craven.

'Are you saying it were one of us? Bloody coppers. Why don't you just f—'

'Norman, just shut it. The bloke's only doing his job.' This was from the first man who'd spoken. He had a greying moustache, seemed slightly older than the others and had an air of authority. Craven suddenly remembered who he was: Pete Dukinfield, a caver and an expert in subterranean photography who had become quite famous in the local area. Some of his footage had been shown on television.

Craven hastened to correct himself.

'No, I didn't mean it like that but,' Craven tried to stay firm, 'you know, stories get around, don't they? Have you heard anything unusual?'

There was silence and a few shaken heads.

'Do you think anybody could have got that body down there unless they knew a bit about caves?'

Still nothing apart from a few murmurs. The shaved head and the shaggy head both looked down. They all knew Craven was right, and that made it so much worse. The murderer had to be a caver.

'Did any of you know him?'

'I don't even know who it was.'

'David Atkins from Burnthwaite.'

'Why don't you ask them all over in Wharfedale; that's where he'd be a member, wouldn't it?'

'We are, don't worry, but I wanted to ask around a bit, you know. We need all the help we can get.'

There were one or two murmured conversations.

'Aye, we knew him a bit,' said another of the group. 'Bit of a bugger by all accounts.'

'How did you know him?'

'He came on a few trips with us. Him and that big bloke who runs the garage in Burnthwaite.'

'Aye,' laughed another. 'Have you seen that place? It's a right crap 'ole, falling to bits and piled up wi' old cars and stuff.'

'You mean Sam Cartwright.' Craven was on the alert. He'd had a report of Oldroyd and Carter's encounter with Cartwright in the Red Horse.

'Aye, that's him. The only problem is, he can only go on certain routes he's such a big fat bastard.' This produced raucous laughter.

'He nearly got stuck when he went down with us. Martin had to push the bugger from behind. You should have heard the bloody language.'

Craven's bacon sandwich arrived. He opened it and applied a liberal amount of brown sauce to the bacon.

'Would he get through the Jingling Pot system?'

'I haven't seen him for a bit but I don't think so. He's a good caver, don't get me wrong, but he's just too bloody big.'

'He's strong, though; he could lift a body?'

'I suppose so, but I don't know about moving it by himself. Bodies are heavy, especially dead ones. We've handled a few in Cave Rescue.'

Craven briefly considered this gruesome image before continuing.

'So you think it must have been the work of more than one person?'

'Aye, must have been, mustn't it? But why is a different matter.'

'Did they seem good friends then, Atkins and Cartwright?'

'Can't tell really, didn't know them well enough, but you don't go caving with people you don't get on with, I can tell you that.'

There were nods of agreement around the table. Craven continued.

'You see, we know that Cartwright and Atkins had had a big fall-out. Atkins owed him money.'

'That's no surprise. I hear he was a right slippery sod where brass was concerned.'

Craven took a drink of his neglected tea, which was already cooling. A sullen quiet had descended on the table.

'Is there anything else you know about Atkins, or about why any-one should dump his body down there?'

Pete Dukinfield replied.

'I think I speak for everyone, Inspector. We're baffled by it all too. It's a bad enough business when anyone dies caving but a murder's just . . . terrible. We hope you find out who did it. And when you do, just take 'em to the edge of Gaping Ghyll and push 'em down. That's what they bloody well deserve.'

There was another chorus of 'ayes' around the table. The hurt they felt at this betrayal of the caving fraternity went deep.

At this point the door opened and a group of three bedraggled-looking cavers came in. They were wearing mud-stained fleeces over wetsuits. Their faces were dirty and they looked exhausted. Craven suddenly ceased to be the centre of attention as the whole table greeted the newcomers.

'Bloody hell, you're back soon. What happened?' said the shaven head.

'It's a bloody dead end, should have known, went all round the pool, black as pitch and bloody freezing, but there's no way through.'

'Shit! I'm not surprised though.'

'Had to pack it in early, Steve's not well. He's out in the car, puked up when we got back out.'

'Was he on the piss last night?' This caused general sniggering. Craven decided that this was the moment to make his escape and he left them reflecting over another failed exploration. That must be the story most of the time, thought Craven as he walked back through the village. How rare it was to find new tunnels and passages, the holy grail of caving.

The visit to the café had been as disappointing as the cavers' failed underwater explorations except for the interesting information that Cartwright and Atkins had once been friends. The investigation, like the dead end in the pool, seemed to have no way forward.

In Burnthwaite, a solitary and anxious-looking figure was sitting in a corner of one of the bars in the Red Horse. John Baxter was also a member of the caving fraternity and another one of the team who had helped the police to bring Atkins's body to the surface. He had been very quiet while the police had been asking all the questions because disturbing thoughts were beginning to trouble him even then.

Since yesterday morning it had been hell. He didn't know what to do. Should he tell the police what he suspected? If he was wrong it would cause no end of trouble, but how could he be wrong? There was no other explanation. A shiver went through him as he faced again the significance of what he knew.

He finished his drink and looked nervously about him. It was quite early and the pub was half empty but he didn't want to bump into anyone he knew, one person especially. He took a deep breath and decided he must take action. He couldn't go on like this; he would have to ring the police. They'd all been given the telephone number of that inspector who was in charge of the murder enquiry: Inspector Oldroyd. He would go back home and ring him now.

Casting furtive glances around him, Baxter moved quickly out of the bar and down the short, narrow corridor where Oldroyd and Carter had been confronted by Cartwright. Unfortunately for him, he was seen leaving by a figure standing in the shadows in the lane at the side of the pub and quietly followed.

Outside it was a warm, still evening but, as it was late August, the light was already starting to fade. Baxter walked quickly along the streets until he reached his house, a large converted barn tucked behind a row of cottages. He was a joiner by trade and his van was parked in the short lane leading from the road. Inside the house he hesitated again and then walked through a wide hall into his sitting room. A bachelor, Baxter was extremely house-proud and everywhere showed ample evidence of his professional skills. He had done most of the work of the conversion himself and was particularly proud of this room, which had a wooden spiral staircase up to a mezzanine floor above. Through large patio doors there was a panoramic view across the fields and the drystone walls down to the River Wharfe and the fells beyond.

Baxter opened these doors as the room was a little stuffy and stepped outside. There was an eerie silence in the late summer evening and, looking up, he saw the black fluttering shape of a bat outlined against the fading light. He paused to take in the view and then returned to the sitting room. He sat in a large low leather sofa, took the phone and dialled the number.

Oldroyd had finished his ravioli and was sipping his coffee and gazing at the unusual décor. The restaurant was a converted music hall and the proscenium arch was still there. The tables higher up were on what would have been the stage. He was just trying to imagine some Edwardian music hall artistes performing up there when his phone rang.

'Hello, Chief Inspector Oldroyd.'

'Oh, hello, er, my name is John Baxter I'm ringing from Burnthwaite.' The voice sounded hesitant and a little afraid.

'Yes.' Oldroyd tried to be encouraging.

'You won't remember me but I was there on Monday when Dave Atkins's body was brought out of Jingling Pot. I was one of the rescue team who helped to bring him up.'

'Yes.'

'You're in charge of the investigation aren't you?'

'That's right.'

'Well.' There was a long pause. 'I think I can help you.'

'OK.'

'You see I'm pretty sure I know who did it and how the body came to be where it was.'

Oldroyd sat upright and immediately forgot about music hall artistes.

'You do, but how?'

'Yes,' the voice cut in, 'but I can't tell you over the phone. It's just that there's a bit too much to explain as to how I know who it is, I mean, if I do. I can't be completely sure and I know you'll understand that I can't explain it over the phone,' he repeated, sounding rather agitated.

'Yes, I do understand. Look, give me your address and I'll be in Burnthwaite in half an hour.'

Baxter put the phone down with relief. He blew out air to release his tension and went to the kitchen to pour himself a beer. He returned and switched on the computer; there was something he wanted to check before the chief inspector arrived, although he was pretty sure of his facts.

He had just located the site he was looking for when he heard a loud crash from his garage workshop, located through a door from the kitchen. His immediate thought was burglars. There had been a spate of break-ins in the area recently. Without further pause he unlocked the door and entered the workshop. It was dark inside, and he reached for the switch and pressed it, but no light came on. In the light from the kitchen he could make out a box of tools upended on the floor, the contents scattered.

The step he took towards the toolbox was his last. He hadn't seen that the cable from the light switch had been cut and he didn't realise that the toolbox had been deliberately dropped to make the crashing noise which lured him to his death; a death which was administered by a savage hammer blow to the back of the head, very similar to the one that had killed Dave Atkins.

Four

If tha slips and slides on t'Devil's Cup,

That monstrous 'ole will eat tha up.

Oldroyd was looking down at the body of John Baxter when Andy and Steph arrived. They'd not been long back in Harrogate when the call had come to return to Burnthwaite.

The lanky figure of Tim Groves was stooping over the body like a question mark. Oldroyd was crouched down beside him examining the head wound from which blood had trickled across the concrete floor. They were so engrossed that neither man acknowledged the arrival of the others. The scene had been sealed and a PC was keeping a log of who went in and out.

'Head smashed in by the famous blunt instrument, Jim,' pronounced Groves. 'Very possibly the same blunt instrument as the one which finished off our poor friend in the pothole.'

His long, sensitive fingers in their thin plastic gloves felt around in the blood-matted hair of the head and into the nasty depression in the skull, which was leaking blood and brain matter. The body lay crumpled on the floor of the garage in a way very similar to the body in the CSI's photographs of Jingling Pot. Strange, thought Oldroyd, as he had many times before, how quickly and irrevocably death could strike. He had been talking to this man only hours before and now he was reduced to a mass of flesh: a carcass, inert and no longer human. It was not an idea he liked, so again he brought his mind back to the situation.

'I've no doubt you're right,' said Oldroyd. 'Our killer has struck again.' He was suddenly aware of the presence of the newcomers. 'Ah, come on, you two, look at this.'

'You seem to be well on with things, sir,' said Carter, also looking down at the body.

'Yes, Carter, Tim lives here in the dale not far away so I was soon able to get him here. The victim's only been dead a couple of hours.'

Steph looked puzzled.

'How come you were here so quickly, sir? What happened?'

Oldroyd moved away from the body, stepping over a congealing pool of blood and the tools scattered over the floor.

'I was already on my way here. This unfortunate chap phoned me and asked me to come straight over. Said he knew about the murder of Atkins.'

'Obviously he did, sir.' Steph moved around the room to view the body.

'Indeed. In fact he told me he knew what had happened, how the body had ended up in the pothole, but he wouldn't tell me over the phone.'

Carter whistled.

'So you arrived here to find the body?'

'I did; someone beat me to it and you can bet your life that that person is the one we're already looking for.'

'How did the killer know that this bloke was about to spill the beans?'

'Difficult to be sure but I suspect that they were already suspicious for some reason and probably tracking him. It's our bad luck that they decided to move in just before he got to us.'

'Who is he anyway, sir?' asked Steph.

'He told me his name was John Baxter and you and I have met him, Andy.'

Carter glanced down at what could be seen of the face.

'I don't recognise him, sir.'

'He said he was there at Jingling Pot when Atkins was brought out. In fact, he was part of the team that did it. I don't recall him either but he must have been one of those who didn't say much. He was probably already beginning to piece together what had happened but didn't feel he could say anything. You don't go around accusing people of murder without being pretty certain of your ground. Maybe the murderer was actually there. He told me over the phone that he couldn't be absolutely sure. He must have been agonising since that day about whether or not to come forward.'

'Poor sod,' said Carter. 'Just a bit longer and he would have been safe.'

'Yep.' Oldroyd sighed. 'I'm afraid it's another MTAP.'

'A what, sir?'

'Malignancy of time and place,' replied Steph. 'One of Sir's acronyms.'

'Well remembered, Steph.' Oldroyd turned to Carter. 'I like to create a few of my own acronyms to counter the idiotic ones that come from the morons that spout management speak. At least mine have some practical meaning. This one refers to the reality of so many murders: that the fate of the victim depended on being in the wrong place at the wrong time or acting in the wrong way at the wrong time. Think how many unfortunate victims of serial killers just happened to present an opportunity to the killer without knowing it.'

'But he must have known the killer, sir.'

'Yes, but here the malignancy lies in the fact that he didn't speak out earlier before the killer got to him. He's had since yesterday morning but only decided when it was too late.'

Oldroyd paused. He often mused on the ironies of time and place. Did the lucky accidents in life balance the unlucky ones or was fate governed by a Hardyesque malignity? Maybe the victim lying on the floor now in a pool of his own blood refused when he was seventeen to get in a car that later crashed. It was one of the many intractable mysteries of life that circled around the main one: death itself.

'Better rouse the neighbourhood, you two, and see if anybody saw or heard anything suspicious. But before you do, come and look at this.'

He led Carter and Johnson to the living room and the computer, which was still switched on.

'He must have been looking at this when the killer arrived. What do you make of it?'

Carter looked at the screen to see weather reports for the area. There were columns of figures giving temperature, wind velocity, rainfall etc. for the Wharfedale area going back a couple of weeks. He shook his head.

'Weather reports, sir? I don't get it. Why would he be looking at them? Unless he was a weather nerd, you know: "The average temperature this month has been higher than for any August since 1935 and nobody gives a toss" kind of thing.'

'Well, don't be so dismissive of the weather, it can sometimes tell you some useful things,' replied Oldroyd, who could be a bit of a weather nerd himself, 'and I have an idea it could be an important clue here. I think he was checking things before I arrived.'

'Checking the weather, sir?' said an equally puzzled Steph.

'The weather records,' replied Oldroyd with emphasis on the last word, but would say no more.

Carter went to look around the workshop.

'It's pretty tidy in here, sir, apart from that box of tools scattered around. That must have made a hell of a racket if it fell off that shelf. I wonder if that's how the murderer lured him in here?'

'I would think you're right, Andy. The killer was already in here, that's for sure; got in through that small door at the back there, forced the lock.'

'They must have known a bit about the layout of things; that there was a door there and another one from the house.'

'Yes, all confirming that the killer knew him and had visited this place.'

There was the noise of vehicles drawing up outside.

'This'll be the SOCOs and probably Bob Craven too.'

Steph looked down at the body.

'Does this take us any further, sir? I mean, we're already pretty sure that the killer was a potholer. I suppose that must be confirmed now.'

'If one potholer was killed because he knew too much about the circumstances of the murder, it is reasonable to assume that what he knew was something to do with the caves. And that would also be known by another potholer who is the murderer.'

Carter followed the logic, but was still sceptical.

'Are you sure he was telling the truth when he called, sir? I mean, how do you know that he wasn't an accomplice who got scared and wanted to rat on his mate?'

'I can't be sure, and Steph's right: it doesn't tell us very much more than we know because we'll probably find that most of the caving fraternity knew this poor bloke, so it hardly narrows it down much. It still leaves us with plenty of suspects.'

'Right Jim, I've finished.' Tim Groves was removing his rubber gloves. 'I'll send the report as soon as I can; doesn't sound as if it will be much help; cause of death obvious and you have a pretty good idea of the time of death already.'

'Still need to have it confirmed, Tim, you never know on a case like this; something unusual is always likely to happen.'

Tim Groves left and Oldroyd sighed.

'Come on, we'd better get back too. I need to get ready for the media. We can't keep away from their friendly embrace for much longer after this.'

~

As Burnthwaite was about to learn of its second murder within a matter of days, Geoff Whitaker returned to work in the kitchens of the Red Horse. This was not a particularly stressful prospect as, to be honest, he'd been producing the dishes on the menu for so long that he could do it almost blindfolded. It was the standard stuff of pub cuisine: steak-and-kidney pie, battered haddock with Yorkshire mushy peas, lamb Henry, roast beef, vegetarian lasagne, pork casserole with peppers, various filled baguettes with chips. The monotony was broken by the daily specials: today it was Cumberland sausage in onion gravy with mustard mash, and fish pie with salmon and prawns. Not a great deal to tax his culinary skills there. Nevertheless, he enjoyed his job as a chef. The issue was money: it didn't pay well and he was always a bit short.

This problem was compounded by his fondness for a little online gambling. In truth, a little would have been OK, but as with all addictive activities, a little soon became a little more and so on. As with all gamblers who are genuinely hooked, the illusion of huge gains that never actually materialised became compulsive. The losses mounted up, all to be wiped out when the big win came . . . and so on.

Helen was aware of his gambling. They'd had a serious discussion about it that had ended with him promising to kick the habit that was now damaging his family. The thing that had affected him most deeply was not having enough money to buy the kids what they wanted for Christmas.

Everything had been fine for a while, but, like an ex-smoker who starts to drag furtively on an illicit cigarette, he had quietly slipped back on to the fatal websites where the temptation was too much to bear. He was now well and truly hooked again, but this time it was all in secret. Even worse, his losses had led to him becoming involved in things he now regretted.

He entered round the back of the pub through a grubby doorway next to the bottle bank and rubbish bins. People were already at work in the kitchen. One or two looked up and he received some muttered 'Hi's in greeting, but he felt a tension in the atmosphere. Did people find it too ghoulish to talk to someone who had stumbled on a murder victim? Maybe there was a suspicion that somehow if you found a body you might have had something to do with it. Only Penny, a young sous chef, came over and quietly asked him if he was OK.

'Yeah, fine. I suppose.'

'Can't have been much fun, finding a body like that.'

'No, especially when you know them.'

'I know; God, that must have been awful.'

'I've had better trips underground.'

He'd been putting on his working clothes and apron while he was talking. 'Anyway, better get on. I'm late.'

He was glad that people would think he was not himself because of his experience in Jingling Pot. The truth was that other things were on his mind.

He began to assemble the prepared ingredients for the lasagne, trying to concentrate on what he was doing, but after a few minutes he looked around the kitchen and checked that everyone was working. He slipped back out unnoticed to where he had come in and stood behind the bottle bank. He called a number on his phone. He was expecting the usual recorded message, but this time there was an answer. Whitaker looked round sharply, checking there was no one in hearing distance.

'Where the hell have you been?' he hissed.

As he listened to the reply, his face contorted with contempt.

'Needed to get away! Wouldn't we all bloody like to, but there is no getting away from it, you bastard; you're in this too!'

Whitaker began to pace around, trying to avoid the shards of broken glass as he listened to another reply.

'Well, that's pointless now, isn't it? Because the police will be on to it soon so there's no point running away and . . .'

He suddenly pulled the phone away from his ear and jabbed at it with his thumb.

'Bastard!' he shouted, but then stuffed the phone in his pocket and glanced nervously at the door. He stalked back to the kitchen, kicking an empty wine bottle against the wall in his frustration.

The next case meeting at West Riding Police HQ found Oldroyd and his team under much greater pressure.

'I'm expecting the super to call me at any moment,' confessed Oldroyd. 'It's all over the press now.'

On the table were some of that morning's tabloids with lurid head-lines: 'Is There a Serial Killer in This Idyllic Village?' over pictures of Burnthwaite with insets of photographs of Atkins and Baxter. 'Caving Community Rocked by Second Murder' screamed another headline, followed by 'A second caver was found brutally murdered last night only days after the body of local man David Atkins was discovered in Jingling Pot, one of the most popular potholes with experienced cavers.'

Carter frowned, picked up one of the papers and scanned the article.

'"A spokesperson for West Riding Police said investigations were ongoing." We can't hide behind a statement like that for much longer, can we, sir?'

'No. I've arranged a press conference for this afternoon. I'll have to throw them something to feed on. You come along; it'll be a good introduction to the local media circus.'

Carter was not intimidated by this, being familiar with the relent-less media scrutiny placed upon the Met.

The telephone rang sharply. Curious, thought Oldroyd as he picked up the receiver, how we ascribe a voice to the telephone depending on who we think is calling. This would almost certainly be Tom Walker. It was; the conversation was fairly brief.

'Ah, Jim.'

'Tom.'

'It's a bad do, this caver business, now isn't it? Have you seen the papers?'

'Yes, I'm having a conference this afternoon.'

'Good man. Are you getting anywhere with it?'

'It's not long since we spoke, Tom. The first bloke was really unpopular, but we're narrowing the list of suspects down. The second bloke called me just before he was done in. He was going to tell me who he thought did it. I was on my way over there.'

'Bloody hell, that's bad luck; killer got to him before you did. Keep that away from the bloody hacks; it's just the kind of thing they like: "Killer Outwits Police" and rubbish like that.'

'I know. Only my team and Tim Groves know what happened.'

'OK. Well, they're good people, but tell them to keep their mouths shut. You know Burnthwaite's in Archibald Ramsay's constituency. That little Tory bastard will be bleating to the Home Secretary that the crime investigation's damaging the tourist economy; can't the police ensure the safety of his tax-paying constituents etc. etc. Then the Home Secretary will be on to Watkins and he'll carpet me.'

'Yes, Tom.'

'So what I'm saying, Jim, is I know you're doing your best, but get your skates on for all our sakes.'

'As you say, Tom, I'll do my best.'

'Do you need any more help?'

'I don't think so, thanks, but I'll let you know if we do.'

'Good; off you go then.'

The super rang off. Oldroyd sighed as he put down the receiver. Power structures were always the same: everyone gets kicked by the people above them and then kicks the person below, especially in an organisation like the police force where rank is all-important. He looked at Steph and Andy; he should now give them a blast, but he wasn't going to destroy his relationship with those below by taking out on them his frustration with the people above. This was probably why he wouldn't rise any higher in the force, not that he particularly wanted to; he wasn't ruthless enough. Also, he sympathised with Tom Walker having to deal with the politicians and a repulsive specimen like Matthew Watkins. Why was it that professionals in the service ended up being told what to do by people who knew nothing about the job? It was the one thing he hated about his work: having to justify himself to people he didn't respect. At least he was lucky with his – what was it called now? – his *line manager*. Tom Walker was an old pro and he was glad about that. He turned his attention back to the task in hand.

'Right, where were we?' He realised he'd got to his feet while talking to the super and had been striding round the room.

'Sit down, sir; I'll get you a cup of coffee.' From experience, Steph knew how Oldroyd would be feeling after a tense conversation with his superior.

'Thanks, Steph.'

So, fortified by coffee and the usual chocolate biscuits, the three detectives, impelled by a greater sense of urgency, grappled with the mystery again.

'Let's have another run through the main suspects,' Oldroyd began. 'I take it nothing's emerged from all the screening we've done of the other people who knew Atkins?'

'Our detectives have been working with Craven's people and they've interviewed just about everyone in the Caving Club and in Burnthwaite who knew him. He was universally unpopular but nothing's come up that gives us any better leads than the suspects we've got at the moment.'

'Nobody else who had a motive?'

'Not stronger than the people we're pursuing.'

'OK, let's start with who we've got. Take me through them, you two, and treat me to your latest theories.'

In preparation for the meeting, Carter had drawn up a chart listing the chief suspects and the evidence for and against. He consulted the sheet.

'I suppose top of the list now must be Bill Watson, as he disappeared on the day the body was discovered. He was probably the one who shouted out that Atkins was a bastard. Do you think he could have been the bloke tracking us near that limestone walkway?'

'Pavement,' corrected Oldroyd. 'Quite possibly, we'll know more about that when Craven's people have done a bit of exploration. Do we have any further information on his possible whereabouts?'

Steph replied, 'Not yet, sir; officers from the Ripon station have interviewed the sister but she claims not to have had any recent contact. She could be hiding him, of course.'

Oldroyd frowned. 'His behaviour is clearly suspicious, but somehow it's a bit too obvious.'

'Why, sir?' argued Carter. 'It must have been a shock when the body was discovered because, as you say, it wasn't meant to be found there.'

'But would the person who planned this murder suddenly lose his nerve and bolt off in a panic?'

'Or her nerve, sir,' interposed Steph.

'Absolutely,' replied Oldroyd. 'They could still have panicked in the circumstances, and if we're talking about Bill Watson, we don't know him and how he would have reacted.'

'He certainly had one of the strongest motives,' said Steph. 'His wife confessed straight out to having an affair with Atkins. Also, sir, if he wasn't the killer, why has he disappeared? His wife seemed genuinely concerned, as if she couldn't explain it and maybe suspects he's involved. I got a photograph of him, by the way, as he's now officially reported as missing.'

'Good. He may also have been involved with Atkins himself in some way, like so many other people. That man clearly had all kinds of things going on and his death will have stirred up the bottom of a murky pool. There're bound to be more repercussions.'

Carter turned to Steph. 'The other problem you're forgetting is the second murder. Unless Watson had an accomplice, he must have returned to Burnthwaite to kill John Baxter. He couldn't have done that without tracking him, so he would have had to be well disguised and concealed if he didn't want to be recognised.'

'It's all possible,' said Oldroyd, 'but unlikely. If he had the determination and the nerve to protect his skin by getting rid of John Baxter, then why draw attention to himself by running off in the first place?'

'What about his wife, sir?'

'Go on.'

'She had an affair with Atkins, but he was a womaniser. We know he was talking about starting an affair with another woman when he disappeared so he may well have dumped her for someone else. She also doesn't have a very good alibi for that evening, claims she was just at home.'

'So she could have killed him out of jealous revenge?' observed Carter.

'Yes.'

'Well, that's a powerful motive; women certainly don't like being dumped, do they?' continued Carter. Steph flashed him a look of annoyance and her reply was a little sharp.

'No, and neither do men, in my experience.'

Oldroyd interjected. 'But you're not suggesting she did this alone? She doesn't sound like the type of woman who would know about potholes and be able to drag a body underground.'

'No, but there are enough of Atkins's enemies in Burnthwaite for her to form an alliance with someone. I think she could be pretty deadly if she felt cheated. She seemed to be sincerely upset at Atkins's death and worried about her husband's whereabouts, but that could have just been an act. It didn't strike me as very consistent. She obviously didn't think much about her husband as she cheated on him, but she seemed to be laying on the concern once she admitted she didn't know where he was.'

Oldroyd frowned and gave a slight shrug of his shoulders.

'OK, well, that makes both the Watsons suspects. Now, who else have we got?'

Carter took a chocolate biscuit and consulted his list.

'Sam Cartwright, mechanic. We've already established motive and now we know he is a potholer so he would know the system. Craven also reported that Cartwright and Atkins had been potholing together with caving groups over in the Ingleton area.' Carter looked up from his notes. 'Where's that?' he asked.

'Over in the western Dales.'

Oldroyd was thoughtful.

'That's strange; I wouldn't have expected that. So it seems they were friendly at one point, despite Cartwright calling him all the names under the sun to us at the Red Horse. Atkins's relationships seem more complex the more we find out about him.'

'The big reservation I have,' continued Carter, 'is still the obvious one of his physique. He must have had an accomplice to get the body down there.'

Steph added, 'From the way you describe him, he also doesn't sound like the sort of bloke to plan a murder. He'd just lose his temper and smash his victim over the head.'

'That's what I thought; he's got a real temper all right and it could have happened that way. Cartwright admitted being in the Red Horse and seeing Atkins about the time he disappeared. He could have ambushed him later, hit him over the head, hastily hidden the body and gone to his accomplice for help in disposing of it more permanently.'

'In that case he or they were extremely lucky not to be discovered at any point. I tend to agree with Steph; Atkins's murder was carefully planned. And what about Baxter?'

Carter continued to develop his theory.

'Maybe he saw something and Cartwright had to silence him.'

Oldroyd frowned again and shook his head. 'It doesn't really hang together. Baxter certainly knew something, but I'm sure it was more complicated than seeing Atkins battered over the head outside the Red Horse. Carry on with the list.'

Carter briefly consulted his notes again. 'The Hardimans.'

'Do we have any further leads on them?'

'Not really, except it did occur to me when I was interviewing Cartwright. He mentioned seeing a woman outside the Red Horse that night. I wondered if it could have been Caroline Hardiman.'

Oldroyd raised his eyebrows. 'That's interesting; any particular reason why?'

'Just a hunch, sir. Atkins was bragging about getting another woman and you said you weren't sure whether Caroline Hardiman was telling the truth about her relationship with Atkins. Maybe she changed her mind and was going to meet him that night. If the husband found out, he'd have been furious, because we know he'd already got rid of Atkins for pursuing his wife. Also, he'd certainly be capable of carrying out the murder and getting the body into the pothole. I assume from his job he must be pretty strong and fit.'

'Yes, but I still think he would have needed an accomplice. Not even he could have done it alone.'

'The problem is,' observed Steph, 'not only do we not know if it was her outside the pub, but we don't have any corroboration of Cartwright's story; he could have made it up to put suspicion elsewhere.'

'That's possible,' said Oldroyd, 'but I think that makes our friendly mechanic rather more sophisticated than he is.'

'Of our main suspects that just leaves the Whitakers,' said Carter, coming to the end of his notes.

'Yes, any further thoughts on them?'

'Not at the moment. One of Craven's people interviewed the other caver who was with Whitaker leading that expedition when the body was discovered and he confirmed everything Whitaker said about the circumstances down there. We should be getting the report from the IT people shortly. I'm still convinced that he or his wife was involved in something with Atkins.'

'There's one more thing,' said Oldroyd. 'Craven has located Atkins's wife over in Burnley and he's going over to interview her as we speak; that might yield something.'

He did a little formal summing up. 'Right, well, thank you both for your thoughts. We can't eliminate any of our suspects yet and they'll all have to be interviewed again to find out who's got an alibi for last night. That might reduce the list a little, but the problem with alibis in a small place like Burnthwaite is that everything's close together. Someone would have only had to nip out for a few minutes from wherever they were to go over and kill John Baxter. I'll ask Craven to get his people to find out if anyone was seen near Baxter's house, but I don't think they'll come up with anything. Whoever planned and executed these murders is pretty clever. It's getting tough, but all we can do is press on and wait for the breakthrough. If necessary, we'll have to go back and interview people again and again until we find the opening we're looking for.'

Carter and Steph nodded.

'I'm going on a televised news conference in about an hour so I'd better get a few things done before then.'

'What kind of format do they take, sir?' asked Carter.

'Oh, the usual: ask for anyone with any knowledge to come forward; police are following some lines of enquiry and so on. Then the journalists ask me a lot of questions which they know I can't answer and I don't answer them.'

'I see,' said Carter with a smile.

'It's all a bit of a charade. The thing is presented as if it's us asking everyone for help but the real reason is to satisfy media interest and to give them an opportunity to find some juicy detail for their headlines.'

Oldroyd sat back, stretched, then relaxed into his chair.

'Anyway, the pressure's mounting,' he observed, but he didn't look like a man under pressure as he lazily reached for a biscuit and then sipped his coffee. 'We'd better get on with it. I might pay my sister a visit later. I usually go and see her when things get tough.'

'Your sister, sir?' asked Carter as they all got up to leave.

'Yes, she's a vicar in Kirkby Underside, a little village near here. I always find it comforting to talk to her. It puts a lot of things in perspective and she's got a fine mind. I like to think of her as my Mycroft.'

'Yes, sir, er, right.' Carter didn't understand Oldroyd's reference but thought it better not to pursue it at this point.

Oldroyd walked on quickly to meet with the people organising the press conference, leaving Carter and Steph together.

'What was he talking about?' asked Carter.

'Mycroft Holmes was Sherlock Holmes's brother in the stories; supposed to be even cleverer than Sherlock, I think. I've heard him make the comparison before.'

'Is his sister really a vicar?'

'Yeah, in a village just south of here. Quite a character, by all accounts, and Sir dotes on her.'

Steph seemed rather subdued.

'By the way, I'm sorry if my remarks about women being dumped seemed sexist, but do you really think a woman could have got that body down there?'

Steph stopped and turned to look at him.

'You've got some pretty old-fashioned views about women for a modern city guy. It's all those urban girls in London. Couldn't imagine them dragging a body along muddy tunnels, could you? What would they do with their designer handbags? There are lots of women strong enough to do something like that, or at least help. We've established that even a man couldn't have done it alone.'

'I suppose you're right.' Carter was forced on to the defensive but he didn't mind. He liked a woman who was strong enough to put him down.

~

Oldroyd sat behind a table with a barrage of microphones in front of him. Andy and Steph were at either side. He surveyed the ranks of serious-faced reporters and composed himself before making a statement. At pressurised times like this he sought his inner calm by imagining himself at Barden Towers by the River Wharfe on a quiet morning in May, the shallow waters drifting over the rounded stones on the riverbed and chaffinches in the trees singing notes that descended into a sweet blur of noise.

These images made the flashing cameras and jostling reporters seem insubstantial as he made his standard statement about the case: outline basic facts, several lines of enquiry, request for assistance from the public. Then he faced the questions. A loud-mouthed reporter from one of the tabloids was the first to speak. With his head shaved, and wearing an earring, he looked and behaved like a yob and personified the kind of bullying, cynical arrogance Oldroyd most detested in the media.

'Is it true that the first body was stripped naked and had cuts on it?'

Here we go, thought Oldroyd.

'No, the body was not naked, but it was dressed in ordinary light clothes: jeans and T-shirt and not in the special clothing and equipment required for caving. The main mark on the body was the head injury that was the cause of death. There were also some minor abrasions suggesting that the body had been dragged.'

The reporter bounced back.

'But why the hell was it down there, Chief Inspector? Don't you think it's weird? We've heard rumours of some kind of satanic rituals going on in the village. Do you think he could have been a victim of that? You know, taken down there as some kind of sacrifice?' This prompted some murmurings and quiet laughter.

Even Oldroyd was shocked by the outlandishness of this suggestion. My God, he thought, are there no limits to their desire for sensation? He moved in sharply and adopted a fiercer tone.

'We have absolutely no reason to believe that anything of a sinister nature such as you suggest has taken place in Burnthwaite, or that it had anything to do with the murder.'

There was something supremely authoritative about Oldroyd's powerful Yorkshire voice when he spoke in this vein. The reporter was momentarily cowed and Oldroyd went on. 'Why the body of Mr Atkins was discovered in the situation it was remains one of the mysteries of the case, but we are confident that we will solve it.'

'So it's "The Body in Jingling Pot"?' another reporter retorted to some amusement around the room.

Oldroyd smiled. 'Well, it sounds like the title of a good thriller, but if you people wish to call it that it's fine with me. It'll make a good headline, I'm sure; certainly better than "Human Sacrifice in Jingling Pot".'

There was quite raucous laughter at this and the tabloid reporter looked sheepish.

Oldroyd took a drink of water and folded his arms on the table in front of him. He relished the control he had of the situation. He usually came out on top in these tussles, however difficult the case and no matter how embarrassingly slow the progress. The fact was that he was just too damned clever for them.

'Are you sure the two deaths are connected?' This sensible question was Oldroyd's reward for slapping down the more sensational comments.

'Absolutely,' he replied. 'In fact, I can tell you that Mr Baxter had contacted me before he died and offered information about the murder of Mr Atkins.'

Oldroyd had decided to go against Walker's advice for a good reason, which the super would respect. It caused a minor sensation.

'You mean he was silenced?'

Eager eyes were fixed on Oldroyd from all over the room. He paused to create maximum dramatic effect.

'It appears so. I'm deeply sorry we couldn't get there quickly enough to save him.'

'Did he tell you anything?'

'I cannot comment at this stage of the investigation but suffice it to say that the conversation we had was interesting.'

'Did he tell you anything important?'

'No further comment on that.'

'So you're dealing with a conspiracy here. A number of people are involved in these murders?'

'Conspiracy is not quite the word I would use. It was clear from the outset that more than one person was involved in the murder of David Atkins. There is no evidence, at this stage, that John Baxter was involved in that murder. He was presumably killed because he had information which could lead us to the killers.'

Oldroyd was using an old technique to put pressure on the killers. It was a huge bluff: Baxter had in fact said nothing but Oldroyd had implied the opposite. The newspapers would not make pleasant reading for whoever was behind all this. They would sweat and might be panicked into some rash action.

'What about the question of motive? Is it true that the pothole victim was hated in the village?'

Oldroyd winced at the tabloidese exaggeration. His reply was diplomatic.

'I cannot comment on the personality of the deceased, but it does seem that he was involved in a number of relationships in the area and that some of these relationships caused resentment.'

The tabloid reporter perked up again.

'Sex,' he said in the manner of someone relieved to be on familiar territory.

'Maybe,' said Oldroyd, 'but we have evidence of financial dealings of a possibly dubious nature. So I ask once again for anyone with any information regarding this or any other of Mr Atkins's activities to come forward.'

'Do you believe they will strike again?'

This question came from the back of the room and it was a tricky one. Oldroyd didn't want to panic the community; he could see the headlines: 'Living in Fear in a Dales Village'. It was not impossible that other people could be at risk, but this was not the work of a deranged serial killer.

'Clearly there is a dangerous person or people at large, and while that is the case, it would be complacent of me to pretend that there was no danger. On the other hand, I consider it safe to say that these crimes are both associated with Mr Atkins, the first victim. We are not talking about some killer who could strike at random, which is why I ask yet again for anyone with knowledge to speak to us.'

Oldroyd had only just arrived back in his office when Superintendent Walker was on the phone.

'How did it go? Did you manage to keep the bastards at bay?' Walker's hatred of the media could be traced back, as Oldroyd knew, to the mauling the West Yorkshire police received during the terrible years of the Ripper investigation when Peter Sutcliffe was allowed to slip through their hands and continued to rampage around the industrial towns of the area.

'I think so; they obviously love the idea of murder coming to a sleepy Dales village, but we've got them under control. I did tell them about Baxter's call, by the way. It's worth trying to flush the murderer out.'

'As you think best.' Oldroyd smiled; he knew the old boy would trust him. He didn't go into details about the satanic rituals. If Walker heard about that, he would probably have an apoplectic fit.

'Keep at it then. Let's hope for a breakthrough soon. Send me a full report on your progress.'

'Aye, Tom, I will.'

Oldroyd put down the phone. Under pressure like this, there was only one thing to do. Go home and listen to a string quartet.

Later that day Carter went to see what the experts had discovered on Atkins's computer files. He sat in a large, overheated room in the basement of the building surrounded by monitors, hard drives and half-dismantled machines. It looked like a robot-servicing laboratory from a science-fiction film.

Carter sat sweating, enduring the noisy buzzing of fans and monitors and the vague smell of oil and electricity. An expert in analysing computer files for illegal financial transactions – or 'nerd', as Carter preferred – was explaining what they had found. He had longish greasy black hair and spectacles that were repaired with tape. Why did these people conform to their stereotypes? thought Carter.

The man seemed oblivious to the discomforts of his surroundings despite the fact that he had to raise his voice slightly to be heard above the din of the machines.

'It's clear that this bloke was up to no good. We found loads of files which give us evidence of suspect dealings in property, and equities, stuff like that.'

'Suspect in what sense?'

'Oh, you know, the usual thing: properties sold for more than they were worth due to the defects being concealed; shares bought following advice obtained illegally.'

'It was a bit risky, leaving all that kind of stuff on the computer, wasn't it?'

'Ah well, that's where we come in. These guys use a kind of code to conduct their activities and they use special programs to conceal where emails are coming from, but we can crack them.'

Carter was very interested, and relieved; at last, some progress!

'Did he do all this himself?'

'He wasn't alone. It seems there were two other people involved. We can detect two sets of emails on the files but we need longer to trace them.'

'Right, we'll need you to do that. This could be vital information.'

Carter was enjoying himself. He liked this kind of thing. Unlike Oldroyd, he was of the IT generation and some of his most exciting times at the Met had been working on big fraud cases. He wasn't a real techie, but he enjoyed the chase using the information from the experts to trap the cheating bastards. Carter despised white-collar crime. Most of the perpetrators were pretty well off before they embarked on their criminal careers. It was sheer greed that made them defraud their own companies or the pension schemes on which some poor workers were relying for support in their old age. He had much more sympathy with shoplifters and burglars, people from the hard parts of London who'd never known anything except a tough struggle for survival.

'How long before you get those details to me?'

The man frowned.

'It's not easy. We'd have to put in a concentrated effort and we have to run a special program on the F drive which . . .' He launched into a highly technical explanation, which Carter cut into impatiently.

'DCI Oldroyd needs this urgently. We're under pressure on this case to make a breakthrough.'

The mention of Oldroyd's name provoked the reaction Carter expected: a mixture of fear and respect crossed the technician's face.

'Oh, right. Well, we'll make it a priority and it should only take us a day or so.'

'Great,' replied Carter and with some relief left the underground lair feeling optimistic that he was on to something.

When he arrived back in the office, Steph was at the computer tapping away at the keyboard with a frown on her face.

'You don't look happy,' he remarked as he sat down at his workstation near hers.

'I'm not; something's really bothering me and I can't bloody find anything about it.' She closed her eyes and sighed. 'Oh, it's so frustrating!' She banged her fists either side of the keyboard.

'Temper, temper,' he said. Privately he thought she looked even more attractive when she was angry. 'What is it?'

'Ever since we started investigating this case I've been having this strange feeling that I've read something or there was something in the news a while ago that's got something to do with it.'

'Sounds vague.'

'Exactly. I can't pin it down, but I've got a feeling it might be important.'

'It'll come to you when you least expect it.'

Steph sighed.

'I'm getting nowhere. I can't spend any more time on it now.'

She moved the mouse pointer on to the cross at the top of the screen and clicked emphatically. It seemed like another dead end.

Carter looked at her.

'We've not got very far yet, have we?'

She returned his look.

'Oh, I don't know. Don't underestimate the boss. I told you; he doesn't always share everything as you're investigating but he'll have plenty of theories.'

'You really admire Oldroyd, don't you?'

Steph looked at him condescendingly as if he had asked a rather silly question.

'Everyone does. He's known and respected everywhere round here. He works things out when you think there's just no evidence, nothing at all to go on. And he has such an incredible knowledge of Yorkshire and all its different areas and people. Anyway,' she changed the subject, 'how are you doing? Do you still like it up here? It's been pretty hectic since you arrived. I don't suppose you've had a chance to settle in.'

'Not really,' Carter replied, 'but I'm enjoying it.' He thought for a moment; maybe it was worth another try. 'Look, do you fancy coming out for a drink after work, you could tell me more about what it's like round here?'

To Carter's surprise, her expression changed completely. She looked worried and confused and glanced away from him.

'Sorry, I can't, I – I've got something else on.'

It was just like in the pub the other day. One minute she was all friendly and then she went cold. The sparkle and confidence Carter found so attractive went out of her. What was the problem? He found this coldness a turn off but also puzzling because he sensed she liked him.

'OK. Well, maybe another time.'

'Yeah.'

She got up and went out of the office and Carter watched her go. He shrugged his shoulders regretfully; plenty more fish in the sea was his motto, so unfortunately it seemed time to move on.

As the day progressed in a fairly humdrum manner, Carter was left contemplating again how different things were in this part of the world from the one he'd left. He wasn't used to this rootedness that so many people seemed to feel. His whole experience of life was of a shifting urban scene, a vast, energetic but amorphous environment with nothing deep that tied you to a particular place.

In the afternoon most of his new colleagues were out of the office and it went rather quiet. He felt a tinge of nostalgia for the constant bustle at the Met and for his old, fast life in London. He decided to take a break and call Jason. He smiled when he heard the familiar cheery voice above the usual buzz of noise in the background.

'Hey, how's it going, me old mate? Can't talk for long, I'm run off my feet here. It's chaos; one minute they're pressurising you to make the deals and the next they're panicking that someone's going to break the rules and lose the company millions.' He didn't sound in the least concerned about it.

'I'm OK; it's a bit quiet here today.'

'Nothing doing up there then, just a few people stealing clogs or mistreating their whippets?'

'Not exactly, but, you know, I don't really know many people yet so it's a bit sort of low key.'

'Oh, the poor chap's lonely! What you need, mate, is a woman; what's the talent like up there? There must be something worth chasing.'

Carter was about to tell him about Steph, but decided he didn't really want to talk about her in the way Jason would expect.

'Give me a chance; I've only been here a few days.'

'That should be long enough for a stud like you; get your finger out! When I think of all those women police officers in their uniforms with the tight skirts I could almost join the police force myself.'

'That would be a joke: you in the police force. You'd be more pissed than the drunks you were supposed to be arresting. "I'm sorry, sir, but it is my duty to arrest you for not drinking enough this evening. You're a disgrace to the male sex. How dare you walk the streets in this sober condition?"'

Jason seemed to love the image.

'Too right, mate; anyway must be off, I have to press a few more computer keys and shift a bit more money around the world. It's called work and at least it pays well. I'll give you a call soon. Ciao.'

Carter smiled at the phone; he felt better. However wild and morally dubious his friend was, he was also undoubtedly good for the spirits.

In his flat overlooking the Stray, Oldroyd decided to play a quintet instead of a quartet. Schubert's Trout Quintet for piano and strings always put him into a good humour. It was the young Schubert, exuberant and happy, celebrating his visit to Steyr in 1819 before the despair caused by contracting syphilis had engulfed him. Oldroyd pushed the remote and the first soothing bars were heard on the piano.

He looked out of the window across the Stray. It had been a bright day but clouds had gathered and heavy rain was beginning to fall. It spattered against the window as Schubert's music suggested the tumbling waters of the trout stream.

Oldroyd felt calmer as he sat down, closed his eyes and listened. His father had been a competent amateur cellist and had taken Oldroyd and his sister to chamber concerts. An abiding love of the unique sound of the string quartet and other chamber groups was the result. He listened to the rippling notes on the piano and sank deeper into the chair.

And then suddenly his eyes popped open. He sat up straight, thought for a moment and then got up quickly and switched on his computer. He logged on remotely to the system at work and, with some excitement, he opened the file of photographs of the Jingling Pot crime scene and looked again. On one particular shot he zoomed in and, after a long gaze, he nodded. A satisfied look appeared on his face. He remembered something Tim Groves had said to him that afternoon and things fitted into place. He sat down again and reabsorbed himself in the Schubert with a smile on his face. Chamber music truly was inspiring and in the most unexpected ways.

In the house next to the gift shop in Burnthwaite, Anne Watson was also looking out of a window at the rain. A grey mist concealed the fells across the dale and water ran down the grey stone tiles of the roof opposite. Her face contorted with disgust. She took a long pull on her cigarette and a gulp of the gin and tonic she held in the other hand. She thought how she hated this bloody place. It was tedious enough in the good weather, but when it rained it was the dreariest place in the world.

Why on earth had she ever allowed Bill to persuade her to come here? She was a city girl from Manchester, who had then gone to art college in Leeds. She and Bill had been fellow students and their relationship in those early years had been passionate and exciting. Practically all they ever did all day was have sex, smoke dope and go to bars and the cinema.

They got married after graduating but problems began almost immediately with work and money. Then she fell pregnant with Alice and there was a more serious need to earn cash. Bill started to evolve money-making schemes, one of which involved trying to get loans to buy properties and renovate them. After a while, he seemed to tire of it and then suggested they move out of Leeds into the Dales.

She had been sceptical from the beginning but Bill said it would not be a 'crappy gift shop'; they would sell proper art and craftwork by local artists, potters and jewellery makers. He thought it would be nice for Alice, who was still only a baby, to grow up in the countryside. She knew another, more selfish, reason was that it would give him the chance to indulge his hobby of cave exploration.

She had agreed because she hoped it would anchor him, give him a purpose. It might also improve their relationship, which was starting to deteriorate owing to Bill's restlessness and his recklessness with money. He was fond of Alice but, like a lot of men, pretty useless with babies and toddlers. They had to take on a huge mortgage to get the place, and Anne found that things were actually very much as before. She was landed with running the shop while Bill swanned off talking to local artists and weavers. He continued to devise ever wilder financial schemes.

So here she was, running what was effectively a 'crappy gift shop', despite his promises. Was it for this that she had studied Art? What had happened to all her career aspirations? All sacrificed to him! Tied to a shop in a claustrophobic little village, miles from anywhere, full of Tory-voting farmers and retired couples and infested with gossip. The only positive thing was Alice, who had taken to living in Burnthwaite straight away.

She thought she was going to go mad selling Kendal Mint Cake to hikers and hearing from the locals about how so-and-so parked his car outside their window and they had no right to. It was like being in *The Archers*, a programme she despised. She had started the affair with Dave Atkins more out of boredom than anything else. Dave had a sense of fun and shared her view of the village. Having an affair was exciting; the only exciting thing she had ever done in Burnthwaite. She knew she wasn't Dave's only lover, but she didn't care. Ironically, it was through Bill that she had met him. They knew each other through caving, another ridiculous activity she couldn't see the point of; those dark dripping places just gave her the creeps. Dave could laugh at it, saying it was really a lot of hairy men (and women) proving they were hard by crawling through tunnels and getting covered in shit.

Anne took another drink from her glass and sighed. The problem with Dave was that he knew too much about everybody, including her husband. She lit another cigarette and frowned. Surely Bill would contact her soon? As if on cue, the telephone rang.

'Where the hell have you been?' she snarled into the receiver. She could barely contain herself to listen to the reply.

'Great, that's wonderful for you, isn't it? Yes, of course she's wondering where you are. Why the hell did you run off like that? I think you're completely spineless, that's what I think. And what about the weekend? Oh, I see. Who do you think you are? A spy from a James Bond movie? Why don't you get real for once?'

She dragged hard on her cigarette and tapped her foot on the floor while listening to his reply.

'That's pathetic. It's typical of you to leave me in the lurch, isn't it? What's all this about anyway? Yes, the police have been. What do you expect when there've been two murders and you knew both victims? No, I didn't cover for you. Why should I? I said I didn't know where you were, which was true. Well, of course, she's asking me every day: where's Daddy? So you'd better think of something quick before Saturday.'

She slammed down the phone and gulped her gin and tonic.

∼

After his fruitless conversation with the cavers at Johnny's café, Inspector Craven was hoping for better results when he tracked down Atkins's ex-wife. Ex-wives and husbands, in his experience, were always good suspect material, especially if there was money or infidelity involved. Where Atkins was concerned, it seemed that there was often both.

Sylvia Atkins had been found over the Pennines in Burnley, where she was a nurse in the local hospital. Craven and DC Angela Denby arrived at the house, a small semi in a modern estate. The paved-over garden was tidy but characterless. The wooden front door and window frames were in need of a coat of paint. Craven got a sense of struggle. It hadn't been easy for the owner to keep this house going.

Mrs Atkins had been contacted, so the police officers were expected. She opened the door before Craven could knock and gave them a curt, 'Come in.'

They followed her into a small living room, again tidy, but rather shabby. She indicated a place for them to sit but offered no drinks. Craven introduced himself and the PC and then began.

'Mrs Atkins, we're here to . . .'

She immediately interrupted. 'It's OK; I know you're here about my husband. I got to know as soon as his body was found.'

'How?'

'I still know people in Burnthwaite. One of my old neighbours rang. Our kids are about the same age. They went to Burnthwaite Primary together. Anyway, it's all over the telly and the newspapers now, isn't it? Dave and that other poor bloke, John Baxter wasn't it? I knew him too, a bit. He was in the caving club with Dave; I used to see him in the pub. Bad stuff; it won't be going down well in Burnthwaite.'

Craven looked at Sylvia Atkins before replying. She wore jeans and a T-shirt. She had short dark hair with a face that must once have been pretty but was now rather lined and careworn.

'Was it right that Geoff Whitaker found Dave's body?'

'Yes.'

'God, that's ironic!'

'Why?'

'It's just that Dave was involved in something, a long time ago now. Geoff's wife's brother was killed in a caving accident.'

Craven raised his eyebrows. If true, that would need to be passed on to the chief inspector.

'I see. What happened?'

'Helen's brother was just a teenager. Dave and another bloke took a party of them down and something went wrong. The boy was killed; I can't remember his name. It was nobody's fault though.'

She looked up at Craven.

'I'm not saying Helen had a reason to, you know, or anything.'

'No, well, we need to ask you some questions about your ex-husband, Mrs Atkins. Can I ask you when you last saw him?'

She got out a cigarette from a packet on the coffee table and lit up.

'It's over a month. I can't remember exactly which day. It must have been a Thursday because I was on the early shift. He was here when I got back at about two o'clock in the afternoon.'

'Why did he come?'

She took a long drag and exhaled the smoke.

'Not to see me, I can tell you that; he came to see Paul, our son. He still lives here with me. My daughter's married; she's in Manchester.'

'Did he get on well with your children?'

'Yeah, he did. Amy wasn't too keen on her dad, to be honest. She's the eldest and she remembers the split better than Paul; he was too young to really understand, but he gets . . .' She stopped herself.

'I keep saying "gets" – it seems strange. He got on with his dad well; he's devastated, actually.' She stopped again and looked thoughtful. Craven detected some inner conflict.

'What did you think about that?' he asked.

'Huh,' she shrugged. 'I wasn't delighted. Paul's too much like his father as far as I'm concerned; brings his girlfriends back here all the time. I can't tell you what it sounds like in the middle of the night. He's got no bloody shame at all and neither have those bloody little tarts he goes with.'

'I take it your marriage broke up, shall we say, acrimoniously?'

She laughed, but Craven continued, 'So did you bear any bad feeling against your husband?'

She took another drag and replied sarcastically.

'No, I thought he was a bloody great bloke. What do you think, Inspector? He was cheating on me with every bloody woman in Burnthwaite, and he'd been doing the same for years with any woman he could.'

'So it was never a really happy relationship?'

She paused again. 'Look, I was going out with Dave when we were a couple of wild teenagers. We dropped out of school and were into everything: sex, drugs, you name it. My parents banned him from the house so we ran off together. We had a great time living on the road, sleeping on people's floors, but I was pregnant with Amy by the time I was eighteen and it was never the same after that.'

'How did you end up in Burnthwaite?'

'Long story. We eventually got married. Dave had an uncle who ran an outdoor-pursuits centre up in the Lakes and he gave him a job. That's where he learned all about caving and potholing and stuff like that and it was where he started shagging other women.'

'I see.'

'We lived in a little flat in Ambleside: a beautiful little tourist town, but not the kind of place for me. I was stuck inside all the time with a little baby while Dave was out enjoying himself. He didn't care who it was; sometimes he seduced young women who were on courses at the centre. He was always good-looking and a great charmer, but I was stuck. I had the baby and no job.'

'So what happened next?' If nothing else, Craven was finding out a lot of useful information about Atkins's background.

'Dave got into computers in the mid-nineties, when PCs were starting to take off. Then he fell out with his uncle. He didn't like Dave messing about with the girls and women at the centre and there was some argument about money. He accused Dave of fiddling something.'

Craven raised his eyebrows. 'Was that the first time, to your knowledge, that he may have been involved in fraud?'

'No, not really; you always had to watch Dave with money. He could be generous, but if he needed money for a night out or for, you know, some stuff . . .'

'Drugs?'

'Yeah, well, he'd pinch it or he'd borrow it from someone with no intention of ever paying it back.'

'So you left Ambleside?'

She crossed and uncrossed her legs and seemed uncomfortable in the chair. She was speaking very bluntly as if to show she was tough and didn't care any more, but clearly talking about her past life with Atkins was not pleasant.

'Yeah, Dave said it was too far out. We came to Burnthwaite and rented that house Dave still lives in – there I go again. From there he could commute to Leeds or Bradford if he got work in computers, but we were still out in an area where he could get outdoor-pursuits work as well.'

'Did it work out?'

'Work-wise it did. He seemed lucky. He got temporary jobs in computers, and if they came to an end he got work doing canoeing or potholing. Sometimes he did a bit of both. He also stopped doing drugs, said it was a kid's game.'

'What about the . . . relationships?'

She took another drag, finished the cigarette and stubbed it out.

'Oh, he didn't stop that. I was still very young and naïve, of course. I thought when we left Ambleside we would have a fresh start. We had

Paul as well by then. I thought he would finally accept his responsibilities. No bloody chance; he was up to his tricks again in no time.'

'We understand he worked for Simon Hardiman.'

'Yes, that was a few years ago.'

'Did they get on?'

'Why, is he a suspect?'

'Along with many others.' Did she realise that meant her too? She was trying to appear relaxed and not intimidated by the situation, but the smoking and fidgeting told another story.

'They did to begin with, but then he tried it on with Caroline and Simon got rid of him.'

'Sorry to press you on this, but what about the final breakdown in your marriage?'

She lit up again and blew out smoke.

'It's OK; I know you're only doing your job. I've been expecting this. It doesn't bother me any more. I've built a life of my own.'

Craven looked around the room in a different light. What seemed rather shabby and basic to him was, of course, a source of pride to her: her independence, hard won after years of relying on an unfaithful, crooked husband.

'I put up with it while the children were little, for their sake; classic, isn't it? But then he started trying it on with friends I'd made in the village and I'd just had enough; he was making a fool out of me. It was nasty for Paul and Amy but better for them in the long run. They came with me and he stayed in Burnthwaite.'

She flicked ash into an ashtray on the coffee table.

'So that was it, Inspector.'

'And how do you feel about him now?'

She shrugged.

'I don't feel any sense of loss if that's what you mean. My feelings for him died a long time ago.'

'Do you hate him?'

She looked away from Craven and into the distance as if thinking deeply about her current feelings about this man who'd had such a massive effect on her life.

'No,' she said at last. 'He treated me badly but, as I say, I've no feelings for him now. I didn't kill him, if that's what you're driving at. I've moved on. I trained to be a nurse as a mature student and I've got this palace.'

She glanced around the room and smiled at her own sarcasm.

'Dave doesn't – didn't – mean anything to me any more. I didn't need him.'

'Can you account for your whereabouts on Monday the seventeenth of August?'

Here there was another pause and the sharply observant Craven saw a worried look pass fleetingly across her face. It was the first time she didn't answer directly and had a hesitant note in her voice.

'Look, Inspector, I know I've told you how Dave treated me but I didn't hate him enough to kill him. He was my children's father.'

Craven was insistent.

'Yes, Mrs Atkins, but you will understand that we have to eliminate every possible suspect from our enquiries.'

She thought for a moment.

'That would have been when I was staying with my sister in Leeds.'

'Why were you there?'

'I visit her now and again to have a break from routine, you know. It's hard being a single mother. Jane's husband's a barrister; they live in a big house in Roundhay. It's very relaxing.'

'I see. Well, if you could give your sister's details to DC Denby – we'll obviously have to check your alibi.'

She nodded.

'Was there anyone else you can think of who disliked your husband enough to want to kill him?'

She laughed in her grim way again.

'You could start with all the husbands of the women he had affairs with.'

Then she looked more serious, as if she realised the gravity of the question.

'He was not a popular man, but I can't think of anyone who'd actually want to bump him off. I don't know anything about what he was up to on the money side. It could have been someone who had been cheated out of money rather than made a cuckold. A lot of men value their money more than their wives.'

'True,' agreed Craven, who concluded the interview and left the house feeling a combination of admiration and suspicion. He started the car but sat thinking for a moment before driving off. Sylvia Atkins had clearly had a difficult life for a very long time, which had given her a hard and bitter edge. First trying to cope with a rogue for a husband and latterly struggling as a single mother. But something in her story didn't quite ring true. Many of her replies seemed to come a little too easily, almost as if she'd been expecting the interview and had prepared herself. Her real attitude to Atkins was difficult to determine. The alibi would have to be checked and he could not eliminate her from the investigation.

Sylvia Atkins watched from the window as the two police officers got into the car. As they drove off, she picked up the phone and quickly dialled a number.

'Jane, it's Sylvia. Listen, I've just had the police round. Yes, about Dave, but listen. I told them I was with you when he disappeared. Yes, I know, I'm sorry. They'll be coming to see you . . . Yes . . . Jane, just stay calm and tell them I was with you Monday the seventeenth of August. Just remember, that's all you have to do. What? Of course not; what exactly are you saying? You don't think I would ever do anything like that; I can't believe you're saying this. OK, fine, just tell them what I said . . . Yes . . . Bye.'

She put down the phone, sat at the edge of the armchair and lit yet another cigarette. After a while, she picked up the phone again. It rang for a while before someone answered.

'It's me. The police have been. Yes, they wanted to know where I was when Dave disappeared . . . I know they've nothing on us but I think we ought to play safe. I've been on to Jane; she's going to say I was with her that night. OK . . . No, nobody saw us, I'm sure.' Suddenly she looked exasperated.

'Well, what do you suggest? Me being there with you doesn't look good, does it? . . . How will they find out? We can trust Jane . . . Yes, I'm sure. Anyway, they're bound to get on to you soon and they'll be over to see you so just keep your nerve and keep to the story: I was in Leeds, right? . . . OK, back to the cows.'

Simon Hardiman had spent an exhausting morning cleaning various items of equipment while Caroline was doing an excellent job of showing a group of sceptical-looking teachers around the hall. Why the teachers looked so negative, he couldn't understand; the teaching staff from the school had a great time while the kids were being looked after by the hall staff and taken out to do various activities. Anyway, he was able to make his escape for a couple of hours. He and Caroline periodically allowed each other these breaks as being cooped up at the hall all the time could get very oppressive. Sadly, they were very rarely able to go out together these days as it was nearly always necessary for at least one of them to be on duty.

He drove down into Burnthwaite and parked the van in the car park of the Red Horse. Inside there was the usual lunchtime bustle of people, mostly tourists, drinking and eating. From behind the bar, Trevor Booth saw Hardiman and came over.

'Well, stranger, we haven't seen you for a bit.'

'Too busy, Trevor, can't get away.'

'I thought this was your quiet time, you know, school holidays.'

Hardiman laughed.

'No such luck. When you've got fewer bookings you've got to take the chance to service all the equipment or decorate the rooms and stuff like that. Anyway, I'll have a pint of bitter.'

When the pint was pulled, he took a long drink and found it very refreshing. Turning round to survey the bar, he was slightly surprised to see Stuart Tinsley by himself eating a sandwich and drinking a pint. He went over to the table.

'Hi, Stuart, didn't expect to see you here at this time. Has Fred Clark let you out for the afternoon?'

'Bloody hell no; he doesn't know I'm here. He doesn't like his workers drinking at dinner time, or after work, for that matter. In fact he doesn't like anything which involves enjoying yourself; tight, miserable git.'

They both laughed.

'I only come here a couple of times a week, pretend I'm going home and I suck these on the way back.' He produced a packet of extra-strong mints. 'I'll have to be getting back soon.' He sighed and rubbed his eyes. He seemed worn out.

Hardiman sat down.

'It's pretty bad with these murders, isn't it? You went down with some of the team, didn't you, to bring Dave Atkins up? I was over in Skipton when the call went out.'

'Yeah.' Tinsley looked down and chewed on his sandwich. Like all the cavers who had been down to retrieve the body that day, he was not keen to talk about it.

'Where was he, you know, in the cave?'

'Right down at the bottom of the system, laid across Sump Passage.' He took another bite of his sandwich; Hardiman had another drink of his beer.

'It was bloody hard, I can tell you, getting him out; right through that Mud Crawl bit we had to just drag him through. It's not much fun with a dead body.'

'How do you think he got there?'

Tinsley looked at Hardiman. 'No idea,' he said shaking his head.

'Bloody hell,' said Hardiman. 'Then there's John Baxter. Have you heard anything about that?'

'Nothing, only what was on the news with that chief inspector bloke. Seems he was smashed on the back of his head in his garage. That's a lot worse; he was a good mate of mine in the club, though he kept himself to himself most of the time. I don't think many people will be crying over Atkins.'

'Do you think it could have been a burglary that went wrong? There's been a few break-ins recently. John might have caught the intruder, you know, who panicked, hit John and ran off.'

'Could be, but didn't you see that inspector on the telly? Said he thought John was about to tell him something about Dave Atkins, but the murderer got to him first; they seem to think the murders are linked.'

'Maybe, you never know with the police. Have you had them round to see you yet?'

Tinsley looked startled.

'No, why should I?'

'Well, with you bringing the body up, you know.'

There was another reason but Hardiman didn't want to mention it. Most of the village knew and the police were bound to get on to it soon.

'They've been up to the hall.'

'Who has?'

'Same chap, that Chief Inspector Oldroyd. He was asking about when Atkins worked for us.'

'You got rid of Atkins, didn't you?'

'Yeah, well, he was after Caroline, you know what he was like. That Oldroyd was also asking about the caves: Jingling Pot and Winter's Gill.

Seemed to think there might be a link between the two systems, but I told him there isn't, is there?'

'No, there isn't; Winter's Gill's just a dead end.'

'That's what I told them.'

Tinsley stretched out, sighed, then drained his beer.

'Well, it's all a funny do, but life has to go on. If I don't get back, Fred will have me. I'm already in his bad books for being late, so I'll see you.'

With that, he got up and briskly left the pub by the back entrance, leaving Simon Hardiman to contemplate matters alone.

Tinsley had just got outside the door and closed it when a voice said, 'Stuart.'

Startled, he glanced round. The barmaid – who was also his wife – was standing at the side of the door close to the wall. He looked at her with a mixture of emotions.

'What do you want, Susan?'

'You've heard about what's happened?'

'Obviously, I helped to bring his body up, and I've heard about John. It's all over the village, isn't it? Not to mention the news.'

She looked down as if too ashamed to say the next words.

'Stuart, did you have anything to do with it?'

He laughed with bitterness and sarcasm. 'Oh yeah, sure, I bumped them both off. Stuffed that bastard's body into the cave and then went down with the police to fetch it up again. And I killed John Baxter for no reason, even though he was a mate of mine. What the hell are you talking about? And what's it to you anyhow?'

She was still looking down and started to cry.

'I . . . I was just worried that she might have . . .'

Tinsley said, 'Oh, for God's sake, I'm not listening to any more of this,' and walked off up the road to Fell Farm.

After crying for a minute, Susan Tinsley wiped her eyes, composed herself and returned to the bar.

As the afternoon went on, the Red Horse became relatively quiet as the lunchtime crush receded, leaving just the odd tourist and a number of locals, mainly of the older retired type. The atmosphere was notably subdued and conversations more hushed as the gruesome events of recent times were discussed.

In the evening it started to fill up again. Sam Cartwright was sitting at the bar. His large grubby hands picked up his pint glass and he drained the contents in two enormous gulps.

'Trevor!' he called out. The landlord came over. 'Another pint in there, ta.' He handed over his glass. As the host obliged he asked, ''Ave those coppers been back again?'

'Haven't seen any sign of them for a few days.'

'I hope they keep out o' t'way for t'Feast. We don't want 'em prowling round and spoiling it, but I expect there's not much chance they'll stay away now. It's a bad do about John, in't it?'

The landlord shook his head. 'I'll say.'

'They'll be back no doubt, forever asking all their bloody questions. They'd like to pin it all on me but they've no bloody chance.' He rummaged in his pocket and took a cigarette out of a filthy packet. 'Oh, bugger it, I forgot. We can't bloody smoke in here any more, can we?' He stuffed the cigarette back into the packet. 'I mean we're all glad to see t'back of Atkins, but John's another matter. He wor a good bloke.'

Trevor Booth set the pint on the counter. He looked at Cartwright rather quizzically as he handed over the money.

'I thought you didn't get on with John Baxter all that well? I've heard you cursing him as well for not paying his bills.'

Cartwright looked uncharacteristically taken aback.

'We sorted all that out, it wor only because I got that drive shaft new. I told him I couldn't get one second hand; he paid me all right.' He frowned and turned on to the offensive, his language becoming broader as he got angry. 'What's bloody well got into thee? You sound like t'bloody police.'

The barman laughed.

'You sound like you've got a conscience.'

Cartwright realised Booth was joking but was uneasily pacified by the laughter.

'Gerroff wi' yer, yer bugger.'

At this point there was a newcomer to the bar. Cartwright turned; it was Geoff Whitaker. He had just finished work in the kitchens and had stopped at the bar for a drink before going home.

'Oh, it's you.'

'Pint of bitter, Trevor. Hi, Sam.' Whitaker's face still looked drawn.

'Are you over t'shock yet?' asked Cartwright sarcastically.

'Of what?'

'Finding that bastard dead.'

Whitaker shook his head. He looked tired after his shift and also with the weight of other things on his mind.

'Not really.' He paid for his beer.

'So it was right down in Sump Passage?'

Whitaker sighed. He didn't want to get on to this topic again but, obviously, people were going to ask him.

'Yeah. It's the last thing you'd expect to find so far down. I was just thinking about the party I was taking through and how far we had to go when, bang, I stumbled on him. It gave me a bloody fright, I can tell you.'

The barman shook his head. 'How do you reckon he got down there?'

Whitaker took his newly pulled pint and drank from it. 'I've absolutely no idea and that's what I told the police.'

'I'll bet you did,' laughed Cartwright. He had almost drained his glass again and was getting slightly tipsy. 'We're suspects, you and me, aren't we?' He nodded at Whitaker and leaned over towards him. 'The police think we could have done Atkins in, but I told them, I made no bones about it, we're all glad to see t'back o' t'bugger.' He laughed again, rolling on his bar stool, but Whitaker seemed angry.

'Speak for yourself.'

'Ger away wi' yer. Yer know bloody well everybody 'ated him. What about you, any road? Wasn't he after that wife o' yours?'

'No.'

'Well, he were after every bugger else's.'

'Look, I don't want to talk about it, OK?' Whitaker took up his pint and walked off into another part of the pub. Cartwright turned back to the bar.

'What the bloody hell's the matter with him?'

Trevor Booth was drying glasses and waiting to pull Cartwright's next pint.

'Don't know; stress, I suppose. Can't have been a nice thing, finding a body like that.'

Cartwright tapped the side of his nose. 'Bit weird though; maybe he knows more than he's letting on.'

'Geoff Whitaker? You're joking.'

Cartwright grunted. 'Yer never know; ever thought it funny that he stumbled on t'body down there? Maybe him and some of his mates in t'club cooked up a plan to bump Atkins off.' He exploded in laughter immediately, realising he had made a weak joke. '"Cooked up", him being a chef, get it?'

'Yes, absolutely hilarious. And then what happened? He led the police to the body? I don't think so.'

'Well, I don't trust him anyway, I'm sure Atkins were knocking his wife off.'

'That may be, but just lay off Geoff. I can't afford to have him off work with stress or something because people like you are making out he might have done it.'

The big mechanic took up his glass and drained it again. 'Off with stress, my bloody arse. Anyway, I'm off. See you tomorrow.'

'See you, Sherlock, leave something for the police to do.'

'Bugger off!' Cartwright called out good-humouredly as he lurched off down the passageway where he'd confronted Oldroyd and Carter.

Trevor actually felt rather deflated when Cartwright left and he followed him down the passage to get a bit of air. He stood looking out into the night at the dark mass of the fell opposite. Cartwright could be a nuisance, but he was what was usually known as a colourful character and some relief was needed. Tension hung over the village like winter mist on the fells. Two murders discovered within a week; it was enough to shake any community, but especially a small one like this where everyone was known to everyone else. And there was the terrible question that no one liked to contemplate: who next? Booth shook his head and returned to the comforting light of the bar where he served himself a whisky and continued to dry the glasses.

As Cartwright walked across the village green opposite the pub, his mood darkened as he remembered that there was very little prospect of ever getting back the money that Atkins owed him. And these bloody murders making everyone jumpy and whispering in corners. What the hell for? Surely they weren't sorry about Atkins. John Baxter maybe, but people were looking worried as if they thought they might be next. He laughed grimly to himself; they were just a bunch of cowards.

He made his way to his small terrace house on the edge of the village. Here he lived a bachelor existence and the inside of the house was as chaotic and filthy as his garage workshop. In fact, he had so many tools and bits and pieces of engines strewn around that the two places were almost indistinguishable.

His route home took him past his garage and he usually stopped to have a quick look round and check if everything was OK. It was an overcast night and very dark as he approached the garage, which appeared as a black shape against the sky. He had a quick glance down either side of the building and was about to carry on home when he noticed a light flashing through a dirty window. He frowned and unconsciously clenched his fist. There was someone in there; someone had broken in.

Cartwright had no thoughts about phoning the police. He was going to tackle 't'bugger' himself. He edged his bulk as carefully and quietly as he could down the side of the building, picking his way between the just-visible car bodies and piles of old tyres and scrap metal. As he reached the back, he saw that the padlock on the somewhat rickety door had been forced. He peered into the workshop and saw the back of a figure who was shining a torch on to tools stored on a roughly made rack on the greasy wall. He burst angrily inside.

'What the 'ell do yer think yer doin' in 'ere!'

The figure turned. It might have frightened a more easily scared person than Cartwright. It had a stocking over its face and it immediately grabbed a hammer from the rack.

'Put that down, yer bugger, and piss off.'

Cartwright had picked up a much more impressive sledgehammer that was lying by the door and looked ready to use it. The figure dropped the weapon and darted out of the workshop; Cartwright could hear footsteps sprinting down the road. Muttering 'bastard' to himself, he checked to see if anything was missing but it seemed not. As he searched for a replacement padlock in a tin under his workbench, he suddenly smiled to himself. The break-in had given him an idea.

Five

Don't go thinking tha's bold and brave,
Tha'll tremble and shake afore Yorda's Cave.

The next day found Oldroyd driving across the hills from Harrogate to Skipton. It was a beautiful late-summer day; the sky was blue and huge billowing white clouds were blowing in from the west. As Oldroyd drove over Blubberhouses Moor there were wide views across the moorland landscape. It was an open, airy scene and Oldroyd felt invigorated as he contemplated the contrast between this lightness and space and the dark constricted world of the caves that was the focus of the investigation. More prosaically, it was good to get away from the office and the pressure to get results.

He passed the sinister golf ball radomes of the Menwith Hill American intelligence base from where, it was rumoured, every telephone conversation in Britain could be monitored. The idea amused Oldroyd, who imagined innumerable Americans wearing headphones and chewing gum while listening to tedious and, to them, incomprehensible conversations.

'I'm just popping into the Bell for a swift half.' 'It's a fortnight since I saw the in-laws.' And so on.

Today Oldroyd was pursuing a different kind of intelligence. He needed to know more about the cave systems around the area of the crime and his visit to the Hardimans had yielded little in that direction. He was going to Skipton to visit a bookshop run by a classic Yorkshire eccentric, Gilbert Ramsden. He was a man who might be able to help.

Oldroyd liked to browse in the shop whenever he had the time and was in the area. This time he had a professional reason for his visit. Ramsden specialised in books about Yorkshire. No one living knew more about the county. His bookshop was a legendary place: a rabbit warren of dusty rooms and passageways. No point in looking for bestsellers or romantic novels; most of the stock comprised old editions of local history and ancient maps. As the shop was usually almost deserted, exactly how Ramsden made a living was a mystery, but he was always there to welcome you and answer any kind of questions about Yorkshire. Oldroyd planned to put him to the test today.

He arrived in Skipton to find that it was market day and stalls lined the main street leading up to the parish church and castle. He walked past the greengrocers and crockery sellers and stopped briefly to buy some Wensleydale cheese at a specialist stall. Then he headed off down one of the passageways or 'ginnels' that led from the main street down towards the canal, a picturesque section of the long route from Leeds to Liverpool.

The bookshop was almost hidden in an old cobbled square, deliberately avoiding the brasher commercialisation of the High Street as if ensuring that only the genuinely interested and persistent would discover its treasures.

The building was very old. Above the door was the date 1659 carved into the stone, and the initials 'WD', presumably those of the builder. Oldroyd went in and, sure enough, there was Gilbert Ramsden sitting behind a table by the door. He wore a tweed flat cap and a waistcoat with a pocket watch. His precise age was difficult to determine, but Oldroyd remembered coming into the shop with his father when he was a boy and Ramsden being there then, and scarcely looking any different. He had to be well over eighty. His long sideburns and rimless glasses gave him the appearance of a Victorian antiquarian, which in a sense was what he was: a relic from a different age, a pre-digital, book-based, literary age. He was eating wine gums from a paper bag on the table and reading an ancient-looking tome, which seemed, going by the illustrations Oldroyd could see, to be about Yorkshire church architecture.

Oldroyd surveyed the shelves crammed with volumes of different colours, shapes and sizes and felt a reassuring familiarity. To a man whose formative years were in the pre-computer age, it felt good to escape the keyboard and the screen, if only briefly, and re-enter the sensuous, physical world of books you could hold and feel the weight of as you turned the pages. There was also the texture and pungent musty smell of the paper. How long would it be before people who enjoyed browsing in places like this were regarded as being as odd as Gilbert Ramsden himself? It was a strange feeling to be on the cusp of such a profound change after five hundred years of the printed book.

'Good morning, Chief Inspector. Can I help you?'

Ramsden had a remarkable memory for faces and seemed to remember everyone who came into his shop. Oldroyd came out of his reverie and turned to the bookseller, who was looking at him curiously.

'Good morning. I hope so, Mr Ramsden.' Oldroyd maintained a certain formality with people of Ramsden's generation. 'By the way, I enjoyed your talk to the Harrogate Local History Society on the Pilgrimage of Grace.'

'Ah yes, I remember. Last March, wasn't it? Very nice people.'

His speech was slow and precise, rather genteel with soft Yorkshire vowels.

'Was it about the Pilgrimage of Grace you wanted to ask me? I understand research is still going on into how many joined Robert Aske from the Dales area. There were some very nasty reprisals from Henry after he'd betrayed Aske and had him executed at York.'

Betrayal and exploitation of the north by the south: that was a familiar theme over the centuries, thought Oldroyd, and not just in 1536. But there was no time to pursue that. The problem with Ramsden was that if you got him on to one of his favourite topics, of which there were many, it could be difficult to get him off it again.

'No, it wasn't that. I'm currently investigating the murders in Burnthwaite and I believe you can help me with the enquiry.'

'Oh.' Ramsden looked rather surprised. Oldroyd hastened to reassure him.

'I don't mean in the normal sense of that phrase. You must have read that the body of the first murder victim was found in a pothole system in Wharfedale.'

Ramsden offered the bag of wine gums to Oldroyd, who thanked him and selected a bright green one.

'Yes. Very strange; I read about it, of course. The body was found a long way into the Jingling Pot system, wasn't it? Those caves are unique, you know, nothing like them anywhere else in England or even the world, for that matter; beautiful, awe-inspiring. Do you know how it got there?'

'Sorry?' replied Oldroyd, who had followed Ramsden's ramblings with interest.

'I beg your pardon, I mean the body. Do you know how it got into that cave system?'

'We don't. That's the question that's still baffling us. But I think the answer lies in the system itself, and if we find the answer I believe that will also lead us to the murderer.'

'I see.' Ramsden looked impressed but puzzled. 'But I'm not sure how I can help you.'

'Look . . .' Oldroyd began.

'Please sit down, Chief Inspector.' Ramsden got up heavily and shuffled across the room to bring over another chair. He was wearing a faded corduroy jacket and a waistcoat that fitted tightly around his ample belly.

'Thank you. You see, the thing is, as I'm sure you will appreciate,' said Oldroyd, speaking in Ramsden's quaint, ornamental, circumlocutory style, 'that you have to approach the whole thing logically and eliminate the possibilities. We're reasonably sure that he wasn't murdered down there, or carried all that distance to be dumped in the main passage. That only leaves one possibility.'

Oldroyd's conclusion seemed to send Ramsden off into the realm of whimsy.

'Well, there were many legends in the past of supernatural creatures living in those caves like fairies and boggarts; evil spirits you know, who could whisk you off into the depths. You know those potholes on the slopes of Ingleborough called Boggarts Roaring Holes? That gives you the idea.'

'I think I know how my chief superintendent would respond if I suggested that the victim was magically transported down there by a cave spirit.'

Ramsden smiled. 'I wasn't serious, Chief Inspector; what you're thinking is that there must be another way to get to that point in the system, a shorter and quicker way.'

Now it was Oldroyd's turn to be faintly surprised. The old boy's mind was still very sharp beneath his seemingly inconsequential reflections.

'Yes, that's right. But I have been assured by two authorities on the subject that there is no way to reach this Sump Passage, where the body was found, other than the direct route.'

Ramsden thought quietly for a moment.

'I'm sorry to disappoint you, Chief Inspector, but it's not a subject I know a great deal about. Whatever you've been told by the experts is probably true. Was one of them Alan Williams by the way?'

'Yes. He was one of the rescue party that brought up the body.'

'I know Alan. He comes in occasionally; he's bought a few books on caving and mountaineering. I keep a few volumes on local hobbies and pastimes.'

Oldroyd was a little deflated. Was this going anywhere? It was always difficult to tell with Ramsden.

The old man continued, 'However, who was it, Chief Inspector, who said that a well-educated person was not someone who knew the answer to every question, but someone who knew where to find the answer?'

'Go on,' said Oldroyd with a knowing smile.

Ramsden paused again, slightly enjoying – like myself, thought Oldroyd – a sense of drama.

'Taking your logical approach one step further, if there is no known alternative way into the Jingling Pot system there must be an unknown one. Dear me, I nearly quoted Donald Rumsfeld then and I wouldn't want to imply that it was possible to derive any wisdom from that notorious warmonger.' Ramsden's eyes glinted fiercely.

'I see the logic, but I've been assured that Jingling Pot has been thoroughly explored and there are no links to other systems.'

Ramsden raised his eyebrows and gently shrugged his shoulders, suggesting scepticism.

'Maybe,' he said. 'Now, I'm not an expert, as I said, but I went down into those caves a few times with a couple of friends of mine who were keen – years ago, you understand, but I remember it vividly. Have you ever been down, Inspector?'

'Only some of the show caves and I've been down the Gaping Ghyll winch.'

'Just so. Now, one thing I noticed while going through those systems is that you have this lamp on your head and a tunnel of light in front of you but all around is darkness. The walls of the caves are completely irregular, so shadows are cast all over.' Ramsden paused as both men recalled the scene. 'You can't tell whether those black areas are just shadows or openings; other caves leading off to other systems.'

'I agree,' said Oldroyd, 'but we're told by the experts who have explored the system that there positively is no cave leading in.'

Ramsden leaned his head to one side. 'The experts, Inspector? Now I know a man like you is too perceptive and wise to believe everything that the so-called experts say. Experts can develop a pride in their knowledge and think they can't be wrong. Just think of these cases recently of those poor mothers put in jail for supposedly murdering their babies largely on the testimony of experts.'

Oldroyd was continually surprised by the range of Ramsden's knowledge and interests. Beneath the eccentric appearance lay a very perceptive mind with an extraordinary capacity to store information.

'All right, so what are you saying?'

'That they can't possibly be completely sure. Aren't new links always being discovered?'

'Yes.'

'So, although the experts would appear to be right, the fact of the body's position suggests otherwise.'

'Yes, but what did you mean when you referred to an unknown way?'

'Ah.' Ramsden's eyes widened and he nodded; he seemed to be enjoying a mild teasing control over Oldroyd.

'I meant a way unknown to the caving fraternity as a whole but known to the murderer, who, I take it, must be a caver too.'

'Certainly.'

Ramsden leaned forward.

'But also maybe known to people in the past.'

'Exactly,' said Oldroyd, 'which is why I'm here to ask if you have any books on the early history of caving.' He sensed that Ramsden did and was enjoying the lead-up to a dramatic revelation. In the circumstances, Oldroyd didn't mind being on the receiving end as he was just as fond of leading people on like this. In fact, the two men had a lot in common. Oldroyd would have loved to own and run a bookshop like this.

'Well, as I said, Chief Inspector, it's knowing where to find things that counts. Now just wait a minute.'

He shuffled off and disappeared into a room behind the desk, and returned soon after, blowing the dust off yet another ancient-looking volume.

'This might be what you're looking for.'

He handed the book to Oldroyd, who read the embossed title: *Explorations of the Caves of the Craven District of Yorkshire.* A vague memory stirred in his mind as he turned to the title page and smelled the distinctive and fusty aroma of an old book that had remained closed for some time. Underneath the title was written as a kind of subtitle: *With Reflections in Verse Written in the Vernacular by Joseph Haverthwaite.* The author was Sir William Ingleby.

'That's one of the first books ever to contain any detail about caving in Yorkshire, although the caves are mentioned in travel books as far back as the eighteenth century. It dates from the 1850s, long before caving became popular.'

'Who was Sir William Ingleby?'

'A Victorian gentleman of the time who had leisure to pursue his passions. There were quite a few of them round here.'

'You mean people like Reginald Farrer.'

'Yes indeed, the famous plant collector of Clapham – went all over the Far East collecting plants and bringing them back to Ingleborough Hall; eventually died out there in Upper Burma.' Ramsden could not resist giving even the shortest exposition on any subject raised. 'Well, Ingleby was like that, but his passion was caving.'

'What does this subtitle refer to?'

'It's curious, isn't it? It seems Ingleby didn't actually explore the caves himself; maybe not the kind of thing an English gentleman did in those days. He got the locals to help him and one man in particular: the Joseph Haverthwaite referred to there. He was what you'd call a local character, apparently, and a blacksmith; got to know Sir William when he was repairing iron fences on his estate at Garthwaite Hall. They were both interested in caves and it seems they struck up an unusual friendship across the great chasm, pardon the expression, of the Victorian class system. Haverthwaite seems to have been a complete daredevil. He and a group of his friends had already done some exploring.'

'How did they do that?'

'Simply with hemp ropes and candles; very dangerous, there's evidence that some were killed. It was quite something when you think it wasn't long after the time when there was still a lot of superstitious fear about potholes. As I said before, people thought they were inhabited by witches and devils and probably if you went too far down you'd reach Hell itself.'

A memory flashed into Oldroyd's mind of standing on the fellside below Ingleborough and gazing into the horrible black mouth of Gaping Ghyll. No wonder people thought it was a way into the Underworld.

'So you think I might find something useful in here?' Oldroyd sensed that Ramsden knew more than he was prepared to admit.

'Quite possibly. It's an odd assortment, mostly descriptions and anecdotes plus Haverthwaite's dialect poems. It's not that well known among modern cavers; most people don't like the style: ornate, Victorian, gentlemanly stuff. You have to be a patient reader. You're welcome to borrow it to help with your investigations, but please look after it, I'm not aware that there are any other copies in existence outside some of the library special collections.'

'Well, thank you, and don't worry, I'll take good care of it,' reassured Oldroyd.

'The main reason I think it could be useful,' Ramsden went on, 'is that after Ingleby and Haverthwaite there's a bit of a gap in caving history. It could just be that something they knew about was forgotten.'

The last sentence was delivered with a knowing twinkle in his eyes. Oldroyd saw a ghost of a smile on Ramsden's face. Clearly, also like me, he loves a bit of enigma, thought Oldroyd as he left the shop.

On the limestone fells above Burnthwaite, two figures were trudging across the fields. Two PCs had been instructed by Inspector Craven to search the area where Oldroyd and Carter had encountered the mystery person. PC Ward enjoyed any break from the routine of traffic patrol on the A65 and was a member of the local branch of the Ramblers Association, but PC Taylor was resolutely sedentary. He was finding it difficult to drag his beer belly over the rough terrain.

'What are we looking for, anyway?' His grumpiness got more pronounced the further they went.

'Nothing in particular, you know that. Craven just said do a general search of the area around the limestone pavement.'

'Around the what?'

Ward turned to his sullen companion.

'Do you come from round here or what?'

'Yeah, you know that. I was bloody well born in Keighley; somebody had to be.' He laughed at his own joke.

'Well, you ought to know what a limestone pavement is then. Didn't you ever do any geography at school?'

Taylor thought for a moment. His education had been rather disrupted in his teenage years when he started to do labouring work for his dad, who was a plumber, and he sometimes skipped school.

'I never liked all that stuff about rocks and weather.'

'It shows.'

They reached the point where Oldroyd had seen the figure behind the wall.

'Anyway, Craven said that Oldroyd and his new DS . . .'

'You mean that cockney bloke?' News travelled fast in the West Riding Police.

'Yeah. They saw someone acting suspiciously round here and one of the suspects in that pothole murder is missing.' Ward looked up at the drystone wall. 'Apparently he could have been the person who ran off behind that wall.'

'Why didn't they run after him then? London boy probably wearing his designer shoes, didn't want to get them scuffed. What the hell were they doing up here anyway? That Oldroyd's a clever bugger, but he does some weird stuff sometimes.'

'Ours is not to reason why. We'd better have a look up there then.'

They walked across to the wall meandering around weathered outcrops of limestone and followed in the tracks of the mystery person. The wall swung over a rise and joined another wall at right angles. They were in another even more isolated and quiet dry valley.

Taylor came puffing up behind Ward.

'Bugger me if I know why people want to come walking up here; there's nowt to see.'

Ward gave him a glance of contempt. He shared Oldroyd's love for these strange landscapes. He scanned around for any clues. Across the dry, flat valley, the fell rose almost vertically and there were sheer limestone cliffs with grey scree slopes below. Ward suddenly had an idea; he could see the black opening of a cave.

'Come on, let's have a look over here.' Taylor looked in the same direction.

'Where? There's nothing over there except rocks.'

'Look to the right of that rock face, there's a cave.'

'Oh, bloody hell!' Taylor complained as he followed Ward through patches of stinging nettles and then up the steep rocky slope, slipping on the scree.

Ward was already in the cave before Taylor was halfway up the slope. Luckily, he had a small torch with him as the cave proved to be quite deep. He swung the light around and saw that there was a bend at the far end of the chamber. Shining his torch around the corner, he found the remains of a recent fire and scraps of litter on the floor. Nearby was a frayed and discarded blanket. It all suggested that someone had been living rough there, and quite recently.

Taylor came into the cave and promptly tripped over a rock in the dark.

'Shit!'

'Never mind,' Ward replied to this expletive, 'we've found what we're looking for.'

Carter's arrival had not gone unnoticed at West Riding Police HQ. He had particularly caught the attention of DC Nicola Jackson, a curvaceous brunette with a predatory reputation. She'd immediately decided that Carter was going to be her next conquest. Luckily for her, she was catching him at a vulnerable time; he was not the kind of man to go long without a relationship.

Nicola saw Carter sitting by himself in the canteen, just finishing his lunch. Seizing her opportunity, she grabbed a cup of coffee and went over.

'Mind if I join you, Sarge?'

She had a range of techniques for seduction at her disposal. There was a little pause before the 'Sarge', which created a rather demure effect. She sensed that Carter might be quite turned on by a woman like her playing the submissive role. It was one of the intricate ways in which sex and power were connected.

'Sure.'

She sat down and crossed her legs. Her tight skirt inched up a little. Carter was looking at her deeply cut blouse and enticing cleavage. She saw the hunger in his eyes.

'I saw you were on your own so I thought I'd take my chance before anyone else.'

'Glad you did; who else do you think might want to sit there?'

She looked at him and her eyes widened slightly as she leaned forward.

'Plenty of women, I would think, if they've any sense.'

It wasn't subtle, but it was effective. Carter felt the raw sexual energy and found it invigorating.

'I'm glad it was you,' he said.

Knowing she had already aroused more than a little interest, she pulled back slightly and sipped her coffee; not a good thing to appear too eager.

'So how are you finding it up here? Missing the girls in London?'

'Not at the moment.' Carter grinned back, glad to be taking part in some sexual banter again. It had been difficult with Steph, not getting a response and not knowing why. Here things were much more clear-cut.

'Do you fancy some more of these moments then?'

'I'm ready anytime you are.'

At that moment Steph walked into the canteen and immediately saw Carter and Nicola together. She caught Carter's eye and gave him a long hard stare before turning abruptly away. It was obvious what was going on. She bit her lip and felt like crying. It was always the same. She attracted men, but then her stand-offish behaviour drove them into the arms of women like Nicola Jackson.

She got herself a slice of pizza with salad and sat by herself, eating moodily and glancing over to their table. Nicola was giggling about something and she could see the Cheshire cat smile on Carter's face as if he couldn't believe his luck.

After a while, Nicola got up and left by a door on the other side of the room. Carter, heading in the opposite direction, passed Steph's table on his way out. He nodded to her and smiled.

'You look as if you've been enjoying yourself,' she said sarcastically.

'Yeah, is that a problem?'

'No, but it's a bit predictable.'

'What do you mean?'

'You won't be the first or last enjoying yourself there.'

'Oo, bitch, bitch.' It was Carter's turn to be mocking. 'So what? She obviously knows how to have a good time.' He pointedly emphasised the 'she'.

Steph turned away, stung by the remark, and Carter walked off, rather regretting his cruelty.

At Garthwaite Hall, Simon Hardiman finished work for the day and trudged into the gloomy kitchen through an old wooden door from which the paint was peeling. He pulled a can of lager out from the fridge and went into their small private sitting room.

He sat down in an armchair by the window that commanded a view across the fells. The slanting evening light fell on the green hillside dotted with sheep and criss-crossed by limestone walls.

He only had to look at that view to restore his faith that, when things were hard for himself and Caroline, it was all worth it. The other thing he could do was think about his time teaching in secondary school. He remembered it almost as a time of incarceration. Bells went and a group of thirty plus reluctant adolescents trooped into the room. He drank from the can and looked out over the fells, drew a deep breath and frowned. The truth was, he was worried about Caroline; lately she seemed depressed and weary with the struggle. At that moment, she came into the room and sat down heavily opposite him with a sigh.

'Hi.' He tried to be bright and encouraging, but there was little response. After a little while he said, 'Are you OK?'

She sighed. 'Yes, just tired, that's all, as usual. Did you fix the window?'

Someone had attempted to break in the previous night through the window of the downstairs office.

'Yes, fine. I suppose we ought to report it to the police, but I can't really be bothered; interviews and signing forms, you know.'

'I wonder what they were after?'

'Who knows? Probably just an opportunist thief.'

She didn't reply.

'Look, we'll get through this. The schools will be back soon. We'll get plenty of bookings this autumn, you'll see. We'll just get stuck in.'

She looked at him. He was always optimistic and she drew strength from that.

'Just look over there.' He pointed to the fells. 'That's worth anything, isn't it? We couldn't possibly leave and go back to the city.'

She glanced out of the window and managed a weak smile.

'No, we couldn't; you're right. But there's such a tense atmosphere in the village now after what's happened.'

'That's one advantage of being up here away from things.'

'Yes, I think I'll be better when the school term starts and things get busy again. I forgot to tell you, that party I showed round the other day?'

'You mean the miserable-looking lot?'

'Yes. Well, they were obviously more impressed than we thought; they rang up this morning to make a booking. We've not had anyone from their area before. If it goes well they might recommend us to other schools.'

'That's great, so things are looking up already. I told you, if we stick at it, things will work out.'

'Unless people are put off by what's going on in Burnthwaite.'

'I don't think so, and any publicity's got nothing to do with us, that's the important thing.'

'I still think it'll be better when the police aren't swarming all over the place.'

'Maybe, but don't worry.'

He put his arm around her shoulders. They kissed and watched as the sun went down behind the fells.

On his way back from Skipton, Oldroyd called in to see his sister Alison at the vicarage in the village of Kirkby Underside, a few miles outside Harrogate. Brought up as an Anglican, Oldroyd's faith had progressively weakened until he was in that perpetually tormented state of agnostic doubt. He prided himself on solving difficult puzzles, but he knew that the ultimate puzzle of life itself was not solvable. Luckily, he had a spiritual adviser who was a considerable help when he felt particularly down, but he envied those who were happy believers or cheerful atheists.

Alison was three years older than Jim and had preceded him at Oxford, where she'd read Theology. Strong willed and rebellious, she was also very highly principled from an early age. Vegetarian before it was fashionable and active in numerous campaign groups from her early teens, she threatened to drop out of sixth form because A levels were just part of 'bourgeois education for people who wanted to have a steady job, a nice house and 2.4 children'. Unfortunately, this dismissive comment neatly expressed the Oldroyd parents' aspirations for their daughter and thus caused fierce rows.

Then one weekend she disappeared to her room. A thoughtful teacher at school had given her a book about Trevor Huddleston, the Anglican monk from the Community of the Resurrection at Mirfield in the industrial West Riding. The book told of Huddleston's struggle against apartheid in South Africa in the 1950s and the high Anglican beliefs that underpinned it. She came out of her room once to ask Jim where Mirfield was and also the location of various towns in South Africa. Geography was not her strong point.

Finally, she emerged properly on Sunday afternoon and announced she had become a Christian. She was going to study Theology at university and then campaign for the ordination of women, among other things. She was going to the local church to Evensong that very evening.

Her mother was ready to dash upstairs and search Alison's room to find out what drugs she'd been taking, but her father, despite his shock, realised that at least this was better than some of her other schemes, such as going to live in a commune run by the Guru Maharaji-whatever-his-name-was, where the members shaved their heads and gazed at crystals.

Against all expectations, Alison never faltered in this new ambition. All her energies had found a moral focus. She was transformed at school; her teachers didn't know what to make of it and neither did St Mary's, the local Anglican church. The Oldroyd family were members of the congregation, although Jim and his father were infrequent attenders. Alison had not been seen in the place since she refused to attend Sunday School because 'it's all stories about Jesus and his friends and they're all boys'. Suddenly they had an eager but feisty teenage girl who wanted to take an active role in things and get the church involved in every social-action campaign going. They found her rather overwhelming and Alison found them boring and middle-aged.

It came as some relief to everyone when Alison departed for Oxford, whose dreaming spires had enticed her with the promise of deep theological investigation. After getting her First in Theology she stayed on to do postgraduate studies for a while before, in typical impulsive fashion, suddenly throwing it up and deciding that her faith demanded practical action.

She worked for various charities and campaigning groups for many years before becoming one of the first women priests to be ordained in the early 1990s. She occupied a place on the liberal wing of the Church, scathing of the literalist theology of the evangelicals and of the stuffy conservatism of the middle-of-the-road traditionalists. This often made her an uncomfortable person to have around at deanery or diocesan meetings. The current Bishop of Ripon and Leeds was terrified of her. In Oldroyd's view, this was because he feared for his job.

Oldroyd drove up the steep road and could see the village overlooking Lower Wharfedale, with the spire of St Bartholomew's prominent on the ridge. Alison had begun her ministry in inner-city Leeds but had raised so many uncomfortable questions about the Church's commitment to alleviating poverty, and been involved in so many controversial campaigns, that pressure had been exerted on her to move to quieter pastures. She would never have agreed had she not been exhausted owing to personal problems and in need of what she still saw as a 'sabbatical in the countryside'.

It was in her response to those problems, reflected Oldroyd, that you saw the strength in her, the depths of her faith, which sustained her when others might crumble.

It began years before when she and her husband, David, a university lecturer, discovered that they were unable to have children. Oldroyd knew this had been a terrible blow to them both. They'd fostered, but for some reason unknown to him had never adopted. Then, five years ago, David had been diagnosed with pancreatic cancer. It was far advanced and very aggressive and he'd died within the year. The memory hurt Oldroyd, who had been close to his brother-in-law: a gentle, quiet but wise man who was often the only person who could counsel Alison out of some impetuous course of action.

Alison was not only his sister and spiritual adviser but also, as he had said to Carter, his Mycroft too. More than once her comments had given Oldroyd an insight and helped to progress the case to a satisfactory conclusion.

Oldroyd drove past the church and turned sharp left. His tyres scrunched over the gravel of the drive up to the rectory. Grass and weeds grew through the gravel and leggy rhododendrons hung down and nearly brushed the windscreen. The rectory was a spacious and beautiful Georgian building straight out of Jane Austen, but certainly designed for a different era. Neither Alison nor the Church of England itself had the time or resources to maintain the building and its gardens in their original splendour.

An area of flat lawn to one side of the house was all that remained of an Edwardian tennis court. At the rear were broken greenhouses and tumbledown sheds that had once been a stable block.

The door of the rectory was flung open and Oldroyd was greeted with a big hug.

'Jim! Wonderful to see you. What's been going on recently? You haven't rung!' Alison was a large woman with short greying hair and glasses. 'Come in!'

Oldroyd was ushered inside, through the wide hall past the winding staircase and into the kitchen. The kettle was put on and they both sat at the table.

'You look tired. Is it work or family?'

'A bit of both.' Alison was the only person whom Oldroyd talked to in any depth about his private life. He looked uncharacteristically uncertain of himself and nervously drummed the table. He wanted to talk to his sister about Julia but it was difficult, even to her. They chatted awhile about Robert and Louise before he broached the subject.

'I saw Julia the other day; she came over to Harrogate, just for a chat, you know.' He shook his head. 'Can't really make any sense of it. We keep meeting; we're supposed to be discussing Robert and Louise, but we just have a pleasant talk and off she goes. It feels like a brief date somehow, but I've no idea what she's really thinking.'

Alison gave him a searching stare.

'Maybe that's exactly what it is. I don't think she's given up on you, Jim. She still wants to see you, but she's not sure about things. She wants you to woo her again. She wants you to make an effort, to show that you really want her back.'

'She knows I want her back.'

'Yes, you want her back in theory and because you love her, but are you prepared in practice to give her what she needs?'

Alison was also the only person who could give Oldroyd a lecture. He looked uncomfortable.

'You know that what happened was your own fault. I've told you before and you know it's true. Relationships have to be worked at; you can't take them for granted.'

'Yes, I know all that.'

'But would you change?'

'How?' Oldroyd sounded weak and despairing; although he'd raised the subject, it was painful.

'You know how: make your marriage central, and not work. The trouble with this Protestant country is that it's too bloody Protestant when it comes to the wretched work ethic.'

The kettle boiled and she got up to make the tea.

'It's linked in to consumerism, of course: work harder, make more money, spend it, work harder and so on, and meanwhile we're destroying our health and our relationships. Look at this.'

She went over to a pin board and removed a postcard. It was a Christian Aid card and showed rats running down tracks following notices that read: 'Work Harder, Buy More Goods, Happiness Just Around the Corner'.

Oldroyd smiled and grunted.

'Very good, but you know the problem with me is that work is endlessly fascinating. I can't tear myself away once I'm immersed in a case. I feel it's my duty.'

He remembered all the times he had stayed working until very late in the evening and through the weekend. What else could you do if there was a killer on the loose and people were depending on you to catch them? But then he knew that this was partly egotism: the unwillingness to allow other people to take a more prominent part in the investigation. Too often it became his personal struggle with the criminal and he wouldn't delegate to others. Alison placed a mug of tea in front of each of them, and a plate of chocolate brownies. She seemed to have read his thoughts.

'There's more than duty involved though, isn't there? It's also a matter of pride with you that you're the one who cracks the case, even if everyone has to suffer. Anyway,' she pointed to the brownies, 'these are Fair Trade; try them, they're excellent. I hope you're still buying Fair Trade goods?'

'I've lapsed a bit since we split up. You can't always be bothered, you know, with shopping when it's just for one, can you?'

Alison nodded.

'I know what you mean. It's not like shopping for food together.' Conversation lapsed as each contemplated their unwanted solitariness. 'Tell me more about what's going on in this fascinating world of work of yours? You said it was tiring you.'

Oldroyd drank his tea.

'It's this Jingling Pot business. You must have seen something about it.'

'Yes, I saw you on the local news, actually. You were lucky. I don't often get a chance to see TV news. A chap found dead in a pothole and then another caver killed. Sounds unusual.'

'Very. Needless to say, now that it's hit the media the super's on my back all the time.'

'So what've you been up to today?'

'Out to Skipton, got an old book on potholing from that chap Gilbert Ramsden.'

'It's always worth a good browse in there, isn't it? I've found some very obscure theology books. Do you remember when Dad used to take us in and we played hide-and-seek in all the little rooms and corridors?'

'Yes. We weren't that interested in the books then, were we? Anyway, I'm hoping I get some clues from this book. I have an idea that this mystery is maybe tied up with the past.'

'I see. What about the motive?'

'No shortage there; it's harder to find someone in Burnthwaite who didn't want him dead.'

Alison looked thoughtful.

'Whatever exactly happened, it was obviously carefully planned. Premeditated violence like that indicates a terrible degree of hate.'

Oldroyd thought of the cuckolded husbands in Burnthwaite and the people cheated out of money.

Alison continued, 'They may have felt threatened in some way and needed to get rid of him. People turn on their tormentors sometimes and often unexpectedly. And a lot of things go on in these country villages, I can tell you. There's one not far from here; couple of years ago a quiet old lady left her cottage one summer's evening, walked through the village, into the garden of an elderly man about her age and promptly sunk her garden shears into his back. Killed him instantly. It turned out he'd been blackmailing her about something, can't remember what, on and off for forty years and he'd just made one demand too many. Nobody suspected a thing, but it was all building up over all that time and everyone has their breaking point. We're surprised when some genteel person does something so raw and violent, but that's only because the middle classes are mostly protected from real stress and live very cushioned lives, so we can develop all these polite ways of behaving. Beneath the veneer we're the same animal that can lash out to defend itself if provoked too far.'

'I suppose that's one of the reasons why Agatha Christie had such success setting her Miss Marple stories in little chocolate-box villages,' said Oldroyd. 'The violence is more shocking because of the prim exterior. Anyway, how's the parish?'

'Pretty quiet as usual. It's a typical rural backwater; the events in the outside world hardly impinge. Maybe we could do with a murder here to liven things up. I find it very restful at the moment, but then I am meant to be resting. What will happen if I decide to stir things up a bit, we'll have to see.'

Oldroyd saw a glint in his sister's eye.

'You mean like coming out as a lesbian and preaching on gay marriage services in the Anglican Church?'

Alison laughed.

'Not quite. I was thinking more of twinning the parish with one in inner-city Leeds and getting us more involved with Christian Aid and Oxfam campaigns. Do you know, there wasn't even a Traidcraft stall when I first came here?'

'It doesn't surprise me. Living in these villages is a kind of fantasy, isn't it? The poorer parts of Leeds might as well be a hundred miles away instead of fifteen. And Africa might as well be on another planet.'

'True; they're perfectly nice genial people round here at one level and the Church must minister to them, but we also have a duty to challenge. Let's see how people respond when their comfort and complacency are questioned.'

'I await the sensational headlines in the *Church Times*. "Minister hounded out of Yorkshire village after being branded a heretic and socialist."'

Alison laughed again.

'That sounds like fun to me.'

The conversation reverted to family matters before Oldroyd reluctantly decided that he'd better be getting back to HQ.

'It's the PCC meeting tonight,' said Alison as she saw him out. 'I don't know how I stand the tedium of who will serve on the flower rota and whether we continue to have sidesmen – sidespeople, of course, as I insist.'

'All part of the rich tapestry,' teased Oldroyd. Then he caught sight of the church spire, an elegant black outline against the sky, reaching up to God. 'It would be sad, though, if it wasn't there, you know, an Anglican church in every village. We'd miss it.'

'I don't think you need to worry. It'll survive in places like this longer than in the cities, where we're going to lose it, and fast, if we don't change.'

'Do you think it can change that quickly, the dear old C of E? I mean, it always seems to me a bit like turning the *Titanic* to miss the iceberg. It's already too late, but you can be sure everyone will stand gallantly on the deck and salute as the ship goes down. I think most members over sixty would rather it died than changed.'

Alison shrugged.

'Maybe. We'll have to see.' She seemed remarkably sanguine about the prospect. 'Don't make the mistake of equating Christianity with the Anglican Church or any other organised denomination. They're all very largely human constructs which may have had their day, but if they disappear, God's purposes will continue.'

'"He moves in mysterious ways His wonders to perform."'

'Indeed.'

Sadly, he didn't have time at the moment to pursue with her what she thought those purposes might be.

The same evening, after darkness fell, two figures could be seen quietly entering the small backyard of Dave Atkins's terrace house in Burnthwaite. As they approached the back door they could be heard arguing, each urging the other to be quiet.

At the door, they stopped and looked around furtively. One of them produced a screwdriver and tapped hard on the glass panel.

'What if the door isn't just on the Yale latch? The other lock could be on too.'

'Then we won't bloody get in, will we? But Dave never bothered with the other lock; you'll see.'

There was another tap on the glass panel and it shattered. The sound of glass falling on the inside was unexpectedly loud.

'Shh, bloody hell, you stupid bastard! Why did you hit it so hard?'

'Shut up. I didn't. Now then.'

The speaker put his arm through the gap in the panel.

'Oh shit!' The arm was quickly drawn out.

'You daft sod, you've cut yourself, haven't you? I told you to be bloody careful.'

'Fuck off. I'd like to see you do this.'

The arm was gingerly placed through the hole again and fumbled behind the door.

'Got it!' The other arm turned the handle and the door opened.

'Thank God for that; let's get in quick.'

Both figures entered the house and closed the door quietly behind them. They moved into the small hall and away from the door. A torch was switched on which revealed the faces of Gary and Carol from next door. As Gary held the torch, he was sucking the wrist he had scraped on the jagged glass.

'Oh shit, Gary, this is bloody awful, let's get on with it.'

'Calm down, you silly bitch. We've got to search a bit.'

'I thought you knew where Dave kept it?'

'I've a good idea but I can't be sure.'

'What? That's not what you said when I agreed to do this.'

'Keep your bloody voice down!' Gary hissed in a harsh whisper. 'And get your torch out.' Carol fumbled in her pockets.

'What if the police found it? We don't know if it's still here.'

'Well, let's get looking then. You look in that cupboard in the hall, right at the bottom. I have an idea about upstairs.'

Reluctantly, Carol opened the hall cupboard while Gary's fat frame plodded up the stairs. After a few minutes of prodding, poking, bumping into things and cursing, Gary called down in a stage whisper.

'Up here, I think I've found it!'

'Bring it down then and let's have a look!'

Gary came back down the stairs and Carol pronounced herself very satisfied with what he had found.

'Come on, then, let's get out. Oh, shit! Turn off your torch quick!'

Everything went dark again and they both froze as they heard a sound outside. Someone was approaching the door! Then they heard a voice.

'What the hell! It's bloody open,' and then footsteps in the hall. They had no time to hide before a torch came on and a deep voice laughed.

'Looks like someone's bloody beaten me to it.'

In the dim light they saw the bearded face and bulky figure of Sam Cartwright. He peered at the sheepish-looking pair.

'You two live next door, right? You burn them joss sticks and crap like that, don't yer?'

Gary turned his torch back on and shone it at the new intruder. Any desire to remonstrate was stifled by the sight of Cartwright's huge frame and the compromising situation in which they found themselves. The silence seemed to encourage Cartwright. He shone his torch in Carol's face.

'Hey, watch it!' she complained.

'Look at you love, you've got more pins in your face than my mother used to put our nappies on.' He gestured with the torch towards Gary. 'Does it turn him on then? Where else have you got things stuck through you then?' He broke into lewd guffawing laughter.

'Look,' began Gary but Cartwright went on.

'Anyway, what yer doing in here?'

'We could ask you the same question,' retorted Gary, trying to go on to the offensive.

'Aye well.' Cartwright became more subdued. 'That bugger Atkins died owing me money, so I thought I'd come here and try and find some. I'm not paying some bloody grasping solicitor to get it for me. I suppose t'coppers have taken everything out.'

Carol and Gary glanced at each other and saw a way out of the situation.

'Same here, Atkins owed us money as well.'

'Have yer found owt then?'

'Not a penny, honest, you can search round if you want.'

Cartwright shook his head.

'No point; I wouldn't be surprised if there's been others here before us. I'll bet the bugger owed brass all over.'

'Yes,' said Carol. 'Look, if you don't say anything about this, we won't. Is it a deal?'

'Aye, you won't catch me blabbing owt to t'police.'

With that he turned and walked out of the house leaving Carol and Gary both heaving a sigh of relief. As he walked out of the small garden, Cartwright thought he saw a figure hiding in the bushes across the lane. He decided not to investigate, as he was in too incriminating a position himself to confront any other interlopers.

Steph Johnson drove herself home from West Riding Police HQ in her Mini Cooper. Although she loved Harrogate, she'd decided to move out and away from her family when she had the means, and she'd bought a small flat for an exorbitant price in one of the new waterfront developments in Leeds. The fifteen-mile distance was enough for her to establish her independence without losing contact with her mother and sister, with whom she was close.

This closeness was partly the product of adversity. When she was twelve years old and her sister Lisa only ten, her father had left the family after years of drunkenness and violence. Even now, she didn't like to think about the three years before he went, particularly the nights. She and Lisa would be in their bedroom waiting terrified for him to come home and wondering what sort of mood he would be in. Sometimes he would be all sentimental and would cover them both with slobbering kisses, his breath stinking of beer. A wave of anxiety flooded over her at the memory. At other times, the outside door would crash open and the shouting would begin almost as soon as he entered the house. When this happened, they pulled the bedclothes over themselves, partly out of fear and partly to pretend they were asleep so he wouldn't hit them.

In truth, he seldom did, but with their mother it was different. They got used to seeing the bruises on her arms or face the next morning, but she would never say much about it other than to tell them not to worry, Daddy loved her really. It was just that he got a bit angry when he'd had a drink.

One night Steph heard loud cries and, telling Lisa to stay, she crept downstairs, unable to bear it any longer. In the kitchen there was a terrible struggle; her mother, with a cut lip, was pulling at her husband's arm and crying.

'Don't, Kevin!'

Steph saw that her father was holding a kitchen knife and seemed about to use it. She screamed and both adults abruptly turned to her and froze in a terrible tableau that she would never forget. The shock seemed to bring her father to his senses. He threw down the knife, brushed roughly past her and went straight upstairs to bed. Her mother collapsed sobbing on the floor. Steph wanted to go to her, but was so horror struck by what she'd seen that she also turned and went quickly back up to bed. She told Lisa everything was OK, turned out the light and lay crying silently until the early hours, when she finally fell asleep, exhausted.

She still felt guilty about that night. She kept telling herself that she was only twelve at the time and couldn't cope with the situation, but she felt she'd let her mother down, not gone to her when she most needed her. By suddenly appearing, of course, she might have saved her life, but it had put a barrier between them for many years: that night and the awful possibility of what could have happened was literally unspeakable. Even now, she had not really talked in depth with her mother about how she felt about those times, but at least it was not a totally taboo subject any more.

Less than a year after that incident, her father had left and they'd had very little contact with him since, other than cards and presents at Christmas and birthdays. He had disappeared back to London to the relief of them all.

Steph had been deeply scarred by the experience. At the age of twenty-five she'd had no long-term relationships with men and she knew it was because she didn't trust them. She tended to see her father in them and had always ended a relationship when it threatened to become serious. Deep down she felt that she would end up being hurt like her mother.

As she drove up the hill past Harewood Castle and into Harewood village, she thought with a combination of guilt and frustration about Andy and how she had treated him since he had arrived. She liked him a lot. He was good-looking but not arrogant about it. He had a sense of humour and could take a joke against himself. Unfortunately, he reminded her all too much of her father: another handsome blond-haired Londoner.

This was why she had gone cold and remote on Andy and it wasn't his fault. He must be extremely confused; she couldn't respond to someone who was so like the man who had made her life miserable for so many years. But she did like him and the situation made her angry and frustrated. Now her behaviour had pushed him away and he was turning his attention elsewhere.

She reached Alwoodley Gates and the rural scene abruptly changed as she entered the suburban outskirts of Leeds. She sighed and tried to think positively. One thing was that her experiences were in a big part responsible for her deciding to join the police force. The burning sense of injustice that she felt about her mother's suffering and the terrible power she saw that the strong wielded over the weak. Maybe she was living out her family battles in her work. So what? She loved the job and she knew she was good at it. Chief Inspector Oldroyd thought so too. She had a great respect for his ability and was slightly in awe of him, as everyone was. But she'd worked with him long enough now to have seen the more vulnerable side beneath the surface of the charismatic detective. She was fond of him and tended to think of him as a father figure.

She hit heavy traffic by the West Yorkshire Playhouse, but soon she was parking in the basement of the converted warehouse that contained her flat. Once inside, she put on some music and made some coffee, which she sipped as she looked out of her window across the River Aire. The evening light illuminated the river and the people sitting outside at cafés. It might not be Venice, but it looked surprisingly good for a stretch of river that had been filthy and derelict only a few years before.

She thought about Andy again. This felt like a big opportunity, so what was she going to do about it?

That evening Oldroyd opened a bottle of red wine and put a Marks and Spencer's lasagne in the microwave. Although he liked good food, he'd never developed any culinary skills, something which, living alone, he now regretted. He could manage a bit of salad: tomato, rocket, cucumber and red onion, and he'd called for a small baguette on the way home.

He finished his solitary meal quite quickly; he found it difficult to eat slowly when there was no one to talk to. Half the pleasure in eating was in the conversation. As his waistline seemed to be thickening, he'd recently given up desserts, but he found it hard to cut down on the red wine. He poured himself another glass and took it into the living room with the book he'd borrowed from Gilbert Ramsden.

He put on a CD of Mozart piano sonatas, which created a relaxing background as he began to examine the book carefully. The sense of age was intensified by the weight of the binding and the thickness of the pages compared with contemporary books. Oldroyd had always liked browsing through old bookshops as much for the atmosphere as for anything else. He remembered the old Thornton's second-hand bookshop in Broad Street in Oxford, which had a positively Dickensian atmosphere and was full of impressive-looking old volumes just like this.

He opened it at the first page, which contained a preface written in typically elaborate Victorian prose.

> *Whereupon it has seemed to me that the subterranean explo-*
> *rations of recent times in the Caves of Yorkshire should be*
> *recorded for posterity, I have, in a manner which I hope will*
> *be deemed modest and of the utmost moral earnestness, taken*
> *it upon myself to undertake and present to the world the afore-*
> *mentioned recording.*

And so it went on in its near impenetrable circumlocutory formality, much to Oldroyd's amusement; he loved this leisurely manner redolent of a much slower age. He read on selectively through verbose and flowery descriptions of the Yorkshire Dales countryside. Sir William's description of Gordale Scar was typical:

> *The visitor must walk up a path alongside a stream which*
> *can be exceedingly muddy in wet weather, but if he persists*
> *he will be rewarded, as he turns a sharp corner, with a truly*

dramatic view, one which has inspired both the poet William Wordsworth and the painter JW Turner. Awe inspiring rocky cliffs dripping with water, overhang a darkening and narrowing path and ahead water cascades through a hole in the rock and over a huge boulder on the floor of this collapsed cavern, for so it is and the imagination is thrilled to contemplate how the stream must once have passed through an enormous dark tunnel to emerge further down into the pleasant grassy fields full of light and tranquillity after its gloomy journey through the depths of the underworld.

Well, the old boy certainly had some imagination himself, thought Oldroyd, and tremendous enthusiasm. Further on, he found the section where Sir William began to describe the caves of the region in a manner that suggested they were not very well known to the outside world at that time.

These caves or 'potholes' as they are often described in this region, have been known to local people for centuries and held in some fear as the haunt of fairies, goblins or as entrances into the nether regions. Many do not have horizontal entrances, but terrifying vertical openings on the fell sides. These shafts are often concealed by thick moorland grasses and by stunted trees and the unwary traveller can come within a few feet of a shaft dropping hundreds of feet into the darkness without ever realising it.

He then gave an account of how the *speleological endeavours* or *subterranean explorations*, as he called them, began, and prominent in this was Joseph Haverthwaite. ·

Haverthwaite, it seemed, was a local blacksmith who was employed by Sir William in his stables and to repair ironwork around the estate.

The Victorian gentleman clearly had a high opinion of the skilled worker.

> *My admiration for Mr Haverthwaite is of the highest order. His abilities in several fields are most remarkable; not only in his trade as a blacksmith in which he is very skilled but also in cave exploration in which his courage and fortitude are unsurpassed. He is also, in my opinion, a gifted poet. His verse would not be acceptable to many in the established literary circles because he writes using the dialect language spoken in this part of the world by the ordinary people. Notwithstanding this, and in fact because of it, his verse contains an unusual power and verisimilitude and I have included several examples in the present volume.*

Oldroyd applauded Sir William's defence of the local poet as he carried on his search for material that could help him in the case. Eventually, in the middle of a description of the basic equipment the early explorers used, Oldroyd found what he was looking for.

> *Mr Haverthwaite was always indefatigable in inventing solutions to the ever present need for devices which would enhance our speleological endeavours. On one occasion he produced a small iron contrivance, curved to form the appearance of a thick hook. Mr Haverthwaite used these to support ropes in a manner which enabled an explorer to use longer ropes in greater safety. This involved attaching these iron pieces to the wall of a cave and tying the ropes to them. When arranging a steep descent, he would attach a ladder to the hook and a safety rope in case the ladder failed.*

Oldroyd got up and went to his jacket in the hall. He searched in the pocket and brought out a plastic bag. He opened it and handled again the rusty piece of iron recovered from the crime scene. He had carried it around with him since that day, convinced that it was an important clue. Surely this was an example of Haverthwaite's 'iron contrivance'? But how did it get into Sump Passage? Oldroyd read on, and luckily the answer was not long in coming.

> *Mr Haverthwaite first used these implements in his exploration of Winter's Gill Hole.*

Oldroyd's pulse raced. He had discussed Winter's Gill Hole with Simon Hardiman: it was the adjacent system to Jingling Pot.

> *This exploration ended tragically with the death of Mr Alfred Walker. Sadly he was not the only one to die. A year later Mr Harold Lazenby also met his death. Neither body was ever recovered. I was never a party to these explorations of Winter's Gill Hole. Mr Haverthwaite advised me against it, insisting that it was too dangerous and I believe that, in the end, this cave was abandoned by all explorers, even the most redoubtable.*

Oldroyd paused and laid down the book. That was curious. He realised now what Ramsden had been implying.

Unfortunately, that seemed to be the end of Sir William Ingleby's comments on Winter's Gill. But there must be more. What about Haverthwaite's poems? Oldroyd turned back to the section that contained Haverthwaite's dialect verse. These turned out to be an odd miscellany of ode-like celebrations of the Dales landscape, eccentric bits of dialogue in dialect such as a conversation between a shepherd and a sheep that didn't want to graze on a certain fell. Then he found a terrifying poem about what it must have been like to go down a deep shaft on the precarious wood-and-rope ladder which Sir William had described, with only one of Haverthwaite's 'safety ropes' to save you if the ladder snapped.

Dangling on t'Rope

If thi ladder breaks
Thi only hope,
Is to cling on hard,
To thi safety rope.

W'i out that ladder,
Tha'll swing and dance,
Out o'er darkness,
To take thi chance.

Will that rope hold thi firm
And save thi precious breath?
Or will it be a hangman's noose
On which tha'll meet thi death?

Will thi mates haul thi up
While tha swings around?
Grab tha and pull tha
On to safe, firm ground?

Or will tha slip into t'blackness,
Screaming out a long cry,
As tha falls on to t'jagged stones
On which tha'll die?

It makes tha pause on t'ladder,
And move on quickly in th'ope,
That tha'll not be left th'ere,
Danglin' on t'rope.

Oldroyd felt positively dizzy after reading this. It seemed to carry you out over the void in a startling way. There was something powerful about its rough rhymes and bluntly expressed images.

Doggedly, he kept on turning the thick leaves of paper and scanning the brown musty pages for information relevant to his theory, and after a while he was rewarded with the discovery of a curious short riddle-like verse.

> Some men say and it maht be true,
> That t'Devil's Passage can get tha through,
> From Winter's Gill Hole to Jingling Pot,
> 'appen it's reight, an' 'appen not,
> Listen hard, but stay afee'ard,
> Those who've tried it are mostly dee'ad.

Oldroyd shouted in triumph.

'Yes!' He could scarcely contain himself. At last, some confirmation. This was a strong hint that there was indeed another way into the Jingling Pot system. Despite Haverthwaite's teasing equivocation, Oldroyd had no doubt. A link must have been discovered in those early days of exploration from Winter's Gill Hole and that link must still be there. For some reason it had been lost to the modern cavers. Oldroyd read the verse again. Behind its sardonic Yorkshire humour there seemed to be something sinister. Maybe this was the origin of the cavers' superstition about Winter's Gill that Hardiman had mentioned. Calling a cave the 'Devil's Passage' might be a reminder of how caves were associated with evil, but Oldroyd sensed there was more than that.

There was a warning of real danger.

Six

Tha'll think tha's dee'ad and gone to t'devil,

If tha tries to climb down Ibbeth Peril.

The sound of Carter's mobile phone ringing disturbed the quiet. He was lying in bed. He groped over to pick it up and glanced at the time. It was 2.30 a.m. and for a moment, still in the haziness of sleep, he panicked. Then he looked at the number and smiled.

'Hey, Jason!'

'Hey, mate, how're you?'

'I'm good.'

There was a stirring in the bed next to him as Nicola turned over. In fact, I'm very good, he thought to himself, grinning.

'How're you?'

'The usual: skint and pissed. What a night!'

'Just got in, I suppose. Where've you been?'

'Up the City; started out at Malone's – they've got some new fancy Czech lagers in there, five quid a bottle, mind you – had a bite to eat, moved on to that little bar near Lamb's Conduit; stayed there most of the evening, then on to a club or two or three.' He laughed. 'It all gets a bit hazy after that.'

'Any luck?'

'Naw, nothing about, at least not available; there's too many of these skinny blokes around; thin legs and arses, not a hair on their chests or faces. They look about seventeen but women seem to like them.'

'You mean they don't fancy old, fat, hairy gits like you?'

'Hey, watch it! You're not exactly the slim type yourself. Anyway, what's going on up there? Dying wi' boredom i' Yorkshire?'

The last phrase was delivered in a grotesque parody of a Yorkshire accent.

'No, actually.' He glanced over. Nicola had gone back to sleep. 'I'm more successful than you.'

'Lucky bastard; that didn't take long. Are you stunning the Yorkshire lasses with your sophisticated London ways?'

'I've stunned one, anyway,' he lowered his voice, 'but I can't say any more at the moment.'

'Why's that? What the— You're in bed with her now, aren't you, you randy bastard!'

'Shh!'

Jason laughed raucously down the phone and mimicked a female voice.

'Oh, Andy, do it to me again, please; stick your long London dick up me and—'

'Shut up!' said Carter in a stage whisper, but he couldn't help giggling. Jason, struggling with his own laughter, shouted even louder.

'Oh, Andy! I never come like this with a Yorkshireman. I . . .'

Carter pressed the button and ended the call.

Nicola stirred again.

'Who was that?' she asked in a sleepy voice without turning to look at him.

'Just a mate of mine in London.' He laughed again and shook his head. You couldn't beat Jason for the old banter.

Suddenly a mixture of feelings came over him. He felt a twinge of nostalgia for the old life in London, but he'd caught sight of his stomach, which was indeed on the fat side and hairy. He was pushing thirty, no longer in the first flush of youth. Jason's failure to pull was a kind of wake-up call.

He glanced at the figure beside him and felt a wave of self-disgust. How long could he go on behaving like a young lad, sleeping around like this? A lot of men would envy him, in bed with an attractive woman like Nicola, but the experience, despite his laddish joking with Jason, seemed rather empty. The last thing he wanted to be was a sad bloke nearly forty trying to pull women in bars.

Unexpectedly, an image of Steph came to him and he regretted his last conversation with her even more bitterly.

When Carter arrived at headquarters on Friday morning, he received a call from Inspector Craven.

'Tell the DCI that I'm following up some useful leads with Atkins's wife and I'll report back as soon as I know more.'

'You interviewed her then?'

'Yes, over in Burnley. Very plausible, but I wasn't convinced; she's hiding something.'

'Good luck then.'

'Thanks. Also I've just had confirmed some information she gave me about Helen Whitaker.'

'The wife of the bloke who found the body?'

'Yes, it seems her brother was killed in a caving accident, and Atkins was involved. You and the gaffer will want to follow that up. How's he doing, anyway? The pressure's hotting up, isn't it, with all this in the press?'

'Yeah, OK I think, but he's not in yet; he disappeared yesterday over to Shipley, is it? To a bookshop or something?'

'Skipton. What was he doing there?'

'Something about research into the caves.'

Craven laughed. 'He'll have been to Gilbert Ramsden's shop; it's the best place to do any research like that. He's a funny old chap; has a bookshop down by the canal, full of mouldy old books about all kinds of stuff, but mainly Yorkshire.'

'There's a lot of pride in this part of the world, isn't there?' said Carter.

'Oh yes, God's Own Country, as we like to call it. Stay here long enough and you'll feel the same way. Speak to you later.'

Carter smiled. 'God's Own Country' – not a modest title.

At that point, Oldroyd appeared clutching a large, heavy-looking book.

'Andy, you're looking a bit tired, lad. Busy night?' He held up the book. 'Very interesting things in here that I want to share with you and Steph.'

Carter couldn't imagine how an old tome like that could possibly have anything to do with the investigation but didn't feel he could say anything.

'Right, sir, but I spoke to Inspector Craven just before you came in and he had some important information about Helen Whitaker. I think you'll probably want to go over and speak to her.'

He told Oldroyd about the accident.

'Hm. That *is* interesting. And she never mentioned it to you?'

'No, nothing.'

Oldroyd put the book down and looked at his watch.

'Well, no time like the present. This could be a very important lead. We'd better get over there and have our case meeting a little later. Leave a message for Steph.'

It was typical of Oldroyd's impulsive behaviour, and soon both detectives were driving along the route to the Dales, which was rapidly becoming quite familiar to Carter. On the way, they discussed the latest finding.

'Of course, we can't be sure about Sylvia Atkins's motives, can we, sir? I mean, she might have told Bob all this about Helen Whitaker just to try to incriminate her and deflect attention from herself.'

'Most certainly a possibility, but I've had the feeling for some time that events in the past have a lot to do with this case, as they do with many murders that have been carefully planned. The problem here is that there's so much "past" with Atkins it's difficult to know which bit has formed the motive for his murder.'

'If she blamed Atkins for her brother's death that's a pretty power-ful motive.'

'True, but why wait so long to do something about it? Did she recently acquire an accomplice who could help her? We'll have to see what she says and decide what we make of it.'

They were both quiet for a while. Then Oldroyd said abruptly, 'I hear you're a big success with the women officers, one in particular.'

Carter was surprised and rather embarrassed, but he could hardly tell Oldroyd to mind his own business.

'I hope you haven't heard anything bad about me, sir.'

'No, not particularly, but I thought you might have had better taste, especially as I think there's another person interested in you who would make an infinitely better partner,' he said sharply.

Bloody hell, thought Carter, does nothing escape him?

As if he realised that he'd gone a little too far, Oldroyd continued apologetically.

'I know it's none of my business, but I've worked with Steph for quite a while, since she was a young lass, and I've grown quite fond of her.' He turned to Carter. 'I just don't want to see her hurt.'

'OK, sir,' said Carter and there was an awkward silence for a while. Carter couldn't help smiling at his boss's paternal concern for a young woman who he was convinced was quite capable of looking after herself.

∽

'I suppose you know why we've come back to talk to you again,' said Oldroyd. He and Carter were in the sitting room of the Whitakers' house with Helen Whitaker. Geoff Whitaker was at work at the Red Horse. She sighed and pursed her lips.

'You've found out about Richard.' She gave Oldroyd a look of defiance.

'Yes. So, why didn't you mention it when Detective Sergeant Carter here interviewed you before?'

'I thought he was interviewing Geoff, not me. I don't see why I should have brought that up. I don't like talking or even thinking about it, Chief Inspector. It was a long time ago and I don't see what it's got to do with anything now.'

Carter looked carefully at her. She seemed different this time; not the wife desperately trying to defend her husband and making accusations against people. This time there was the sense of a quietly strong character and one quite difficult to read. There was definitely some anger beneath the controlled exterior.

'We understand that your brother died in a caving accident and that . . .'

Oldroyd stopped; she had turned away and put a finger up to her eye.

'I'm sorry, that was rather abrupt.'

'It's OK.' Her voice broke slightly, then she regained control.

'Richard was only seventeen. It killed my mother; she never got over it,' she said simply and starkly.

'I'm sorry to have to bring those memories back to you, but I believe David Atkins was involved, and you understand that everything concerning him is relevant to our investigation.'

She exhaled a deep breath and, like most people faced with Oldroyd, realised there was no escape from giving him the information he wanted.

'It was fifteen years ago. Richard was in this youth club; we lived in Grassington then, although I'd just gone away to start my training in

Liverpool. I'm a physiotherapist though I'm not practising at the moment. I work part-time in the Wharfedale Gift Shop. The club leader arranged for a small group to go potholing with a caver from the Wharfedale Club.'

'David Atkins?'

'Yes; the youth club leader had done some caving himself and there were only six from the youth club so I suppose the adult supervision was technically adequate.'

'So what went wrong?'

A pained look passed across her face.

'They were abseiling down a waterfall underground. It was Richard's turn and apparently he was doing fine when . . .' She paused as she confronted the awful memory. 'There was a rock fall, unexpected; it was supposed to be a safe area. A large piece hit Richard on the head. He was wearing a helmet but he must have been stunned. He lost his grip on the rope and went down too quickly. The combination of the blow to his head and the fall killed him. By the time they got him to the surface he was dead.'

'I'm sorry.'

'The post mortem showed that his skull was thin at the point where the rock hit him otherwise he would have survived.'

Oldroyd glanced at Carter before he continued.

'Mrs Whitaker, I'm sorry to say this straight out to you, but it's probably best if we get to the point: do you believe anyone was to blame for your brother's death?'

Helen Whitaker seemed to struggle with the question.

'I don't suppose so. The verdict at the inquest was accidental death. They'd done everything right, given them training beforehand. There was nothing wrong with the equipment. It was a rock fall; things like that happen in caves. All the parents had signed consent forms. My mother never forgave herself for signing one.'

'And yet?'

She shrugged.

'Nothing. Except I don't think it would've happened but for David Atkins.'

'Why's that?'

'After the inquest I spoke to the youth leader. He was a bloke called Mike Wentworth. He left soon afterwards; the whole thing upset him so much. He came from the north-east and went back up there; Newcastle, I think.'

'What did he say?'

'He said although he couldn't blame Atkins directly for anything, he was still angry with him because he thought he was pushing them on too fast; you know, all that macho stuff. In other words, if someone else had been in charge they wouldn't have been at that point going down that waterfall. They were only kids.'

'But the accident could have happened anywhere, couldn't it? And your brother had a physical weakness.'

'Yes, but a rock fall is more likely to happen where there's water, so I understand, because it dislodges the rocks. Anyway, the fact is, I did blame Atkins for Richard's death. I think I still do.'

'But he didn't do anything wrong.'

'No, but somehow to me he's responsible. It was because of him they were there.' She put her hand to her head in frustration as if she could never get past this fact, however unfair or irrational it might be.

'So do you hate him enough to want him dead?' asked Oldroyd.

She thought for a while before answering, as if analysing her feelings.

'No,' she said. 'It's been too long. I don't feel as strongly about it now and I know I was probably unfairly imposing all my grief and anger on to him. But I still miss Richard; I can see him in my son, Tim. He never got the chance to become an adult; you know, have a family of his own and things like that.'

'How does your husband feel about all this, Mrs Whitaker?'

'He sympathises, of course, but he never knew Richard.'

'So how did you feel about your husband getting involved with Atkins with this money business? I understand when you were interviewed before, your husband admitted to lending Atkins money and getting into an argument with him about it.'

She hesitated and Oldroyd thought she was considering her answer carefully.

'I wasn't pleased, obviously, but Geoff and Atkins were in the same caving club and went on caving trips together. He didn't feel the same way about him. In fact, more than once he took Atkins's side, said the accident wasn't his fault, caves are always dangerous and all that, but he knew I still felt differently.'

'I have to ask you where you were on the night of Monday the seventeenth of August?'

'Why?'

'That was the last time David Atkins was seen alive.'

'I don't know. A Monday evening, was it? Geoff would have been working so I would have been here with the kids.'

'Can anyone confirm that?'

'No. I suppose I could have gone out to murder him and then come back to check if the kids were still asleep.' It was stated calmly but with sarcasm, implying that it was a ridiculous idea.

'Did you know John Baxter?'

'Not really. He was a bit of a loner; only went around with other cavers.'

A silence followed and Oldroyd looked at her. She would have obviously needed an accomplice, but there was a deep hurt that had been festering a long time and 'still waters run deep', as his grandfather would have said. Had she carefully planned her vengeance over many years? If so, there was still the question of why she'd struck now.

'Thank you, Mrs Whitaker, that's all for now.'

~

After she had shown them out, Helen walked slowly back into the sitting room and opened a drawer in a sideboard. She took out a photograph album and sat down. Inside were photographs of herself and her brother when they were growing up. In one, they were very young getting dried after their bath and ready for bed. In another, they were going off to school together in the snow. Tears came into her eyes. She always found this album unbearably moving, but the tears were only partly due to the memories of her brother. She was increasingly anxious about the whole business of the murders.

Carter drove on the way back. It was raining very heavily and he had the headlights on. He went slowly to negotiate the country roads. He wasn't used to this kind of driving, weaving along between drystone walls.

'What did you make of that, sir? Did you believe her?'

Oldroyd had been rather quiet and thoughtful since leaving Burnthwaite.

'I'm not sure. She was quite open about blaming Atkins, but then she knows we're on to the business of her brother and we would eventually track down this Mike Wentworth. Steady, Andy, there's a narrow bit here.'

Carter slammed on the brakes and pulled into a passing place as the road became too narrow for cars to pass. A van came past, flashing its lights in appreciation, and they moved off again.

'He'll presumably verify that she was very bitter against Atkins so there was no real point in her denying it.'

'The question is whether she's telling the truth about her feelings now.'

'Exactly, and as we know, her husband was somehow involved with Atkins, and we don't know the truth about that yet, they may have both had a motive for killing him.'

'It would have been a kind of poetic justice from her point of view, wouldn't it, to have Atkins dead in a cave like her brother?'

Oldroyd feigned surprise.

'What a morbid imagination you have, Andy, but yes you could be right and – watch it!'

Carter braked hard again as the dark shape of an animal loomed up in the road ahead. It turned and Carter saw two green eyes stare at him accusingly before it ran across the road and leaped over the wall.

'A fox,' said Oldroyd.

'We've got some of them in Croydon, sir, believe it or not,' replied Carter as he picked up speed again, 'but you don't usually meet them crossing the road.'

The next day saw the weather fining up as Bob Craven drove over from Skipton to Burnthwaite. He'd been pursuing a line of enquiry that had developed from his interview with Sylvia Atkins. The sister verified the alibi, but not without a little discomfort, according to the detectives who interviewed her. Craven was not convinced. Sylvia had one of the strongest motives after all those years of abuse by Atkins.

The only way forward was to find out more about her time in the village. For him and his team this would mean the hard slog of interviewing as many people as possible until they found someone who could help the enquiry. This was the unglamorous part of detective work that didn't figure much in TV detective series. In those, he thought, with a wry shake of his head, investigations proceeded smoothly and rapidly to a conclusion with a minimum of effort and every interview was dramatic and charged with meaning.

As it happened, Craven was about to get the first piece of luck in this case in which everything seemed against an easy solution. He'd got his team to trawl through the list of Burnthwaite residents and identify people who might know Sylvia Atkins, anyone who'd lived there when she was in the village. While distributing the names to be interviewed among the team, Craven saw the name Susan Tinsley, who worked in the bar at the Red Horse. She was about the same age as Sylvia and it was highly likely that they would have known each other, given that there were not many women of that age in the village. Craven's hunch was that she should prove an interesting source of information. He decided to interview her himself, and set off to find her at the Red Horse.

Craven parked in Burnthwaite and entered the pub to find it bustling with visitors consuming bar meals at the tables and locals propping up the bar. How many of those visitors, mused Craven, were here now because of fascination with Burnthwaite, the 'Murder Village', as it had been garishly depicted in one tabloid headline? On one wall were some black-and-white photographs of grinning potholers standing outside caves and underneath was a collection box for Cave Rescue. This all now seemed a little macabre.

He then saw Sam Cartwright, his large bulk perched on his usual long-suffering bar stool, and thought how key this popular local pub was proving in the investigation. Not only was it the last place in which both murder victims were seen alive, but it was also where suspects seemed to gather. Here was Sam Cartwright, and in the kitchen was Geoff Whitaker. If the barmaid, Susan Tinsley, proved a fruitful lead, what might this mean? What about the landlord, Trevor Booth? He had implicated Geoff Whitaker while claiming not to want to, maybe . . . Craven pulled himself up; he was allowing his imagination to race ahead of the facts, but the Red Horse did seem to be taking on a kind of ghoulish significance.

He walked up to the bar and tried to catch Trevor Booth's attention. Before he could do so, he was spotted by Cartwright, who, like many people in the area, knew Craven.

'Bloody 'ell, not t'police again. Trevor! Yer wanted.'

The landlord was at the other end of the bar talking to a couple of farmers. He glanced over with a worried expression as he saw Craven and immediately broke off the conversation and came over.

'Inspector Craven, isn't it?'

'Yes.'

'Is it just a drink you want?' he asked hopefully.

'No, I'm afraid not.'

'It's not about Geoff again, is it? I told the chief inspector and his sergeant what I know. They've spoken to Geoff; he wasn't too pleased with me for saying what I did to the police and . . .'

'No, sir,' Craven hastened to reassure him. 'It's Susan Tinsley I need to speak to. I understand she works behind the bar here.'

Instead of being reassured, Booth's face dropped even further.

'Susan? Why? She's got nothing to do with anything, surely. It is the murders you've come about?'

'Yes.' Craven glanced around the busy pub. 'Look, if she's here, it would be better if I came behind the bar; it would cause less fuss.'

Booth looked extremely harassed. How many more of his employees would the police want to interview about these terrible goings on?

'Yes, she's here; she's serving in the other bar.' He sighed. 'You'd better come through.'

He lifted the counter up at the end of the bar and Craven followed him between the line of beer pumps on the bar and the optics on the wall containing various malt whiskies. Cartwright's eyes followed him all the way but he didn't say anything.

They passed through the archway into another bar with a near-identical set of pumps and optics. This was the public bar and games room. No food was being consumed here, but a darts match was in progress in one corner and a lively game of pool was ongoing in the centre of the room.

A woman behind the bar was talking and laughing with a group of young men who had pints of lager in front of them.

'Susan!' Booth called out.

The woman turned and the smile died on her face. Did she recognise him? Craven was not sure. She had long auburn hair tied back and was wearing a low-cut, tight-fitting top that emphasised her ample bosom in the classic buxom-barmaid style.

His long experience of encountering a wide variety of human types and probing their motives had enabled him to develop a sort of sixth sense about people and their basic take on life. Here was a woman who needed and enjoyed attention, maybe because she'd not succeeded or been allowed to develop a fulfilling role for herself: very good material for a predator like David Atkins who must have seen her a lot in here.

'This is Inspector Craven,' continued Booth. 'He wants to have a word with you; you'd better go up into the back room.'

Susan Tinsley exchanged a perfunctory greeting with Craven but said nothing more as she led the way through the kitchens where a number of people, including Geoff Whitaker, were hard at work. Whitaker noticed the pair and watched them as they passed through. There was a cacophony of sounds from sizzling pans to extractor fans whirring and people shouting orders and instructions across the room. The heat, despite the fans, was intense and there was a strong smell of hot cooking oil. It was a relief to Craven when they left the room and went up a flight of stairs and into a small sitting room.

They both sat in rather worn armchairs and Susan immediately went on the defensive.

'I've been expecting you, with all these detectives asking questions about who knew Sylvia and Dave Atkins, but I don't know anything about how Dave was killed and I didn't know John Baxter at all.'

Craven smiled. She'd made the fundamental error of denying what she hadn't been accused of and thereby admitting to a great deal. However, it also suggested that she was a very inexperienced criminal, if she was one at all. Craven was more than ever satisfied that he was on to something.

He settled his large frame in the chair and stroked his moustache, a habit when he was thinking carefully.

'I'm right in assuming then, Mrs Tinsley, that you did know David Atkins fairly well, and his wife Sylvia?'

She squirmed in the chair a little and scowled.

'Yes, fairly well,' she said, repeating Craven's phrase.

'Is that all? Would you like to explain that in more detail?'

She flared in anger.

'No, I wouldn't; it's none of your business and I've told you, I don't know anything about him being killed and put in that pothole.'

Craven looked up sharply.

'How do you know he was killed before he ended up in the pothole?'

The sudden directness disconcerted her. She raised her voice.

'Well, it's obvious, isn't it? Everyone round here knows that you couldn't kill someone in a pothole like that; I mean it's daft, isn't it?'

'I see.' Craven paused, considering the best way to handle her apparent volatility. 'Look, Mrs Tinsley, the reason I'm here is that I thought you might have some useful information about David Atkins and his wife Sylvia.'

He saw a look of hatred pass across her face.

'Why?'

'Because we're interviewing everyone who knew Dave Atkins, and Sylvia when she lived in Burnthwaite. You must have known them, you're the same age as Sylvia, you work in the bar and it's a small place.'

She didn't reply, looked extremely uncomfortable and seemed to be wrestling with a decision. She looked out of the window, then down at the floor. Finally, uttering a sigh, she seemed to resolve it; her demeanour changed. The hostility left her, and she seemed to relax a little. She took a deep breath.

'You're right, Inspector, I know both Sylvia and Dave very well. In fact, I'm not living with my husband at the moment, and that's because a while back I had an affair with Dave.'

Craven maintained his composed professional expression, but privately he was delighted to have struck gold; it looked as if the list of suspects was about to lengthen still further.

'The affair's been over for quite a time now. You've probably already found out that Dave liked to "move on", as it were.'

'Yes.'

'We tried to keep it all as quiet as you can in a place like this. One advantage of working in the pub: they can't gossip about you because you're there behind the bar. Anyway, I don't feel any bitterness, at least not against him. It's a different matter with that bitch of a wife of his. Stuart and I might be back together by now, but she had to have her revenge.' She looked directly at Craven. 'A lot of people would say I deserved it, but she went for Stuart when he was down; she behaved just like her husband, seemed to know when someone was vulnerable. But . . .'

All the sullenness was gone and unexpectedly she burst into tears. Craven sat with the same impassive expression. 'As far as I know he's still seeing her and I'm frightened because I don't know what she might have persuaded him to do.'

'In what way?'

She went quiet again and her hand nervously twisted the handkerchief. She seemed to be trying to summon up the will to say something important. Then it was as if the dam burst and she blurted out her fears to Craven, who was startled at how accurate his hunch had proved to be.

'Because I saw them, Inspector, Stuart and her, in Burnthwaite when Dave disappeared; and before you ask me, it was in the paper that he was last seen in the Red Horse on the seventeenth of August. I remember that night because I was in here too, working, though I kept out of Dave's way. Trevor was very understanding and let me work in the back bar when Dave was around. I had to go in there when Stuart came in too. It's been awful. Anyway, I remember walking home and seeing a car parked by the green. I recognised it straight away as Stuart's, and inside,' she stopped to wipe her eyes, 'I saw them: Stuart and Sylvia, just sitting there.'

'Are you sure it was that particular night?'

'Yes, because it was the last night that Dave was in the pub and I remember thinking how odd it was that all four of us were so close to each other at that moment; I was in the street, Dave was in the pub and they were in the car.'

'Why was he still in the pub if you'd finished working?'

'I finish at 9 p.m. on Mondays because I do a lunchtime shift as well.'

'So I take it you're saying that they could have been lying in wait for him.'

She twisted her handkerchief again and now she couldn't face Craven.

'I hope to God not, Inspector. I'll never forgive that woman if she's talked Stuart into . . .' She was unable to complete the sentence. Her hands were shaking.

'Why are you telling me this now?'

She shook her head.

'I can't stand it any longer; had to get it off my chest. I knew you'd find out sooner or later; I just want it over and done with, whatever . . . happened.' Her voice trailed off.

Despite her obvious anguish, Craven found it hard not to smile. People had watched so many crime dramas on television that they believed the police always got their man. It would be a shock to them to know how many crimes remained unsolved, so in a curious way maybe this presentation of an invincible organisation by the media was a help to the police force. He decided he'd got enough from Susan for the moment and allowed her to compose herself and return to the bar, slipping out himself through the back entrance, past the rubbish bins where Whitaker had conducted his angry phone call.

Driving back to Skipton, he felt that at last here was something tangible to pursue: a bitter story of love and betrayal, of jealous revenge that could have ended in murder. If so, who were the guilty ones? Was it Stuart Tinsley, egged on by his lover to kill her husband to get revenge for years of mistreatment? Or could it be Susan herself with another accomplice, resentful at being rejected by Atkins? They murder him and then she has a convenient story that implicates her husband and his lover, a nice double revenge? Her distress about her husband's possible involvement seemed genuine, but you never knew. However, what about Baxter? How did he fit into this lurid scenario? He didn't seem like the kind of person who would be involved in steamy tales of lust and adultery.

He smiled and shook his head. Once again, his imagination was working overtime. It sounded more like material for a tabloid story or for one of the crime dramas he'd been thinking about rather than a rational and objective theory. But at least things were getting interesting.

The early evening found Steph and Andy at Giuseppe's in Harrogate, at the very same restaurant in which Oldroyd had consumed his ravioli. This unexpected date was a result of Steph deciding that she was not going to give up and leave him to women like Nicola Jackson. Late in the afternoon, she'd found Andy in the office by himself.

'How's it going?' she asked as she sat opposite him at her work desk.

He sat back from his computer and stretched. She watched admiringly as he flung his arms wide and revealed his broad chest.

'It's good. I've got that IT report for the boss. It confirms there was all sorts of dodgy stuff on Atkins's computer, but they're still working on cracking the code; should be interesting when they do.'

After a pause she said, 'How's it going with Nicola?'

He looked over quickly in surprise and frowned. She bit her lip: should she have said that?

'Why, what's it to you?' He sounded a little angry and obviously resented the question.

'Nothing. I just wondered.' As she said this, she gave him a very meaningful look.

Carter was surprised but cautious. He'd given up on the idea that anything would happen between them and he was not sure whether this was another example of her blowing hot only to go cold on him again later. But he had to admit that he was glad that she was still interested in him, especially as the answer to the question was that Nicola had turned out to be nothing more than a one-night stand. She'd made it clear that she had other priorities; rumour had it that she was using her skills to seduce a DCI, a colleague of Oldroyd's and a married man with a family.

'It's finished, actually.'

'Oh, why's that then?'

Steph was not really surprised at this news, but her heart leapt: he was available!

'It was never really on, you know; just a bit of fun.'

'Is that what all your relationships are like?' She looked at him archly. 'Just fun?'

'No, it depends.'

'On what?'

'Dunno, on the person, I suppose, and how I feel about them.'

Carter looked at Steph with renewed interest. The signals were very positive, so why not give it another go? She beat him to it.

'OK, so as you're free at the moment, how about us going out for a pizza after work?'

'Fine.' He gave her one of his dazzling grins.

And so here they were, sitting under the former proscenium arch. Steph looked around and smiled.

'This place has been here for ages. We used to come here when we were kids; they're good with children, look over there.'

She pointed out various stuffed birds hanging from the ceiling and a model of Pinocchio's house. Carter liked her to talk about her family life; she seemed to do it so naturally. He looked dutifully around the restaurant, but to be truthful he was finding it difficult to keep his eyes off her. He was usually quite confident with women, but on this occasion felt a little nervous.

The waiter brought starters of garlic prawns and Italian bread.

'Tell me about your life in London. Did you have a wild time?' Steph's eyes were sparkling and teasing. She was trying hard not to link him with anything painful in her past.

'Well, not really, too hard working, that's my problem.'

'I'll bet.' She laughed. 'So it's no great loss to come up here?'

'On the contrary,' he replied, looking at her. 'It's a big gain.'

'Very charming,' she replied with light sarcasm, but in truth she was charmed.

'What about you? Do you want to get on in the force, you know, get a promotion and stuff?'

'Maybe, although I don't fancy getting too far into management. I can't stand all that corporate managerial rubbish.'

'Performance targets, mission statements, value for money; all bollocks, isn't it? You'll never get me to bow down before the great god Mission Statement.'

He mimicked an act of obeisance and she laughed again. She liked a man who could make her laugh.

'Are you missing your mates, then?'

'Not much so far; doesn't take long to go back down there if I want to. You have to make sacrifices if you want to get anywhere.'

'What about your family?'

She felt an unusual desire to get to know more about him. He was still a rather exotic stranger to her.

'My mum's retired now and my sister's a nurse. They're OK. Mum's coming up to see me soon.'

'What about your dad?' There was a pause and she realised she may have said the wrong thing.

'He's dead.' Andy looked down at his plate.

'Oh, I'm sorry.'

'No, it's OK. It was a long time ago. I was telling the chief inspector about it. He was in the police too, got killed on duty.' Carter looked up a little nervously, but he didn't seem offended by the question. 'Are any of your family in the force?'

'No, Mum works in a jeweller's shop and my sister works in the bank. My dad's . . . not around, as I told you.'

Sensing this was also a sensitive topic, Carter didn't pursue it and instead picked up the bottle of red wine to defuse the slight tension.

'Look, this is getting a bit heavy, have some more wine.'

As they walked back from the restaurant to Steph's car, Harrogate looked picturesque and romantic with coloured lights illuminating trees along the edge of the Stray. She was parked down Montpellier Road near to the famous Betty's Café. Carter was a little unsure about how to play the situation, but he decided to go for it.

'You could come back with me.'

She looked at him and he smiled in what was, for him, an unusually coy manner.

'It would be easier for work tomorrow.'

She laughed. She had done a lot of laughing throughout the evening and it had done her good.

'Thank you, gallant sir; only thinking about my convenience, very noble, but I have to get back.'

She looked at him again. The fact was that part of her wanted to go back with him, but it felt too much too soon. She was desperate that he didn't get the wrong message, so she smiled meaningfully and said, 'Not yet.'

It was a test for Andy and he passed it. Laddishness gave way to his more mature and sensitive side. He sensed that she was not being awkward or moody, but that she needed time. He was prepared to wait.

'That's fine,' he said. He didn't even attempt to kiss her, but put his arm around her shoulder and gave her a gentle squeeze.

'See you tomorrow,' he said quietly and walked off back up the hill.

It was the right thing to do. As Steph got into the car and drove off, she felt relieved: relieved that the evening had been so enjoyable and relieved that he obviously understood and didn't feel she was rejecting him. This sensitivity made him even more attractive.

The next day Carter's mood was much jauntier as he strode through the early morning streets of Harrogate. He felt he was settling in now and there was nothing like the excitement of the start of a relationship to improve the mood. He was the only one of the team in the office when Craven rang.

'Tell the chief inspector we need to add Sylvia Atkins to the list of suspects and a couple called Susan and Stuart Tinsley.'

Carter was eating a doughnut he'd bought as breakfast on the way to work and washing it down with coffee. He quickly swallowed a mouthful.

'Why's that?'

'I've tracked down a former friend of Sylvia's in Burnthwaite, a Susan Tinsley. As soon as I spoke to her I sensed something was up. She admitted straight away that she'd had an affair with Atkins.'

'Hasn't every woman in Burnthwaite?'

'Just about, but listen to this. Sylvia Atkins returned the compliment. She's involved with Stuart Tinsley. The Tinsleys have separated, but he is still living in Burnthwaite. Now here's the really interesting bit: Susan Tinsley says she's sure that Sylvia was in Burnthwaite with her husband at the time Atkins disappeared; claims that she saw them in Tinsley's car on the last night Atkins was seen alive. She's clearly worried that her husband was persuaded into murdering Atkins.'

'She could have made that up to implicate her husband and his lover – you know, the jealous wife – even though she was knocking off Atkins.' Steph was right, thought Carter; it was unbelievable what goings on there were in the countryside. He wouldn't be surprised if sex turned out to be at the bottom of this case as well.

'That's definitely a possibility,' continued Craven. 'I'm working on getting some corroboration for her story. My feeling, though, is that she's probably telling the truth. I'm more interested in Sylvia Atkins when you think of the motive she had: all the years of abuse. She could well have persuaded Tinsley to do her husband in. Also, she spun this alibi to me about being with her sister in Leeds, which I didn't buy. I think the sister had covered for her several times in case questions were asked.'

'Could they have killed the other bloke, Baxter?'

'That's the problem; I'm not sure how Baxter's murder would fit into any of these scenarios yet. Maybe he saw something suspicious. Anyway I'm on to it; I'm going to interview Tinsley.'

'I expect he was a potholer too; nearly every bloke in Burnthwaite is.'

'You're right, he was. In fact, he was part of that Cave Rescue team that brought the body up.'

'What? Not another! I'm beginning to think about conspiracies again: half the suspects brought the victim's body out of that cave. It's a bit weird, isn't it? Anyway, I'll tell the boss.'

'How is he?'

'Fairly quiet at the moment.'

'He's like that, likes to work on his theories and expects you to do the same. At some point he'll reveal his ideas and surprise you. OK, speak to you later.'

Carter finished his doughnut, brushed the crumbs on to the floor, screwed up the paper and threw it at the bin. His luck was in and it disappeared into the rubbish. Craven had had a bit of luck too, but they could do with some more in this case, he thought rather glumly. So far, none of the leads amounted to anything really substantial. Everybody seemed to have a motive. Maybe Oldroyd was quietly on to something. He hoped so.

Carter's hopes were realised because, at the next case meeting, Oldroyd had a confident demeanour and a slightly self-satisfied look on his face, which Steph knew was an indication that he had something interesting to impart. However, he seemed content to wait. Coffee and chocolate biscuits were being consumed in the usual manner. Steph and Andy smiled at each other. There was a much better atmosphere between them now.

Carter reported Craven's discoveries about Sylvia Atkins and the Tinsleys.

'This all just makes it seem more complicated, sir. The list of suspects seems to grow. I've been thinking about that last night in the pub, the last time Atkins was seen alive, and it seems most of the suspects were around there if we believe what people are telling us. The only suspect who wasn't was Bill Watson, unless he was also lurking around outside somewhere.'

'Or on an extended visit to the Gents,' joked Oldroyd. 'But you're right, and I think it confirms the likelihood that those people are the serious suspects and that the killers will turn out to be among them.'

'Also,' continued Carter, 'I was saying to Craven, it's weird how many people involved with Atkins brought his body out of the cave, and that's after Whitaker found the body. Bill Watson and Stuart Tinsley were there that day, and John Baxter.'

'What significance do you think that has?'

Carter didn't want to sound too imprecise as he suspected Oldroyd would disapprove of vagueness.

'I'm not entirely sure, sir, but I think I'm coming back to the notion of this being the work of a group. Maybe Atkins's enemies formed some sort of alliance to get rid of him.'

'One thing you've got to remember,' said Steph. 'In a small village like Burnthwaite, the same names do keep cropping up in different contexts; it doesn't necessarily mean that there's some conspiracy going on; it's not like an anonymous city.'

'Yeah, I know, but it doesn't mean there wasn't one either.'

'Anyway,' said Oldroyd, who could contain himself no longer. With a flourish, he produced the Victorian volume that had caused him such excitement.

'This is what I've discovered,' he announced.

Carter looked dubiously at the heavy book, but Oldroyd continued enthusiastically.

'This was written by Sir William Ingleby, a very early explorer of the limestone caves. He included in it some poems by a local man: Joseph Haverthwaite.'

This is even worse than his fuss over the old bit of metal, thought Carter. What could some old Victorian geezer and a crappy local poet from God-knows-when tell them about anything?

'What does this have to do with the case then, sir?' he asked, trying hard to keep the scepticism out of his voice. Oldroyd put the book down.

'Remember on the first day when we went to Jingling Pot and they brought the body up? We were confronted by a puzzle: how and why would anybody drag a body so far into a cave system?'

'We don't know the answer to that yet, do we, sir?' said Steph.

Oldroyd paused and took in a breath. He enjoyed the drama of these moments.

'I think I do have an answer to that now. Listen to this.' He read Haverthwaite's cryptic verse.

> Some men say and it maht be true,
> That t'Devil's Passage can get tha through,
> From Winter's Gill Hole to Jingling Pot,
> 'appen it's reight, an' 'appen not.
> Listen hard, but stay afee'ard,
> Those who've tried it are mostly dee'ad.

There was something sinister in this curious little verse that made a chill pass through Steph. Carter was bemused by the language but picked up enough of the meaning to start to see where this might be going.

'You'll have to translate most of that, sir, but was it saying something about a link?'

'Exactly. I knew there was some rational explanation as to how the body got there. That was why I was questioning those potholers about links between Jingling Pot and other systems. They were all adamant that there was no other cave that could get you more quickly to that point. But when I thought about it, I decided that there simply had to be, but it could be a way which maybe no one knew about except the murderer.'

'But that's not possible, is it, sir?' said Steph. 'Lots of people know those systems.'

Oldroyd pointed his finger at her.

'Yes, but what if there was a way that was known about in the past, *but had been lost and forgotten for some reason*? It could have been redis-covered recently, and by the very person who became the murderer.'

He turned to the book.

'So I decided to do some research. What this little rhyme hints at is that there is indeed a link between Winter's Gill Hole and Jingling Pot. I knew from the maps that that system was the most likely because it runs close to Jingling Pot, but everyone denied there was a connection.'

'What's all that about listening hard and, what was it, "stay afee'ard"?'

'"Stay cautious, don't be overconfident." Haverthwaite calls this link the Devil's Passage. In his indirect way, he's saying it's dangerous. In the book, Ingleby says that Haverthwaite and his companions tried to explore Winter's Gill Hole but after two of them were killed, they abandoned it. I think those men died in this Devil's Passage, which is why Haverthwaite says that those who've tried to go through are mostly dead. Simon Hardiman was telling me that cavers are superstitious about this system: they think it's haunted. Maybe that all dates back to this.'

'Why "listen hard", sir?' asked Steph.

'I think that's the clue as to how we can find where the link is.'

'You mean go down to the cave and just listen for something?' Carter was even more perplexed.

'Yes. For what, I'm not sure, but there's only one way to find out.' Oldroyd looked at his two assistants and his smile broadened.

'We're going down there.'

'What, right down into the cave system, sir?'

'Yes, Carter. I know you're not used to things like that, but I think you said you came up to join us for the challenges and we can certainly provide you with plenty of them. Anyway, Steph here will look after you.' He looked briefly from one to the other in a knowing way. 'And we're not going down by ourselves; we'll have experts with us. I'm going over to see Alan Williams and get him to come down with us. He'll take a bit of persuading that it's worth it, but I'm convinced it is.'

Craven arrived at Fell Farm with DC Denby mid morning to interview Stuart Tinsley. At the sound of the car coming up the lane, Fred Clark appeared from behind a shed, where he'd been tinkering with a tractor engine. He stared in a characteristically surly way at the officers as they got out of the car. He didn't trust 't'bloody police', as he dubbed them with his usual bluntness. They were usually here to harass you about licences for this or that, or to check up on you because someone had reported a spillage or that your muck heap smelled too strong: what the hell did they expect a pile of shit to smell of? Police were like the rest of officialdom generally: they interfered with your work and made things difficult with their regulations and bureaucracy.

Luckily, Craven's long experience with Dales characters had taught him how to handle people like Fred Clark. He walked straight up to the big farmer.

'Morning, Mr Clark, sorry to interrupt your work, but I understand you have a chap working here called Stuart Tinsley.'

'Aye.'

'Is he here today?'

'Aye.'

'Then I'd like to speak to him, please. I won't keep him from his work for long.'

Clark's frown deepened.

'Is he in bother then?'

'Well, I'm sure you understand I can't go into details on the matter. I just need to ask him a few questions.'

Clark pointed to the cowshed.

'He's in theer.'

'Thank you.'

Craven and the DC walked briskly over to the building where they found Tinsley cleaning the milking machines.

'Stuart Tinsley?'

'Yes.'

'Inspector Craven and DC Denby.' As he showed the ID, Craven thought he saw fear, quickly controlled, in Tinsley's expression.

'What's all this about?'

'We're investigating the murders of David Atkins and John Baxter. We need to ask you a few questions. Can we go somewhere?'

Craven noticed that there was no instant denial of anything. Instead, he silently led them into a small shed-like room nearby, which obviously acted as a kind of rough dining room for the farm workers. There were a few battered chairs and a Formica-topped table. In the corner there was a grubby sink piled with dirty mugs. They all sat down without a word being spoken. Tinsley slouched and crossed his arms defensively as Craven began.

'I've spoken to your wife, Mr Tinsley, and to Sylvia Atkins, the deceased's wife.'

'What's Susan been saying to you?' He sat up and there was anger in his voice.

'We'll come to that, sir; it will be much easier if you let me ask the questions.'

Tinsley's anger seemed to subside; he still looked tense and sullen, but then he sighed and seemed to relax a little as if he'd decided that it was no use resisting.

'OK.'

'It's true your wife had an affair with David Atkins?'

'Yes.'

'And that you are separated from her?'

'Yes.'

'And is it also true that you were having an affair with Sylvia Atkins?'

Again came the monosyllabic answer.

'Yes.'

Craven paused; he hadn't expected such straight answers. Maybe that indicated that Tinsley had nothing to hide.

'We have reason to believe that Sylvia Atkins was with you on the night of Monday the seventeenth of August. Is that true?'

Tinsley looked puzzled.

'What, two weeks ago? Can't remember. Maybe. What's so important about that?'

'We think it was when Atkins was murdered.'

Tinsley laughed.

'Oh, I see, and you think Sylvia and I did it?'

'We're just making enquiries at the moment.'

'Who told you Sylvia was with me?'

'So you admit she was here in Burnthwaite that night?' said Craven, ignoring the question.

Tinsley started to sound angry again.

'It was Susan, wasn't it, Inspector? You have to understand that Susan's very bitter, even though it was her that cheated on me first.'

'Mr Tinsley, can you just answer the question, please?'

Tinsley didn't reply; he was considering what to say. His face contorted with anger, and then he looked at Craven, who was waiting for a reply.

'All right, I suppose you'll find out soon enough. Besides, I'm useless at lying, any road. Yes, she was here with me in Burnthwaite, but we didn't kill him, Inspector.'

'Sylvia Atkins's sister,' Craven referred to his notebook, 'Jane Edwards, has stated that Sylvia was with her in Leeds at the time we're considering.'

'It's not true, Inspector. Sylvia's frightened that it will look bad if she was with me in Burnthwaite when her husband was murdered, and Jane is just under her sister's thumb: she'll do anything Sylvia tells her.'

'The fact is that it does look rather suspicious if you were together here, doesn't it? What exactly happened that evening?'

Tinsley had laid his hands on the Formica table next to a large stain made by a coffee mug. Craven saw the hands curl and tighten into angry fists.

'We just stayed in that night, I think. Wait, we might have gone over to Grassington and then come back at about nine o'clock. I don't stay out late in the week. I start work very early. The neighbours knew she was there.'

'Your wife claims she saw you both in the car by the village green at about the time you mention.'

'That's probably right. I was dropping her off. Her car was in the car park by the river and she was going back to Burnley.'

'You weren't waiting to attack Atkins when he came out of the pub?'

'No. Is that what Susan told you?'

'Even though you must have been very angry with him.'

'You're right there.'

Craven decided to pull back and explore the wider context.

'So how did you find out that your wife was having an affair?'

'Susan told me herself when I confronted her.'

'And how did you feel?'

'Isn't that obvious? Humiliated: the village cuckold. You wonder how many people had known but never said anything.' Tinsley shifted uneasily, remembering the embarrassment.

'So what happened?'

'She packed a suitcase and went to her parents.' That memory clearly hurt.

Craven scrutinised Tinsley's face.

'So I wonder if you started the affair with Atkins's wife as revenge?'

Tinsley met Craven's gaze.

'I suppose there was a big element of that, and for Sylvia too. She was the one who actually turned up at the house and told me what was going on. God, she's had a lot to put up with over the years from that bastard. No doubt she gets satisfaction from telling the partners of his conquests.'

'And how did it develop?'

'Is all this relevant?'

'It is to me and to the enquiry, Mr Tinsley. I'm trying to establish how you were feeling about things and how strong a motive you had. The best thing you can do is answer my questions honestly.'

Tinsley looked down.

'I did find her attractive, but it also felt good to stick two fingers up at Susan and Atkins. It made me feel less stupid and trodden on.'

'And was that feeling of vengeance enough or did you need more?'

Tinsley seemed to be finding this increasingly difficult.

'Look, Inspector, Susan and I were married when we were nineteen. People think it must always be wonderful in these little Dales villages, but it's not brilliant if you're a teenager and you don't know anything different. We were at school together and our parents knew each other.'

Craven nodded; he understood the patterns of rural life.

'We sort of fell into marriage. Round here it's either marry someone local and stay where you were born for the rest of your life or leave and go to the towns and cities. It was all right for me, I had a good job tending the dairy herd, but Susan never had the chance to do anything but bar and shop work. If we'd had kids, things might have been different. We tried, but she never got pregnant. She just got bored.'

'So you're saying you understood why she had the affair with Atkins?'

'I knew Atkins from the caving club. He knew when a woman was vulnerable. He was entertaining and charming, you know. Yes, I was bloody furious and I hated that loud-mouthed, bragging bastard and . . . and it's all a bloody mess. But it's taught me that I do care about Susan.'

He stopped and looked exhausted. 'All I want now, Inspector, is for her to come back to me.'

Craven decided to wrap up.

'So going back to that evening. You left Sylvia Atkins by the green and went home?'

'Yes, and straight to bed. That's all I can tell you, Inspector. I've no one to give me an alibi. We could have stayed in the car and killed Atkins when he came out. We didn't, but shall I tell you something?' He looked at Craven with a grim smile. 'I almost wish we had done.'

Oldroyd enjoyed the journey over to Ingleton. It was one of the great perks of his job that he regularly got to drive across the Dales land-scapes. At a stressful time like this when there was pressure to get results, he was able to relax and try to rest his mind. Today he listened to a CD of Elgar's violin concerto as he coasted through the scenery. The prob-lem was, if he got his mind off the case, he then tended to ruminate on his personal issues – in particular, what could he say or do that would persuade Julia that he was serious about renewing their relationship? Alison was right, she hadn't completely given up on him, but it was unnerving to feel that he had to make the right moves because he didn't really know what they were. Maybe it was time to invite her to some-thing, but he winced at the prospect. What if she refused? He would feel rejected and further away than ever. When he got to Ingleton, it was quite a relief to have to think about the case again.

He arrived at Johnny's Café to find it surprisingly quiet. It seemed as if the shock of a second murder in the caving community was too painful even to get together to talk about. A couple who looked more like tourists than cavers sat in a corner drinking tea and looking at guide books. Alan Williams himself was taking a break from behind the serving hatch and was sitting at another table reading a local newspaper with a mug of coffee in front of him.

Oldroyd went over. Williams recognised him immediately from the day that Atkins's body was retrieved from Jingling Pot.

'Sit down, Chief Inspector, I've been expecting you. We had Inspector Craven in here a few days ago. Things are obviously much more serious now; we've gone up a rank.'

Oldroyd smiled at Williams's sardonic humour.

'You'll be pleased to know that there is a way you can help.'

Williams put the paper down and Oldroyd saw that the attempt at being light-hearted was, as he suspected, a desperate one. His face was taut.

'Well, of course I'll help, but I don't know how. I mean John Baxter, he's the second member of our Caving Club to be found murdered. I don't need to tell you that everybody's devastated and some are downright bloody scared. Who knows who might be next? Where's it going to end?'

'I understand how bad it is for you,' replied Oldroyd sympathetically. 'You're quite a close group, you cavers, aren't you?'

'Yes, I was telling Inspector Craven about that. There's a kind of fraternity develops. Even when you don't like a person, it's a shock when something bad happens. Nobody liked Atkins much, but nobody wants to bring a caver out of a cave dead, whoever he or she is.'

'But it's much worse when it's not an accident and they've been murdered by someone who must be a caver themselves.'

Williams was silent and looked down.

'Yep,' he said tersely. 'And now it's two.' He looked at Oldroyd quizzically. 'Maybe I shouldn't be talking to you. I understand John had information he was going to give you but he got murdered first. It could be me next.'

Oldroyd moved to reassure him.

'Unless you know something about the murders, I don't think you have anything to fear, and that goes for anybody else. I'd be grateful if you got that message out. I said at my press conference, this is no deranged serial killer. John Baxter knew something and I'm pretty sure he was killed because of that. How well did you know him, anyway?'

Williams considered for a moment.

'Pretty well, been on a lot of trips with him. He wasn't very sociable; didn't come in here much, just to the pub now and again. He was a very keen caver, though, and he loved diving, and that's not for everybody.'

'Because of the risks?'

'Too right, it's bloody dangerous. You dive into total darkness, not knowing what you're going to find. People get killed all the time. John was a quiet sort of bloke but very brave in some ways, some would say daft. He'll be missed.'

'Did he have any enemies? Can you think of any reason why someone would want to kill him?'

Williams laughed, again rather grimly.

'It's the opposite of Dave Atkins, isn't it? Loads of people won't be sorry to see him dead, but John, no, he was a nice bloke. Didn't have any family, caving was his life really, but he got on well with everyone as far as I know. Good builder and joiner too; did lots of work for people, extensions and stuff.'

Oldroyd nodded; this seemed to confirm the theory that the murder was to silence him.

'Did he have any special friends, people who could help us a bit more?'

Williams took a drink of his coffee and thought for a moment.

'Not particularly, except for the blokes over in Burnthwaite, you know, Geoff Whitaker, Simon Hardiman, Bill Watson. He used to go on trips with them a lot. They used to talk about it when we had Cave Rescue meetings.'

Not very helpful, thought Oldroyd, as those are all the people who are already suspects in the Atkins murder anyway. He sighed. This wasn't getting him very far in narrowing the list down.

'I know everybody must be as jumpy as anything and wondering who the killer might be. Are there any particular people or ideas that keep being mentioned?'

Williams shook his head.

'Naw. I've heard some wild stuff about strange people being seen around the caves; some think that he could have been a victim of some gang warfare, maybe he got too deeply into something he couldn't handle, but nobody believes it. I know what you blokes would think about it and you're right: why look for strangers who might have a motive when there's so many people round here who would like to see Atkins dead? Anyway, Chief Inspector, you said I could help.'

Oldroyd explained about the proposed trip down Winter's Gill Hole. Williams frowned.

'Winter's Gill Hole. Well, you've chosen a right one there. You know it's supposed to be haunted; a lot of people won't go down it.'

'You don't believe that, do you?'

'Well, who knows, Chief Inspector? Of course, I'll get one or two of the lads and we'll take you down. It won't be pleasant but there's not much to it if you show respect, like any other cave, but you want to be careful.' He leaned over closer to Oldroyd. 'Many people believe those caves have evil spirits in them which can lure you down to your doom.'

Oldroyd was never sure exactly how serious Williams was on this subject.

'Not nowadays, surely.'

'Why not? Maybe these deaths are a kind of curse, the spirits telling us they don't want us down there. Go up on Leck Fell at dusk and stand near one of the potholes that open up on the moor. You can hear tap, tap, tap down in the darkness, and it gives you the shivers, I can tell you. It's the sound of the water dripping, but all the same.' He shook himself as if from some ghostly memory.

'Very atmospheric; are you trying to frighten us off from going down?' remarked Oldroyd.

Williams laughed too; his little joke a release from the tension he felt.

'No, but I think you're wasting your time. I can't see how the caves are going to solve this crime for you.'

'I think you may be wrong there,' said Oldroyd.

He thanked Williams and left. As he approached the door, a group of men with the tousled hair and muddy faces of cavers came in. They appeared to recognise Oldroyd and immediately went silent, drew back and looked at him suspiciously as he left the café, as if he might be the murderer himself.

Seven

T'watter goes dahn and niver comes back,
And nather will thee, swallowed up bi' t'black.

Oldroyd woke up early on the next day feeling tired and deflated. He'd been turning things over in his mind all night and not slept well. He got out of bed, made a pot of tea, switched on Radio 4 and heard the farming forecast. He sat at the table rubbing his eyes and decided that he might as well go into work; he would never get back to sleep now. He was desperate to get down into the cave and see what they could find, but that would take a few days to organise. It was a long shot and he knew it might turn out to be an embarrassing failure, but he trusted his own judgement, at least in these matters.

He left the flat in the early morning quiet. It was a sunny morning and there was a heavy dew on the Stray, the first sign of approaching autumn. Few people were around other than some joggers and dog walkers. The shops, bars and cafés were all still closed.

When he arrived at HQ he found three reports waiting for him. The first report was of the discovery of the cave and its contents by the two officers from Skipton. It was highly likely that the person who had squatted in the cave had also followed Carter and himself across the fields, and, as Bill Watson was the only suspect missing from Burnthwaite, it was also highly likely to be him.

The second report was from forensics and concerned the piece of metal found in the cave. It confirmed what he thought. The hook was made of cast iron and not of recent construction. It was at least a hundred years old. He was even more convinced that he had found one of Haverthwaite's 'iron contrivances'.

The final report was from Tim Groves, and this was the least helpful: the post mortem on John Baxter. It confirmed the time and cause of death but contained nothing else of note.

He was just musing on all of this information and feeling that things were beginning to gather momentum a little when his phone rang. On the other end of the line, Craven sounded rather excited.

'Tip-off from Trevor Booth, landlord of the Red Horse; says he saw the elusive Bill Watson early this morning in the village. Watson didn't see him.'

'What was he doing?'

'Sitting in a field behind a wall, obviously still in hiding; didn't realise he could be seen from a window at the back of the pub.'

'Anything else unusual?'

'Said he wouldn't have recognised him if he hadn't had a good long look; he was scruffy and bearded, as if he'd been living rough.'

'That ties in with our theory; he's obviously the one who's been living in the cave. Any idea why he's decided to come back to civilisation?'

'Yes, Jim. It's Burnthwaite Fair and Fell Race today. They have all those children's races on the green every August bank holiday. I wonder if he's turned up to see his daughter taking part. It's just an idea, but you know what kids are like.'

'Well done, lad, I'll bet tha's reight.' Oldroyd and Craven also liked to use a bit of matey dialect, especially when things appeared to be going well.

'Let's get over there, plain clothes, no marked cars, park outside the village.'

'I don't think we'll have any choice, Jim; Burnthwaite will be packed.'

'Of course, I was forgetting; well, that's to our advantage. We'll park in one of the fields they open up; the one by the bridge. Make sure everybody's seen that photograph my DS got. I've put it on the website so we all at least have an idea who we're looking out for.'

'Will do. By the way, Jim, before you go, I interviewed Stuart Tinsley. He confessed to having the affair with Sylvia Atkins and that they were both in Burnthwaite the night Atkins disappeared. It confirmed what I thought about her story, so she's in trouble for misleading us.'

'Do you think they could have done it?'

'Not impossible, plenty of motives between them. Tinsley doesn't strike me as the vicious sort, but he could have been driven by the Atkins woman. That's exactly what his wife was afraid of when I interviewed her.'

'OK, the plot continues to thicken but at least it's speeding up a bit; no one's been eliminated but I have my theories.'

'Knowing you, Jim, I'd be surprised if you didn't. See you later.'

Oldroyd rang off and felt some excitement himself. Although the list of suspects seemed to grow ever longer, at last things were moving. Today they should finally make their first arrest, and of someone who might lead them on still further.

Preparations for the Burnthwaite Fair had been going on for some time. It was the usual type of rural village fete with local produce stalls, ice-cream vans, bouncy castles and other children's games. The fair itself dated back to Elizabethan times, and since the nineteenth century, at the end of the afternoon, there had been a now-famous race up the steep fell that rose opposite the village green.

Oldroyd drove into the village on a back road, avoiding the crowded centre. Beside him, Carter looked round at the bunting and the families heading for the large village green. The village fair, he thought, how quaint! Not really his scene. The only time he'd been to anything remotely like this was when a couple of mates had taken him off to some village in Surrey where there was a beer festival. All he remembered was a huge tent that stank of beer, and then downing one pint after another of potent stuff with names like Dragon's Puke and Devil's Piss before reeling out and collapsing in the corner of a field. He turned to Oldroyd.

'Do you really think he'll turn up here, sir? Why would he risk being seen at something like this?'

'Pester power, Carter.'

'You mean his kid?'

'That's right. You haven't got any kids yet. Before you do, you have all these ideas about discipline and how you'll never give in to them. Then it all goes out of the window when the little things plead with you. If Craven and I are right, Watson's been away from his family since Atkins's body was discovered. That daughter will have been on to her mother all the time, and if she's been in contact with her husband, which is highly likely, he's probably promised to come and see her in the race.'

'How's he going to manage that?'

'That's the interesting bit, and the challenge for us; he's not going to stand at the side of the races shouting out her name. Anyway, let's meet up with Craven.'

Oldroyd turned the car through a gate in the drystone wall. A flat-capped farmer was standing by the entrance and Oldroyd lowered the window.

'Afternoon.'

The farmer nodded.

'Two pounds fifty, please; tha'll have to go reight to t'bottom o' t'field near t'river.' He pointed down the lines of cars.

'Right.'

Oldroyd drove slowly and bumpily down the slope past line after line of cars. It's going to be busy over there, he thought.

Ten minutes later, he and Carter were walking back to the village with Craven, who was parked near to them.

'I've briefed all my lot and they're positioned around the village. They've all got radios but they know to be careful how they use them. Do you think this bloke's dangerous?'

'If he's the murderer he could be.'

'Do you think he is?'

'Still too soon to say. He was mixed up with Atkins all right, but we're not sure how. They've all seen the photograph?'

'Yep.'

They walked across the bridge and Carter looked over to where Oldroyd had demonstrated skimming on the first day of the investigation. Today the grassy banks near the water were full of families picnicking and children paddling in the shallow edge of the river.

As they neared the village green, the sound of a brass band drifted over from the far side. They began to walk past the stalls selling sweets and homemade cakes. Oldroyd stopped.

'Better split up now,' he said quietly. 'Just wander round and stay alert.'

They went their separate ways and merged with the crowd. Oldroyd looked beyond the village, contemplating the broad sweep of Burnthwaite Fell shortly to be scaled by the racers. The upper slopes were reddish purple with the late August heather. It all looked grand and impressive, dwarfing the happy human activity below. The scene was so beautiful and inspiring that it was difficult to believe that they were investigating two brutal murders. The bustling fair was testimony to the doggedness of the human determination to carry on normal life whatever had happened. Surrounding it was an awesome landscape, indifferent to human affairs.

As Oldroyd mused on the scene, Carter was occupied by a group of medieval knights reconstructing a battle. He was more used to the music and energy of street festivals like the Notting Hill Carnival. This was a quiet affair compared with that. Nevertheless, he found himself interested in the sword fights and jousting, and on the edge of the 'arena' he encountered the best thing of all: a medieval cannon. This was loaded with powder, then a taper was held to the touch hole and the cannon gave off a formidable crack, smoke and sparks belching from the front. An elderly man in costume with a grimy face seemed to be in charge of the cannon. Carter could imagine scores of men looking just like that on some battlefield in the past: smoke drifting over the brutal scene, the smell of gunpowder and the screams and cries mingled with furious clashing of metal.

Returning to reality, he walked on to another part of the green and encountered a scene far removed from a battle, but still competitive. Children's races were taking place. At the moment it was the egg-and-spoon race and a line of eight-year-olds were running along trying desperately not to spill the precariously balanced eggs, to shouted encouragement from their parents and siblings. It seemed curiously twee and 1950s to the city-bred Carter, but there was also something touching about kids who could enjoy something old-fashioned and harmless. As he saw them giggling with the wholesome fun of it, he was saddened to think of some of the young kids he'd encountered in London: foul-mouthed, sophisticated beyond their years, knocking about estates and getting into trouble. Not for the first time recently, he found that everything he knew in London seemed a long way away.

Across the other side of the green, Oldroyd was strolling past stalls selling homemade cakes and chutney. Further on he came unexpectedly to one manned by the Hardimans which was advertising Garthwaite Hall and the facilities it offered.

'Afternoon, Inspector, what brings you here?' said a surprised-looking Simon Hardiman as Caroline spoke to an enquirer.

Oldroyd was anxious not to have his identity broadcast too widely so he moved close to the stall and spoke softly.

'Just a bit of undercover work, so I'd be grateful if you just kept quiet.'

'Oh, right. Well, we're just here for the publicity, you know; every little helps.'

'Quite,' said Oldroyd and moved on. He began to watch the egg-and-spoon race on the opposite side to Carter and at the same time look around the crowd. If Craven's theory was right, this was where they needed to be alert.

The egg-and-spoon race came to an end with a round of applause. Around the green, various sideshows were in full swing. Some unfortunate individual, probably a teacher from the local primary school, was having wet sponges thrown at him. There was a big tombola stall and someone in a clown costume, which included a large headpiece. This caught Oldroyd's attention; could that be Bill Watson? It was certainly a complete disguise, but surely too risky. If he was challenged, the whole thing could come unstuck. No, he would want something much quieter, in the background.

A voice came over the public address system.

'The next race is the fifty-metre sprint; boys under eleven. Next after that will be the same race for girls. Boys, come up to the line, please.'

Oldroyd nodded discreetly to Carter across the green. The second race would be the one in which Alice Watson would probably run. Boys in shorts and running vests received pats on the back and words of encouragement and walked over to the starting line. Carter and Oldroyd were not watching them. They were scanning the crowd for Anne Watson and her daughter.

Oldroyd was the first to spot them. He moved behind the other spectators to avoid being seen. He spoke quietly into the radio.

'Carter, they're coming over on my side to my right. Try to stay inconspicuous.'

'OK, sir. She won't know us, will she? It was Steph who interviewed her.'

'Yes, but she must expect that the police are out looking for her husband. Let's not take any chances.'

Oldroyd watched the elegant woman wearing dark glasses and her daughter in a tracksuit and T-shirt. They came towards him but then veered off towards an ice-cream van. They stopped. Oldroyd looked hard. A starting gun went off and the boys' race began. Oldroyd hardly noticed. That was not Bill Watson serving in the van, it was a ginger-haired man with a full beard. He handed the girl a can of cola and the mother paid. Oldroyd expected them to move on past him to the starting line, but they stayed by the van. The girl didn't open the can. She was looking up and appeared to be talking to the man who had served her the drink.

Oldroyd frowned. There was something about this that wasn't right; somehow, the angle of her posture was strange. She seemed to be facing further to the right as if she was talking to someone at the side of the ice cream seller, someone who was out of sight.

That was it! Watson was hiding in that van, standing to the right so he couldn't be seen at the window! Oldroyd grabbed his radio.

'Carter, he's in that ice cream van, I'm pretty sure, hidden to one side. The girl's talking to him now.'

'Right, sir, shall we rush it?'

'No, tell the others that we think we've got him. But we've got to do this carefully. If we pile into the van now it's going to cause a terrible scene, ruin the show and the races and I might be wrong. We've just got to keep watching the van and go for it when the time's right.'

'OK.'

As Oldroyd finished speaking, the girl left the van and walked with her mother behind him to the starting line.

The boys' race finished to great shouts and applause. A poor lad who had fallen was led away crying by his father. As the girls lined up, Oldroyd moved behind a tree so that he could keep the van in view without being seen.

'On your marks, get set . . . Go!' The starting gun blasted again. The girls shot off, pigtails bouncing, and Alice was near the front. Oldroyd kept his focus on the van and as the girls passed it a second figure came into view inside, craning forward to see what happened at the finishing line. As Oldroyd suspected, Bill Watson's eagerness to see how his daughter did in the race had briefly caused him to betray his hiding place.

Alice came in second and then ran over to her mother, who was applauding enthusiastically. Oldroyd got on the radio again.

'He's definitely in there, Carter; I've seen him. I'm going to stay in this position. Tell the others to form a perimeter around the van, but at a distance.'

The detectives got into their positions and waited. The children's races continued and in the distance, by the Red Horse, the sound of a piano accordion and a jingling of bells indicated that a Morris Dancing team had started to perform.

Oldroyd turned to Craven. 'What do you think he'll do?'

'I'm not sure, Jim. He'll probably just stay in there and be driven off.'

'That's what I'm expecting; we'll have to stop the van as soon as it gets away from here, keep the fuss to a minimum. Do we know who owns this van? He's obviously helping Watson to conceal himself.'

'Almost certainly a bloke called Jack Armstrong; bit of a wild character; yet another potholer. He's got two vans, this and another he lives rough in.'

'He hasn't come up in our investigations, has he?'

'No, but it could be just that he owed Bill Watson a favour, no questions asked. I can imagine Jack Armstrong having to lie low himself now and again.'

'So he'd understand?'

'I think so.'

'OK, stay in position. I don't want a big scene and pictures in the paper: "Police Ruin Burnthwaite Fair" and all that.'

Slowly the afternoon progressed. The van stayed put and did a brisk trade with the children and their parents. The green seemed to be full of people licking ice cream cones, some with enormous chocolate flakes sticking out of them. Carter was sorely tempted himself, but knew it was out of the question. The detectives stayed in their positions maintaining a weary vigilance while everyone around them was enjoying themselves, unaware of the cordon of police waiting to pounce.

Late in the afternoon, families started to drift away and the stalls began to shut down. It was time for the climactic event of the day: the fell race. The start of this was on the road that ran alongside the green. Some people started to line the edge ready to cheer the competitors and others, who looked like serious runners, started to appear and gather on the road.

Still the van remained where it was but with a decreasing number of customers. As a group of men and women in running shorts passed the van, the rear door opened and a man stepped out quickly and joined the back of the group. He was also dressed in running gear.

Oldroyd grabbed his radio.

'Watson has just come out of the van; he's joined a group of runners going up to the line. Now we know his escape route: he's going to run out of the village with the others, pretend he's part of the race. Get to him before the race starts.'

'Why didn't he just stay in the van until it drives off?'

'I don't know. He probably knows we're on to him, maybe he's seen someone he recognised and this is his emergency option: try to escape before we stop the van to search it.'

Carter had moved across to the road where the runners were gathering. He saw Craven and his men moving over carefully. He pulled out the photograph of Watson and searched the faces around him. There was now quite a big crowd milling together; trying to locate one face was extremely difficult.

Suddenly Oldroyd was by his side.

'I've tried to keep my eye on him since he left the van. He's in that group there, I think.'

He pointed to a group of men in the middle of the crowd, but in running gear they all looked the same.

The race was about to start. Some local dignitary said a few words about this historic race and then a starting gun went off yet again. The runners moved off at a fairly slow pace, conserving their energy for the steep climb ahead.

At that moment, Oldroyd got a clear view.

'He's there! Craven! He's by you in the red vest!'

People turned in surprise as the detectives burst into action. Craven ran forward, but Watson realised he was being pursued and ran off to the left into the spectators, pursued by Carter. They ducked and weaved through the crowd, Carter trying desperately not to lose track. There were angry shouts as some people were brushed aside.

'What the hell's going on?'

Watson was heading for the Red Horse, at the front of which the Morris Dancing team were performing. He darted quickly to the side of them, but Carter blundered straight in. Suddenly he was surrounded by dancing men waving handkerchiefs and then he collided with an outlandish figure dressed as a clown.

'What the . . .'

Carter crashed to the ground and lay flat with a pig's bladder on a stick resting on his head. The dance stopped and angry faces were looking down at him.

'You dickhead; are you pissed or what? Are you OK, Martin?'

The clown was sprawled at the side of Carter. His cap, decorated with streamers, had fallen off. He scowled at Carter.

'Aye, no thanks to him.'

Carter was already on his feet. He had no time to explain.

'Sorry, but I have to catch that bloke, police.'

He barged his way through the group and ran off, much to the consternation of the Morris team.

Meanwhile, Watson had bolted down a lane between two cottages with Craven in pursuit.

'Head him off!' shouted Craven to one of his detective constables, who shot off down another alleyway.

Watson was heading for a stile that led into a field, but the detective's route was more direct to the same point. Soon Watson was trapped between the detective and Craven. He tried to push through but was wrestled to the ground. Oldroyd came up behind.

'Mr Watson?'

'Yes. Ow!' he muttered sullenly and then grimaced with pain from Craven's arm lock.

'Detective Chief Inspector Oldroyd.' He showed his identification to Watson, who did not look surprised.

'We need to question you about the murders of David Atkins and John Baxter.'

'I don't know anything about it.'

'Which is why you're running away from us now and why you've disguised yourself as a runner.'

'I am a runner. I was doing the fell race. I didn't know who you were. You frightened me.'

'And why you've been hiding in an ice cream van all afternoon.'

'I wasn't hiding. I was helping.'

'From a concealed position, very likely. Take him away. He'll be more cooperative when we get him back to HQ.'

Watson was bundled off to a nearby police car as Carter arrived looking somewhat dishevelled.

'What happened to you?' said Oldroyd.

'I ran into those Morris men or whoever they are by mistake.'

Oldroyd chuckled. 'The Morris Dancers? I didn't have you down as someone who would dress up with bells around his ankles. I would've thought that was too middle aged and rural for a young cosmopolitan type.'

'Very funny, sir. Did you get him?'

'Yes, he's in the car.'

They walked down and re-emerged into the road. Luckily, the incident had done little to disrupt the proceedings. Most people had wandered back on to the green and a small number were watching the runners. Oldroyd glanced up the fell at a line of figures toiling up the slope between the rocks and on to the upper fell. Over by the Red Horse, the piano accordion could be heard again. .

'Never mind, Andy, the Morris Dancers seem to have survived their clash with modernity.'

'Yes, sir,' replied a rueful Carter.

Bill Watson was sitting in the interview room waiting for Chief Inspector Oldroyd to arrive, his solicitor at his side. A PC with an implacable expression stood at the back.

Watson looked down at the table in front of him in despair. This was exactly what he'd been trying to avoid. Damn that Atkins! If only he'd not got involved with that bastard, he wouldn't have ended up here. Now it was a game of cat and mouse with the police trying to work up a plausible story, and that detective looked a bit formidable.

At that moment, the said detective burst into the room, closely followed by his blonde cockney sidekick.

Oldroyd sat down opposite Watson and the PC pressed the button on the recorder.

'The time is 5.30 p.m.; start of the interview of William Watson, suspect in the murders of David Atkins and John Baxter. Also present Detective Sergeant Andrew Carter, PC Lauren Clifford and Derek Smith, acting for Mr Watson.'

Oldroyd turned to Watson and began in quite a mild manner.

'Do you prefer Bill or William, Mr Watson?'

'I don't mind.'

'But you're known to everyone as Bill?'

'Yes.'

'Including Dave Atkins.'

Watson sighed. 'Yes.'

'Did you kill him?'

Watson looked up sharply and directly at Oldroyd.

'No.'

'Did you kill John Baxter?'

'No.'

'Can we progress from the monosyllabic replies? Perhaps you can explain why you've been living rough in caves up in the limestone fells since Atkins's body was found?'

This time there was no quick reply. Watson remained silent.

Oldroyd's eyes suddenly blazed and his face took on a fierce, hawkish expression. His voice became deeper with a controlled but menacing power. Carter was rather taken aback by the abrupt transformation.

'Mr Watson, would you agree that it is rather suspicious? The body is discovered and you disappear without explanation? We know your wife had an affair with Atkins, which places you as a chief suspect. Now give us some clear and detailed answers and maybe we can sort this out. Otherwise you'll be staying in here.'

Watson had edged back further in his chair before this onslaught, but he tried to fight back.

'It was for personal reasons. My wife and I weren't . . . getting on.'

Oldroyd grunted.

'I see. Your relationship with Mrs Watson wasn't going well, so you went to live in a cave. It's not quite the normal place to go in such circumstances is it?'

Watson glanced at Carter and the PC as if appealing for help.

'I . . . wanted to be by myself. I like being outdoors. I've been on a lot of solo expeditions up in Scotland and places and camped outdoors for days on end.'

'That would be in a tent, though, wouldn't it? Why did you choose a cave?'

Watson paused.

'It's true. I didn't want to be found. A tent is too obvious.'

'Why didn't you want to be found? Was your disagreement anything to do with Atkins?'

'No, but Burnthwaite's full of gossip. It would soon have been round the village that I was living in a tent up on the fells.'

'So how long did you intend to stay up there?'

'Don't know. For a while, until things had cooled off and were better between us. I've done it before and it does us good for me to, well, go away for a bit.'

'But your little daughter didn't like Daddy being away?'

'No, she didn't.' Watson seemed to relax a little as if he felt his story was hanging together. 'She pleaded with me on the phone to come home and see the races.'

'Hmn,' murmured Oldroyd, 'but you still weren't ready to . . . reveal yourself, as it were?'

'No, I was going to go back up to the cave again. Until you stopped me.'

'Why were you watching us near the limestone pavement?'

'Who? What do you mean?'

'Detective Sergeant Carter and myself. We saw you behind the wall. It was you, wasn't it?'

Watson frowned. 'Yes, it was. Well, I knew what had happened to Atkins and I was a bit nervy. Then I saw your police car parked not far from where I was hiding and—'

'That's the real reason you did a bunk, isn't it? Because the body had been found and you were scared. It was nothing to do with your wife.'

'No, that's not true. I didn't kill him.'

Derek Smith intervened.

'Chief Inspector, you are adopting a very hostile manner, and you know you can't make an allegation like that without evidence. My client has explained to you why he was living in the cave.'

Oldroyd ignored him and continued to pin Watson down with his penetrating stare.

'So what exactly was your relationship with Atkins? How did you know him?'

'It was through the caving club.'

'And how did you get on with him?'

'OK, up to a point. It's not easy to like a man who has an affair with your wife.'

'No, but did you have any other dealings with him yourself, other than through caving?'

There was a slight pause before Watson answered.

'No, well, we both invested some money together once in, you know, property. He was good at finding investments; spent a lot of time searching online.'

'So just a little investment?'

'Yes.'

'Did your wife know about this?'

Watson flinched.

'No, and I'd be grateful if you didn't tell her. Money is what we mostly argue about and she doesn't think that all the things I do with money are sort of, you know, prudent.'

'Was anyone else involved in these deals?'

'No.' But again there was a pause, which told Oldroyd a lot. He remained silent for a few moments and then his demeanour changed again. He suddenly seemed bored, as if he'd had enough of the interview.

'OK.' He waved to the PC. 'Let him go.'

Carter was astonished. 'But, sir . . .'

Oldroyd spoke right over him.

'Go home,' he turned to Watson and pointed at him, 'and mind you stay there; no more going wild. We might need to speak to you again.'

Carter noticed Watson smiling to himself as the PC led him and the solicitor out. As soon as they were alone, he turned to Oldroyd.

'Sir, that story was the biggest load of bollocks I've heard in years. He must be one of our main suspects: disappears after Atkins's body is found and while he's "away", as it were, Baxter is murdered. There's also something going on with money. Couldn't we have pushed him further?'

Oldroyd was thoughtful but unmoved. He turned to Carter.

'I agree; the story was rubbish. He's obviously hiding something, but whether it's murder I'm not sure. It's an unconvincing story, but it's also an unconvincing thing to do if you are the murderer. Atkins's murder was carefully planned and cold-bloodedly executed. As I said before, it doesn't seem like the person who carried that out would suddenly panic and bolt into a cave on the fells.'

'But you said yourself that we weren't meant to find the body. Maybe he was so sure that nobody would that he didn't have any plan about what he would do if they did, so he did panic and run off.'

'You could be right; I'm not eliminating him, but there's also the question of who was helping him. I'm still convinced we're looking for at least two people, so what's happened to his accomplice? Why didn't they feel the need to run off? Anyway, for the moment we've no evidence to link him to the murders; suspicious behaviour isn't enough. I'm going to ask Craven to keep an eye on the Watsons' place in case he tries to disappear again. Maybe the accomplice will turn up too.'

Both detectives trudged rather wearily back up to Oldroyd's office.

'That seemed to be a lot of effort for very little, sir,' said a discouraged Carter. 'The problem with this case is that there are too many bloody suspects and we don't seem to be able to narrow it down.'

Oldroyd poured out coffee.

'I think we're a little closer than that, Carter; just have patience.'

He handed him a cup, opened the biscuit tin and sat down in his big armchair.

Steph had been doing some routine work at her computer and now she joined them. She saw the frustration on Carter's face.

'How did it go?' she asked.

Carter sighed and scratched his head, for once leaving both coffee and biscuits untouched.

'We got Watson, but apparently not enough evidence against him; he's been released.'

Steph sat down. 'Oh, that's disappointing. Are we back to square one, then, sir?'

Oldroyd looked tired after his poor night's sleep and the hectic events of the afternoon, but as he lounged in his chair, he still had a twinkle in his eye.

'Buck up, you two, don't get downhearted. We've got an adventure ahead of us.' He sipped his coffee and took a bite from a chocolate digestive. 'I think we'll know more when we've been down into that cave and it's revealed its secrets.'

The dramatic arrest at the Burnthwaite Fair had been observed by someone else who had taken a keen interest in Watson's disappearance.

Geoff Whitaker was serving at the Red Horse food stand grilling sausages and burgers over a smoky barbecue when he saw the commotion over at the start of the fell race. As he stuffed a sizzling burger

into a bun, doused it with tomato sauce and mustard and handed it to
the next customer, he kept his eye on what was happening. Luckily for
him, the chase ended not far from the stall. As he was serving the next
customer, he saw the figure being bundled into the car and thought he
recognised Bill Watson.

'Hey, I don't want so much sauce!'

Whitaker looked down and saw that he had completely covered the
burger in a pool of red.

'Sorry, Anna will get you another.' He turned to his colleague from
the Red Horse kitchens. 'Can you cover for a minute? I have to take a
quick break.'

'OK.'

Anna prepared another burger for the disgruntled customer as
Whitaker ran the short distance across the field to the road. He was
just in time to see the police car pass. He was able to get a clear view of
the person in the back and it was definitely Bill Watson.

'Oh, shit!' he exclaimed loudly, to the disgust of a woman passing with two small children. So Bill had reappeared just to get himself
arrested. He was not only a coward but a bloody fool as well!

He found it difficult to carry on serving burgers after this and was
glad when the fair ended. When he arrived back home, Helen was sitting at the kitchen table, looking morose. It seemed as if she was waiting
for him.

'How did it go?' she asked in a voice that conveyed no interest.

He filled the electric kettle and switched it on.

'OK. We made quite a bit; gets monotonous after a while though;
right now I don't want to see another burger or hot dog sausage ever
again.'

She did not respond to his attempt at light-heartedness.

'I hear Bill Watson was arrested.'

He turned to her sharply to see an accusing expression.

'How do you know?'

'Paula rang; she was at the fair with Terry and saw it happen.'

'Yeah. Apparently he was hiding in an ice-cream van and then pretended he was in the fell race. Do you want tea?'

He poured boiling water into the teapot.

'Geoff, we can't go on like this.'

He turned to her again. 'What do you mean?'

'You didn't tell the truth to the police, did you? You didn't just lend Atkins money, there's more to it than that. And Bill Watson's got something to do with it, hasn't he?'

'What the hell is all this? What are you talking about?'

'I overheard you on the phone talking to Bill when he was missing and you were talking about money. Atkins's name came up.'

He said nothing but turned away from her.

'It's been bad enough all these years with you going off caving. You know how I feel about that after what happened to Richard; I worry all the time. Then what made it worse was Dave Atkins going with you, and now you've got involved in something with him, haven't you?' She was shouting at him now. 'Haven't you? He's a curse on my life, that man. I'm glad he's dead but did you . . . ?'

'I don't want to hear any more of this!' Whitaker shouted back and stormed out of the house.

It was a still, sunny day in Upper Wharfedale with large white clouds drifting slowly overhead. On the fells, the tiny figures of walkers carrying rucksacks could be seen from the bottom of the dale making their ant-like progress to the summits. By the river, oyster catchers kleeped and sand martins twisted and dived over the water.

By a cluster of police cars in a lay-by could be seen the figures of Oldroyd, Carter and Steph, dressed in an unusual fashion. They had abandoned their normal clothes for what looked like boiler suits and crash helmets. They were standing among a number of other figures who seemed to wear the clothing more easily. Oldroyd was consulting a map with Alan Williams, who was shaking his head.

'I still think we're wasting our time, Chief Inspector; Winter's Gill's nothing of a system, it just peters out into a muddy dead end. Nobody bothers with it and it has a kind of nasty, claustrophobic feeling.'

'Yes, but have you seen this?' Oldroyd produced a photocopy of Haverthwaite's poem. Williams read it and raised his eyebrows.

'What's all this about then? I've never heard of anything called the Devil's Passage.'

'It's an old dialect poem by a man named Haverthwaite. He was an early cave explorer.'

'Yes, I've heard of him. It was all primitive stuff in those days; they never got very far in, didn't have the equipment.' Williams looked rather pityingly at Oldroyd. 'So you think this suggests that there might be a link from Winter's Gill to Sump Passage? It's not a right lot to go on, is it?'

'No, but I'm convinced that link must be there; it's the only explanation of this case that makes any sense. It won't be easy to find or you lot would have found it years ago. It'll be well concealed or almost blocked up or something, but it is possible, isn't it?'

Williams had to concede the truth of this.

'Yes, it's possible. These caves aren't static even if most of the change is very slow. Rocks fall, some passages are blocked, and some open up, things get wider or narrower. A hundred and fifty years is a long time.'

Oldroyd imagined the subterranean world below their feet. It was mostly moving with the slowness of geological time where a stalactite and a stalagmite could take a thousand years to meet. But occasionally there were swift and dramatic events that could instantly change the configuration of a system. He pointed to the map.

'Look at this point here. This is where the two systems are at their closest, if I'm reading this correctly. Crucially, it's not far into the

Winter's Gill system because, remember, we're talking about the body being carried in.'

Williams was still sceptical.

'Yes, that's where the two systems are closest and Sump Passage is near that point. Sounds plausible but . . .' He shook his head. 'So what do you want us to do?'

Oldroyd shrugged. 'Take us down there and let's see what we find.'

Carter went over to Steph and looked her up and down. 'It suits you.'

'Thanks,' she laughed. 'What does that mean? I've got an awful figure so I might as well conceal it under this shapeless thing?'

'No, but you look right in it. You look as if you'd have no trouble down there. Whereas me, the only underground I know is the Piccadilly Line, and that's dry and well lit.'

'You'll manage; stay close to me and I'll protect you.'

This sent a frisson of excitement through Carter, who had to remind himself firmly that he was on duty; no unprofessional conduct down in the caves.

At that moment, Oldroyd called everyone together and they set off on a short path across a field towards a stream. Carter looked around but there seemed to be no sign of any cave or pothole, only the velvety sheep-grazed grass and grey-white weathered outcrops of limestone.

They reached the course of the stream and Carter could see that there was no water, just another dried-up stream bed. Water was constantly appearing and disappearing in this mysterious limestone country. Alan Williams walked over towards what looked like an old metal dustbin lid lying on the ground and lifted it up.

'After you, Inspector,' he said to Oldroyd, who promptly climbed down into a hole and disappeared.

'What the . . . !' Carter was flabbergasted.

Steph laughed. 'Some of these cave entrances have been excavated by the cavers and they put these lids over to stop water flooding in.'

Carter shook his head at this bizarre eccentricity. When it came to his turn, he switched on his lamp as instructed and manoeuvred himself down a short stairway constructed from chunks of limestone.

Immediately he was in a different world. The only experience Carter could compare it to was going scuba diving on a holiday in Majorca. One second you were in the hot air of the Mediterranean with a breeze blowing across the water, everything light and airy. Then suddenly you plunged into a darker, cool world under water. It was silent except for your own breathing, and movement was slow against the pressure of the water.

As he disappeared below ground, the light was shut out; the noise of the wind and the bird calls abruptly ceased. The drop in temperature in the clammy air was instantly noticeable. The vivid colours of the fells and the sky were replaced by a damp world of dirty rock and mud.

He trudged along for fifty yards or so along a narrow tunnel, the beam from his lamp illuminating the passage ahead. He was already feeling tired with the effort of walking while crouched and was wondering again what on earth made people do this for a hobby, when the tunnel suddenly opened out and disappeared.

This came as quite a shock. He was in an open space but it was impossible to say how big because the darkness confused his bearings. The beam of light from his helmet shone up indistinctly into the void. The muffled quality of sound in the tunnel changed to a frightening echo suggesting depth and height. Was the ground about to fall away in front of him? Was he in some mammoth and terrifying cathedral-like chamber?

Carter anxiously moved his head around to direct the light, which he eventually got to hit the walls. It turned out to be a relatively small chamber with no bottomless pit. There were several beams of light criss-crossing the dark. He looked over to where he could hear voices. The shadow of a man's head wearing a helmet was projected by Carter's lamp on to the wall behind. The head belonged to Oldroyd, who was again consulting with Alan Williams. Carter moved over to them. Williams was shaking his head again.

'There's nothing here, Inspector. It's a dead end; just damp and nasty.' Although he was an experienced caver, he looked genuinely uncomfortable to be in the system. Carter looked round and saw the rocks were glistening with water that was seeping from the walls. As he moved to get a closer look he stumbled and fell.

'Watch out!' called Williams. 'The water makes all the rocks unsteady down here; it's constantly eroding the joints, so watch you don't turn your ankle.'

'But that's the point, isn't it?' said Oldroyd. 'The rocks are unstable so that means they move; other passages could open up.'

'Yes, but no one's found one here.'

Oldroyd had brought a copy of Haverthwaite's poem. He looked at it again and his eyes narrowed in thought. He turned to the group, who were now all gathered in the chamber.

'Now, everyone, I want you to be absolutely quiet and listen.'

One or two of the cavers glanced at each other, looking bemused.

'Sir,' said Steph who was standing just behind Oldroyd, 'what are we listening for?'

Oldroyd made a gesture with his hands and shrugged his shoulders.

'Look, I'm not sure, but what I *am* sure about is that this poem,' he held up the paper, 'daft as it might seem, holds the key to this whole business. It was written by a man who explored this cave a long time ago and he talks about the possibility of a link to Jingling Pot.'

This was Oldroyd at his most charismatic. Everyone was listening now. Carter looked at his boss with admiration. He made you believe in what he was saying. It took a lot of guts and self-confidence; if he was wrong, he was going to look a fool.

'We know from the maps that at this point the Jingling Pot system is close to us. I believe the murderer, most likely with help, dragged the body of David Atkins down here, and that couldn't have been done over a great distance.' Oldroyd paused and looked round the chamber again.

'Everything points to here. So please, silence now, and listen.'

Everyone went dutifully quiet; some sat down, some stood in the centre of the chamber.

Carter listened. The silence was eerie. So rarely was quiet like this attainable in the modern world that it felt unnatural; some permanent background noise had become the norm. He moved quietly into the centre and paused. He could hear absolutely nothing. He looked at a rock face streaming with water. Could that tell him something? He moved across, stumbling again and being 'shushed'. He reached the rock and touched it. Cold water trickled over his finger. The rock was covered in limescale deposited over hundreds of years by the constantly oozing water. Carter looked up. The water seemed to be coming from a ledge about fifteen feet up. Could water talk? Maybe anything was possible in this strange world.

He put his ear near to the rock surface. At first nothing, but then, just faintly, he did hear something. It was as if the rock was carrying a sound. He heard a gentle rushing noise. It was far away, but surely it was the sound of running water.

'Sir, over here, I can hear something.'

Oldroyd came over. 'What, Andy?'

'Listen here, sir. Put your ear near to the rock. It sounds like water in the distance.'

Oldroyd followed the instruction.

'Yes, I can hear it.' Carter could hear the excitement in his voice.

Alan Williams had also come over. Oldroyd turned to him.

'What do you make of it?'

Williams listened, drew back from the rock and looked up.

'Yes, there is something, it's coming from up there.' He suddenly exploded into action. 'Bloody hell! Barry! Keith! Over here!'

The shouts echoed around the chamber.

'What is it?' asked Carter.

'It *is* the sound of running water. I'd say quite a powerful force, but not here. You get these peculiar effects with sound down underground; it seems to get carried distances through the rock.' He turned to Oldroyd, looking very animated. 'I think that old bloke was right. There must be a way through up there to Jingling Pot. What we can hear is the stream in that system.'

Oldroyd pulled out the map and looked at it with Williams.

'Correct me if I'm wrong, but we're about here, so a link would bring us to here.'

Williams considered the map.

'My God. You're right, Inspector: Sump Passage!'

Oldroyd turned to Carter and Steph with an expression mingling satisfaction and relief.

'Where the body was found.'

Williams and the others were scaling the rocks in front of them with the eagerness of those about to put their hands on the greatest prize in caving: not just a new passageway but a new link between two systems. They stopped at the ledge and, as the detectives watched, one of the cavers edged around into the shadows and disappeared. Suddenly they heard his voice.

'Alan, here!'

The others moved round to join him and they all disappeared from sight, leaving the detectives tense and waiting.

After a while, Williams reappeared and climbed down quickly, jumping the last few feet to the floor of the chamber.

'There's definitely a passage up there. It's round a twist in the rocks in the shadows, impossible to see from here, and someone's been up there before us. There are some anchor bolts in the rocks so they've been using ropes. They've put the bolts in in quite a clever way so that you'd never notice them from down here.'

Oldroyd nodded. 'That's probably from when they hauled the body up there.'

'They must have used a harness and they must have been strong, whoever they were. But the other thing is, the passage is nearly blocked off; you can't get through at the moment. It's what we call a boulder choke.'

'Yes, the murderers will have tried to block it off after they dumped the body as an extra precaution. I don't think that boulder choke happened naturally.'

'Right, well, I'm off back to the surface to get some tools. I think we can knock a little of the rock away and make a hole big enough to crawl through.'

Oldroyd, Steph and Andy sat on the floor of the chamber and waited. Above them, they could hear assorted bangings and scrapings as the cavers worked to create a way through.

Carter spoke. 'So the body was brought down through where we've walked, then through that tunnel up there into Jingling Pot?'

'Yes, this way the much shorter distance makes it possible. They could have done it in an hour or so.' Oldroyd looked around. 'But I'll bet it was still a terrible struggle to get the body up there.'

'Worth it though, sir,' said Steph. 'It's an unbelievable hiding place.'

'Yes,' said Carter, 'but aren't we forgetting something? The body was found in the middle of that Sump Passage. Geoff Whitaker walked into it. It wasn't exactly hidden, was it?'

'No,' replied Oldroyd, 'but I have a good idea how it came to be there. I'm just waiting to confirm my theory.'

'You like to keep us guessing, sir,' said Steph.

'Well, it's all part of the training; use your brains to work it out yourself. I'm not going to spoon-feed you. You've seen all the evidence I've seen.'

At that moment there was a call.

'OK, come on up here, we're through.'

After scrambling up the side of the chamber, Carter found himself squeezing through a small hole between a boulder and the rock wall. As he puffed and panted, he again lamented his lack of fitness.

At the other side, he stood next to Oldroyd and Steph.

'Be careful,' warned Oldroyd. 'Don't forget that phrase "stay afee'ard"; I'm convinced there's some danger here. "The Devil's Passage" he calls this, don't forget.'

Carter moved his helmet lamp around. They were in a narrow tunnel and would have to crawl forwards. What danger could there be? This wasn't *Lord of the Rings*; there couldn't be trolls, orcs or dragons. As he crawled along, Carter noticed that the sides of the tunnel were streaming with water; he was crawling and splashing through watery mud. Also, the roof and walls looked less solid, as if there could be a rock fall at any moment.

The sound of water was getting louder and louder. Water dripped on to Carter's head; the passage widened slightly and he slipped on the muddy stones and lurched to the left. He banged his head on a huge boulder and his lamp was dislodged.

'Shit!'

His hand scraped painfully on the rock and as he steadied himself, it slid down to the base of the boulder. With a shock, he felt something strange. Surely it was fabric, material? He adjusted his helmet and shone the light down. What he saw shocked even the experienced copper from the hard streets of inner-city London: it was a human arm partly covered with very frayed and tattered material. The arm itself was dried and wizened like an Egyptian mummy and it ended in a bony claw. It was sticking out from under the boulder.

'Sir! Down here!' Carter called out, but Oldroyd was further down with no possibility of turning round. Steph, however, was behind him.

'Look at this!'

She looked down and her eyes widened. 'God, what is it?'

'I don't know; it looks human.'

'Barely. It's like something out of *The Mummy*. This whole bloody place gives me the creeps. We'll have to move on and tell Sir when we catch up.' She moved on past him.

Carter took a last look at the arm and further down the side of the boulder he caught sight of something white that looked like part of a rib cage.

He went on, feeling shaken by the fall and by what he'd seen. But worse was to follow. Steph was crawling on just in front of him as the sound of the water grew louder. The others were now some distance ahead. The tunnel twisted and turned sharply and all the time the roaring sound was getting nearer, louder and more menacing. This section was even wetter; water was pouring from the roof and the floor was virtually a stream. Carter was crawling over muddy rocks and slopping through the wetness. He saw Steph grasp an outcrop of rock to pull herself along but the rock seemed to move away from her. She fell away to her left and out of view.

For a moment, Carter was too stunned to react. The whole thing had happened so quickly and was almost bizarrely comic, as if she had fallen off the side of a stage in a comedy sketch.

Then he heard her shouting frantically. 'Andy!'

He launched himself down the tunnel. When he reached the point where she'd disappeared, he saw that a section of the tunnel wall had collapsed, revealing a black hole. In the light from his helmet, Carter could see water dripping down, but could hear nothing landing anywhere. Steph was clinging on to a rock with her legs dangling into the blackness.

'OK, hang on, I'll get you.'

He looked into Steph's terrified face and, reaching over, he gripped her around the arm near the shoulder and heaved. Steph gave a muffled scream, but pushed herself up on the rock with the other arm. Stones disappeared into the hole as she was dragged to safety. She lay shivering with shock and Carter put his arms around her. They were silent until they heard a voice calling down the passage.

'We'd better move on; the boss'll wonder where we are. I'll go first this time.'

'OK. And thank you,' said Steph, giving him a warm smile.

They carried on down as the passage continued to twist. Carter turned a corner and almost crashed into Oldroyd and the three cavers who were crouched together on a ledge. The narrow tunnel had entered a much larger passage.

'Steady,' warned Oldroyd, 'or you'll fall into that.' He nodded over the ledge. Carter looked over and his lamp shone on a fearsome sight. A deep black torrent of water was swirling at terrifying speed through the larger passageway below. The deafening roar echoed around the chamber. Steph joined the group and gasped as she looked down.

'My God! You'd never get out of there alive.'

'You're right,' replied Williams. They were all virtually having to shout in order to be heard.

'But, sir, if your theory is right, isn't this the place the body was found?'

'Yes.'

'But how? This is an underground river; you couldn't walk through there at all, never mind find a body.'

'It's completely flooded now,' replied Oldroyd, 'but I think Alan here will confirm that normally this is a passage with a shallow stream running through it.'

Williams turned to Carter.

'What you've got to remember is that the water levels change a lot in these systems and they can change very quickly, that's why they're so dangerous. It's one of the greatest hazards we face. You never go down a deep system which is known to flood if rain is forecast. Once it starts to rain, the water can rise in minutes, flooding the system and cutting you off. The number of times we've had to rescue people trapped like that.' He shook his head. 'Some of them haven't made it and we've had to pull out the drowned bodies.'

'It was raining all last night and that's what caused this torrent. It's a good job too, otherwise we wouldn't have heard the water back in Winter's Gill,' said Oldroyd.

Steph turned to him.

'So, sir, you think the murderers brought the body down that passage we've come through and left it there somewhere?'

'Yes, as you said: what an amazing hiding place.'

'But in that case how did it get down there?' She pointed down into the flooded Sump Passage. 'Surely the body would have been left back up here; the whole point was to conceal it in a passage no one knew was there.'

Oldroyd nodded.

'Yes, you're right. Do you remember me saying, Andy, that I didn't think we were meant to find the body where we did?'

'Yes, sir, but who moved it then?'

Oldroyd gave a wry smile. 'Nobody moved it.'

'What? You've completely lost me, sir.' He shook his head. 'I remember you also saying that we're detectives who don't believe in magic.'

'We don't,' continued Oldroyd. 'I remember Tim Groves saying to me that the body got there somehow. And I realised we'd been assuming that some*one* moved it, but in fact some*thing* moved it.'

Steph exclaimed and pointed to the torrent.

'You mean the water! That's powerful enough to move a body.'

Carter frowned.

'Yes, but it's below our level, it's not high enough.'

'It's not high enough now, but remember how it rained and rained over the weekend before the body was found. The water level in here must have been even higher, and the force even stronger, and it would have got up to where we are now and into the tunnel we've come through.'

He glanced solemnly at the underground river as if acknowledging its awesome power.

'The body of David Atkins would have been picked up like a straw doll, swilled down into the main passage and then, of course, it got stuck further down where the passageway narrows. And that was where it was found when the water had subsided.

'It was water, the thing that moves and changes everything in these caves. There's no other force down here. It was listening to Schubert's Trout Quintet that gave me the idea. I could hear the water coming down the stream and suddenly I realised what the answer might be.'

There was silence except for the roar of the water.

'But sir . . .'

Oldroyd smiled. 'Go on, Andy, good on you, keep pressing me.'

'Well, how come the water was so low when Geoff Whitaker and his party came through not long after?'

'That's not difficult. The water subsides almost as quickly as it builds up. Once it's not being fed by heavy rains, it quickly returns to normal levels. Whitaker would have monitored the weather situation and after a couple of dry days he would have known that the water would have been down and that Sump Passage was passable.'

Steph turned to Oldroyd. 'Another thing, sir: you knew how the body had been moved down there, didn't you, before we came down here?'

'I was pretty sure. Remember the photographs taken by the CSIs? They were standing down there and some of the shots took in the whole passage up to the roof. Shine your helmet lamps up there.'

The beams of light moved up like searchlights raking the sky and they halted on the rocky roof of Sump Passage.

'What can you see up there?'

The roof was cut with fissures and stalactites hung from the dripping rocks. Then Carter's lamp illuminated something weird jammed into one of the cracks.

'Up there – it looks like a log, a piece of wood.'

'Yes,' said Oldroyd, 'and around it there's a brownish foam stuck on the roof. That means that the water can sometimes reach to the very top of the passage. At some time or other that bit of branch or something has been brought down and it's got caught up there.'

'Very good, Chief Inspector,' said Williams. 'You're right. It looks like this passage gets completely submerged when the weather is really wet. We knew this passage was impassable after heavy rain, but obviously no one's ever seen just how high the water rises. We've found things like that in the roofs of other tunnels, sometimes quite high ones: the volume of water which passes through must be tremendous.'

'Do you remember also,' continued Oldroyd, 'that John Baxter had been looking at the weather records on his computer just before he was murdered. I think he'd come to the same conclusion that we have and was checking on the rainfall in that crucial time before the body was discovered.'

'So he knew about this passage?'

'Most probably, and that was why he was killed. He must have rediscovered it with someone else and for some reason they'd kept quiet about it. He worked out how the body got into Sump Passage and so he knew who the murderer must be.'

'That other person.'

Oldroyd nodded.

Carter was silent in admiration.

'There's something back here you need to take a look at, sir,' said Steph.

Carter had been so mesmerised by the dark horror of the river and the unveiled truth of what had happened to Atkins that he'd forgotten what they'd discovered in the Devil's Passage and Steph's narrow escape.

Steph led the way back. Oldroyd and Williams examined the gruesome remains.

'Poor bastard,' said Williams, 'but he's been here a long time, I can tell you that.'

'How long, do you think?' asked Steph.

'Difficult to tell,' said Oldroyd. 'It's weird down here. Tim Groves told me that things don't rot in the same way in this cold and dark, they go like mummies, you know, all wizened up. There's not much left on him. He could have been here a very long time; over a hundred years even. We'll get a team down here to take this away for analysis. We may not be able to prove it, but I think we're looking at the body of either Alfred Walker or Harold Lazenby, and I dare say the body of the other one is nearby.'

'Who were they, sir?' asked Steph.

'Cavers from the time of Haverthwaite, the man who wrote that poem. Sir William Ingleby refers to them in his book. Walker and Lazenby were killed in the Devil's Passage and then Haverthwaite and his friends abandoned exploration of it.'

'Now we know why this was named the Devil's Passage,' said Williams. 'It's one of the most dangerous tunnels I've ever seen; it's streaming with water everywhere and that's made everything loose and liable to fall anytime. There's shafts underneath it too, by the look of that one that's just opened up; if you don't get crushed by rock falls you could fall to your death.'

'And with two bodies in here, there's no wonder the tradition came down that this place is haunted. Now that is interesting.' Oldroyd was crawling down the side of the boulder that had obviously crushed the unfortunate victim.

'Steady on, sir.' Carter was behind his boss, who was straining to reach something. After Steph's experience, he was terrified of another hole opening up in this treacherous place.

'I can see the remains of an old coat or something, Carter. I just want to feel around inside it and . . . Yes!' Oldroyd shouted in triumph and reversed out of the narrow crevice.

The triumphant smile was on his face again and he held something up.

'Hold that, Carter. I think we'll find it's very similar to this.'

He felt in his pocket and brought out the plastic bag he had been carrying around with him since the first day of the investigation. Inside was the rusty iron hook and Carter held up the other, almost a replica.

'Sir, you were right,' said Carter shaking his head.

'What are they?'

'Let's ask our friend here. What do you think these are?' He handed them across to Williams, who looked at them with renewed curiosity.

'You showed me one of these on the day we brought the body up. I haven't seen anything like it before, but from the look of it, and now we've seen all this, I'd say it's some kind of iron hook they were using.'

'You mean to tie their ropes to?' asked Carter.

'I think so. They seem to have been more advanced than I realised. Where did you say you found the other one?'

'It was found down in Sump Passage, not far from the body.' Oldroyd looked at the hook. 'I somehow felt it was significant. It set me thinking about cavers who might have been down here in the past and if this hook had been brought down with the body somehow.'

'So you think this was swilled down from this passage into the other one with the body?'

'Possibly, or it could have been accidentally knocked or kicked by the murderer. This one was probably found near to where the tunnels join. Also, I noticed in the photographs that there was a pile of stones on the floor of Sump Passage which looked as if they could have fallen recently: it was all consistent with the body being brought down from another passage, but I didn't know how until I saw the branch and foam on the roof. When the body came down it obviously brought some stones with it.'

Everyone fell silent as they continued to stare at the rushing water and contemplate the answer to the riddle of the body. But the other question remained: who had intended its final resting place to be the secret link between Winter's Gill Hole and Jingling Pot?

It was just after closing time at the Wharfedale Gift Shop. The last customer had bought a soft-toy sheep for her little daughter, who had cried petulantly for it all the time her mother was in the shop.

Helen Whitaker smiled falsely at the woman as she closed the door behind her and locked it. 'That's why the little brat behaves like she does, because you always buy her what she wants,' she muttered. She paused a moment and sighed as if gathering her strength to do something, then she walked past the little café area where the floor was being mopped by the tired-looking girl who was cleaner and waitress.

Anne was folding and rearranging a pile of thick woollen pullovers, which were not selling well during the summer season, when Helen came in and stood at the side of her.

'Hello, Helen. Sorry, were you talking to me just then?'

'What? Oh, no, just some silly woman. Look, Anne, do you have a minute? I really need to have a talk with you about something.'

Anne turned to her in surprise and saw her anxious expression.

'Helen? What is it? You look worried. Let's go and sit down. Natalie!' she called to the waitress. 'Just finish off and you can go. Lock the door behind you.'

She put down the pile of pullovers and led the way through to the living room where she'd been interviewed by Steph Johnson. Helen sat on one of the stylish sofas but fidgeted and looked agitated.

'It's about Geoff and Bill,' Helen said finally. 'You must know something about it, Anne. Why did Bill go missing and why did the police arrest him?'

'They suspect him of killing Dave because I had an affair with him.'

'But are you sure that's the only reason they arrested him?'

'I don't know; he wouldn't tell me and I can't be bothered to ask him about it. He's gone off before like that; I'm just glad he's back, and I don't believe he's a murderer.'

'But surely you must know that Geoff and Bill were up to something with Dave Atkins?'

'No, what?'

'Something to do with money. I've tried to find out but Geoff's been very careful to hide any paperwork and he's got a password on his computer. He told the police that he lent Atkins some money but I don't believe him. I think it was more serious and Bill was involved too.'

'What makes you think that?'

'I've overheard phone conversations and I'm sure he was talking to Bill after he'd gone off. I had a row with him but he still won't tell me anything.'

Anne laughed. 'That makes two of them who keep us in the dark.'

'But it's serious, Anne. I'm afraid that they've put a lot of money into one of Atkins's schemes and maybe they've lost it all.'

Anne looked thoughtful. Helen could be right. It would tie in with how Bill had been behaving. He could never face up to difficulties and his instinct was to run away. Perhaps she'd been careless. She and Bill had got into the habit of almost leading separate lives and she didn't ask many questions about what he was doing.

Helen continued, 'There's more than that. What if what they were doing was illegal? The police will have Atkins's computer now and all

267

his papers. They'll find out what was going on. It's only a matter of time before . . .' Tears were forming in her eyes and she took out a handkerchief.

'Wait,' said Anne. 'Calm down. We don't know that it was illegal.'

'Well, why all this jumpiness now that the police are around? And why won't they say anything? But Anne, it could be even worse.' She struggled to continue. 'What if . . . they killed him?'

Anne was shocked. She'd been honest with Steph Johnson when she'd said that she didn't believe that Bill would kill Dave Atkins out of jealousy. When he'd been arrested, she'd assumed the police still suspected him, but she hadn't really been concerned. She hadn't considered that there might be another motive. She needed to confront him at the first opportunity, but first she had to deal with Helen, who was clearly extremely worried.

'No, I'm sure they didn't; Geoff and Bill wouldn't kill anyone,' she said reassuringly, despite her doubts.

Helen, however, was becoming near hysterical and her voice got louder.

'And what about John Baxter? Did they kill him too? The police think the two crimes are linked.'

Anne went over to sit by her and put an arm round her shoulder.

'They probably are, but that doesn't mean Geoff and Bill were responsible, and why on earth would they kill John Baxter?'

Helen quietened as the panic subsided but she still sat nervously rubbing her hands together.

'I don't know. I don't know what to think. What are we going to do?'

Anne took a deep breath; there was clearly some crisis developing and she was going to meet it with determination. Part of her was glad that at last something was breaking the monotony into which her life had fallen.

'There's only one thing we can do. We're going to get the truth out of them. Leave it to me.'

∽

It was quiet now in Burnthwaite. The bright weather in the morning when the team had gone down Winter's Gill had turned overcast in the afternoon, but now the leaden sky was breaking up and the evening sun was creating a colourful sunset behind the fell.

There were few people around. The August fair traditionally marked the end of the high tourist season and soon the new term would begin at the village school. The village green, so recently full of noise and activity, was empty and silent. A gentle breeze lifted the leaves of the horse chestnut trees that lined the edge. The leaves were beginning to turn yellow at the edges, a sign that summer was moving into early autumn.

In the distance the sound of an engine gradually grew in volume and a solitary car appeared, moving down the narrow road between the limestone walls and then over the bridge into the village. It paused outside the Red Horse and the driver looked towards the pub with an expression of contempt before angrily engaging first gear and turning the car down the side of the building and into the car park.

Inside the pub, Trevor Booth was behind the bar as usual, but it was a little too early for Sam Cartwright to be perched on his bar stool. Later in the evening there was going to be a darts match between the Red Horse and a team from a pub in Grassington. Sam was one of the stars of the Red Horse team and was so keen that he stayed at home practising on a dartboard hung behind his kitchen door until just before the match started. As with many skilled darts players, it seemed that having a large girth and consuming numerous pints of beer generally enhanced his performance rather than impeded it. Other regulars were present and Trevor Booth was in conversation with a group at the bar that included Alan Williams and Simon Hardiman. The hot topic of conversation was the arrest of Bill Watson and his subsequent release.

'So he was living rough out in a cave up on Atterthwaite Scar?' Williams was as bemused as everyone else.

'So it seems; no wonder the police were suspicious, especially as he disappeared after Atkins was found,' said Booth.

'But they've let him go, haven't they?'

'Yeah, but he's not been around. Has anyone seen him?'

Numerous heads were shaken.

'Come on, though,' said Williams. 'Surely Bill couldn't have done anything like that. He's a bit useless with money, and I know Atkins was knocking Anne off at one time, but I can't see Bill killing anybody, even Atkins.'

'I agree,' said Hardiman, 'but who knows what someone might do through jealousy, you know? And I've heard he was in with Atkins on something to do with money.' He glanced at the landlord and lowered his voice. 'And Geoff Whitaker was in on it too.'

Booth was again quick to defend his chef.

'Hey come on; what're you saying? They were in it together and bumped Atkins off? I told the chief inspector that Geoff wouldn't . . .'

Williams butted in to taunt Booth. 'Oh, so you know something about this, do you, Trevor? I thought Geoff had been quiet recently. I put it down to the shock of finding the body, but maybe there's more to it.'

'Look . . .' Booth started to reply but was interrupted.

'Trevor, are you serving or what?'

They all turned to see that while they had been so engrossed in their speculations about the case, a newcomer had entered the bar. It was Sylvia Atkins.

'I've just driven over from Burnley and I'm ready for a drink, if anyone wants to serve me.'

'Sylvia!' was all Booth could say. They were all surprised at the sudden appearance of this apparition, a figure from the past who'd formerly been a regular in the Red Horse, but who'd never been back since she left Atkins and moved to Lancashire. She looked extremely grim-faced. The men at the bar looked sheepish. Sylvia had never been an easy person to relate to; it had always been difficult to talk to her when you and the rest of the village knew what her bragging, womanising husband was up to.

Sylvia seemed to know what they were thinking.

'It's all right, you don't need to worry. You can talk to me now. He's not screwing anybody; he's dead.'

No one said anything; they were too embarrassed by the bitter bluntness of the way she spoke.

'Sylvia,' repeated Booth weakly. 'What can I get you?'

'I'll have a half of lager, please.'

'OK.'

Everyone remained silent while Booth drew the half from the electric pump and Sylvia paid. There was something angry and dangerous about her and no one wished to engage her in conversation. She stood at one end of the bar and took a sip of the lager while the men stood in an awkward group at the other end.

'What brings you back to Burnthwaite, then?' asked Booth in an attempt at breaking the ice. She ignored him.

'Is Susan working tonight?' she asked.

'Yes, she's in the other bar. Why?'

'Right.'

She scooped up her glass and marched to the door.

'Sylvia!' called Booth, sensing something was about to happen, and he went quickly through the arch to the other bar.

Here everything was busy as it was the venue for the darts match and filling up with spectators. Susan was behind the bar facing a group of men and talking and laughing as usual.

Booth arrived to see Sylvia enter the bar, locate Susan and walk straight up to her. Susan didn't notice her at first.

'Susan Tinsley!' Sylvia shouted and the conversation at the bar immediately stopped, though there was still the mutter of talk going on further away among people who couldn't see what was happening.

Susan turned and drew back when she saw who it was.

'What do you want?' she said, her defiance tinged with fear.

'What've you been blabbing to t'police?' shouted Sylvia.

'It's none of your business.'

'It is. You've put them on to Stuart and me, said we were here the night Dave disappeared.'

The whole bar was now watching and listening. Booth felt he ought to do something, but couldn't decide what.

'Well, you were. I saw you in Stuart's car by the green.'

'So what if we were? Why can't you keep your mouth shut? I've had the police round calling me a liar and Stuart's opened his big mouth as well.'

'Why should I?' Susan started to cry. 'I don't know what you've made him do.'

Sylvia's anger reached its climax.

'You stupid bitch. Don't you dare go around saying I talked that puny husband of yours into killing Dave. He wouldn't be capable of it, and as for you . . .'

She swung the glass of lager she was still holding and flung the contents over Susan, who screamed.

'Sylvia!' shouted Booth yet again.

But before the shocked audience of this encounter could do anything, Sylvia had stormed out of the bar. Seconds later, her car pulled on to the road in front of a van, which braked and blared its horn. Sylvia's car shot over the bridge and up the hill out of Burnthwaite.

Eight

So say thi prayers and save thi soul,
And keep thi body from t'dark pot 'ole.

Two days after Bill Watson had returned home following his sojourn in the cave, his subsequent arrest and interview by the police, he was still tense and quiet and wouldn't do anything except lie in bed late and watch television. To Anne's angry and exasperated questions, he would say only that he'd gone off because he had some issues that had got to him and he needed to be on his own for a while. He'd kept going upstairs by himself to call someone on his mobile phone.

Anne entered the living room to find her husband sprawling on the sofa watching some inane early-evening game show. After her conversation with Helen Whitaker, she was in no mood for any more prevarication. Alice was at a friend's house for tea. It was time to have it out with him.

She marched over and turned off the television.

Watson looked up, puzzled. 'What're you doing?'

'We can't go on like this, Bill; I'm sick of it. Tell me what's going on.'

Watson just sighed.

'I know it's something you and Geoff Whitaker are involved in.'

Watson looked up sharply. 'How do you . . . ? What makes you think that?'

'He rang a few times while you were on your little holiday, but wouldn't say why. It's him you keep ringing, isn't it? Now tell me what it's about.'

Watson considered for a moment.

'Look, you're right, Geoff is involved, but I can't tell you what it's about. It's better if you don't know. Geoff and I will sort it out.'

He went to switch the television back on.

Anne frowned. She was having none of this. Her ex-lover is found dead, her husband disappears and the police come sniffing round. Her husband is arrested and questioned, comes back home and has the audacity to try to fob her off with patronising remarks. She was going to get to the bottom of this and the only way was to be direct.

'Don't patronise me. Did you and Geoff kill Dave?'

Watson swung round and gave her a filthy look. 'What? What the bloody hell did you say that for?' he shouted. 'Of course we didn't. Why would we? Geoff found the body and I went down to bring it out, didn't I?'

Anne remained firm and cool.

'That could have been a useful cover.'

'For what?'

'For the fact that you did him in in the first place. Look, I don't know exactly what's going on with Geoff, but Dave was in it as well, wasn't he? I know something was going on with money.'

He looked at her suspiciously. 'How do you know? Have you been going through my stuff?'

'Why not? You disappear without a word. Alice is really upset. Why shouldn't I find out what it's all about? You've put a password on your login on the computer, so there was nothing I could find there, but you printed out some emails and you left one or two in the bin. They were from Dave and they were about some investments or something.'

Watson murmured 'Shit' to himself and sat down on the sofa again, frowning.

Anne continued her onslaught. 'That's not the only thing, is it? There's a history there after I had that affair with Dave. That's all over, but I don't really know how you feel. Are you still the jealous husband? That would give you another reason to kill him.'

She sat down herself, exhausted with the effort of getting all this off her chest.

Bill looked at her sombrely, but also with some admiration. 'You have been doing some searching and thinking haven't you?'

'I've had plenty of time, haven't I, while you were in your cave,' she said contemptuously. 'I couldn't say anything while Alice was here, but I'm not sure I like some of the possible conclusions I've come to.'

For the first time she showed some weakness and looked at him pleadingly.

'In fact, they scare me, Bill.'

Watson shook his head and sighed.

'OK. Well, you're not going to like this, but you've asked for it.'

Steph Johnson was at her computer again. Ever since the start of the investigation something had been nagging away in the back of her mind that she'd been struggling to recall. Her experience in the cave had brought it closer to the surface, but it was still irritatingly just beyond her grasp. She was more than ever convinced that it would help the investigation. The only way was to keep searching the archives of the local papers.

She was fairly sure it had been early in the summer, about three years ago. She began to search methodically, but without a clear idea of what she was looking for. She slogged her way through accounts of new schools being built, fires in fish-and-chip shops and reports of agricultural shows until she felt dizzy. Then she had an idea. She started searching under a different phrase and, before long, she came to the front page of an edition of two and a half years before. Suddenly there it was. A smile of satisfaction and relief came to her face as she read the headline. She was right.

The final case meeting took place in Oldroyd's office that evening.

Carter had at last received the final report from the IT people.

'They've cracked the code, sir, so we know who was in with Atkins on the illegal financial stuff. It makes interesting reading.'

Oldroyd had been scanning the report as Carter spoke.

'It does indeed, Andy, and it ties in with what I was beginning to think about that aspect of the case.'

Steph presented a printout of the newspaper article she'd found.

'I don't know how important this is, sir, but it's the thing I've been trying to remember for some time.'

Oldroyd nodded his head as he read it. 'Brilliant work,' he said.

Steph was pleased but a little unsure. 'Thanks, sir. You think it's really important, then?'

'I do indeed. In fact, I think we'll find that this is the final piece of the puzzle.' He looked with satisfaction at his two detective sergeants.

'Get a good night's sleep tonight because we're going to be busy tomorrow. It's time we made some arrests.'

That night, Stuart Tinsley had just arrived home from work exhausted after another day at Fell Farm. Fred Clark had been particularly demanding and he was beginning to wonder how long he could go on working for the bloody slave driver. He was slumped on the sofa with a can of lager when there was a knock at the door. To his surprise, it was Susan.

'Hi,' she said.

There was an awkward silence.

'You'd better come in.'

She sat in a chair opposite him. She looked tired and nervous.

'Do you want anything to drink?'

'No, I'm fine.' There was an awkward pause. She seemed to be summoning up her courage to say something. She was nervously playing with her wedding ring and couldn't look him in the face.

'I . . . I've come to say I'm sorry. I . . . I want to come home.'

Tinsley was unable to speak. She looked at him for the first time, but timorously, as if she feared his reaction.

'Do you want me to come back?'

'I never wanted you to go.'

She looked away again.

'I know, but I want to come back now.'

'I see.'

'Knowing you were with Sylvia, it made me feel awful. I realised . . .' She started to cry a little, then controlled herself.

Tinsley looked at her for a while but was again lost for words. Instead of speaking, he went over and kissed her gently on the top of her head. She reached out and grasped his arm, then started to cry again.

'There's just two things,' she said between sobs. 'Can we leave this village? I can't stand it here any more.'

He nodded and led her over to sit with him on the sofa.

'We'll go to Skipton and I'll get another job. I don't want to stay here either after all this, and I've had enough of Clark. What's the other thing?'

'I've already made an appointment for us at the fertility clinic. I want to have a baby.'

'Are you sure?'

'Yes, I want us to be a family.'

Tinsley held her tight. He was never going to lose her again.

Thursday dawned fine for the last day of the investigation, which started in an unexpected way for Inspector Craven. He was at Skipton police station, and about to leave for Burnthwaite as part of the operation organised by Oldroyd, when he was called to the front desk. He was surprised to see Anne and Bill Watson and Helen and Geoff Whitaker. The two women were looking serious but composed and the two men rather sheepish. Craven saw immediately what was about to happen.

'These two have come to turn themselves in, Inspector,' said the desk sergeant.

'I see, and what are you turning yourselves in for?'

The two men looked at each other and then Bill Watson spoke.

'We were involved with Dave Atkins and his property schemes. We knew they were illegal. We put a lot in and we lost it. The bastard told us that our money was safe, but it wasn't.'

He glanced at the angry face of his wife but she looked away.

'I'm sure you know all this already; you'll have been looking at Atkins's computer and his bank account and stuff.'

'Yes, quite right,' replied Craven who had had a full briefing on this from Carter. Atkins had probably never made an honest penny in his life, but more fool these two for getting involved with him.

'It looks as if you've saved me a job today. By the way, if my memory serves me right, that's the second time you've called Atkins a bastard in my presence.'

Watson looked puzzled.

'At the entrance to Jingling Pot – you were there with the others who brought out his body. And you shouted it out. I don't forget things like that in an investigation like this.'

'But Inspector,' said Geoff Whitaker in an urgent and pleading manner, 'we didn't kill him, and we didn't kill John Baxter. When I found the body and he'd obviously been murdered, we knew you'd find out about us and we thought you might think we'd done it; we sort of panicked and didn't know what to do. Bill ran off and hid.'

'I thought you might also suspect me because of what happened with Anne and Atkins. I managed not to give much away when they arrested me,' said Watson. 'But they,' he nodded to the two women, 'persuaded us that it was only a matter of time before you were on to us, so here we are. But we didn't kill him,' he repeated.

'I know you didn't,' replied Craven. He turned to the sergeant. 'Take them in and get them in a car to Harrogate. DCI Oldroyd will want to speak to them later.'

With that, and excusing himself politely to the two women, he left the station, giving the impression that he had much more urgent matters to consider.

Anne and Helen sat in Anne's car in the police station car park, rather stunned by what had happened, but also quite relieved now that it was over.

'It could have been worse, Helen; at least they didn't kill anyone.'

'Yes, they've just ruined us, that's all.'

Bill Watson had borrowed heavily to put money into Atkins's schemes and had lost everything. Geoff Whitaker had lost just about all the family savings and would also now lose his job if he received a prison sentence. Both men had resisted confessing to the police, but their wives, particularly Anne, had pointed out that as the police now had Atkins's computer, not doing so was pointless. The only way they could claim any mitigation or hope for leniency was to turn themselves in and plead guilty. Reluctantly, they'd got into the car and Anne had driven to Skipton.

'What will you do now?' asked Helen.

'I'll have to sell the shop, of course, to raise the money to pay off Bill's debts. I'm sorry about your job. Then I'm going to get out of Burnthwaite and back to the city. Can you imagine what it would be like here now? The gossip! The nudges and pointing: "There's that Anne Watson whose husband's inside; bet she knew more about it than she lets on, and she had it off with that bloke who was murdered." It would be impossible. Anyway, country life's not for me. How about you?'

'We'll manage somehow. My mum and dad'll help me. I'll have to leave Burnthwaite too; get a job in a hospital somewhere. I still can't believe he would do this to me and the kids; gamble our money away like that.'

'Dave Atkins could be very persuasive.'

'But Geoff's a compulsive gambler and I thought he was cured; apparently not. He was an easy target for Atkins.'

'Yes.'

'I still can't believe they would get involved with that man. Geoff knew about what happened with Richard and you'd had an affair with Atkins and still both of them were persuaded by a man they'd no reason to like.'

'It's greed. Some people will always be suckers for someone who comes along and promises a fast buck, even if it's someone they don't like or trust; their judgement seems to go. Anyway, come on, we'll go over to Grassington and into the King's Arms for a drink. At least we know the worst now and we'll recover. I know we will.'

She put her hand on Helen's arm reassuringly. Their partnership in this adversity had made them closer as friends.

'OK,' said Helen, and smiled for the first time that day.

❦

Inspector Craven was driving at the head of a fleet of police cars towards Burnthwaite. He felt quietly confident that the operation would go smoothly; he always had the greatest confidence in Oldroyd who, with his two detective sergeants, was driving over from Harrogate. They were all to converge on the unsuspecting Dales village.

As he drove along, Craven thought about similar surprise operations like this he had worked with the chief inspector, such as the time he and Oldroyd had hidden in a Dales barn covered in straw in order to surprise a gang using the barn to conceal their stolen loot. There was never a dull moment when you worked with DCI Oldroyd, he mused, as the police cars entered Burnthwaite. They pulled up sharply near Atkins's house and a number of officers piled quickly out of the cars and ran down the lane. Craven jogged down after them. When he got to the bottom, a burly officer was banging on the door next to Atkins's deserted residence.

'Open the door; police officers.'

There was no response so the officer rapped again. He shouted, 'There are police officers at the back too. Do not try to escape. Open the door.'

Muffled shouts came from inside and then the door opened. Carol Anderson stood looking defiant with Gary peering sheepishly at the officers from behind her.

'What the hell's this about?' she demanded. 'It's not about Dave Atkins again, is it? We didn't kill the poor bugger; we've told you all we know.'

'Carol Anderson?' replied a police sergeant with a stern, unyielding face. 'We have a warrant to search these premises. Just let us in, it will be much less trouble for us all.'

'Search for what?' was the defiant reply. 'What do you think we've got here?'

'We can't discuss it on the doorstep; we need to come in.'

With this the sergeant, followed by two constables, barged into the house.

'Bloody hell!'

Craven remained in the hall while the couple exchanged angry glances.

'It was your bloody idea, was this.'

'Shut up, you bloody little coward! You were keen enough, but you didn't have the guts without me.'

'No point falling out about it,' said Craven.

More officers had entered from the back door and soon there was the sound of searching in every room in the house. Craven ushered the couple back down the hall and into the gaudy living room. They had only just arrived when there was a call from upstairs.

'Sir, I think we've found it.'

'Good, that was quick work. Let's have a look, bring it down here.'

An officer came quickly down the stairs. He was wearing gloves and carrying a plastic bag. Craven looked inside and smiled.

'I thought as much: cocaine.' He took the bag and whistled as he felt the weight. 'Well, quite a little pile you've got stashed away here. Were you going to use it all yourself or sell it, or maybe a bit of both?'

There was no reply from the sullen couple.

'Clearly, I'm going to arrest you for possessing this. It will help if you answer my questions truthfully. Did you acquire this from David Atkins's house?'

'Yes.' Gary decided to cooperate. 'It was one of his many sidelines. He did a bit of drug dealing.'

'Did you help him?'

'No,' replied Carol firmly. 'But we knew he had the stuff because . . .' she stopped.

'Because occasionally you got some from him.' Craven finished the sentence for her.

'How did you know about this, anyway?' snapped Carol.

'We've known for a while that someone was peddling drugs in this area. Then we found out about Atkins and his various nefarious activities.'

'Ne-what?' said Gary.

'Bad,' Craven clarified. 'We suspected he might have some of this hidden and that someone might lead us to it.'

He looked from one to the other. 'So I really need to thank you both for breaking into the house and bringing this out for us.'

'How did you know?'

'We've been watching the house ever since the body was found, partly to see if anyone we suspected of the murder turned up. But we just got two neighbours with a penchant for illegal substances.'

'Pon-what?'

'Shut up!' shouted Carol.

'So we watched you go in and come out with a bag. We were pretty sure what was in it. My officer also saw Sam Cartwright make an appearance that night. Was he in this with you?'

'Naw, he was just trying to find some money.'

'We thought as much. I take it he didn't find any?'

'He only came to the door and gave up when he saw us there.' Gary had no desire to get Cartwright into trouble just for trying to take some money that really belonged to him anyway.

'There's quite a lot of burgling goes on around here, isn't there?' continued Craven. 'We've just arrested a gentleman from Skipton who made quite a living out of driving out to Dales villages and breaking into houses and shops. Terrorised people with a stocking over his head, but ran off at the first sign of trouble.'

Carol had had enough of Craven's breeziness.

'OK, really clever; I'm dead impressed. Pity you're not clever enough to find who murdered Dave and John Baxter.'

'Oh, I wouldn't be so sure about that,' replied Craven as he led them out of the house and into one of the waiting police cars. 'I think we'll see some interesting developments shortly.'

Oldroyd, Carter and Johnson were driving through Burnthwaite just as Craven was talking to Gary and Carol. They were followed closely by another police car containing three detective constables.

The cars passed through the village and up the hill towards Garthwaite Hall. Carter was driving the lead car.

'How long have you suspected the Hardimans, sir?' he said to Oldroyd.

'From the beginning,' replied Oldroyd. There was no attempt to be superior or boastful; it was purely a factual statement.

'There was something too calm and organised about their manner and their responses, as if they'd worked it all out and were playing their parts. I put them in a terrible situation, of course, bringing the news that Atkins's body had been found; they weren't expecting that. I have to hand it to them, they put on a great show, but an old hand like me could sense the strain.' He paused as the cars entered the drive and the old house came into view.

'I remember when I left seeing them together in the rear-view mirror, holding hands. They gave the impression of having faced some great difficulty together.'

'It's amazing how your body language conveys so much,' said Steph from the back seat.

'And you get used to picking it up. I knew that Anne Watson was hiding something, no matter how cool and sophisticated she tried to appear.'

'So it was that book about the caves that really made you suspicious, sir?' asked Carter.

'Yes. It seemed to me, from the first day when we had all the peculiar details about the body and where it was found, that there had to be another entrance into that system, one that the modern cavers didn't know about.'

'So you went to Garthwaite Hall pretending to do some research.'

'No, I actually was doing some research. I was told Simon Hardiman might be able to tell me what that piece of iron was that was found by the body. It was clear he was known to be a bit of an expert on the history of the caves and that aroused my interest, if not my suspicion. Then he took me into his office to get me a map of the system and I saw a number of old volumes on his shelves, old caving books.'

'And you saw the same book as the one you got from that bloke in Skipton?'

'Yes, although I didn't realise it until Ramsden took that book from the shelf and immediately I knew I'd seen it before. They're probably the only two volumes in existence outside libraries. The author, William Ingleby, lived at Garthwaite Hall. I would imagine the Hardimans inherited that copy along with a lot of other dusty old volumes when they bought the place. That was what you'd call pretty convincing circumstantial evidence. I knew there was a strong possibility that the Hardimans knew about the Devil's Passage. OK, we're here.'

The police cars had drawn up at the faded entrance to Garthwaite Hall. As the engines stopped, there was silence. Oldroyd got out, gazed sombrely at the edifice and then walked quickly up the wide stone steps, followed by the others.

Before he could ring the bell there was the sound of shouting inside and then a scream. A door slammed at the rear of the house.

'Round the back, quick.' Oldroyd gestured to a couple of the DCs, who ran off down the side of the building. They had just reached the drive to the rear of the house when a van came tearing round the corner, scattered the DCs, and shot off down towards the entrance gate. Oldroyd reacted quickly.

'That's Hardiman; Andy, take one of the cars and get after him.'

Calling to one of the DCs to join him, Carter leaped into the rear car, started it up and swerved to start the pursuit.

'Be careful!' shouted Steph. She knew this was not professional, but Oldroyd ignored it and turned back to the house.

'They obviously know the game's up. No point standing on ceremony.'

He went back up to the door and tried the handle. The door swung open.

Carter and DC Robinson struggled to get their seat belts on as the police car tore down the drive leaving a cloud of dust behind. Carter had done training in vehicle pursuit and quite relished the challenge. He was less clear about what they would do if they managed to catch up with Hardiman. This was a dangerous man.

'He turned left out of the drive, Sarge,' said the DC.

'Yes, I saw him. Any idea where he might be heading?'

'Not a clue, Sarge.'

The van had a reasonably good start, but Carter was confident he could catch it up. He turned left and accelerated up the road.

'Where does this go?'

'Over to Ribblesdale, I think. It goes right over the moors and comes out at Selside.'

'What's that?'

'It's just a little village on the road between Settle and Ribblehead.'

'Right.' Carter turned on the sirens and the flashing lights and settled in for a long pursuit.

Oldroyd, Steph and DC Carol Jones burst into the entrance hall just as Caroline Hardiman emerged sobbing from the rear of the house. Her face was distorted with anguish. When she saw Oldroyd, she called to him in desperation.

'Inspector, oh my God! Inspector, stop him, please! He'll do something to himself.'

'My detective sergeant's gone after him.'

Oldroyd turned to Steph and DC Jones.

'Take her in there.'

The two detectives, supporting the distraught figure at either side, led her into the shabby living room and sat down on either side of her on the big sofa. Oldroyd waited a long time for her to calm down.

'You know why we're here?' he eventually said, gently.

She nodded.

'I have to arrest you for the murders of David Atkins and John Baxter.'

She nodded again, but seemed incapable of speech. She was shaking badly.

'Would you like a drink?'

'No, thank you.' She managed the words between sobs.

'You do not have to say anything but it may harm your defence if you do not mention, when questioned, something which you later rely on in court. Anything you do say may be given in evidence. Do you understand?'

She nodded, and finally the sobs stopped and she looked up at Oldroyd, realising that he wasn't hostile to her; just a man doing his job. She took a deep breath and, for a moment, a look of relief passed across her face. She was glad to be letting go of this guilty secret at last.

'It was all a terrible mistake. I let Simon talk me into it, but I'm not blaming him. I played my part.'

'Was it to do with this?'

Steph produced a printout of a newspaper cutting. The date was some two and a half years before:

Narrow Escape for Schoolgirls

Two schoolgirls from Manchester narrowly escaped being swept away by floodwaters on the River Ribble yesterday.

The girls were walking up the river on a stretch which is normally shallow, when a sudden increase in water levels caused them to lose their footing and fall. They were carried downstream a hundred yards before adults leading the party were able to pull them to safety.

The girls were on an Outdoor Pursuits holiday at Garthwaite Hall Outdoor Pursuits Centre. The owner of the centre, Mr Simon Hardiman said, 'It was a freak accident; we have taken lots of parties of schoolchildren into the river at that point. We call it river walking. The kids love it. It's usually very shallow. Clearly, we will have to review our policies and practices.'

The girls were suffering from shock, but were otherwise unharmed. They have returned home to Manchester.

Caroline glanced at the article and a spasm of anger crossed her face.

'Yes, it was.'

'Dave Atkins was blackmailing you about something, wasn't he?' asked Oldroyd.

She nodded and pointed to the article. 'It happened while he was working for us. We were terrified of the bad publicity, how it might damage our business, but we managed to contain it. The girls weren't injured, so there was nothing the press could get their teeth into. We even changed the name of our centre to avoid the link in people's minds with the incident.'

Steph turned to Oldroyd.

'That's why it took me so long to find this. I kept searching under Wharfedale Outdoor Pursuits, but the name at that time was Garthwaite Hall Outdoor Pursuits.'

Caroline's eyes were wet, her face strained beyond recognition. She twisted a handkerchief as she struggled to tell the story.

'You're right, and then . . .' She broke down into tears again. 'If it hadn't been for that bastard everything would have been all right.'

Oldroyd waited for her to regain some control. 'What did he do?'

'At the time we had two students working for us, you know, just temporarily. They were out on that expedition with the school party. They helped to drag the girls out by the river only . . .' She paused to blow her nose. 'One of them wasn't properly qualified. Oh my God!' She broke down again. 'It was so unfair. I swear to you it was just an oversight. There's this supervisory qualification and he only had Level 1. To go out with a party of children like that you have to have Level 2.'

'And Atkins found out?'

'Yes. I don't know whether the student told him at the pub or something but he went into the office and pulled out the staff records. Then he confronted us with it.'

'He threatened to report it.'

'Yes, said he'd go to the press. What could we do? The press would have loved that: "Girls in river supervised by unqualified student". We'd have been finished overnight, no one would have come here; our dream would have been ruined.' Her face crumpled again. 'Now it's ruined anyway.'

～

Carter gripped the steering wheel and kept his foot down on the throttle. They were chasing the van on a narrow road that climbed over the fell. There were no walls or hedges and occasionally they rattled over a cattle grid.

'He's driving like a lunatic,' said DC Robinson as there was a blare of horns and the van, which was not far ahead of them now, forced a car coming in the opposite direction off the road.

'He's driving like a man who doesn't care if he lives or not,' replied Carter grimly.

The road dipped down again with drystone walls at either side. It twisted and turned down the fell, approaching vivid green fields grazed by cows as the wide expanse of Ingleborough, dark and majestic against a distant bank of cloud, came into sight.

They were right behind the van now. Carter banged his fist repeatedly on the horn. Suddenly they went under a bridge, turned a corner and were at a T-junction with a main road. The van hardly slowed but screeched and swerved out and turned right just in front of a lorry, which braked and skidded, the horn sounding angrily. The collision just avoided, lorry and van continued, leaving the police car behind.

'Bugger it!' shouted Carter, blasting the horn again. Valuable seconds were wasted until he managed to overtake.

The van had drawn ahead but Carter was making progress again as they entered a small cluster of old limestone buildings. The name 'Selside' on a wooden board was attached to a gable end. Luckily, there was no one walking on the narrow road as the van hurtled to the left with a screech of tyres followed by the police car, siren still blaring. The van bounced up a track for several hundred yards and then stopped. The two policemen saw Simon Hardiman jump out, climb over a gate and run up a path which crossed a field. Carter switched off the engine and was out of the car almost before it came to a halt.

He ran to the gate and shouted, 'Mr Hardiman, stop; you can't escape.'

But it was futile. There was a terrible determination about the figure running across the field. It seemed to be heading towards an isolated clump of trees on the lower slopes of the fell.

'Where's he going? What's over there where those trees are?'

'It's Alum Pot, Sarge.'

'What's that?'

'It's a nasty deep pothole, a two hundred and fifty foot drop, one of the deepest in the Dales.' DC Robinson looked at Carter.

'If he's thinking of doing himself in there's no better place to do it.' Carter responded by climbing the gate.

'We'd better get after him then.'

'What did Atkins want from you?'

Caroline had calmed down again. 'Not much to begin with. An occasional payment of a few hundred pounds; but then about six months ago he started to demand bigger sums, said he'd lost money on some property investments.'

'We know all about that,' said Oldroyd. 'It was all illegal stuff.'

'We just couldn't pay. We're struggling enough as it is, but he wouldn't listen; kept saying this place was a little gold mine and we must have plenty stashed away.'

'We were desperate, but particularly Simon. He just couldn't bear to go back to the city, lose this place.'

She was becoming agitated again.

'My detective sergeant is following him,' repeated Oldroyd.

DC Jones brought a glass of water. Caroline sipped at it before continuing.

'One day Simon came back from one of his potholing expeditions with John Baxter. He was very excited; said he'd been reading an old book he'd found here in the hall about a lost passage from Winter's

Gill Hole to the Jingling Pot system. They'd found the passage; it was narrow and dangerous but Simon thought it would be a great place to hide a body. He'd agreed with John that they wouldn't announce their find until the next meeting of the cave group – you know, to make it more dramatic. He looked at me strangely and I knew straight away what was on his mind.'

'It was his idea.'

'Yes, but I agreed. I know it was wrong but we were so harassed by this . . . this terrible man. We'd got to the point where we'd do anything to get rid of him. He was ruining our lives.' She paused as the anger welled up in her.

'So we made up a plan together. I got Atkins to come up to the hall saying I wanted to ask him about something and I came on to him, pretended I fancied him and was willing to have an affair, but we'd have to be careful.'

'He didn't suspect anything?'

'No, of course not; he was a womaniser, thought he was God's gift. It was too flattering to his pathetic ego. This particular night I agreed to meet him in Burnthwaite, near the Red Horse.'

Oldroyd glanced at Steph and nodded. Sam Cartwright was right: he had seen her waiting near the pub.

'I told him that Simon was away. I parked the van down a back lane; told Atkins this was so we wouldn't be seen. Simon was hiding nearby; when we got to the van he came up behind Atkins and smashed him over the head with a hammer.' She grimaced as she recalled the scene.

'It sounds terrible, but all I felt was relief that our tormenter was gone. I couldn't feel sorry for him.'

'What did you do next?'

'Loaded the body into the van and drove back here. It was completely dark by then. We waited until the early hours, then got our caving gear on and drove to Winter's Gill. I kept asking Simon why we had to hide the body down there; why we couldn't bury it. He said bodies always turned up. There was even a bloke who threw a body into a lake in the Lake District but it was found over twenty years later. He said no one would ever find it down there, though. Turned out he was wrong.'

'Go on,' encouraged Oldroyd.

'It was pitch black. We carried the body over to the Winter's Gill entrance and dragged it down the cave and into that Devil's Passage. We had a difficult job getting it up from the chamber, but Simon's tremendously strong and he rigged up a harness using anchor bolts. We were absolutely exhausted when we got back. He wanted to take the body to the far end so that he could get to it from the Jingling Pot side if he needed to; check it was still there, I suppose.'

It was a familiar pattern, thought Oldroyd: the murderer hides the body but feels a compulsion to return to check it. And what a strange and gruesome irony that they were unaware that other bodies were hidden there, bodies from the distant past.

'That was another mistake, if we'd left it further towards the Winter's Gill end, the water might not have moved it out into Sump Passage. After you'd gone that day we worked out that it must have been the water that moved it.'

'Wasn't he worried that John Baxter would go back to the Devil's Passage?'

'His plan was to start a rock fall and block the entrance at the Winter's Gill end, then tell John he'd been back but the entrance was blocked. It all went smoothly until you came that day and told us the body had been discovered. Simon had been out in Skipton, otherwise he might have been called out to bring the body up. I don't know how he would have managed that.'

Oldroyd reflected on how those caves were always capable of springing surprises, even on the experts. He said, 'I knew it was a shock when I told you. You tried hard but I'm afraid I wasn't fooled. You never asked me how Atkins was killed because, of course, you knew.'

Caroline laughed harshly. 'And I thought we did well to conceal it all.'

Oldroyd continued, 'After that you soon realised that you had a problem with John Baxter, the only other person who knew about the Devil's Passage.'

Caroline bowed her head. 'We had a terrible row about it. I said we couldn't kill an innocent man and it was all Simon's fault for hiding the body there. He said, what else could we do? We'd lose everything . . . I . . . just gave in in the end, but I refused to have anything to do with it. Simon went round and killed John himself. It didn't make us feel any better, of course, because we saw your press conference and we weren't sure what John had said to you. Simon went down a few times to the Red Horse to see if he could find out anything from the locals.'

'Even if the body hadn't appeared, didn't he think people would want to open the passageway up again, like we've done, once they knew about it?'

She looked at Oldroyd.

'He never mentioned it but now you've said that, I think he must have been planning to kill John anyway to make sure no one else ever knew about the passage. He was waiting for a good time to tell me because he knew I wouldn't approve. When the body turned up, it just brought everything forward and he had to kill him quickly.'

She put her head in her hands.

'Why did I ever agree to it? I wasn't thinking clearly.'

She looked up.

'That was why we didn't deserve to get away with it: killing John Baxter. I still don't feel sorry about Atkins, but John Baxter is different.'

Carter ran up the path towards the clump of trees but he had no chance of catching the fit Simon Hardiman. DC Robinson was close behind.

They reached a wall surrounding the trees and Carter began to climb over a stile.

'Careful, Sarge, it's steep, a sheer drop.'

Both detectives climbed over and then stopped, panting for breath. Carter looked around. He couldn't see anything beyond the foliage but, as he listened, there was the tinkling sound of water falling away in a manner that was somehow sinister. A preternatural instinct sent a shiver through him. Some menacing change in the acoustic gave him an apprehension of a void, a terrible danger that turned his legs weak. He crouched down and grasped a branch on the nearest tree.

'Did you see where he went?' He found he was whispering to DC Robinson.

'No, Sarge. I think we'll just have to walk around the edge.'

Carter got up and walked gingerly along a narrow path that wound between some trees. Then he saw it. The jolt made his legs collapse again and he grabbed for another branch. The ground fell away quickly into an appalling black void, a horrifying, wide chasm to which no bottom was visible. At one end, a small stream flowed to the edge and disappeared down into drops and spray. He felt a powerful desire to lean over and look down, but DC Robinson put a firm hand on his shoulder.

'Keep back, Sarge.' He looked down himself from his safe position. 'Mesmerising. You want to lean over and look into it; it's deadly. My dad was a sailor. He said some people look over the side of the ship at the sea so long, they feel a compulsion to jump in and sometimes they do.'

Carter dragged his gaze away and looked up at the grassy fell rising away from them for a few moments. Then he allowed himself to look just at the edge again. Ferns were growing on the damp limestone and a bird fluttered across the chasm, its gift of flight totally removing the terror of the drop.

Suddenly DC Robinson pointed across.

'He's there, Sarge!'

Carter saw a grassy bank at the other side. It sloped down steeply to the very edge of the chasm. Near the bottom was the figure of a man lying on the bank, head facing away from the drop.

'Let's get over there,' said Carter.

They edged their way carefully round, glancing frequently at the figure, which remained still.

Eventually they were standing at the top of the bank, several feet directly above Hardiman. Carter crouched down again and leaned forward.

'Mr Hardiman!' he called out. 'Mr Hardiman, can you hear me?'

The figure turned its head. 'Leave me!'

Carter lay flat on the bank and inched further down head first towards Hardiman.

'Watch it, Sarge!' Robinson clutched Carter's foot.

'Mr Hardiman,' Carter called again. The two men were facing each other twelve feet apart. It was close enough for Carter to see an expression of the most intense anguish on the other man's face.

'I told you, go. You can't do anything. I'm not trying to escape.'

'Mr Hardiman, don't do it. Atkins had some hold over you, didn't he? Was it something to do with those schoolgirls who were swept down the river? Come back with us. Put your case to the court.'

'What case? I've killed two men; one was innocent. I'd go down for the rest of my life.'

Carter desperately tried to think of something else to say. The man was inches away from plunging over the edge.

'What about your wife?'

'She's not to blame. I talked her into it. It's my responsibility.' He paused and shook his head. 'We tried hard but it was all against us.' He looked up at Carter. 'I'm sorry about John Baxter, but I'm not sorry about that bastard Atkins. May he rot in hell for all the lives he's ruined!'

Carter could see that he was crying.

'Tell Caroline I love her. Tell the court it was my fault, do you hear? It was my plan and my mistakes.'

'Sir, you don't want to die like this.'

To Carter's horror, Hardiman struggled to his feet. He was standing with his back to Alum Pot on the very edge. He laughed.

'Oh, but I do,' he said and made a strange gesture with his hands. 'Look at these fells, the wild beauty of it all. I can't go to prison; I'd go mad cooped up in a cell. I can't leave these hills and these caves; I'd rather die in them.'

As Carter clung on to the bank, time seemed to slow down. Hardiman stood up straight and fell backwards. The body appeared to fall in slow motion, silently away from Carter, diminishing in size until it disappeared from view. An agonisingly long time seemed to pass before a muffled thump was heard far below.

Carter felt dizzy and Robinson had to help him back up to the top of the bank.

He found it impossible to say anything for several minutes. Finally, he looked at Robinson.

'Did you hear what he said?'

'Yes. To be honest, I can understand it.'

Carter stared again at the fells. The eerie silence that had fallen was broken by the poignant bubbling cry of a curlew. Large white clouds drifted over, creating patches of light and shade on the limestone pavements leading over to Gaping Ghyll. He turned to Robinson.

'So can I.'

Steph and DC Jones were leading Caroline Hardiman out of Garthwaite Hall. Oldroyd was waiting for Carter to ring.

'You won't arrest Simon,' she said. 'He couldn't stand being in prison.' She seemed to accept it now.

'What did he say?'

She stopped as she was getting into the car.

'When we saw your police cars we knew it was over. Simon held me tight and told me he loved me and . . .' She started to cry again. 'Then he said it was all his fault and I was to blame him, but he had to go and I knew why. Then he said goodbye.'

She nearly broke down but struggled into the car. She looked up at the hall for the last time with a tear-stained expression of agony.

'God, I hate this place!' she cried, and then slumped into the seat as the door was shut.

Oldroyd usually felt some satisfaction in bringing the criminal to justice, but now he found himself feeling some sympathy for this tragic couple and their broken dreams. And he felt contempt for the first victim: a despicable man who'd destroyed so much.

DC Robinson led a very shaken Carter back to their police car, where they radioed for help.

'They're calling the Cave Rescue team and ambulance out, Sarge. Not that they'll be able to do anything.'

'No.'

'Chief Inspector Oldroyd's driving over here to meet us.'

'Right.'

Carter was uncharacteristically quiet. He was too stunned to do anything; he just had to let Robinson get on with it. He sat on a grassy bank by the car and tried to forget the image of Hardiman disappearing into that appalling hole.

'Are you OK?'

'Yes.'

'You did all you could. He didn't want to live.'

'I know.'

Carter remained still and silent until he heard the sound of the second police car arriving. He got up, not wanting Oldroyd to think he was weak.

Oldroyd, however, was impossible to deceive. As soon as he saw Carter's white face, he knew he'd been through something pretty bad. He sensed he might not be the right person to talk to Carter at the moment. He motioned to Steph to go over while he spoke to DC Robinson.

'Hey, how are you?' she asked softly. Carter looked up and saw the warmth in her expression.

'Not brilliant. I've seen a lot of bad stuff, you know, but nothing like that.'

'What happened?'

'We got right to the edge of that bloody pothole or whatever it is, and he just fell back deliberately into it. One second I was talking to him, and the next he was gone. He just sort of fell away; it was horror-movie stuff.'

He looked down and shook his head. She put her hand on his arm.

'That's horrible, but I'm so glad you're OK. I was worried when you drove off.'

Carter looked up at her again.

'I knew Hardiman was desperate; I thought he might pull a gun on you or something.'

'So was that just a professional concern?'

Steph moved closer to him. This was her chance to show what she felt and she wasn't going to miss it.

'No, it wasn't; you know that. I . . . I care for you, Andy.' Though she knew she definitely shouldn't while on duty, she leaned forward and kissed him on the cheek.

'That's nice to know,' he said. 'I feel the same. I kept remembering when I pulled you out of that hole when we went down with the boss and how awful it would have been if . . .' He put his head in his hands.

'Let's talk about it later. I think Sir wants us now.'

From across the lane Oldroyd saw the brief bit of unprofessional behaviour, but decided to overlook it in the circumstances. He walked over.

'Well, come on then, we'd better get this poor woman back to headquarters.'

He smiled at them knowingly.

'I'm glad some good has come out of today.'

That evening, Oldroyd was back in the rectory at Kirkby Underside. He and Alison were again sitting in the kitchen, which, though spacious by normal standards, was still the cosiest room in the house. The rectory was absurdly too large for his sister and a testimony to the luxury in which the clergy once lived. Up on the wall near the door were a number of defunct bells that would have rung to summon servants to various rooms. He reflected on how different his sister's conception of her role was: she saw *herself* as the servant to her parishioners and to anyone else who needed her help, for that matter.

Oldroyd sipped his tea and ate one of the scones which Alison somehow found time to bake.

'You actually gave me an idea on this one, you know.'

Alison was putting dirty pots in the dishwasher but stopped and turned to look at him when she heard this. She was always delighted when she'd helped, even if it was usually inadvertently through some comment she made on the people or the situation.

'It was when you were talking about how people can turn on their tormentors. It made me think that maybe the motive behind the murder was something deeper than the jealousy of a cheated husband. That might have explained Atkins getting beaten up or even killed in a fit of rage, but this was a well-planned murder with more than one person involved. There must have been more at stake. He was a serious threat to someone so I started to think about blackmail and who had the most to lose. The Hardimans struck me as being vulnerable; they were struggling to keep their business and their lives afloat.'

Alison sat down looking thoughtful.

'Attachment,' she muttered.

'What do you mean?'

'It's the old problem of attachment to material things; it's a fundamental aspect of all the world's faiths. That poor couple, so attached to that place and their life that they killed to preserve it.'

'We're all attached to our possessions like that, aren't we?'

'Oh yes; we all like to think we could give them up if necessary, but it's all nonsense. They control us, not the other way round. The gospels are very strong on warning us about that.'

'So we shouldn't judge the Hardimans?'

'We should never judge, really; we never know the full circumstances and it's easy to become self-righteous. We should always think: "There but for the grace of God".'

'So are you saying we're all capable of murder?'

'I'd say yes, in certain circumstances. For most people those circumstances would have to be very extraordinary, but we're all capable of lashing out and hurting others. In some cases, it just goes a bit further. Some people act out what others only think, but it's merely a difference of degree. Murderers aren't a separate order of being, evil monsters, despite what the tabloids say.'

'I can see that in the case of the Hardimans. They just seemed an ordinary couple to me. They'd got desperate and one thing led to another.'

'That's what Hannah Arendt called the "banality of evil". She was talking about Adolf Eichmann, an unremarkable bureaucrat whose day at the office involved organising the transportation of Jews from Budapest to Auschwitz. Evil's very ordinary; it's close to us all the time, just as goodness is. It's a dangerous illusion to preen ourselves up on our feelings of superiority to those who commit these awful crimes.'

'To me the Hardimans were like the Macbeths,' said Oldroyd. 'They embarked on an evil course together, and they still loved each other, right to the end. They suffered so much because of what they'd done, and they're still human and normal in many ways. I think that's what *Macbeth* is about. Shakespeare never lets us forget that Macbeth is human, however evil he becomes. We never entirely lose sympathy with him because he's still connected to us; we still recognise him.'

'Exactly. We must never forget that we're all connected.'

This made Oldroyd think about all the interconnected tunnels and passageways under the Dales and the hated figure of Atkins, who himself ended up immured in that dark far below.

The next day Oldroyd arrived at West Riding Police HQ feeling the sense of anticlimax that nearly always came to him at the end of a case. All the odds and ends were tied up. The murder weapon had been found at Garthwaite Hall and traces of Atkins's blood in the van.

As he entered the office, the phone rang. It was Tom Walker.

'Just wanted to say good work, Jim, spoke to the new lad earlier; turned out to be blackmail, I hear?'

'That's right.'

'Bloody amazing, isn't it, what goes on in those little villages? And they say all the trouble's in Gipton and Chapeltown.'

'I know.' Oldroyd didn't really have the energy to listen to one of Walker's rants.

'Anyway, you did a bloody good job. Chief Constable Watkins, of course, doesn't think so.'

'Why, what's wrong?'

'The press are having a field day with that bloke throwing himself into Alum Pot.'

'Carter did his best to stop him.'

'Don't think I don't know that, but Watkins was bleating on to me saying it makes the police look fools when the perpetrator escapes and commits suicide.'

'That's not fair, Tom.'

'Jim, I know. You don't need to tell me; the man's a complete bastard, knows nothing about real policing.'

Walker didn't worry about loyalty or protocol where Watkins was concerned.

'I sometimes think he never did any police work, just went on the bloody fast track to the top.' He laughed. 'Somebody ought to have derailed the bugger. Anyway, tell everyone involved they did an excellent job. It can't have been easy for any of you. I know you had to go down into those caves.'

'We enjoyed it, it made a nice change from interviewing people in their living rooms.'

Walker grunted sceptically.

'They're bad news, those bloody potholes. I remember Blackfell Caverns, 1976. Five cavers got drowned; Cave Rescue couldn't get to them. I was just a young bloke. Press were saying why didn't the police stop people going down, as if it was our bloody fault. Then if you do try to stop people doing things, the same newspapers complain the police are interfering with people's rights and we're living in a nanny state.'

There was a pause. Oldroyd stayed silent so as not to encourage him.

'Right, well, I'm sure you've got work to do. I'll read your report and make it right with Watkins, don't worry. Are we still OK for that drink tonight?'

Oldroyd's heart sank.

'Er, yes, absolutely; looking forward to it,' he lied.

He put down the phone and sat for a while. Then he picked it up again. The number he dialled rang for a long time and he almost put the receiver down. Then suddenly he heard a voice.

'Hello?'

'Julia. It's me.'

'Oh, Jim.'

'Yes, I, well, I didn't think you'd be in, but, you know.'

'I'm not going to work today; don't feel brilliant.'

'What's wrong?'

'Nothing, just a bit headachy and stuff. Classes don't start until next week. How about you?'

'Fine. Well, a bit down actually, you know what I'm like at the end of a case. The adrenalin flows and then it's the big let-down.'

'Yes, I remember.' She paused. 'Still the brilliant detective then. I saw it all on the local news. That must have been traumatic for that sergeant of yours. Isn't he new?'

'Andy Carter? Yes, he is. He'll be good, very keen. Look, I was wondering if you fancied going to the theatre. *Hedda Gabler*'s on at the West Yorkshire Playhouse.'

There was another pause.

'Well, thanks, but I saw that last week with some college friends.'

'Oh, right.'

'Maybe another time.'

'OK.'

Another pause. Oldroyd found it excruciating.

'I'd better go. I've got to get a bit of housework done, then I'm going to lie down for a while.'

'OK, I hope you feel better.'

'Thanks, bye.'

Oldroyd sighed as he put down the receiver for the second time. And so crashed his latest attempt at wooing his wife back, as his sister had encouraged him to do. It was going to be an uphill struggle.

Epilogue

Several weeks later, on a crisp and clear autumn day on the fells north of Burnthwaite, two figures were moving up a path that climbed directly and uncompromisingly up the hillside. Oldroyd was slightly ahead of Carter, who wore a new pair of walking boots that Oldroyd had persuaded him to buy. As these were slightly stiff, he was hobbling a little and felt as if he was developing blisters.

Oldroyd turned to him.

'Not far now, just round that spur.'

Carter looked back and was surprised how quickly they'd climbed from the dale bottom. Oldroyd had persuaded him to go fell walking with him and he'd never walked on paths like this, which rose steeply out of pastoral softness into the different world of a wild moorland terrain. He looked down at the boots and smiled. Who would have expected that he would have exchanged his stylish shoes for a pair of walking boots? What would Jason say if he could see him now? He didn't care; he liked it here and he liked his new boss. He looked around; police work here was so different and fascinating and somehow this landscape was part of it.

Suddenly his phone rang. It was Jason. There was a lot of background noise.

'Hey, Andy my old mate!'

'Jason! I was just thinking about you. Where are you? Obviously getting wasted, as usual; how come, in the middle of the day?'

'Long lunch hour, you know how it is; did some good work this morning, you know, pushed some money around; here with the team to celebrate, might go back later if we feel like it.' He laughed in his usual raucous way. 'Anyway, I've done over seventy hours this week already so they can piss off. What're you up to?'

Carter looked around him and felt the contrast between the world he was glimpsing through the phone and the world he was standing in. Would he like to be with Jason now? Did he miss the buzz, the camaraderie, the excitement of the city? He looked down over the green fields and limestone walls and thought of Steph. To be honest: no.

'I'm climbing up a fellside in a pair of walking boots.'

'What the fuck!' Jason laughed again. 'Up a what?'

'A fellside; a hill to you.'

'What for? Is there a free lap-dancing club at the top? Hey, Alex, have you heard this? Andy Carter's up a hill in Yorkshire in a pair of walking boots.'

Carter heard roars of laughter in the background and he could just make out someone say, 'Oo, Andy's doing it in walking boots; is that how they do it in Yorkshire?' to the sound of bawdy laughter.

'That northern air's getting to you, mate, or is it all the gas in the beer? Have you got that bit with you? Has she got her boots on as well? Give her one from me when you get to the summit!'

Another explosion of laughter in the background.

Carter could only shake his head. They would never understand. Before he could reply, the signal faltered and the London world faded away.

He stuffed the phone back in his pocket as they rounded the corner and Carter saw another of those strange disappearing streams. This one seemed to come down a rocky course and plunge into a hole at the base of a cliff. Oldroyd contemplated the water and then turned to Carter. They both looked out over the desolate moorland beyond. Where the stream met the limestone, it plunged underground to carve caves out of the softer rock.

'There's something over here, Carter, which I think you'd find interesting, but are you fully recovered after that do at Alum Pot?'

Carter still found the memory quite disturbing, but didn't want to admit it to Oldroyd.

'I'm OK. It shook me up, you know, but I can cope.'

'Well, look at this over here.'

He led the way to a flat slab of stone on a grassy bank and Carter saw there was writing on it. It was a memorial to a group of cavers who'd died underground.

'These hills hold some terrible secrets, I'm afraid; they're beautiful but deadly,' said Oldroyd rather solemnly. 'Alan Williams had a point about respecting these caves.'

Carter was shocked to read the ages of the men who died. One was only sixteen.

'That's horrible, sir. How did it happen?'

'One of Britain's worst ever caving accidents: Blackfell Caverns. A party of cavers went on a trip down there and five were drowned; the caves flooded after a thunderstorm. This place is notorious: there's a whole network of caves under here but they fill up with water completely when it rains. Apparently it can take as little as thirty minutes.'

'They were all so young.'

'Yes, it was a dreadful day. Superintendent Walker reminded me about it.'

'What beats me, sir, is why they do it; you know, keep going down when it's so dangerous. It just seems daft to me.'

'Why do people climb mountains, Carter? Why do they hang-glide off huge cliffs? Why do they try to beat the land-speed record? It's the challenge, isn't it? And the danger's part of it.'

'I'm a city bloke; can't see the point of it. A good challenge for me is how many bars you can visit in one evening. But,' he looked around again at the landscape, 'why go down there when there's all this to see?'

Oldroyd looked at Carter and raised his eyebrows.

'Well, maybe he's not such a city bloke after all.' He took a piece of paper out of his pocket.

'This also might explain it. I copied it out of that old Victorian book on caving. It's by that eccentric local poet, Haverthwaite. Some of it's in dialect I'm afraid, but listen to this.'

Carter listened attentively; he was getting used to Oldroyd's sense of drama.

Lost in t'Caves

T''candle flickers and t'watter drips,
T''stones are muddy and t'cold air nips,
We want to get aht but we can't find t'way,
Now that we're 'ere are we 'ere to stay?

Afee'ard o' t'shadders but we can't thoil t'black,
We can't go forrard and we can't go back,
We're tired and cold and we've nowt to eat,
We're weary, freetened and dead on us feet.

Stumbling round t'corner we can hardly cope,
But we see a light and it gives us 'ope,
It's nobbut tiny, but th'end is nigh,
We stride on upwards with us spirits 'igh.

We all reach t'daylight and we sing and shout,
To God Almighty who's brought us out,
Rolling on t'grass we laugh and cry,
Screwing up us een at t'bright blue sky.

Will we go dahn age'an? Only time'll tell.
We think o' that darkness as t'depths of 'ell,
But t'wonder and t'mystery and t'sheer bloody awe,
Will draw us dahn into t'depths once more.

Joseph Haverthwaite 1851

Carter couldn't follow all the dialect but he understood the sentiment. The dark underworld beneath their feet would always hold a fascination that could draw people down even to their deaths. But as he stood next to Oldroyd and looked across the broad fells overarched by a blue sky with fleecy clouds, he knew which he preferred.

Pot 'oles

Unless tha's careful on thi ways,
Providence Pot will end thi days.
Watch out when striding over th'ill,
Especially near to Gaping Gill.
If tha wants to keep all thi bones 'ole,
Don't go fallin' into Boggart's 'Ole.
If on th'edge tha tries to sit,
Tha'll be dahn Hunt Pot, that evil slit.
If tha slips and slides on t'Devil's Cup,

That monstrous 'ole will eat tha up.
Don't go thinking tha's bold and brave,
Tha'll tremble and shake afore Yorda's Cave.
Tha'll think tha's dee'ad and gone to t'devil,
If tha tries to climb down Ibbeth Peril.
T''watter goes dahn and niver comes back,
And nather will thee, swallowed up bi t'black.
So say thi prayers and save thi soul,
And keep thi body from t'dark pot 'ole.

Joseph Haverthwaite 1852

Acknowledgments

I would like to thank my family and friends for all their support and encouragement over the years, particularly those who read drafts and made comments.

The Otley Courthouse Writers' Group led by James Nash has helped me to develop as a writer and given me the extra impetus to get things completed!

Peter Dransfield, formerly of Upper Wharfedale Fell Rescue Association, gave me important advice and information.

There is an actual pothole called Jingling Pot in Kingsdale, but I did not use this as a model for the Jingling Pot in the story. I simply liked the name!

West Riding Police is a fictional force based on the old riding boundary. Harrogate was in the old West Riding, although it is now located in North Yorkshire.

About the Author

John R. Ellis has lived in Yorkshire for most of his life and has spent many years exploring Yorkshire's diverse landscapes, history, language and communities. He recently retired after a career in teaching, mostly in further education in the Leeds area. In addition to the Yorkshire Murder Mystery series he writes poetry, ghost stories and biography. He has completed a screenplay about the last years of the poet Edward Thomas and a work of faction about the extraordinary life of his Irish mother-in-law. He is currently working on his memoirs of growing up in a working-class area of Huddersfield in the 1950s and 1960s.